Eutopian Destiny

Preacher Man

Hope you enjoy!
Rita Dear

by RITA DEAR

The Beginning of the *Eutopian Destiny* Series

Eutopian Destiny – Preacher Man – eleventh printing
Copyright © 2008 by Rita Dear

DBA Eutopian Press

ISBN: 978-1-935015-00-0

Cover photography
© istockphoto.com/DeborahWolfe
Photo reprinted with permission.
Cover design and graphics by Bob McCranie

Book printed by
Minuteman Press
1288 W. Main Street, Suite 206
Lewisville, TX 75067

Dear Reader,

These books are strictly fiction for the fun of fiction. Sometimes it's nice to just let your imagination take you to another place. Eutopian Springs is that place for me. It isn't on any maps — because it doesn't exist — except in my mind.

Nothing in these books is intended to relate to any real person, place or thing. The characters and their individual personalities took on a life of their own as the scenarios evolved.

References to situations in existing cities, jurisdictions, religions, the INS (Immigration and Naturalization Service) and other federal agencies, etc., are as fictitious as the characters I created within them. I don't claim any expertise in anything more than my own imagination.

I hope you enjoy reading this as much as I enjoyed writing it.

Rita Dear

P.S. You won't find Yucca, New Mexico, Pocomesa, New Mexico, or Salttown, Texas, on any maps either. I created them for the stories.

You can order my entire Eutopian Destiny Series online at
http://www.EutopianDestiny.com

Eutopian Destiny – Preacher Man
Eutopian Destiny – The Siege
Eutopian Destiny – Boston
Eutopian Destiny – Pocomesa
Eutopian Destiny – The Blizzard
Eutopian Destiny – The Parish
Eutopian Destiny – Yucca
Eutopian Destiny – Ghostwriter
Eutopian Destiny – The Round Up
Eutopian Destiny – Poetic Justice
Eutopian Destiny – Agraz

EUTOPIAN DESTINY ~ PREACHER MAN

CHAPTER ONE

AUGUST 1998

Joe walked into Jack's office whistling the wedding march. Jack's unit had spent a year in El Paso helping the INS Border Patrol combat a significant surge in illegal activity. The traffic had slowed down to a normal level and management was sending the borrowed units back to their home offices.

"Better get your best suit pressed, Jack," he said. "You've got a bride to give away back in Boston."

He froze when he saw the somber look on Jack's face.

"We're not going back yet," Jack said. "You've been selected for a special undercover assignment."

"What assignment?" Joe asked.

"A highly organized group is smuggling young women into the country and selling them as sex slaves," Jack said.

Joe grimaced. Of all the crimes he'd witnessed, this was one of the worst. The women were usually enticed with promises of good jobs, nice homes and husbands. They didn't learn their actual destination until they were trapped.

"This particular group is especially ruthless," Jack said. "They've left a trail of dead women across the southwest. One of their victims survived long enough to give the police the name of a town she heard her captors mention. It's called Eutopian Springs. It's so small it isn't on most maps. We finally found it on the Texas-New Mexico line. Since it's over two hundred miles from the border, it doesn't seem probable. But it's our only lead. We have to pursue it. We need you to infiltrate the town and become an integral part of their routine while you help us search for evidence."

"Why me?" Joe asked. "I have a bride waiting for me in Boston. I want to go home to her. They can pick another agent for this assignment."

Jack shook his head and said, "Not really, Joe. Your background makes you uniquely qualified for this job."

"What background?" Joe asked suspiciously.

Jack couldn't hold back a chuckle when he said, "Your religious background. We can't get someone in there if we don't have a legitimate cover job for them. The only one available in Eutopian Springs right now is the Baptist Preacher."

"What the hell!" Joe said, tipping over his chair. "You want me to impersonate a Baptist Preacher?"

"No, you wouldn't be impersonating a preacher," Jack said. "You have enough hours in theology to meet the job requirements and we both know you can recite your father's sermons from memory."

"I don't know, Jack," Joe said, as he swept his hand through his hair. "I'll have to think about this one. Let me talk to Angelique and see what she says."

"No," Jack said. "This is the hardest part. You can't tell Angelique or anyone else where you're going or why. You'll give up your apartment, have your mail forwarded to me and literally disappear. I'll be your only contact with your real life. I'll notify Angelique that you're on assignment and can't be reached."

"My God, Jack!" Joe said. "We can't do that to her. I've already walked away from our wedding once. I'm twenty-eight years old. I want to go back to Boston, marry my fiancée and live happily ever after."

"Okay, I'll let headquarters know that you've declined the assignment," Jack said. "I'm sure they can find someone else to break this case. After all, fifty women a month aren't really that many to worry about."

Halfway to the door Joe's shoulders slumped. Jack knew him too well. How could he go back to Boston and live a happy life with the fate of fifty women a month on his conscience?

"Damn you, Jack, did you have to say that?" Joe snapped.

2

"Of course I did," Jack said. "You would've said the same thing to me, if the situation was reversed. Go home and brood about this tonight, I'll need your decision in the morning."

"Oh," Jack added, as Joe turned back toward the door. "I'd start losing the profanity, if I were you."

Joe bit back another curse and walked out of the office.

Jack took a deep breath and started a new mission log. He'd already searched the backgrounds of the other available agents, hoping to find someone else to take this assignment. Joe was the best qualified.

Joe went over to his desk, turned off his computer and left without saying a word to the other men in the unit. He peeled out of the parking lot, picked up the rest of his uniforms from the cleaners and drove to his efficiency apartment.

He hung up his uniforms, started a pot of coffee and sat down on the sofa that doubled as his bed when he was in town. His one window overlooked a little park and shopping center that was bustling with afternoon traffic. Since he was rarely home during daylight hours, he should've found the activity interesting, especially the kids playing with a puppy in the park.

But today was different. The eyes staring out the window were hundreds of miles away – in Boston with Angelique. This last year was the longest separation they'd had from each other and it had been hell on both of them.

Now the INS wanted him to simply disappear. He shook his head and reached for the phone. He was going to tell Jack to find someone else. But he couldn't make himself do it. Jack had played the trump card. He knew Joe's conscience wouldn't let him walk away from those women.

"Damn you, Jack," he said, as he slammed the phone down. He poured another cup of coffee and cursed again. He was homesick and angry – and trapped.

I can't believe they want me to infiltrate as a Baptist Preacher, he thought. He winced at the irony. His family would love to hear this news. He'd spent years under the thumb of the *renowned Baptist Preacher, Jacob Morris.* He and his older brother, Asher, had both been groomed to follow in their father's ministry. Asher not only joined the ministry, he excelled in managing their mother's significant inheritance. Her family was one of the oldest and richest in Boston.

He had never been as pliable as Asher. He chafed under the strictures of being a preacher's son. He'd had to attend *every* sermon his father preached. In fact, he knew most of the sermons by heart – and frequently mimicked his father delivering them. *That's what got me into this mess,* he decided. *If I hadn't recited them to Jack, I'd be on my way home to Angelique right now.*

Memories of Angelique made him smile again. She wasn't just a beautiful young woman, she was an accomplished pianist and vocalist. They'd grown up together and remained best friends and sweethearts. He'd always been a maverick and she never hesitated to help him break the rules.

The worst was the night he slipped out of the house and took her to a high school dance. They'd had a wonderful time and thought they'd fooled their parents. But they got caught trying to sneak back home. Since dancing was forbidden in the Baptist Church, Joe was severely punished for instigating the defiance. He must have memorized half of the Bible before his father was satisfied.

Deacon Baker, Angelique's father, was stern, but fair with him. Angelique's mother was their secret champion. She'd help them slip away to have some fun – and frequently covered for them with both of their dads.

His big plans for a degree in criminal justice were dashed when his father dictated that his college funds would only be available if he pursued a degree in theology. Out of pure spite, Joe enrolled in a Catholic Seminary to study for the priesthood. His father had a fit. But as long as Joe was enrolled in a religion, he had to release the funds.

It took less than a year for Joe to acknowledge his mistake. Although several of the priests expressed dismay at his decision to leave, his Latin teacher emitted a sigh of pure relief. Joe openly admitted he was a dismal failure with the language.

The next semester, he enrolled in a variety of theology classes. But he continued to thwart his father by refusing to study exclusively for the Baptist ministry.

Finally, Jacob relinquished his demands and allowed Joe to pursue his criminal justice degree.

Those theology classes have come back to haunt me, he thought, on his way back to the coffee pot. *I don't even have my books out here. They're back in Boston. I wonder if Jack thought about that.*

He shook his head. He knew he had to stop blaming Jack. Jack was just the messenger – and Joe knew it.

They'd always been a team – a damn good team. Even the first night they met at the Boston harbor, they'd teamed up to cut off some smugglers. He still remembered the stagnant smell of the wharf and the terrified screams that pierced the gunfire when he jumped out of his patrol car.

A group of heavily armed men, hiding behind some shipping containers, had the first row of officers pinned behind their cars. Joe signaled an INS agent to join him. He eased his car into an alley behind the shooters. When they had the thugs covered, they radioed the others to cease fire. Only one more shot was fired. It grazed Joe's shoulder.

While the police were arresting the men, other INS agents broke the locks on the containers and started shouting for ambulances. Joe stared in disbelief as they carried out emaciated women and children. The horror of the inhumane conditions and the terror on the faces of the occupants were permanently burned in his memory – and frequently returned as nightmares.

Jack was the agent who joined him. He encouraged Joe to resign the Boston PD and join his INS team.

Angelique supported the move. She knew they'd be apart while he attended the INS Training Academy in Artesia, New Mexico, but she didn't want to stand in his way. He was the one who had encouraged her to follow her dreams. And he was still her staunchest supporter as she traveled around the world performing concerts.

Aside from the culture shock he experienced when he arrived in the desert southwest, the Spanish language requirement killed him. He called Angelique nightly begging for help. Languages were easy for her. She had to master several to complete her vocal training at Julliard. He could excel at anything physical, but he couldn't twist his tongue around the simplest phrase in Spanish.

When he graduated from the Academy, he was assigned to Jack's Boston unit. They formed a lasting friendship and evolved into a formidable enforcement team.

Since Jack was a widower with no children of his own, Joe and Angelique became his surrogate family. He was with them when her father succumbed to cancer and watched over Angelique and her mother when Joe was out on assignments.

Jack was with him when he bought a stunning diamond engagement ring. When Joe phoned to say Angelique accepted his proposal, she popped a question of her own. She asked Jack to stand in for her father at the wedding.

Jack was stunned and honored.

Two months before the wedding, Jack received the urgent message ordering his unit to El Paso. They postponed their wedding and Joe packed out with Jack.

That was a year ago, he thought, as he looked around his apartment. His few personal items were sitting in boxes by the door. He let out a long sigh, unplugged the coffee pot and tossed a pillow and blanket on the sofa.

He fell asleep dreaming of Angelique, but ghostly visions of hollow-eyed women and children floated across the foreground and obscured her image. He kept trying to push them away so he could see Angelique again, but they just floated back. He woke up in a cold sweat. He was as tired as he was when he laid down. He knew he had to stop fighting the situation.

He cleaned up and headed in to Jack's office to accept the assignment. Obviously, the Agency was expecting that answer. They'd already set up his identity in the Baptist registry and revised his resume to conveniently highlight his religious accomplishments. His years in law enforcement were concealed under a variety of miscellaneous jobs. He sent his application to Deacon Morrison in Eutopian Springs, New Mexico.

Jack obtained some religious books and other memorabilia he thought would help.

Joe carried them home and started reading.

The Agency gave him an old Ford van to use. It didn't look like much on the outside, but it had a rebuilt engine and transmission under the hood. They'd added an air conditioner and a couple of concealed compartments beneath the floorboard to hold his undercover equipment. Some mechanical genius had even installed a special choke that would make it sound like an old rattletrap when he was in town. Once they scuffed up the new black paint, he had to admit it would look like an appropriate vehicle for the *Reverend Joseph Marsh.*

When his application was accepted a week later, he packed up his office and turned his files over to Jack. He cleared out of his apartment and stored his personal items at Jack's place. He loaded his gear bag, firearms and surveillance equipment in the van's compartments. Then he piled *Reverend Marsh's* boxes and clothes on top of them.

He pulled out of the parking lot and onto the highway. Glancing wistfully toward the east, he forced himself to head for a little town called Eutopian Springs.

CHAPTER TWO

MONDAY – FIRST WEEK

When he approached the town, he wondered if *Godforsaken* was in a preacher's vocabulary. It would certainly describe Eutopian Springs. The weather-beaten sign said, Population 100. He doubted it had seen that many people in several years.

He drove Main Street and looked at the faded brick buildings. He only counted seven open businesses – Morrison's Grocery and Gas, Kelly's Barber Shop, Reed's General Store, Thompson's Drug Store, Doctor Stockwell's Office, Jasper's Feed Store and Osborn's Bar. At the end of the second block he was out of town. He wondered how anything this small could even survive.

He drove the roads on each side of Main Street. It was obvious that surviving was about all these people were doing. Most of the frame houses had paint peeling back to bare wood.

The Baptist Church, correction *his* Baptist Church, needed a new roof and some paint, too. The parsonage, *his* new home, looked even worse, but he had to admit they looked better than some of the other buildings.

"Oh well," he muttered. "The sooner I start this assignment the sooner it'll be over." His letter of acceptance told him to meet Deacon Morrison at the grocery store when he arrived, so he drove back to the store. With the choke making such a ruckus, he was sure everyone in town knew he'd arrived.

He walked into the store and people turned to stare. Looking down, he realized he probably looked more like a vagrant than the new preacher. His jeans and t-shirt were sweaty and his favorite sneakers were pretty shabby.

Braving through it, he walked over to the only cashier. She was a pretty young girl with Katherine printed on her apron.

"Hello, Katherine," he said. "Could you please tell me where I can find Mr. Morrison?"

She looked at him with a twinkle in her eye and said, "I think I can do that." She turned back to the store and yelled, "Dad, there's a man to see you. I think it's the new preacher."

So much for formalities, he thought, as she grinned and said, "Hi, I'm Katherine Morrison. Are you our new preacher?"

He laughed and said, "Yes ma'am. I'm Reverend Marsh, the new Baptist Preacher." Although he'd rehearsed the name all the way to town, it still sounded strange when he said it. *Better get used to it*, he told himself, *before you slip up*.

He watched a large man wipe his hands on an apron as he covered the distance to the front. He would've looked intimidating, if it hadn't been for his warm smile.

"Howdy, I'm Ben Morrison and if my daughter's correct, you must be the new preacher," Ben said, as he held out his hand. "You'll have to forgive Katherine. We don't get many visitors in Eutopian Springs. She loves to be the first to announce them."

"Joseph Marsh," Joe said, shaking his hand. "Nothing to forgive, Katherine was absolutely correct."

Ben turned back to Katherine and said, "Go find your mom for me, honey."

"Sure, Dad," she said, as she headed into a coffee shop section of the store.

Katherine returned with a rosy cheeked lady who was rushing to meet him. Alice Morrison welcomed him to town and invited him to join them for dinner. He thanked her for the invitation, but begged off until he had a chance to clean up.

Not to be totally denied, she sent Katherine back to the coffee shop to fix a thermos of coffee and a couple of ham sandwiches for Joe to take home with him.

Ben led him out the other side of the store to meet their son, who was pumping gas for a grey haired lady.

"Well," Ben said, "it looks like you'll get to meet the whole family today." He walked up to the car and said, "Mom, I want you to meet our new preacher, Joseph Marsh." Mrs. Morrison swept her steely grey eyes across his attire, which met with obvious disapproval, before she offered her hand.

Joe acknowledged the reprimand and felt obliged to respond. "How do you do, Mrs. Morrison," he said. "And yes, I promise to clean up before Sunday."

He received what he believed was her best wait-and-see smile, but her eyes definitely challenged his statement.

When she drove off, Ben said, "Mom's a retired school teacher. She taught third grade for thirty-five years."

"No wonder I felt like I needed to go stand in the coat closet," Joe said.

Ben laughed and said, "Yeah, she has that effect on all of us. But she has a heart of gold under that tough exterior. Now come meet one of her biggest challenges – next to me, of course. This is my son, Chris. If he's not pumping gas out here, he's shooting hoops by the hotel."

"Great," Joe said. "I like to shoot hoops myself. Mind if I join you sometime?"

Chris gave him a skeptical look, much like the one Joe just received from his grandmother. Then he said, "Sure, but don't expect any special treatment because you're a Preacher."

"Of course not," Joe said, grinning at him. "And don't expect any in return because you're a Deacon's son."

Chris grinned back at him. He knew Chris was challenging him. But he didn't care. It was a good way for him to get to know the kids. And he knew from his own childhood, that kids know a lot of things they don't tell the grownups.

"I'd really like a chance to clean up before I meet anyone else," he told Ben.

Ben apologized and went after the keys. Following Ben's pickup in his van, Joe mused about the other occupants of the town. *If they're as normal as the Morrison family appears to be, this assignment might not be so bad. Be careful*, he warned himself, *if this town is committing the kind of crimes we suspect, there has to be a corrupt element in here somewhere.*

While Ben unlocked the church door, Joe asked, "How long have you been without a preacher?"

"A little over a year," Ben said. Then he added sheepishly, "Deacon Reed and I tried to continue the services, but we weren't very good." He smiled at Ben's embarrassment.

"Don't feel bad," Joe said. "I've had the same response a few times myself and I am a preacher." *If only he knew how true that statement is*, he thought, as he remembered his sermons in the theology classes.

His smile sobered and he stifled a groan when he stepped inside the church. He reminded himself of the condition of the rest of the town as he looked around the dreary interior. The entry hall was small and dark. It had a row of coat hooks on one side, a long table on the other and a closet under some stairs.

"We had Sunday School in the rooms upstairs when I was a kid," Ben said. "But the congregation's too small to need them anymore."

Joe nodded. He could see someone had tried to clean things up, but the place was dismal. The sanctuary was no better. Someone painted over the varnished pews and the paint was chipping off of all of them. He wondered how many people had ruined their clothes on the rough surfaces. The floor creaked under his feet and the podium was so splintered it looked like it had been used as a goal post in a football game.

Joe had to remember that this was Ben's home church and he had a natural pride in the things Joe was mentally criticizing. Straightening his face he asked, "Who do I need to thank for the cleaning?"

"Alice," Ben said, pleased that he'd noticed. "She's been coming over in the evenings to try to get it ready for you."

"Please, thank her for me," Joe said, as he followed Ben into a closet size office behind the sanctuary.

Ben pulled out a list of the church members and began telling Joe about them. "Your other Deacon is Gene Reed. He and Ginger own the general store. They've got four kids. They're good kids, but they love to get into mischief, so watch your back when they're around. They put lizards in the last preacher's Bible." Joe laughed as Ben described the preacher's embarrassment when the lizards ran down the podium and terrorized the women in the first two pews.

11

"They're a handful," Ben said. "I don't know how Gene and Ginger do it. I only have two and they keep me hopping."

He picked up the list again. "Henry and Nancy Stockwell are the town's doctor and nurse team. They're an older couple with grown kids who live in Ohio and Illinois. They keep our kids patched up and treat the rest of us – unless we have to go to the hospital in Portales."

"Roy and Rhonda Kelly own the barber shop. They have two girls, Barbara and Jeanette. Barbara and my Katherine are best friends. I'm surprised Barbara wasn't in the store when you arrived. I guess her folks had her helping around the shop."

"Otis and Linda Wilson are retired grade school teachers. Their children have grown up and moved away. I'm not sure where they are now."

"Dave and Susan Nelson are our split couple." At Joe's raised eyebrows, Ben rushed to explain. "Not divorced – split religiously. Dave's Baptist and Susan's Methodist, so they alternate Sundays at the two churches. Dave's our Constable. The kids call him the town cop. Susan works at the police station which also serves as our town hall. She handles the utility paperwork, pays the town's bills and monitors the police radio when Dave's on patrol. They've never had any kids, so they spoil ours. He's pretty easy going with the kids, but I've seen him deadly serious a couple of times. If things ever get tough, I want him on my team."

"We have two other families in the church," Ben said. "They both live out of town on the Scott Ranch. Roger and Ellen Scott own and operate the ranch with their five kids. Roger's foreman, Jesse MacKenna, his wife Sheila, and their four kids are the other family. Harry Scott and Richard MacKenna are sweet on Katherine and Barbara. The more the girls ignore them, the crazier they act. In another year or two Roy and I will have to lock the girls up and beat those boys off."

Joe chuckled and thanked him for the information.

Ben looked at his watch and said, "I'd better get you settled in the parsonage and head home before Ma and Alice feed my supper to the dogs. Are you sure you won't join us?"

Again, Joe declined the invitation. When they started back through the sanctuary, he noticed the staircase on the far right. Then he saw an old upright piano on the opposite side of

12

the altar platform. He walked over to it and touched a couple of keys. It was out of tune, but it could still be used.

"Who's our pianist?" he asked.

"No one," Ben said. "We haven't had anyone who could play for several years."

"Well I hope we have someone who can lead the singing," Joe said, "because I've been told I sing best with my mouth closed."

"Don't worry," Ben said. "If you're not too picky, we can get Gene Reed to lead us. He's a pretty good baritone."

"Great," Joe said, with obvious relief.

They locked the church and walked next door to his new home. Joe took a deep breath. After seeing the church, he wasn't sure he wanted to see the parsonage. When Ben opened the door, Joe's face showed his surprise. It was spotless.

"Do I have Alice to thank for this, too?" he asked.

"No," Ben said, grinning at him. "You can thank every eligible female in the county. They're all excited about a new bachelor in the area. Alice had to shoo a couple of them out of here today. They were determined to be here when you arrived."

While Ben watched him for a reaction, Joe tried to remember what his fake resume said about his personal life.

Carefully phrasing his response, he said, "I know we've just met, but I have to ask a special favor. Without discussing my personal life, I need to ask your help in tactfully discouraging these ladies. I want to devote my time to the ministry. I'm not interested in dating or marriage at this time. Could you help me pass the word? I don't want to offend or embarrass anyone."

Ben grinned mischievously and said, "No problem, I'll just tell people you're gay."

"Oh Lord, no!" Joe sputtered before he realized Ben was joking. Ben laughed out loud at the mortified look on Joe's face.

"This will be a very short friendship," Joe said, "if I hear so much as a whisper of that rumor."

"Don't worry," Ben said. "I'll let Alice know you're not in the market and she'll pass the word. I can't guarantee they'll all stop, but we can at least try."

"Thanks," Joe said. "I'd appreciate it. And thank you for everything else you've done. Now you'd better get home before the dogs really do get your dinner." He walked Ben back to his truck. Then he parked his van in front of the parsonage and began unloading.

The parsonage had one large room that doubled as a living room and kitchen. A faded brown sofa with end tables and lamps was centered under the front window. A yellow dinette set divided the room. The kitchen sink faced out a small back window. The counter had been trimmed to accommodate a fairly new washer. The faded linoleum showed where the refrigerator had been until it was moved to make room for the dryer. An old gas range sat on the other side of the kitchen beside the door to the bedroom. A microwave oven was on the far end of the counter. He found dishes, silverware and cookware in the cabinets.

The bedroom had a double bed and a night stand under that front window. A closet and the bathroom were on the opposite end of the room. The house would be small for a family, but it was all the space he needed.

He found freshly laundered towels in the bathroom when he headed for the shower. And he found a stack of extra bedding and linens in the closet when he hung up his clothes.

After putting most of his things away, he sat down at the kitchen table and had the coffee and sandwiches Alice sent over. He'd have to remember to thank her again for those – and everything else she'd done for him. He unpacked his coffee pot and started some more.

Then he opened the box marked *research books* and unpacked his laptop. He hooked it up to the phone line. Thankfully, the town – or probably Ben – had reconnected the phone for him. Logging on under his Agency password, he sent an e-mail to Jack's code name. He advised that he had arrived and started meeting the people. He added the church names he received from Ben and requested any updates available on the issue. He added a personal note requesting information on Goldie, their code name for Angelique.

He logged off and tried to concentrate on the list of names. Instead, all he could think about was Angelique. He was worried about her reaction to Jack's call. He was supposed to be home with her by now. When he closed his eyes, he could picture her long blond hair swirling around her smiling face. Her crystal blue eyes always held him in a trance. He imagined her standing beside him and swore he could smell her perfume.

He shook his head and forced himself back to reality. He knew he couldn't accomplish his mission if he didn't stay focused. Resigned to his task, he headed for bed.

CHAPTER THREE

TUESDAY – FIRST WEEK

When his alarm woke him at five, he stepped into his jogging shorts, grabbed a t-shirt, switched on the coffee pot and headed for the door. Halfway there, he stopped and looked down at his clothes. Remembering Mrs. Morrison's disapproval yesterday, he wondered if the new preacher jogging around town in shorts would cause a scandal.

As he changed, he prayed he wouldn't look equally ridiculous wearing sweats in the August heat.

"Either way I have to run to stay fit for the job," he told himself. "And this will give me a chance to see more of the town before everyone else is up."

In the predawn light, the town looked just like any other small town. Since he hadn't driven all the streets yesterday, he decided to weave up and down the side streets.

The church was at Sage and Second so he started up the north block of Sage. He jogged past three empty houses and the Wilson's home on the west side. Behind those houses he could see a small utility building and a school. The Nelsons, Reeds, Stockwells and Mrs. Morrison lived in the homes on the east side. All four families were in his congregation.

He rounded Sage on First Street, just in time to surprise Mrs. Morrison who was watering her flower bed.

"Good Morning, Mrs. Morrison," Joe said. "I'm sorry I startled you."

"Good Morning, Reverend," she said, scowling at his clothes. "Is this your idea of cleaning up?"

"No ma'am," he said. "This is my idea of getting grimy while I jog. I promised to clean up before Sunday. Since this is only Tuesday, I still have a few days of grace left."

She gave him a very controlled smile, but the twinkle in her eyes said he'd scored a point.

"Well, you'd better get going then before you roast in this heat," she said, turning back to her house.

"See you tomorrow. Have a good day," Joe said, as he jogged off. She just shook her head and stepped inside.

Once he heard her screen door shut, he closed his eyes and silently thanked God that he'd changed out of his shorts. He should've guessed she'd be another early riser.

Turning down Yucca he found Ben's house.

Good planning, he thought when he realized Ben's back door led across the yard to his mother's place. His front door was across the street from the dock to his store. Both the Morrisons lived in older brick homes.

Next to Ben's house was the Thompson's home. He didn't recognize that name. Both of the buildings next to Ben's store were closed. The paint was too faded for him to tell what they had been. The Police Station and Volunteer Fire Department ended that block.

He crossed Second and started on the next block of Yucca. As he passed the Methodist Church, he noticed Reverend Raymond Anderson's name on the sign and decided he should probably make a courtesy call to introduce himself. He passed the back of the general store and another building that faced Main. The block ended with the Church of Christ on the west side and the Osborn Bar on the east side. Since the town was only two blocks long, he turned on Third to jog up Main.

He was surprised to see Jasper's Feed Store open for business, but he realized he shouldn't have been. Their customers would be farmers and ranchers who started work before dawn. He saw three pickup trucks in the parking lot and a semi in the loading dock. Deciding not to jog in front of an open business, he crossed Main, skirted the feed store parking lot and jogged north on Luna.

The Jasper's home was beside the feed store, facing Luna. In fact, the Jasper's house was the only one on the west side of the street. The east side of the block had four smaller stucco homes in desperate need of repair. There were no names on the faded mail boxes, so he couldn't identify the families. He knew at least three of them were occupied because he could hear children inside. He noticed a second row of stucco houses facing a street behind Luna.

He crossed Second again, and found only the Kelly's home on the north block of Luna. The remainder of the block was filled with a large parking area behind the hotel and a storage unit business that appeared to be closed. The east side of the block had a Peanut Buying Station and a large silo that was surrounded with a six foot barbed wire fence and two padlocked gates with big "Closed" signs on them. Judging from the size of the lot, peanuts must have been a good crop at one time. He wondered what happened.

Looking at his watch, he was surprised he'd spent over an hour on these few blocks. He hadn't jogged his normal distance, but he decided he'd better sprint back to the parsonage before he met the rest of the town in his sweaty jogging clothes.

Freshly showered and shaved, he dressed in a pair of casual slacks and a polo shirt. He chuckled and hoped they'd meet Mrs. Morrison's approval. He set out again to explore the town. Since it was so small, he decided to walk over to Main and see who he could meet in the stores.

Heading up Second, he noticed an older lady sweeping the steps outside the Methodist parsonage.

He stopped and said, "Good morning ma'am, I believe I'm your new neighbor down the street."

"Oh," she said, looking up from the broom, "you must be Reverend Marsh. We've been hearing about you. I'm Sherie Anderson." She stretched out her hand and gave him one of the kindest smiles he'd ever seen.

"I'm pleased to meet you ma'am," Joe said. "May I help you carry that?" He gestured at the garbage can he'd seen her drag to the steps. He wondered why the Reverend would leave such a load for his frail wife.

"Oh yes," she said. "Thank you. It gets a little heavy for me sometimes."

He carried the garbage can behind the parsonage and asked, "Would there be a convenient time for me to stop by and visit with you and Reverend Anderson?"

"Oh dear," she said. "I don't guess anyone has told you that Reverend Anderson, Raymond, has been quite ill."

"No," Joe said. "I'm sorry, I didn't know. Is there anything I can do to help?"

She smiled sadly and said, "No, unfortunately not. He had pneumonia last winter and apparently it had a lasting effect on his heart. He's been failing ever since." Then she brightened and said, "The more I think about it, the more I believe he would really enjoy a visit from our new Baptist Preacher. He normally rests until lunch time and then sits up for a while. Could you come back around two?"

"Yes ma'am," Joe said. "I'll be here – and please don't hesitate to tell me if you don't think he's up to a visit when I return. I have an uncle with a bad heart. I know how careful you have to be with that condition." As he turned to walk away he pulled a piece of paper out of his pocket, jotted something on it and handed it to her.

"Mrs. Anderson," he said. "Please put my number by your phone. If you need anything – anything at all – please call me and I'll be here for you."

He saw her wipe away a tear as he turned back to the street. He really did have an uncle with a heart condition and he knew how hard it was for his aunt to handle everything alone.

He walked into Reed's General Store just in time to catch a blond headed little boy racing toward him. He was obviously hoping to escape out the door before the little girl behind him caught up.

"Whoa, partner," he said, picking up the little boy. "Where are you going in such a hurry?"

"Petey stole my dolly," the breathless little girl cried. "He said he's going to throw her in the trash."

Joe looked back at the boy in his arms and asked, "Is your name Petey?" Petey nodded.

"Did you steal her dolly?" Joe asked.

Petey shook his head no.

"So I guess, your shirt is supposed to be this lumpy," Joe said, as he patted Petey's chest. "And your collar is supposed to have doll hair on it….right?" Petey gave him a sheepish look.

Joe whispered in Petey's ear, "If you want to keep her doll and throw it in the trash, I'm going to have to let her get your favorite truck and throw it away."

"No!" Petey said.

"Well that would only be fair, wouldn't it?" Joe asked. "Shall I tell her she can throw your truck away?"

"Naw, I'll give the doll back," Petey said, pulling it out of his shirt. Then he tipped his head up and took a long look at the man holding him. "Who are you?" he asked.

"My name is Reverend Marsh," Joe said. "Can you tell me who this young lady is?" He pointed to the little girl who was now holding her dolly.

"She's my sister, Lily. I'm four. She's seven," he said.

"Hello, Miss Lily," Joe said, bending down to her level. "Can you tell me where your mom and dad are?"

"They're in back," Lily said, pointing to the back of the store. Then she turned to Petey and said, "We were supposed to tell them if anyone came in the store." Before Joe could say another word, Lily raced to the back of the store shouting, "Mommy, Daddy, there's a man in the store."

Petey wiggled out of Joe's arms and joined Lily.

Joe stood still and laughed. He saw two parents scoop up the kids as they walked toward him. Two more kids were behind them. Joe smiled at the picture they made. He stretched out his hand and said, "Hello, I'm Joseph Marsh, the new Baptist Preacher. I just wanted to stop in to meet you. I didn't mean to interrupt your work."

"Gene Reed," the man said, as he shook Joe's hand. "This is my wife Ginger and these are our children, Wayne, Diane, Lily and Peter."

"This man saved my dolly," Lily said. "Petey was going to throw her away."

Joe chuckled at the chagrined looks the parents exchanged and said, "Please relax. It wasn't quite as bad as it sounds. Petey and I reached an agreement and I don't think Dolly lost any hair over the ordeal."

He turned to meet the older kids. When they blended back into the store, he took a few more minutes with Gene. Gene tried to apologize for the kids, but Joe stopped him.

"You have a very nice family, Gene," Joe said. "Please don't worry about it. The kids were just being kids."

Gene looked shocked. Joe was puzzled. Obviously, he wasn't saying what Gene expected to hear.

"I understand you're the other Deacon in the church," Joe said, changing the subject. "Is there a time that would be convenient for you to meet with me to discuss church matters before Sunday? I know I already have one desperate request for you. I met with Ben Morrison when I arrived yesterday and discovered we don't have a pianist. I can't carry a tune in a bucket. I'd be eternally grateful if you'd lead the singing."

Gene relaxed his stiff stance and actually laughed at Joe's assessment of his own singing.

"I'd be happy to lead the singing, at least until we find someone better," Gene said. "I could meet with you tomorrow night around seven, if that's okay with you."

"Sound's good," Joe said. "I'll look forward to seeing you then." They shook hands and Joe left to see what the next business had to offer.

He walked past the empty building beside Gene's store and discovered it had been a second grocery store.

Next was the Osborn Bar that obviously wasn't open before noon. He noticed an advertisement for Saturday Night Dances in the window. He'd be interested in that clientele, but he'd have to be careful. It wouldn't do for the new Baptist Preacher to be seen in the town bar and dance hall.

Crossing the street, he decided to wander into Jasper's Feed Store. The pickup trucks were gone, so he guessed business had reached a midmorning lull. Charley and Mary were cordial, but reserved, when they welcomed him to town and introduced him to their two children, Jerry and Joyce. They seemed bewildered and a little suspicious about his visit. He knew they weren't on his church list. He wondered if they were just surprised that he'd ventured out of his membership.

After a short conversation he left, making a mental note to watch their reaction to him in the future.

He walked up the street to the Doctor's office and introduced himself to Nancy Stockwell. Doctor Stockwell was with a patient, so Joe visited with Nancy for a while.

When the Doctor's door opened a toddler walked out with a bandage on his arm and a lollypop in his mouth.

Joe went down on one knee and said, "That's a big bandage on your arm. What did you do?"

The little boy took the sucker out of his mouth and looked at his mother. He said something to her in Spanish. Joe recognized what he said, but didn't dare expose his knowledge of the language. So he looked at the mother for a response.

"He fall off chair," she said, in broken English. She gestured a cut on his arm.

Dr. Stockwell watched the exchange and said, "We got a little cut from the fall." Then he spoke to the mother in Spanish.

Joe stood up and introduced himself to the Doctor and asked to be introduced to the mother and little boy. He noticed a surprised glance between the Doctor and Nancy, but the Doctor provided the introductions.

The patient was three year old Raul Sena and his mother was Nadina Sena. She was very shy and just managed a quick handshake. Raul extended his hand, too. So Joe went back down to Raul's level and shook his sticky fingers. When they left, Joe talked to the Stockwells for a few more minutes before he walked next door to the Thompson's Drug Store.

He met Doris Thompson at the cash register in the front of the store and her husband, Ralph, back behind the pharmacy counter. Their son, Daniel, was stocking the band-aids and aspirin. Joe noticed a bus pulling up outside, so he wasn't surprised to see Doris selling tickets to some people. Apparently, this was the one source of public transportation in and out of town.

He picked up a magazine and pretended to leaf through it while he checked the open baggage compartments on the bus. The driver stowed the travelers' small bags in one compartment and extracted three large boxes marked Pharmaceuticals from another one. Joe watched Daniel carry the boxes back to his dad. Ralph opened them and verified the contents before he signed the driver's bill of lading. Seeing nothing irregular, Joe walked across the street to the Kelly's Barber Shop.

Roy and Rhonda looked up expectantly. Joe chuckled as he introduced himself and said, "I know I need a haircut. I promise I'll be back to get one before Sunday." They had a short visit and he met their daughter, Jeanette.

Since it was almost noon, he decided to get some lunch at the Morrison's Grocery across the street. He couldn't believe he'd covered every place but Osborn's Bar and the Constable's office in one morning.

When he walked in, Katherine gave him a cheery, "Good Morning, Reverend Marsh."

He grinned and returned her greeting.

She giggled and said, "I hear you startled my Grandma this morning." He groaned internally. He'd forgotten how fast information traveled in small towns.

"Not intentionally, I assure you," he said. "I hope she didn't suffer any ill effects from the surprise."

"Oh, no," Katherine said. "In fact, I think you actually got a brownie point for being an early riser. She's always fussing at Chris and me for staying in bed too long."

"Well, I'll take all the brownie points I can get," he said, as he headed for the coffee shop.

"Oh, Reverend Marsh," Katherine called after him. "Wait a minute. I want you to meet my friend, Barbara." Joe turned to meet Barbara and told her he'd just met her parents and sister, Jeanette. Barbara looked at his hair and frowned.

He chuckled and said, "I've already promised to go back for a haircut before Sunday." He walked on into the coffee shop while the girls shared a spurt of giggles as only teenage girls can.

Alice looked up when he took a seat at the counter. "Hello, Reverend," she said, "how do you take your coffee?"

"Just black, please," he said, "and let me thank you again for the coffee and sandwiches last night. They were great. Since I haven't come over to shop yet, I was hoping you might have some more today."

"Sure," Alice said, smiling at the compliment. "We have three kinds today, ham and swiss, roast beef, and egg salad.

Which kind would you like? We can make them on white, wheat or rye."

"Egg salad on white, please," Joe said.

Alice turned around to the refrigerator, pulled out a bowl of egg salad and made the sandwich while they talked.

"Thank you for all the work you did on the church," Joe said. "I really appreciate it. I know it took a lot of extra effort for you to go over there after working here all day."

She was obviously pleased that he noticed. Then she proved that her husband wasn't the only one with a sense of humor when she said, "It wasn't as much work as it could have been. I had plenty of help with the parsonage."

She laughed when Joe blushed. She quickly assured him that Ben had already recruited her help in diffusing that problem.

Joe was finishing his sandwich when Alice brought out an apple pie. It was still warm from the oven. Tempted beyond reason, Joe lingered over a second cup of coffee and a slice of it.

"This is delicious," he said.

He heard a familiar voice ask, "So you like my apple pie, do you?"

Turning to the kitchen pass-through, he said, "Yes, ma'am, it's wonderful."

Mrs. Morrison's eyes twinkled when she told Alice, "Now that's the kind of appreciation I deserve when I slave in the kitchen. The men in *your* family just take them for granted."

"And who spoiled those men of mine?" Alice asked, grinning at Joe.

"I have no idea," Mrs. Morrison said innocently.

"You've been blackmailing *my men* with your pies for years," Alice said.

"I just used them as *incentives*," Mrs. Morrison said. "I would *never* stoop to blackmail." Alice sputtered.

Joe laughed out loud at the two of them.

Mrs. Morrison suddenly seemed to realize that he was still there witnessing their conversation.

She tried to assume a sterner look.

"Oh no you don't," Joe said. "You're not going to fool me with that frown anymore. I've seen the real you, now."

Mrs. Morrison started to respond when Chris rounded the corner asking, "Is that Grandma's pie I smell?" Then he added, "Hi, Reverend Marsh, how are you?"

Joe barely managed a, "Hi, Chris," before Chris picked up Joe's empty plate and turned on his mom.

"I hope you saved a slice for me," he said.

"Of course I did," Alice said. "But you can't have it all or your dad will divorce me before nightfall."

As if on cue, Ben came in for lunch. He gave his mother and Alice a quick kiss and greeted Joe.

In less than a minute, Ben and Chris were bantering over the remaining pieces of the pie. Ben winked at Joe when Mrs. Morrison laughed at their antics.

Alice gave Joe an exasperated look and said, "See what I mean?" He grinned at the guys and finished his coffee.

When he picked up his check to leave, Chris said, "I get off at four. Wanna join me for some hoops?"

"Sure," Joe said, "see you then."

He looked at the clock on the wall and made a hasty retreat. He was due at the Andersons' in fifteen minutes.

Walking back to the Methodist parsonage, he debated about the best way to approach the other cleric in town. It wasn't in his nature to be pious, but he wondered what Reverend Anderson would expect. When he knocked on their door, he realized he was actually nervous. *Probably too reminiscent of my meetings with Dad,* he thought.

Mrs. Anderson greeted him at the door with a warm smile and ushered him into a small living room similar to the one in his parsonage. Across the room, he could see her husband trying to rise out of his chair to meet him. He gestured to Mrs. Anderson and moved quickly to urge her husband to stay seated.

Extending his hand he said, "Good afternoon, Reverend Anderson, I'm Joseph Marsh, the new Baptist Preacher. Please don't get up. I just stopped by to introduce myself."

Although his body was weak, his voice was still strong.

"Hello, Reverend Marsh," he said. "I've been looking forward to meeting you. I'm sorry my health is so poor that I couldn't come out to greet you when you arrived yesterday."

"Not a problem, sir," Joe said.

Mrs. Anderson brought them two tall glasses of lemonade and started to leave. She was surprised when Joe asked her to stay. She went after her own glass and sat in a chair beside her husband.

"I've spent this morning wandering in and out of the stores on Main Street," Joe said. "It seemed to be the best way for me to start meeting some of the families in your town. I know you've served this community for several years. I'd appreciate any wisdom you'd like to share that would help me in my ministry."

Reverend Anderson leaned back in his chair and stared at Joe for a long minute before he said, "You're not at all what I expected. It's rare for a young preacher to be willing to accept an assignment in such a small town. It's even rarer for a preacher of one faith to ask guidance from a minister of another faith."

Fearing he was failing to meet the religious standards of a preacher in the presence of another one, Joe warned himself to tread softly with this meeting. Reverend Anderson might be physically impaired, but he was mentally alert and astute.

"You're right," Joe said. "Most young preachers probably do want to start in larger churches, but I wasn't sure where I wanted to preach. When I was told about this opening, I thought I might be able to make a larger contribution in a small community. Only time will tell if I made the decision God wanted me to make. As for preachers seeking advice from each other, I believe wisdom is the greatest gift one person can give another – and I value it. We may have different religions, but we share the same faith. I'm sure we both want what's best for the members of this community."

"Well, Reverend, I find your philosophy a welcome change," Reverend Anderson said, still studying him closely. "I hope your congregation will be encouraged to share it."

Joe's confused look prompted Reverend Anderson to add, "Your predecessor, Reverend Phillips, had a much narrower view of his role and his church. One, I might add, that I did not agree with. He was very secular in his opinions and we rarely shared in any community efforts." As Reverend Anderson described the previous situation, Joe began to understand why some of the people he'd met were surprised at his visit.

Reverend and Mrs. Anderson said they'd lived in Eutopian Springs for twenty-nine years. Their children, now grown and living in the Midwest, had grown up there. Before the drought hit in nineteen ninety, peanuts were the major crop that sustained the local prosperity. The Archers, Thatchers and some of the smaller farmers were hit so hard they lost their farms. Then Cozen Oil moved in and the town grew overnight. It actually supported the closed businesses on Main Street. There had even been enough children to fill the school that he'd seen on the west side of town.

He asked about the Church of Christ. They said its membership had dwindled so low that it had to close. There were still a few members in town and they were in Joe's congregation.

"In fact," Reverend Anderson said, "both of our churches are serving very small congregations. Unless the town is able to find a way out of its depressed situation, the town itself might disappear."

Joe mentioned that he'd met Raul Sena and his mother at the Doctor's office. He asked how much of a Hispanic population was in town. Reverend Anderson seemed mildly uncomfortable about the question.

Eventually, he said, "We have seven Hispanic families in town. Unfortunately, the town still has divisive attitudes about Anglo and Hispanic issues. As for their religion, most of the Hispanics are Catholic. Father Romero comes to town on Sundays and provides services for them."

"Where do they meet?" Joe asked.

Reverend Anderson chuckled and said, "They have their services in our church an hour before ours. My congregation wasn't too happy about that decision, but the Hispanics had to drive twenty-five miles to Romero's church each Sunday. It was too hard on the families. I met with Father Romero and we decided it would be better for him to drive over here. We thought about converting the Church of Christ for them, but they couldn't support the cost of the building. So we have both services here. I had hoped it would bring the two cultures closer together. So far it hasn't been very effective."

Joe was so engrossed in their conversations he hadn't realized how long he'd kept Reverend Anderson talking. He looked at Mrs. Anderson and said, "I'm sorry I've taken up so much of your afternoon." To Reverend Anderson, he said, "I was just coming by for a short visit and I've stayed much too long. I hope you haven't become too tired from all this talking."

"On the contrary," Reverend Anderson said, "I'm glad we've had this visit. I believe you're just the type of young blood this town needs. I pray God will bless your mission here."

After Joe thanked them again for their hospitality, he asked if he could help Reverend Anderson back to bed. To his surprise, the Reverend agreed and Joe gently supported him as his steps faltered on the way to the bedroom. Once he was settled comfortably, the three of them shared a small prayer for the Reverend's health. When he left, he reminded Mrs. Anderson of his earlier promise to be available whenever she needed him.

Walking back to his house, he was amazed at the effect that couple had on him. He hoped against hope that the Reverend's health would improve, but he was afraid it wouldn't.

He was so deep in thought he was almost at his door before he saw the young woman sitting on his steps. Shocked, he brought his thoughts back to the present and said, "Hello, I'm Joseph Marsh, the new Baptist Preacher."

"Hi," she said, "I'm Sally Mae Shaw. My family has a farm on the other side of the county. I caught a ride with one of our hands so I could meet you. I came in last week and cleaned your house. I was going to wait inside, but your door was locked. That's really strange. No one locks their doors around here."

Mentally, Joe was trying to digest what this girl was saying. If she was here last week, she was one of the women looking for an eligible bachelor. If he hadn't locked his door, he would've found her waiting inside.

"I'm glad to meet you Ms. Shaw," he said, "and I definitely want to thank you for all the work you did on the parsonage. I'm sorry if you've been inconvenienced sitting out here, but I won't be leaving my door unlocked. Since I'm a bachelor, it wouldn't be appropriate for me to have young ladies inside. I'll get the church keys and we'll go over there if you have a need for prayer or religious guidance."

Sally was shocked. She obviously thought he would be delighted to let her come inside with him. When it was apparent that he wasn't interested, she shook her head and said, "I have to get back to the feed store to catch my ride home."

After a stilted goodbye, she walked briskly down the street. Joe waited until she was a full block away before he unlocked his door. Once inside, he slumped down in a chair and contemplated the close call he'd just had. The last thing he needed was strange women letting themselves in his house – especially women in tight jeans and skimpy halter tops. He'd definitely be locking his door.

A few minutes later, he changed into his jeans, t-shirt and sneakers to go shoot hoops with Chris.

"Hey, Preacher Man," Chris called out, as Joe rounded the corner of the barber shop into the vacant parking lot beside the hotel. Someone had mounted a hoop on the side of the building. Joe looked at the location and decided it was probably the best place in town for the kids to play. Sandwiched between the two buildings, the noises were buffered and most loose balls wouldn't make it back to the street.

"Hi, Chris," Joe said. "I see you've been warming up. What do you play?"

"I usually just shoot by myself," Chris said. "Wanna try some one-on-one?"

"Sure," Joe said, "but don't any of the other kids play?"

"Yeah, some of them come over sometimes, but most of them are too young for any real competition," Chris said. "Harry and Richard used to play when they came to town, but now they just hang around Katherine and Barbara."

"What about Daniel Thompson and Jerry Jasper?" Joe asked. "They're a little younger and shorter than you are, but they'd give you some competition."

Chris stopped dribbling the ball and gave Joe a long look. "What's wrong?" Joe asked.

"You know they're Methodists, right?" Chris asked. "And they let Catholics use their church."

Now it was Joe's turn to stare at Chris.

"Well, I know they aren't in our congregation," Joe said. "But what does that have to do with basketball?"

Chris sat down on the ball and thought for a moment before he said, "I forgot how new you are. But you are a Baptist Preacher, right?"

"That's right," Joe said tentatively. He wondered what he'd done to upset Chris.

Chris shook his head in bewilderment. "Danny and Jerry used to shoot hoops with me all the time," he said. "But Reverend Phillips came down here one day and blasted me for associating with them. Danny and Jerry left and they've never been back. Then Reverend Phillips had a talk with my folks. I think he and Dad had an argument over it. But I'm not sure."

"How long was Reverend Phillips in Eutopian Springs?" Joe asked, silently seething at the damage his predecessor had apparently done to the kids.

"Only a couple of years, more or less," Chris said. "In his last sermon, he told us we were all hopeless sinners and he was giving up on us. I know I shouldn't say this, you being a preacher, too, but I was really glad to see him go."

"I think I can understand that," Joe said softy. "Would you mind taking a few more shots by yourself? I need to run an errand. Then I'll be back to give you the workout of your life."

Hearing the challenge in that last statement pulled Chris out of his dark mood. He grinned and said, "We'll see who gets the workout, Preacher Man."

Joe jogged across the street and into the grocery store. When Katherine looked up, he asked, "Where's your dad?"

She looked at the firm set on his face and didn't say a word. She just pointed to the back of the store. Joe took the distance in five strides and burst through the stockroom doors.

Ben was helping a trucker unload boxes of produce when he looked up and saw Joe. He put the box down and met Joe halfway across the room.

"Reverend Marsh," he said, "is something wrong?"

Joe took a deep breath and tried to control his features. His anger was at Reverend Phillips, not these people.

"I'm sorry, Ben," he said. "I didn't mean to alarm you. But I just heard some disturbing news about my predecessor. Is it true that Reverend Phillips blasted Chris for associating with the Methodist kids in town?"

The cloud of temper that settled over Ben's brow confirmed the facts before he even spoke. "Yes, I'm sorry to say, it's true," he said. "The damage was done before I heard about it. It's one of the few times I've argued with a preacher. In fact, I may be directly responsible for his short duration in this town. As the kids say, he went *ballistic* when the Methodist Minister *allowed the Catholics to take over their church."*

"Well, I'm the new guy in town," Joe said. "I'd hoped to arrive without causing any ripples, but I can't agree with Phillip's attitude. I want to talk to the families and see if we can get the kids back on the hoops lot. Do you have any objections?"

"None whatsoever," Ben said. "The sooner they're back together, the better."

"Okay, I'll get out of your way," Joe said. "I'm sorry I interrupted your work. I should've waited for a better time."

"No problem," Ben said. "I'm glad we finally have someone who cares about *all* the people in this town. I've been hearing good things about your visits to the other businesses."

"Thanks," Joe said. "By the way, Gene Reed is coming over tomorrow night so we can discuss issues we need to cover before Sunday's re-opening. Can you join us about seven?"

"I'll be there," Ben said, "and good luck with the Thompsons and Jaspers."

"I'll talk to them tomorrow," Joe shouted over his shoulder, as he hopped off the loading dock. "Right now I've got to beat that son of yours in a little one-on-one competition."

Ben chuckled and went back to the boxes.

Passing the truck driver, Joe stopped to introduce himself to JJ Simms. Then he jogged back over to Chris.

"I thought you were afraid to come back, Preacher Man," Chris taunted.

"Not on your life, Hot Shot!" Joe said. "Now let's see if you're as good as you say you are." He was.

Joe thought he was in good shape with all his training, but he had to admit Chris had him beat.

Lord! Where does this kid get his energy? he asked silently, as he rebounded another shot.

When they stopped playing, Joe slung an arm over Chris' shoulder and said, "Good game, kid! Do you play on your school team?"

"Yeah," Chris said. "I'm the center on the Yucca High School team."

"That's great," Joe said. "Have you applied for any college scholarships yet?"

Chris shook his head and said, "College costs too much. We can't afford it."

"With your basketball skills, you have a good chance for a scholarship," Joe said. "Then it wouldn't be so expensive, especially if you go to a local college like the one in Portales. You could go to school during the week and come home to help the family on weekends."

He could see Chris considering the idea.

"Think about it," Joe said. "I can help you file the paperwork. Talk to your folks and let me know. We'd have to get your application in before the end of this month."

Chris nodded.

"Same time tomorrow?" Joe asked.

"Sure," Chris said, still deep in thought as he walked over to the store.

Back at the house, Joe collapsed. *What a day,* he thought, as he started a fresh pot of coffee. He was pulling his equipment out of the closet, when he heard a knock at his door.

Braced for another female visitor, he swung the door open and found Chris holding a steaming plate of food.

"Grandma said you probably hadn't cleaned up enough to come to supper yet," Chris said. "But she didn't want you to faint from starvation before you delivered your first sermon, so she sent a plate over for you." The smell of the food made Joe's stomach growl and they both laughed.

"Thank your grandma for me and the rest of your family," Joe said. "I promise to buy some groceries tomorrow. If this tastes as good as it smells, I'll be in heaven before I finish it. Thanks, Chris. Now hurry home to your own dinner. You're probably hungrier than I am."

As Chris crossed the short yard, he shouted back, "I'm going to talk to Dad about that college idea tonight. I'll let you know tomorrow...when I beat you again at hoops."

"Beat me again!" Joe shouted. "Why, you little... I'll show you!" He heard Chris laughing all the way up the street.

Inside, he poured a cup of fresh coffee and sat down to enjoy the dinner. If he wasn't in love with Angelique, he'd be courting Mrs. Morrison – just for her cooking. He thought about Angelique all the time. He wondered what she would've said to Sally Mae today. *Maybe I don't want to know,* he thought, grinning at his memories of Angelique's temper.

Sitting at the table writing his daily report to Jack, he wondered where the Post Office was in this town. Jack was supposed to forward Angelique's mail to him, but he hadn't seen a mail man or a postal sign when he walked around today.

It was ten o'clock. Every bone in his body ached for a hot shower and bed. But he knew he needed to make another sweep of the town to start his night surveillance.

Changing to all black, he slipped out the door – being careful to lock it – before he blended into the shadows.

He moved south around the Church of Christ and over to the bar parking lot. He noticed the same pickups he'd seen at the feed store early this morning. He wondered when those people found time to work. Jotting down the license plate numbers, he continued around the closed feed store and over to the two rows of Hispanic homes. Most of them were dark, only a couple of babies were still keeping their mothers up.

Turning back to Luna, he looked at the hoops lot and smiled at Chris' parting shot. If he was successful, Chris would have his old teammates back tomorrow.

When he scanned the rest of the block, two things caught his eye. The semi that he saw at Ben's store was parked in the vacant lot behind the hotel. Walking closer, he wrote down the license number and checked the cab. Since it was empty, he assumed Simms must be one of the customers at the bar.

The other thing he noticed was a light in what appeared to be a residence on the second floor of the storage units. He thought it was just another closed business, but someone was in there now.

Turning back to Main, he saw the town cruiser coming around the Hispanic section. He hid in the shadows and watched Dave Nelson make his rounds. He hadn't met Dave and Susan yet, but even if he had, he didn't want them to know he was watching the town.

When Dave ran his spotlight over the backs of the buildings on Luna, Joe noticed that he didn't seem to take any interest in the parked semi or the light over the storage units. Maybe this was normal to the rest of the town.

He worked his way back home and added the license numbers to the e-mail he sent Jack.

Then he headed for the shower and bed.

CHAPTER FOUR

WEDNESDAY – FIRST WEEK

Joe decided to jog around the south side of town to see who might still be hanging around the bar. The parking lot was empty and even the feed store wasn't as busy as it was yesterday.

Swinging up Luna, he heard the kids in the small houses harassing their moms. He ran up the second block to check the back of the hotel and the storage units. The semi was gone. Apparently, Simms was back on his route. The storage units looked as deserted as ever.

Circling around to the other side of the units, he saw an older man sweeping out one of the spaces. Joe stopped and called to him, but the man kept sweeping.

Joe waited for him to finish and called again. This time the man looked up and walked over to the fence.

"Hello, my name is Joseph Marsh," he said. "I'm the new Baptist Preacher."

"Hello," the man said. "Wait a minute while I turn on my hearing aids. I turn them off most of the time. No sense using up batteries just to hear myself talk."

Joe chuckled at his joke as the man said, "I'm Max Tipton. I manage these storage units."

Joe repeated his own introduction and asked, "Do you have any to rent?"

"Nope, they're all full," Max said.

"All full?" he asked. "I can't believe this little town has that much to store."

"Oh no," Max said. "They don't use these units. These belong to Cozen Oil. They did a lot of drilling around here a few years ago. They still have some wells north of town. They built these units so they could keep their equipment here."

Not wanting to appear too interested, Joe asked if he could come back and visit sometime.

"Sure, anytime," Max said. "I'll either be down here in the units or upstairs in my apartment."

Joe nodded and jogged on across Main toward Sage.

He saw Mrs. Morrison watering her flowers. He wondered what she was looking at on Sage. Then he realized she was watching for him. Since he'd taken a different path, he was late going around her house.

"Good morning, Mrs. Morrison," Joe chimed, as he jogged up. Startled, she swung the hose and he got a quick shower for his trouble. "Were you watching for me?" he asked, as he shook off the water.

"Not at all," she lied. "I was just watching a pesky bunny trying to eat my irises."

"Well, if I see it, I'll shoo it away for you," he said, grinning at her. He decided not to tease her much more, so he changed the subject. "Thank you for the dinner you sent over last night, I love fried chicken." She smiled and kept watering.

"May I ask a favor, please?" he asked.

When she nodded, he said, "About the only thing I do well in a kitchen is turn on the microwave. So I'm not very good at setting one up. Would you mind making a list of some of the basic items I need for the parsonage kitchen? I never seem to remember salt, pepper, butter, catsup, and stuff until I'm trying to eat something that needs them."

"I think I can manage that," she said, smiling at his comment. "I'll leave the list at the register with Katherine."

"That would be great. Thank you," he said. "I'm coming back later this afternoon to buy some supplies, so I'll just add them to my cart."

She nodded and he jogged on down to his house.

After a quick shower, he dressed for another day in town. He wasn't sure how he was going to meet the bar owner,

Clive Osborn. But it was time for him to meet the Nelsons. And he needed to undo the mess Reverend Phillip made with the kids.

Seeing Mrs. Anderson in the yard, he stopped to ask about the Reverend. She said he was a little tired after Joe left, but he really appreciated the visit.

"Raymond was especially encouraged by the attitude you're bringing to the community," she said. "Could you drop by again in a day or two? Your visit seemed to lift his spirits."

"I'd be delighted to visit any time you think he's well enough," Joe said. "Just give me a call and I'll come over."

She smiled and thanked him.

He visited the Thompsons first. Since there wasn't a bus in front of the drug store, he hoped they weren't very busy. He was right. Ralph and Doris were both in the back of the store discussing some display items. As he approached, he noticed their surprise. They masked it quickly and asked if they could help him find something.

Deciding not to skirt around the issue with small talk, he said, "Late yesterday afternoon, I discovered that my predecessor imposed his religious biases into the friendship your son, shared with Chris Morrison and Jerry Jasper. Although it's not my place to apologize for Reverend Phillips, I can unequivocally state that I do not condone his actions or his ideology."

He waited for Ralph and Doris to absorb what he said.

"I don't want to impose myself on your family or your own religious beliefs, so I won't make any effort to discuss this situation directly with Daniel," he said. "Given his prior encounter with a Baptist Preacher, I'm not sure he'd believe me if I tried. However, I am asking you to trust what I'm telling you. Please tell him that it won't happen again while I'm the Baptist Preacher in this town. Chris and I are going to meet at the hoops lot around four this afternoon. If you and Daniel are willing to trust what I've said, we'd like to have him join us for a game or two." The Thompsons looked at him in disbelief when he finished. Then looking at each other, they turned and smiled – sincere smiles – at him.

Doris was the first to find her voice. "The boys have been miserable since Reverend Phillips separated them," she said. Looking at Ralph she added, "We'll tell Daniel what you said. I'm sure he'll want to join you at four. And thank you Reverend Marsh, for making this effort to re-unite the kids."

"This isn't necessarily the thing a preacher wants to do the first few days at a new location," Joe said. "But I couldn't let this continue to separate friends. Thank you for trusting me enough to talk to Daniel. I know it isn't easy to trust again when someone in the same position caused your family pain. I hope we see Daniel at four."

He walked down to the other end of the block and delivered the same message to Charley and Mary Jasper. Their responses were similar to the Thompsons. He hoped both boys would show up.

As he wandered back toward his house, he decided to drop by the Police Station and meet the Nelsons. Susan was on the radio talking to Dave. When she signed off, Joe introduced himself and they talked for a few minutes before the door opened and Dave walked in. Although he was an older man, Dave's stance still exuded authority. Of course, it didn't take long for Dave to mention Joe's noisy van and suggest he get it tuned up next time he went to Portales.

Joe chuckled and said, "I'll try to get it fixed, but that van's so old I'm not sure how much they can do to it."

Dave nodded and offered him a cup of coffee.

When he discovered that Dave had been the Constable for almost twenty years, Joe asked him what had happened to cause the decline in the businesses and population.

"The drought that still plagues us hit first," Dave said. "Several of the peanut farmers lost their crops and farms. Then the possibility of oil in the area brought oil workers needing housing, furniture and other things for their families. The company drilled for a couple of years in and around town before deciding there wasn't enough oil to justify more than the two or three rigs up north."

"When the drilling company moved out," Susan said, "so did the people who arrived with it." She and Dave reminisced about some of those families. They still heard from a couple of them. Joe made his exit when the phone rang for Susan. Dave walked out with him and reminded him again about the noisy van. Joe chuckled as he watched Dave drive away.

Since he still had some time before lunch, he decided to walk over and meet the two retired teachers, Otis and Linda Wilson. Their house was near the closed school. He didn't need to knock on the door. He found both of them in the back, trying to move a yard swing.

"Hello," he said, "my name is Joseph Marsh. I'm the new Baptist Preacher. May I help you with that?" Mr. Wilson nodded. Joe took over Mrs. Wilson's end so she could help her husband. Together they repositioned it under a large shade tree. By the time they finished, the formalities were over.

Mrs. Wilson brought out a big pitcher of iced tea. Joe pulled up a lawn chair while the Wilsons sat down in the swing. He asked them about their teaching careers. Between them they'd taught every elementary grade level. Mr. Wilson was the Principal the last few years the school was open. He laughed at the stories they told about the kids. He recognized some of the pranks – he'd pulled them on his own teachers through the years.

At noon he wandered back to the grocery store to enjoy another sandwich and if he was lucky, another piece of pie.

Seeing Katherine at the register, he asked if she had a list of groceries for him from her grandmother. "Better than that," Katherine said. "They're already in a box for you."

"Great," he said. "Who did this for me?"

"Barbara and me," she said. "We didn't have much to do this morning, so we thought we'd help you."

"Thank you. That was very nice of you," he said. "By the way, I know Chris likes basketball, but what do you girls do for fun when you're not helping your parents – and me?"

"We just like to do girl stuff," Katherine said. "Listen to music, do our nails and watch videos. Stuff like that."

"Are you looking forward to school starting?" Joe asked.

"I know I'm supposed to say no, but I really am," she said. "I'm one of those weird ones who like school."

"That's not bad," he said. "You're bright. It stands to reason that you'd want to learn everything you can. What's your favorite subject?"

"I like them all, but I guess Literature is my favorite," she said. "I'd love to be able to write like the famous authors do – especially the poets."

39

"Hold on to your dreams," he said. "You never know when they might come true. I'll be back for that box as soon as I finish lunch. By the way, when does school start?"

"Not until after Labor Day," Katherine said.

He nodded and headed for the coffee shop when a shopper moved up to the register. He and Alice talked while he ate another egg salad sandwich and a piece of fresh cherry pie. Then he loaded a cart full of milk, bread, cereal, hotdogs, peanut butter, frozen dinners and coffee. He added those to the box of things Mrs. Morrison ordered and started carrying them back to the parsonage.

"If you don't tell anyone that I'm trying to get brownie points with the new preacher," Dave said, pulling up beside him, "I'll give you a lift."

"I promise not to tell," Joe said, as he put the box in the back seat of the patrol car. "Thanks for the ride. I guess I should've driven over."

"Oh Lord, no," Dave said. "Leave that noisy thing parked as much as you can. I don't want to have to cite you for disturbing the peace. I must've had ten calls the morning you drove into town."

"Okay, I'll try to leave it parked," Joe said. "Anyway, the town's so small, it's really easier to walk to most places. And, I can meet more people when I'm on foot." Dave pulled up in front of the parsonage and Joe thanked him again.

At a quarter of four, Joe jogged over to the hoops lot. He was too anxious to wait any longer. He didn't want the boys to feel awkward if he wasn't there to smooth out the situation. Besides, he wanted to see the look on Chris' face if his old friends showed up. He arrived first and then Chris. They were shooting alternate free throws when Daniel walked by the lot.

Sensing Daniel's hesitation, Joe shouted, "Hey Daniel, come on over and join us."

Chris looked at Joe and then at Daniel. The shock on his face changed to joy when he realized what Joe had done.

"Sure Danny, come on over," Chris yelled. "And you too, Jerry. I see you hiding around the corner. Man! It's good to have you guys back." He gave each of them a hug. Then he

40

turned to Joe and said, "I don't know how you did it, Preacher Man. But I know you're the one who did. Thanks a lot!"

Joe looked at the three boys and smiled.

"Okay, let's play some ball," he said. "Danny, do you and Chris want to challenge Jerry and me?"

Since Joe and Chris were a head taller than the two younger boys, it was only fair that they divide the shorter ones between them. Seeing Jerry's disappointment in not playing with Chris, Joe reversed Danny and Jerry for the second game. They played until dark, and promised to be back again tomorrow.

Before he went home for dinner, Chris ran over and said, "Thanks again, Preacher Man." He gave Joe an awkward hug and ran up the block.

Joe had just enough time to shower and gulp down a frozen dinner before Ben and Gene arrived for their meeting. He grabbed the keys and led them into the sanctuary. While he tried to find the light switches, he heard Ben grumbling to Gene.

"I've invested eighteen years in my son and this guy moves to the top of his list in less than a week."

Gene gave him a confused look.

"Haven't you heard?" Ben asked. "Somehow, Reverend Marsh removed the *Methodist ban* and has Chris, Danny and Jerry back together. Chris was so excited he could hardly eat his dinner – and that never happens. All he did was talk about the Preacher Man." He turned to Joe and said, "By the way, Chris told me about your college scholarship discussion. We'd like to let him try for it, if you don't mind helping us."

"Not at all," Joe said. "I'd be glad to help. Chris has a good chance for a basketball scholarship. He's got a natural talent for the game." Turning to include Gene in the conversation, he said, "Gene, if that little cowboy of yours can carry a football as fast as he does dolls, I'll bet he'll be trying for a football scholarship someday."

Gene laughed at that possibility.

"Okay," Joe said, as he sat down on one of the rough pews. "Let's discuss the church and what we want to do for the re-opening." The men sat down and waited for him to continue.

"I want to keep the sermon simple and let the congregation have time to get acquainted with me," Joe said.

Gene nodded and selected simple, traditional hymns, to add to a sense of comfort.

Then looking at the condition of the church, Joe asked about the boarded sections on the lower level and the other set parallel to the upstairs rooms.

"Those are windows," Ben said. "Someone covered them a few years ago."

"Do you know the condition of the glass behind the boards?" Joe asked. Both men shook their heads.

"What did your other preachers wear for your services?" Joe asked.

"Reverend Phillips wore a heavy black robe," Ben said. "The rest wore suits."

When they mentioned Phillips, Joe stifled a shudder and said, "Speaking of Reverend Phillips, I'd like to know a little more about him. Can you give me some background on him?"

"Fire and Brimstone Baptist," Ben said, much to Gene's surprise. "Well he was," he told Gene. Then he laughed and said, "I don't think we have to worry about our Reverend Marsh being another one, so relax, Gene."

Joe could see he needed to get Gene as comfortable with him as Ben obviously was. "Maybe you'd feel better, Gene, if you had a chance to ask me some questions first," Joe said. "What would you like to know about me?"

"Well," Gene said, "I've read your resume, of course. But I sense a much more relaxed attitude than I'm accustomed to. I'm not saying I'm against it, I'm just not comfortable yet."

"Gene," Joe said, reminding himself to sound like a preacher, "I have a deep abiding faith that I am willing to share with anyone I meet. But I'm not convinced that our Savior wants us to be anything more or less than what we are. Translated, I believe children and adults have God given talents and personalities that we have an obligation to appreciate and cultivate. Your four children have a lot of potential. I want to see us, as a church family and members of the community, help them develop those talents."

Gene thought about that for a minute and asked, "What did you do about the Methodist ban?"

"I spoke to both sets of parents," Joe said. "I explained that I'd heard what Reverend Phillips said to their sons and I

42

knew it affected the friendships of the three boys. I told them it wasn't my place to apologize for Reverend Phillips, but I wanted them to know that I did not condone his decision and it would not be in effect as long as I'm the Baptist Preacher in this town."

Gene nodded and said, "I'm glad you did that. We all had problems with Reverend Phillip's heavy handed attitudes. I need to know how you feel about the Hispanics and their Catholic faith."

"I'm not going to get into the age old differences between their religions and ours," Joe said. "But I will tell you that I see no reason to ostracize anyone because of their race, origin or religion."

"I think you just won some points in my family," Gene said. "Elinda Salazar is Diane's best friend. Reverend Phillips was quite vocal about that friendship, too."

Joe rolled his eyes upward.

Turning to the two men, he said, "Okay, tell me what else the Reverend Phillips did to divide this little town."

Gene answered this time. "He was very strict about the Baptist beliefs. He lectured the children against any form of dance – including square dances at school. As you already know, he roamed through town and freely admonished our children about their friends. When the Methodists allowed the Catholics to use their building, it became an obsession with him. It was the focus of every sermon until he left." Ben nodded in agreement when Joe looked to him for confirmation.

"Well, I'm probably going to be the polar opposite of your last preacher," Joe said. "Is that going to be a problem for the congregation?"

"It'll be a change," Gene said. "But I think most of them will consider it a welcome change. We'll just have to wait and see. Now that we know your personal beliefs, we can give you some support when people start discussing different issues."

Joe heard his phone through the open church door. He excused himself and ran over to answer it.

"I'm sorry for calling so late," Mrs. Anderson said, "but Raymond has slipped off the bed. He's too weak to help me get him back up. Can you come help me, please?"

"I'll be right there," Joe said.

Running back to the church, he said, "I'll be right back. I have to help Mrs. Anderson for a minute."

Once he had Reverend Anderson back in bed, he returned to Ben and Gene. He noticed their bewildered expressions and said, "I promised Mrs. Anderson I'd be available anytime she needed me. Tonight Reverend Anderson slipped off the bed and was too weak to help her get him off the floor. Sorry for the interruption."

Ben grinned at Gene and said, "Our last Preacher wouldn't even speak to the Reverend. This one puts him to bed."

Joe looked at the two of them and said very seriously, "I believe I have an obligation as a *Christian* to help anyone in need. It's not in my nature to turn away from people I can help. If that's a problem, tell me right now and I'll help you find another preacher for your church."

Ben looked at Joe's face and knew his comment had been misunderstood. "No, Reverend Marsh," Ben said softly. "It is not a problem. It is a point of pride that I believe the entire congregation will appreciate. Don't you, Gene?"

Gene agreed and said, "You'll just have to give us some time to adjust to the change."

Joe nodded and forced himself to relax. After lining up the communion trays and arranging the church to be as inviting as possible, given its current condition, the men started to leave.

Gene stopped and said, "I almost forgot, this came in the mail for you today." He handed Joe a large envelope.

"I meant to ask where the postal service was," Joe said. "Is it in your store?"

"Yes," Gene said. "We get it delivered by bus twice a week – on Tuesday and Friday. We have a few boxes on the far wall, the rest we just keep under the counter, like a General Delivery service. We have a box up front for outgoing mail."

Joe thanked him again and the men left. He locked the church and went home.

He ripped open the envelope and searched for letters from Angelique. He found three. He put them in date sequence and started with the first one she'd sent. Although he'd only been in town three days, it had been almost two weeks since Jack

44

told her the news. He read through all three letters quickly, anxious to know that everything was okay in Boston.

Then he fixed a cup of coffee and re-read them slowly. He knew Angelique too well. Her first letter was what he would classify as a 'stiff upper lip' letter. She was full of disappointment, but said she understood and would survive a little longer without him. In the second one, she talked about their families and the concerts she was doing.

The third letter was the real Angelique. She must have written it late at night, sitting alone in the apartment they were supposed to be sharing as a married couple. Although she'd tried to write optimistically, he could tell she was sad and lonely. She needed her best friend and fiancé – who should have been her husband by now.

Knowing her the way he did, he could guarantee that she was no longer sleeping well and had dropped at least fifteen pounds off her slender body. Her music was probably reflecting that same loneliness. He had the *ministry* and the mission to keep him busy. But she was stuck in the same routine she'd endured for years.

Since he and Jack used e-mail for their correspondence, the rest of the packet contained religious fliers, and pamphlets for Joe to leave in the envelope – in case someone was watching his mail. All of it was very appropriate material to receive from the *Reverend Brownstone* listed on the return address.

He chuckled. This was probably the first time the tough Jack Brown had to represent himself as a man of the cloth. *Serves you right*, he thought. *If I have to do this, then so do you.*

Changing to black, he made a quick run through the town. No trucks were behind the hotel and no lights were on in the storage units. The bar was even quiet.

Back home he set up the laptop and checked his e-mail. Jack had the registration information on the license numbers he sent. On the surface, they appeared to be legitimate.

He typed a lengthy e-mail to Jack. He included all the events of the day in both the ministry and the surveillance. He always tried to give Jack as much detail as possible in case something here connected with any information Jack received from other sources. He asked Jack to verify the town history

45

he'd been given and find out who owned the empty houses and businesses in town. He said he planned to ask some questions about them, too. He also asked Jack to get him an application for a sports scholarship to the university in Portales as soon as possible. Then he added a serious paragraph about Goldie.

THE SITUATION IS WEARING TOO HARD ON GOLDIE. CHECK ON HER FREQUENTLY. SHE'S PROBABLY LOSING WEIGHT. HER PERFORMANCES MAY BE SUFFERING, TOO. TRY TO BOLSTER AND REASSURE PLEASE!

He didn't sleep well. He kept dreaming of Angelique, gaunt and depressed. He didn't want her to suffer because of his job. When he finished this assignment, he was going home – job or no job – Jack or no Jack. He hadn't agreed to make his loved ones suffer this much by being out of their lives.

CHAPTER FIVE

THURSDAY – FIRST WEEK

He woke up tired and worried. He jogged around town in a daze. He almost passed by Mrs. Morrison without even speaking to her.

"Either I'm invisible or you're still asleep," she said. "Do I need to hose you down again to wake you up?"

"Oh, I'm sorry, Mrs. Morrison," he said. "I wasn't paying attention. I guess I was thinking about the re-opening Sunday." Mentally he shook himself back to the present. He had to stay focused and trust Jack to take care of Angelique.

"Are you worried about Sunday?" she asked.

"Yes, I guess I am," he said. "Apparently, I'm quite different from your last preacher. I'm wondering how the congregation is going to react to that. I really don't want to offend anyone, but I can't be like Reverend Phillips either."

Mrs. Morrison reacted with an undignified snort and said, "I don't think many of us wanted to see another Reverend Phillips. We expected a new face and we were hoping for a better attitude. From what I've seen so far, we got both in you. You'll never please everyone. So why not focus on pleasing yourself? Let us see the real you, we'll adjust to the change."

"Thank you for the vote of confidence, ma'am," he said. "I guess I needed it more than I realized."

When he turned to start jogging again, she said, "Reverend Marsh, I assume you'll wear a suit Sunday, right?"

"Yes ma'am," he said. "It's in my closet, fresh from the cleaners."

"Then I'll assume you'll be cleaned up enough for Sunday dinner," she said, with a twitch of a smile. "So why don't you plan to join us after the service."

"Thank you, ma'am," he said. "I'd love to…any chance you'll bake another pie?"

Mrs. Morrison laughed out loud. "Lord have mercy," she said. "Do we have another pie addict in our midst?"

"Only if you bake them," he said, jogging on down the street. Realizing he'd been too deep in thought to check the town, he took another loop around the business section.

When he saw a man sweeping up some trash behind the bar, he stopped to introduce himself. It was the owner, Clive Osborn. Although Clive stiffened at the presence of a Baptist Preacher, he was pleasant. Joe guessed he was another one who had received a blast from Reverend Phillips. He tried to remain relaxed and kept his conversation on mundane subjects.

"I'm trying to rearrange my part of the alley," Clive said. "I've had some complaints about the trash piled up on Sunday mornings. It's visible from the Methodist Church. Apparently, it offends them." Then he chuckled and said, "Of course, it doesn't offend them to create the trash on Saturday nights."

"I saw your sign advertising Saturday Night Dances," Joe said. "It sounds like you have quite a crowd."

"As much of a crowd as you can get in this area," Clive said. "We usually have thirty or forty people in there. I have a dance floor on one side of the building and the bar on the other." He gave Joe a quizzical look, obviously expecting a Baptist admonition about both the bar and the dancing.

Joe read the look correctly and said, "Yes, I'm Baptist and we don't advocate dancing or the use of alcohol. However, I'm not naïve enough to believe that people are saints, regardless of their religion."

Clive actually laughed. "You're something else, Reverend Marsh," he said. "Reverend Phillips would roll over and die if he heard what you just said."

Joe nodded and said, "Don't misunderstand, Clive. I'm not advocating either activity. And I won't be one of your customers. But, I can still respect your right to run your business. I'll even go a step further and invite you to attend our worship services any Sunday you're available."

Clive was stunned speechless.

Joe grinned at the look on his face and said, "If you come, I promise not to preach on your *den of iniquity*."

Clive laughed out loud while he watched Joe jog off.

The rest of his second trip around town was uneventful, so Joe decided to concentrate on the condition of the church before he cleaned up.

He grabbed the keys, opened the church door and took a hard look at the gloomy interior. *How on earth can I make this place look more inviting by Sunday?* he wondered.

Going into the office, he looked through boxes and file drawers. He wondered who set up the file system. Each church member had a file folder and each folder contained a personal data sheet with dates of birth, baptisms, marriages, divorces and death. Several had actual copies of baptismal certificates, marriage licenses and death certificates. They looked relatively current. When he became more acquainted with the different families, he'd have to be sure to update the records.

He found three boxes of reference books written by well known Baptist clerics. Judging from the layers of dust on them, Reverend Phillips hadn't put them to use. In fact, it didn't look like Reverend Phillips had even used the office. That was another puzzle. He needed to ask Jack to send him some information on Phillip's background and his current location.

He cleared off a bookshelf in the corner and started arranging the books on it. When he unloaded the third box, he found a bag of fabric in the bottom. He unwrapped it and found an alter cloth, podium cloth and a third one that appeared to be the right size for the table in the entry. All three were beautifully embroidered. But the fabric had yellowed. He wanted to use them Sunday, but he had no idea how to clean them.

He locked the doors and carried the bundle up to Mrs. Morrison to ask her advice.

"I found some beautiful church scarves in one of the boxes at the church," Joe said. "But the fabric is badly yellowed. Can you tell me how to restore them?"

When she saw them, she was surprised. "We used these years ago," she said. "I thought one of the other preachers took them with him. Leave them here. I'll try to clean them up. They'll be my special project for the re-opening."

He thanked her and went back to the church. Brightened by his find, he worked through the other boxes. He didn't find any more special items, but the office definitely looked better.

He walked back into the sanctuary and decided to tackle the two large windows that were boarded shut. He pried off the boards and went outside to open the shutters. Judging from the rust on the hinges, he didn't think they'd been opened in years. *Did Phillips hold services in that dark atmosphere? He probably did,* he thought. *It would fit the mood he brought to this place.* Grabbing some window cleaner and paper towels from the bathroom, he started cleaning the glass. When he finished and went back inside, he was surprised at the change. Things were already looking better.

He was assessing other changes he could make when his house phone rang. It was Mrs. Anderson. "Raymond's having a bad day," she said. "Can you help me, please?"

"I'll be right there," he said. He locked up and ran across the yard. She met him at the door. They both knew things were not getting any better. Reverend Anderson's legs had collapsed under him when he tried to walk to his chair.

Embarrassed, Reverend Anderson said, "I don't know what happened. My legs just quit on me."

"No problem, sir," Joe said. "I'll be your legs. Do you want to sit in your chair or go back to bed?"

"I'd like to sit in my chair for a while," he said. "But I don't know if I'll be able to walk back to bed later."

"Well, why don't I help you into your chair for now," Joe said. "Mrs. Anderson can call me when you get tired and I'll come back and help you into bed."

"Okay," he said, "if you don't mind. I don't want to fall on Sherie. She tries to help, but she's not very strong herself."

"I don't mind at all," Joe said. "I'll be working around the church for another hour or so. Just give me a call when you're ready and I'll come right over."

Outside Joe asked Mrs. Anderson if the Reverend was still trying to deliver his Sunday sermons.

"No," she said. "He had to give them up. Our two Elders, Ralph Thompson and Charley Jasper, are preaching on alternate Sundays now."

"Good," Joe said. "Be sure to call me when the Reverend's ready to go to bed."

Back in the church, Joe looked upward and said, "Great! Phillips didn't just offend the sons of two Methodist families. He offended the sons of both of the Elders!"

He walked over to the old piano, plunked a couple of keys and wished again for a pianist. But that brought back thoughts of Angelique. He forced himself to stay focused.

Alice had already cleaned the altar and pews, so he decided to investigate the rooms upstairs. He found more boards. Apparently, this area was originally a second floor balcony. Someone had enclosed it and divided the space into two small rooms off the landing.

He opened the door to the first room. He could see a rack of folding chairs in the corner and a table with a stack of old Sunday School handouts on it. The dust and cobwebs were so thick, they literally forced him out. He'd have to go get the vacuum and clean it up before he could do much more.

Expecting to find the same situation in the second room, he was puzzled when he found it relatively clean. Each of the rooms had a small window facing the front of the church. The first one was still boarded shut. But the boards from the second one were standing in the corner. Obviously, someone had started to open the window. Since Ben said the church hadn't used these rooms in years, he suspected Phillips had been the last one up here. He found a folding chair, apparently pulled from the stack in the other room, and a bag of trash in the corner. Year old trash didn't appeal to Joe, but he needed to know more about the former occupant – both for the church and his mission. He went over to his house, picked up the vacuum cleaner and tucked some rubber gloves in his pocket. He was heading back to the church when the phone rang. He knew it was Mrs. Anderson. He put the equipment in the church and went back to their house.

While he was helping the Reverend back to bed, he said, "I know Reverend Phillips offended several people in town, but I

51

wonder if he made any friends while he was here. Did you ever notice him having visitors?" Reverend Anderson didn't remember any. But Mrs. Anderson said she used to see a man from the feed store drop by once or twice a month.

"Did you know the man?" Joe asked.

"No, not by name," she said. "He wasn't one of the workers at the store. I know all of them. I think he made deliveries there. He always walked over here so I never saw his truck, but I'm pretty sure I'd seen him unloading it at the store."

"Well, maybe I have a convert in my midst," he said.

When he heard a harrumph from the Reverend, he laughed and said, "Now you wouldn't deny a new preacher a convert, would you, sir?"

Picking up the challenge in Joe's voice, the Reverend said, "Sonny, if I was twenty years younger, I'd give you a run for your money."

"Sir, if you were twenty years younger," Joe said, "I wouldn't stand a chance."

Leaving the Andersons chuckling, he went back to the church and locked the door behind him. He took the vacuum and gloves upstairs and started cleaning – and searching. He went into the second room, first. Putting on the gloves, he sorted through the trash and carefully placed the contents on the floor. He wanted the DNA off the cups and food wrappers.

His search paid off. Two of the potato chip bags had syringes rolled up inside them and a cookie wrapper had white powder residue stuck to it. *Either Phillips was on drugs or he was supplying someone else,"* he thought. He retrieved one of the boxes he'd emptied earlier, lined it with a new trash bag and carefully placed the old trash bag and all its contents inside. He'd have to get Jack to arrange a pick up to take this to the lab.

He scoured both rooms for more evidence. He left the chair in the corner. He'd have to wait until dark to get his finger print equipment out of the compartment in the van. The chair should have Phillips' prints on it, if not others. When he finished vacuuming, he emptied the bag into another clean trash bag and added it to the box. He grinned. He was sure the lab would be cursing him for all the spiders and dust he'd collected. But the machine might have picked up other stuff that could be important. Once the rooms were vacuumed and mopped, he worked across the walls, floors and ceilings. He was looking for any hollow spaces that could be used for criminal purposes.

Back downstairs, he checked the closet under the stairs. Alice had apparently swept it, so he didn't have any dust to collect. He couldn't find any hollow spaces in there either. He went back to the office, moved the file cabinets, desk and bookshelf. All the walls and floors appeared to be solid. The sanctuary had a cathedral ceiling so there wasn't any attic to explore and the slab under the church floor eliminated any crawl spaces. Obviously, there wasn't an area in the church large enough for the smuggling operation. But Phillips was definitely involved in drugs.

He glanced at the clock and was surprised to see it was already three-thirty. Running back upstairs to get the box and vacuum, he peeked out the window to see if the boys were already at the basketball lot.

Shocked, he pulled back from the window and then looked again. Phillips could watch almost everyone in town from this window. The second floor elevation let him see over the top of most of the businesses and the church's location put most of the homes within his line of vision. If he used binoculars, he could see even more.

"Son of a ..." Joe started to say, but stopped. After all he was in a house of God and he was the preacher. Stifling the rest of the profanity, Joe took his stuff back to his house, cleaned up, locked all the doors and raced over to the basketball lot.

When he arrived, the three boys were already warming up and chattering worse than a group of teenage girls. He was sure they wouldn't appreciate that analogy, but it was good to see them together again. The friendships were definitely on the mend. Now all he had to do was keep up with them. They had a lot more energy that he did.

Judging from their greeting, Chris' *Preacher Man* nickname had stuck with the others. It didn't bother him. He knew kids liked to have their own names for people and this one was more respectful than some he'd used when he was their age.

After the game he went home, started a pot of coffee, put some hotdogs in the microwave and threw a load of dirty clothes in the washer.

Then he started writing his e-mail to Jack. He wrote out each step he took and walked Jack through the events of the day. He told Jack about the drug paraphernalia and his suspicions about Phillips. He said he was going back after dark to try to get fingerprints for the lab and he planned to take binoculars up to the window to see what Phillips could see. He said the box for the lab should be ready for a pick up tomorrow.

He suggested a contact in Portales, maybe at an auto shop since the town cop told him to get a tune up. They'd have to be sure they adjusted the noise level to cover the reason for his trip. Also, he asked Jack to arrange to have a used wheelchair for him to bring back to Reverend Anderson. It needed to look like something he could claim he found at a garage sale.

Later he made his nightly run around town. Not seeing anything unusual, he pulled his flashlight, binoculars and fingerprint kit out of the van and went back into the church. He draped a garbage bag over the window to block the flashlight while he dusted the chair for prints. When he finished, he cleaned off the chair and put it back in the corner. He turned off the flashlight, removed the bag from the window and focused his binoculars through the cracks in the shutters. He could see the entire town. He could see families through their open windows and watch the clientele at Clive's bar. In daylight, he could watch every business, person and vehicle on the streets.

What was Phillips doing, he wondered, *watching for 'sinners' he could blast? Or did he have a more nefarious reason for his spying? Whatever it was, he was determined to defrock Phillips and his abuse of his position as a preacher.*

Watch that indignation, he warned himself. *Isn't that the same thing you're doing?* He shivered. He hoped the town wouldn't hate him when this mission was over, but it was something to consider. Exhausted, he collected his equipment and locked the church.

At home, he added the rest of the evidence to the box. Then he finished his e-mail to Jack and went to bed.

CHAPTER SIX

FRIDAY – FIRST WEEK

He was sweating heavily by the time he'd jogged half of his path. The humidity was suffocating in the high temperatures. If it would bring some rain it might be tolerable. But the locals had already told him the moisture would evaporate before it reached the parched earth.

When he rounded the corner of Mrs. Morrison's yard, he held his arms out and begged, "Water me, please, I'm dying." Giggling, she gave him a quick misting and received a very grateful thank you.

"Boy, its hot," he said, "and it's only six a.m."

"Yes it is," she agreed. "Before the drought this humidity would signal a storm and rain. Now, the sun just burns the moisture off before any clouds have a chance to form." He nodded and looked at the sky. There wasn't a cloud in sight.

"Were you able to save the church scarves?" he asked.

She pointed to her clothesline and said, "I think most of the yellow came out. I'm going to let the sun bleach them for a while. Then I'll press them and send them over with Chris."

"Great," he said, moving over to the clothesline. "I don't know what you did, but they look like new. I'm glad we get to return them to their rightful place in the church. The long one went on the entry table, right?"

"Yes, it was made to fit that table and you were right about the other two," she said, pointing to them. "That one's for the altar and the other one goes on the podium."

"Thank you for restoring these," he said. "If I wasn't so sweaty, I'd give you a big hug and have all the neighbors talking." Mrs. Morrison blushed and giggled like a young girl.

"You're welcome," she said. "Now get out of here with your nonsense before I really turn the hose on you."

Laughing, he turned to leave, when she added, "And get a haircut. You're starting to look like a hippie."

"Yes, ma'am," he said. "I plan to do that today."

True to his word, he cleaned up and headed off to the barber shop. It was still early, so he hoped he could have more time to visit with the Kellys. He'd seen Barbara several times with Katherine at the grocery store, but apparently Roy and Rhonda didn't have much time to get out of their shop. Both of them looked up when the door chimed.

"See," Joe said. "I told you I'd be back, and according to Mrs. Morrison, I definitely need a haircut."

Roy grinned and waved him to the empty barber chair.

"So, what do you think of our little town now that you've been here for a few days?" Roy asked.

"I think it's great," Joe said honestly.

"I heard how you got Chris, Danny and Jerry back together. It's good to see them shooting hoops again," Roy said. "It looks like you hold your own out there, too."

"Well, I wouldn't admit it to the boys," Joe said, "but I really have to work to keep up with them. They're good kids. All three of them have great athletic skills."

"It's obvious you like kids," Rhonda said. "Have you considered having some of your own?"

Be careful, he thought. *She's fishing for someone.*

"Yes, I hope to have my own family someday, but not in the near future. I've dedicated myself to the ministry and that's all I want to focus on right now. Sooooo, if you have a specific reason for that question," he said, giving her a knowing look, "I'd appreciate it if you'd help me discourage any of your single friends who might be curious."

She had the decency to blush at being caught. To save her further embarrassment, he said, "I'm sure your customers have a lot of questions about me and probably a lot of speculation, too. It must be awkward for you." She nodded.

Roy had been clipping while they talked. When he turned Joe's chair around to the mirror, Joe said, "You're not just fast, you're good. My old barber never got my cowlick to lay flat." He left Roy grinning at the compliment.

Since it was too early for lunch, Joe decided to drop by the general store to see how the Reed's were doing. The store seemed unusually quiet when he walked inside. Gene and Ginger were putting up some more mail boxes in the back. Wayne and Diane were stocking shelves.

Sizing up the situation, Joe stood at the front of the store, put his hands on his hips and faked a western drawl, "Okay, what've you done with my Cowboy and Miss Lilly?"

Gene and Ginger looked puzzled.

"We sold em to some rustlers," Wayne said.

"Well, get me a horse, pardner, I'm gonna go get 'em and bring 'em back," Joe said. "Course, you're gonna hafta larn me how to ride first."

When everyone stopped laughing, Ginger told him the kids were playing with Alicia and Edmundo. Halfway through the sentence she hesitated and her voice faltered as if she was saying something she shouldn't.

Phillips again, Joe thought. "That's great," he said. "How old are Alicia and Edmundo?"

Warily, Ginger said, "Edmundo's four and Alicia's six."

"I really do think it's great for the kids to play together," he told Ginger. "I think this world would be a better place if we followed their example." To brighten the mood again, he turned back to Wayne and said, "Okay, if'n I don't need to rescue those little buckaroos, I don guess you hafta larn me how to ride."

The kids giggled and went back to work.

He turned to Gene and asked, "Do you know if anyone has a two story ladder I can borrow? I'd like to open the shutters on the second story windows at the church."

Gene thought for a minute and said, "I think Charley Jasper has one he uses on his feed loft. If you can't borrow his, I'll order one for you."

"I'll ask Charley," Joe said. "I hate to buy one when I only need it for a day." He waved to the kids and walked over to the feed store.

When they saw Joe walk in, Mary and Charley gave him a pleasant, but still cautious, smile. Jerry, on the other hand, came in from the back saying, "Hey Preacher Man, what's up?"

Aghast at his familiarity, Mary started to correct him.

Joe held up his hand and said, "I really don't mind the nickname." He faked a jab at Jerry and said, "As long as it's said with the *proper respect* for the senior member of the team."

"Of course," Jerry said. "We're always respectful – even when we beat you." He yelped when Joe faked a grab for him.

Realizing the parents were watching, Joe turned around and said, "Sorry, I get carried away with these guys. They're great kids. I'm talking to Chris about a basketball scholarship for college. In a couple of years, I'll be saying the same thing to Jerry. He's very good. He has great athletic coordination."

Both parents glowed with pride at Joe's comments. Then he told Charley what he was trying to do at the church and asked if he could borrow his two story ladder for a day.

"Sure," Charley said, "I can't spare it this weekend because Saturday is our busiest day and I'm sure you don't want it Sunday. Bart always comes in late Monday night, so we'll need it to stock his load on Tuesday. I can get Jerry to leave some extra feed down and you could have it on Wednesday, if that works for you."

That'd be great," Joe said. "Thank you. My project isn't urgent, so if your schedule changes, just let me know. I'll work around it. Goodbye, Mrs. Jasper. See you at four, Jerry. And, Jerry, you better rest up. I'm getting better every day."

"So am I, Preacher Man," Jerry shot back.

In an aside to Charley and Mary, Joe said, "He is, too." He turned back to Charley and said, "Any time you want to join us, come on over. Then I'll show you the 'aches and pain' section of the drug store. I practically live in that aisle."

Charley chuckled and shook his head as Joe left.

He was already tired of his own *cooking,* so he decided to splurge on another lunch at the coffee shop. Besides, he was burning more calories than he was eating with his two jogs around town and the daily basketball games.

Katherine greeted him as soon as he opened the door. After a quick chat with her, he headed for the coffee shop.

Alice heard Katherine and was pulling out the egg salad.

"Hi, Alice," he said, as he sat down at the counter. "Am I that predictable or are you spoiling me?"

"A little of both," she admitted. "Am I right? Egg salad on white?"

"Yes, ma'am," he said. "It's the only thing on the menu, isn't it?"

"As far as you're concerned it is," she said.

"Hi Reverend Marsh, how are you doing?" Ben asked, as he came around the corner and gave Alice a quick kiss.

"Doing fine," Joe said. "How about you?"

"Getting ready for tomorrow," Ben said. "Saturday's our busiest day."

"Hey, you got your hair cut," Alice said. "It looks nice."

"Thanks," Joe said, "I think Mrs. Morrison was going to lock me out of my own church on Sunday, if I didn't get it cut."

"She's already intimidating you," Ben said.

Joe leaned toward them and said, "Don't tell her I said this, but she's really a sweetheart." They grinned and agreed.

"By the way," Ben said, "I'm glad you found Ma's church scarves. We thought they'd been lost. She was really happy to see them again."

"What do you mean *Ma's* church scarves?" Joe asked.

"Didn't she tell you she made them?" Ben asked.

"No she didn't," Joe said. "They were a treasure when I found them. Now they're priceless knowing that your mother made them. They're going back in the church this Sunday and they'll stay there as long as I'm the preacher."

"Thank you," Ben said. "That'll make her very happy."

"I'm happy I'm the preacher who's going to be able to use them again," Joe said. "Thanks for the sandwich, Alice." Seeing Chris coming around the corner, he added, "I need a lot of good food so I can keep beating that son of yours at hoops."

"Beating who?" Chris challenged, as he swung into the seat Joe vacated. "You're doing a lot of bragging for someone who was huffing and puffing around the lot last night."

"In your dreams," Joe said. "I thought I was going to have to carry you home when we finished." He turned to Alice and Ben and said, "Have mercy on your preacher, give your kid some extra work to do before four."

"No fair," Chris said. "Now you're getting my folks to gang up on me."

"Just pleading for divine intervention," Joe said, waving out. "See you at four."

Back home he checked his e-mail. He had one from Jack. WE'VE ARRANGED A CONTACT FOR YOU IN PORTALES TOMORROW. I LIKE THE MECHANIC IDEA. GO TO THE FOLLOWING ADDRESS AND ASK FOR TOMMY. WE'RE WORKING ON THE WHEELCHAIR – SHOULD BE READY TOMORROW. GOLDIE IS FINE.

He started working on his sermon for Sunday. He was worried. He wanted to keep it short and informal. He planned to give the congregation a chance to discuss their issues with him. Especially since he was overturning almost everything Phillips had done. He'd have to remember to call him Reverend to the congregation, but Phillips had lost that title in Joe's opinion. Mrs. Morrison said to just be himself. He was going to trust her to know the town better than he did. Anyway, he'd never liked heavy handed sermons, so why would he want to use them? He went down the congregation list again. He hadn't met the families from the Scott Ranch. He'd have to make a point to get acquainted with them. He needed to go out there for a visit, too.

When he met the boys, he told them he was going to go to Portales tomorrow. "I may be back by four," he said. "If I'm not, I'll see you guys on Monday."

"Why are you going to Portales?" Danny asked.

"Constable Nelson doesn't like my noisy car," Joe said. "I promised I'd get it tuned up."

The boys hooted and mimicked the noise his car made when he drove into town on Monday. Joe laughed and stole the ball from Jerry. The game was on.

Later that night, after his surveillance run, Joe took out a map he'd drawn of the town. He wondered what Phillips was watching. He needed information from Jack on all the empty buildings. Any one of them could be used to hide illegals. But how would they get them in and out without someone seeing something? This town was too small for that size of operation. Maybe Phillips *was* just looking for 'sinners' – and a drug connection. Hopefully he only fed his habit. Joe couldn't stand the idea of Phillips getting any of the kids hooked on drugs.

He didn't know what was happening with the Hispanic families. He was going to have to find a way to get to know them without violating the Baptist-Catholic battle lines. Maybe some kind of sports would work with them, too. It might be a start, but he knew he'd have to confront the ethnic issues – on both sides – just to get the kids together.

He'd create even bigger waves when the *Gringo Baptist Preacher* visited the families on that block – and he was supposed to just *blend* into this little town. Oh, well. He knew he needed to know all the families if he was going to solve this case. He'd just have to play it by ear – and pray.

CHAPTER SEVEN

He told Mrs. Morrison he was going to Portales to get his car tuned up when he jogged past her house. He showered, put the box in the van and eased out of the parking space. He was trying not to disturb the Andersons or his other neighbors. He didn't dare cut off the choke or he'd be caught in his ruse. Once he was out of town, he turned it off and drove on up to Portales. He had to admit the noise was nerve wracking.

He pulled into the designated garage and asked for Tommy. Once they confirmed each other's identities, he popped the hood and Tommy adjusted the choke. When he finished, it was at least a decibel lower than before.

He asked about the wheelchair. Tommy had it in the back of his truck. Joe pulled his van around to load it and pass the box to him. With the transfer made, he took a moment to look at the chair. It was definitely a used one, but someone had cleaned it up and lubricated the moving parts.

Spinning the wheels, he asked, "Do I have you to thank for refurbishing this?"

"Yeah," Tommy said. "I didn't have much to do last night, so I thought I'd get it ready for you."

"Thanks," Joe said. "I hope I see you again sometime."

"Good luck," Tommy said. "I'll be here if you need me."

Joe stopped at an ATM before he left. He still hadn't found out what the town used for a bank. But whatever it was, he'd only be using it for his church salary. Even the ATM

62

account he was accessing now, was set up under Joseph Marsh's name. At least it kept him in cash during the mission.

Driving back, he wondered how the Andersons would react to the chair. Too anxious to wait, he pulled up in front of their house before he went home. When Mrs. Anderson answered the door, he took her hand like an excited kid and said, "Come see what I found at a garage sale in Portales." He opened the back of the van and grinned at the shocked look on her face.

"We were just talking about trying to find a wheelchair for him," she said, "and you drive up with one."

He pulled it out of the van. She studied it for a moment. He could tell she was trying to figure out how to operate it.

"Is the Reverend up to a visit?" he asked.

"Yes, he's sitting in his chair inside," she said, still trying to adjust to the surprise.

"Then let's take this inside and I'll show both of you how it works," he said. She nodded and ran up to hold the door.

Inside, he had a similar conversation with Reverend Anderson. Then he showed both of them how to operate the chair. A few minutes later, Reverend Anderson took some tentative rolls around the house. Although his legs were weak, he still seemed to have enough arm strength to push the wheels.

"Now that you have a wheelchair," Joe said, "we can roll you over to your church for services tomorrow. But Mrs. Anderson has to promise me that she won't try to wheel you down the porch step. You have to call me or one of the men in your church to help." The Reverend nodded, he was speechless.

After they made several attempts to pay him and expressed their gratitude, he left for his own home. He couldn't remember a time when he felt as happy as he did right now. He'd have to tell Jack and Tommy how much their efforts meant to the couple.

He changed clothes and headed over to meet the boys. He was surprised at the increased traffic in town. Charley and Ben said Saturdays were their busiest days, but he hadn't expected this much. It was easy to see why Clive had Saturday night dances. It was just smart business to take advantage of all the people who were already in town. He knew he'd have a long surveillance run later. He bet Dave Nelson would be busy, too.

He was heading home after the games when Dave slowed his cruiser beside him.

"Hello Constable," Joe said. "How are you doing?"

"Staying busy," Dave said. "But everything's quiet so far. We'll have a few drunks after the dance tonight. Then things will get back to normal again."

"Does the town have a curfew?" Joe asked.

"No," he said. "The Mayor didn't want to be that strict."

"The Mayor," Joe said. "Who's the Mayor?"

"Ben is," Dave said. "Didn't he tell you?"

"No," Joe said. "I guess he forgot to mention it."

"He probably didn't want to tell you," Dave said. "Reverend Phillips didn't like his members getting involved in politics. He quoted something about things belonging to Caesar."

Joe tried to control his expression and just nod.

"I hear you got your van tuned up," Dave said.

"Yes sir," Joe said chuckling. "I didn't like all that noise either. It's still a little loud, but not like it was before."

"That's good," Dave said. "See you around." He waved and rolled on down the block.

Inside his house, Joe shook his head. He wondered how many more of Phillip's edicts he was going to have to rectify. He was also beginning to wonder if he was too moderate for this congregation. Obviously, they were still following Phillip's rules a year after he left town.

He took time for a nap, since he expected to have a long night. He woke after dark, fixed a quick dinner and changed into his black clothes. He stopped by his van and grabbed his revolver and ankle holster. There were still some criminal elements around here somewhere. He wasn't going out unarmed.

Circling the north side of town first, he didn't find any problems. Most of the families had retired for the night. The businesses on Main were closed. Max's apartment was dark and no trucks were in the lot behind the hotel.

As he neared the bar, he could hear the music playing inside. Outside, a group of *good old boys* were tossing back long necks and talking about finding some women tonight.

Sitting in the overgrown brush across the street, he wrote down license numbers and caught fragments of their conversation. He'd seen his share of groups like this. They always spelled trouble. He counted six men, maybe a seventh sitting on the front of one of the trucks. He was furious at the crude language they were using to describe women in general and some young girl they decided they wanted tonight.

He listened closely. He was fairly certain they were talking about one of the Hispanic girls in town. Since he didn't know their names yet, he wasn't sure. Then he heard them say they'd have to get the town cop out of the way first.

That means she's one of our kids, he thought. The men decided two of them would bait Dave into a confrontation and two more in the bushes would jump him. The other two would go grab the girl.

Now what? he thought. *I don't want to blow my cover over a Saturday night brawl, but I can't let Dave get hurt. And I'm sure as hell not going to let these thugs drag an innocent girl off to be raped. I'll shoot all six of them first.*

He worked his way back around the group and picked up some empty beer cans out of the trash in the alley. Then he circled the block and crawled through the field again to get back to the bar. He watched the men and waited. Finally, he heard one of them shout that the cop was coming. Watching as two men baited Dave out of his car, he threw the beer cans behind the two in the bushes. Dave turned, drew, and took cover in one swift motion. *Ben was right,* he thought. *Dave knows how to handle himself.*

With those four exposed, he ran over to catch the two that went after the girl. He found them lurking in the alley between the two rows of Hispanic houses. Apparently, they were trying to decide where she lived. When one of them went out to the street to look for the right house, he knocked the other one out with a trash can lid. He hoped the noise would wake some of the men in the houses. The second man ran back to check on his friend and met the same fate.

When the lights came on in the houses, Joe faded into the shadows. He waited long enough to see two angry Hispanic men drag the drunks out to Dave's cruiser. Then he slipped back to his house.

He locked his door and fell into bed. It was two a.m. and he had a sermon to deliver at eleven. He wanted to be up and dressed before then, in case Mrs. Anderson needed help with the Reverend. He actually hoped she did. It might give him a chance to meet the Catholic Priest who would be ending his services when they arrived.

CHAPTER EIGHT

SUNDAY – SECOND WEEK

He awoke tired and nervous. He showered, shaved and dressed earlier than necessary. He poured a third cup of coffee and started writing his e-mail to Jack. He sent the license numbers and described the events around the bar. He also sent special thanks for the *tune up* and the wheelchair. He put his computer away and decided to go ahead and open the church, even though it was only ten o'clock.

About fifteen minutes later, Chris showed up carrying his grandmother's scarves. "Grandma looked for you this morning, but I guess you don't jog on Sundays," he said. "Anyway, she asked me to bring these over to you." He looked around the church and said, "Wow, I don't ever remember the church looking this nice. Gotta go. See you at eleven."

"Thanks, Chris," Joe called up the block behind him.

He was placing the scarves when he heard a timid, "Reverend Marsh," at the door. Turning, he saw Mrs. Anderson holding a large vase of flowers. "We'd like to give you these for your re-opening today," she said.

Caught speechless, he realized she was waiting to see if a gift from a *Methodist* would be accepted.

"That's very generous of you," he said. "Did you raise these? They're beautiful." She blushed and nodded.

"Thank you very much," he said. "This will make our re-opening extra special."

He set them on the entry table, stood back, looked at them and said, "No, I don't think they belong there." He noticed her face drop when he picked them back up. "I think they'd look better in here," he said, as he placed them in front of the podium. Her smile was radiant when he looked over his shoulder.

Thanking her again for her kindness, he asked, "May I help Reverend Anderson over to his church?"

"I hate to take you away from your duties here," she said. "But if you can spare the time, I'd appreciate it. Raymond's so excited, he's already dressed and ready to go."

Joe looked at his watch, it was ten forty. He could take a moment to help. "Well, let's go take our excited man over to his church," he said.

He was debating about leaving the church open, when he saw Gene and his family walking up the street. "Good Morning, Gene," he called out. "Go on in, please. I'll be back as soon as I help Mrs. Anderson."

He walked over to the Methodist parsonage and wheeled Reverend Anderson around to the side ramp of the church. Because of the hour, both arriving Baptists and Methodists witnessed the event. Most of the Methodists appeared pleasantly surprised, but not all of the Baptists were happy.

Apparently, the Scott Ranch group arrived during his absence. When Joe rushed back to his own church, he overheard Roger Scott muttering something about not being sure the new preacher knew which church he was supposed to serve.

So much for a good first impression, Joe thought. *Good thing I have a day job.* Chuckling to himself, he waited for the congregation to be seated.

Then he moved to the front of the church and approached the podium. Ben and Gene had already taken their places in the Deacon's chairs behind him.

He opened the service with a simple prayer of thanksgiving for the families, the community and the re-opening of the church. Then he signaled Gene, who led the group in a dismal attempt at a simple hymn.

Before his sermon, he told the congregation he had some announcements to make.

Pointing to the embroidered scarves, he said, "I found our beautiful church scarves in the office and discovered they had an earlier history in this church. Mrs. Morrison not only restored the yellowed fabric to its current beauty, she's the talented lady who actually stitched the exquisite patterns. Please be sure to thank her for them." He smiled when she looked surprised that he'd discovered her secret.

Next he said, "I met the ailing Reverend Anderson and his wife this week. Please say a special prayer for the Reverend. His condition is very grave. The vase of flowers in front of the podium is a gift from the Andersons to honor the re-opening of our church."

He continued through his list and thanked Alice for cleaning the sanctuary and supervising the work on the parsonage. Then he thanked Ben, Gene and the other's he'd met this week for helping him get settled in his new church home. To those present, whom he had yet to meet, he offered his assurance that he would make every effort to meet them in the near future.

Reaching for his Bible, he felt *the Word* move beneath his hand when he started to open it. He glanced down and noticed the tip of a lizard's tail. Looking across the pews, he saw Petey grinning in anticipation.

Not today, Cowboy, he thought, as he reached for a plastic bag in his pocket. To the others, he said, "I like to have congregation participation, so I'm going to ask Chris Morrison to read the scripture today."

Chris, caught totally off guard, fumbled with his Bible and rushed through the pages to find the reference. While everyone waited for Chris, Joe slipped his Bible into the plastic bag. He barely managed to trap the lizards as he hurriedly sealed the top. He set it on the podium shelf, pulled his sermon outline out of his pocket and waited for Chris to finish reading the verse.

Joe thanked him and preached a moderate sermon on Christian living. He tried to keep his presentation conversational – not intimidating.

When he finished, they had another hymn, communion and the offering. Then Joe told the congregation he wanted to allow them time to get to know him before he closed the service.

Shocked by the deviation from their traditional service, the group sat quietly for a couple of minutes.

Then a voice in back asked, "Are you sure you're a Baptist – not a Methodist?"

Knowing it was Roger Scott, Joe said, "Yes sir, I'm sure I'm a Baptist. But far above that, I'm positive I'm a Christian. And, as I've already stated to some members of this congregation, I believe I have an obligation as a Christian to help anyone in need. It is not in my nature to turn away from someone I can help." Several people nodded politely.

"Reverend Anderson has been stricken with a failing heart," Joe added. "I will not sit a hundred feet away and let his frail wife struggle with the burden of his care. She cannot and should not be alone in this time of need. Mrs. Anderson has my phone number and knows I am available any time she needs me. Also, for those of you who haven't already heard, I found the wheelchair he's using at a garage sale in Portales yesterday. With it, Reverend Anderson was able to worship in his church this morning. I wish you could've seen the joy on his face when I wheeled him inside."

"How do you feel about Catholics and Mexicans?" Jesse MacKenna asked.

"I don't believe in ostracizing anyone because of their origin, race or religion," Joe said. "I believe exposure to other religions is healthy. The scriptures have had multiple translations through the centuries. Honest questions about our differences lead us to a deeper understanding of the logic we used in developing our own theology. Beyond the differences, however, we frequently find common threads of Christianity that bring us together in our service to the Lord."

Jesse cut a look at Roger and turned back to Joe.

"As for ethnic groups or races," Joe said, "I know of no group the Lord excluded from His love and I endeavor to apply His same standards in my life. We have no more control over our heritage or the color of our skin than we do the color of our eyes. I know I'm probably offending some of your personal opinions on the subject, but I can't perform *my* personal commitment to my Lord by excluding anyone I can serve."

He looked around at the congregation and waited. Everyone looked stunned, but no one asked any more questions.

70

"I'll let you take time to think about the things I've said," he said. "I'd like to have an opportunity to serve as your preacher. However, if you don't believe I'm the right person for the job, let me know and I'll help you locate another one."

With a closing hymn and prayer, a solemn congregation left the church. Joe locked up and joined the Morrisons as they walked back to their homes.

"Thanks a lot, Preacher Man," Chris said. "Why didn't you tell me you were going to ask me to read the scripture this morning?"

"I would've, if I'd known I was going to have lizards in my Bible," Joe said.

Chris laughed and said, "Petey's at it again."

"I guess so," Joe said. "Thanks for the fast save. And thanks, Ben, for warning me about Petey. I grabbed a plastic bag on my way to church this morning. While Chris was looking up the verse, I stashed my Bible in the bag. Remind me to let the lizards out when I get back."

"That's what you were doing," Ben said. "I saw you put your Bible on the shelf, but I didn't know why."

Putting his arm around Mrs. Morrison, Joe said, "Thank you for the beautiful scarves. They truly are treasures."

"You're welcome," she said. "I didn't realize how much I'd missed them until I saw them back in place. You were very kind to recognize me, but it wasn't necessary."

"It's always important to recognize good work," Joe said. "I didn't embarrass you, did I?"

"No, not really," she said. "I was just a little surprised."

"Well, you seem deep in thought," he said. "Is something wrong?"

"I was just thinking about Mrs. Anderson," she said. "Do you think she'd let me visit her? I know how hard it is to watch a husband suffer."

"Madam, I'm going to pick you up and hug you right in front of the entire town," Joe said. "I'm sure Mrs. Anderson would welcome a visit from you. If you let me know when you want to go, I'll join you and keep the Reverend company. Then she'll be able to relax and visit with you. You are such a sweetheart! Bless you for your kindness."

Hearing the conversation, Ben said, "I think we could probably trim their grocery bill a little bit."

"And maybe send a few extras with their next order," Alice said.

"That would be great," Joe said. "Just don't let it look like charity. About the only thing they have left is their pride."

"We'll do it right," Ben said.

"Do you know if Mrs. Anderson likes to read?" Katherine asked. "I could send her a book of poems."

"As a matter of fact, I saw a book of sonnets on her end table," Joe said. "I'm sure she'd love some poetry."

"Hey, you've left me out," Chris said. "What can I do to help them?"

Joe thought for a minute and said, "Their grass is getting a little tall. Maybe you could mow it for a glass of lemonade." He looked at Ben and said, "You have a wonderful family. I know the Andersons will be touched by your kindness."

Ben nodded and grinned at the others.

"By the way," Joe said. "When were you going to tell me you were the Mayor?"

Blushing, Ben said, "That was another bone of contention with Phillips. I didn't want to get off on the wrong foot with you."

"Well, I think it's great," Joe said. "Congratulations. Who was your opponent?"

"Charley Jasper," Ben said.

Joe rolled his eyes and said, "Good Lord. Even the politics in this town are divided by religion."

"Yeah," Ben said. "Charley and I seem to alternate serving. But there really isn't much official business to deal with in this town. I think last night was about the most excitement we've had in months."

"What happened last night?" Joe asked.

"Some rowdy cowboys tried to ambush Dave and break into one of the Hispanic homes," Ben said. "Dave has them all in jail, but he said something was strange about it."

"What was that?" Joe asked.

"The ambushers swear someone threw beer cans at them," Ben said. "And the robbers said someone hit them on the head with trash can lids."

"How many drinks had they had?" Joe asked.

"Too many," Ben said.

"Then I'm surprised they didn't report dancing trash cans," Joe said.

"Very true," Ben said.

"So," Joe asked seriously, "do you think I'll be your preacher next week? I don't think the congregation was very happy with me when they left."

"Give them time to think about what you said," Ben said. "For the record, I think you're absolutely right about our Christian duties, but we've been myopic about our religion for years. They won't wait long to complain about you. But they're going to have a hard time arguing with your position. Don't give up on us yet. We might surprise you."

Ben's home was as warm and inviting as the family. The walls were painted a creamy yellow with multicolored Mexican serapes hung at odd angles on them. The large living room had two tan sofas with assorted tables, lamps and accent pillows. The oversized brown recliner in the corner was obviously Ben's. The smaller green version in the other corner had to be for Alice. Large throw pillows in front of the TV added to the casual appeal.

The living room flowed through a wide archway into an equally spacious dining room with a large oak table and ten chairs upholstered in a compatible serape pattern. The same fabric was used as a table runner. A basket of Indian corn served as a centerpiece for the place settings of practical ovenware dishes. Indian and Mexican accent pieces added splashes of history and color around the rooms. The kitchen was next to the dining room on the right. A hallway off the living room appeared to be the bedroom wing.

Alice was putting a pot roast and vegetables on a platter. Mrs. Morrison was making gravy and Katherine was tossing a salad. Chris was pouring coffee while they waited for the biscuits to finish baking. Joe loved the way the family worked together. When the meal was ready, they asked Joe to say grace.

The food was great, but he enjoyed the relaxed family banter even more. Mrs. Morrison produced an apple pie for dessert and the guys were in heaven.

When Joe got up to leave, he gave Mrs. Morrison a quick hug and thanked her for her kindness – and the pie.

"You're like the Grandma I never had," he said. "Thank you for everything."

"Then you might as well call me Grandma," she said. "I've all but adopted you anyway."

"Grandma, it is," he said, giving her a kiss on her cheek.

"Hey, who's romancing my mom?" Ben asked, joking with Joe, when he heard the exchange. To Alice, he whispered, "I don't know how he's managed to do it in one short week, but we all consider him part of the family." She grinned and agreed.

Joe opened the door to leave, when the phone rang.

Chris shouted, "Wait a minute, Preacher Man. Harry and Richard want to shoot some hoops. Wanna join us?"

Looking at his watch, Joe said, "Sure, I need about an hour to free some lizards and change. Meet you there at three?"

"Got it," Chris said. "I told them you play as good as you preach."

"That can be taken two ways," Joe told the adults. "I guess I'd better go change."

He stopped at the church, retrieved his Bible and turned the lizards loose. *That Petey's a rascal,* he thought. *I'll bet he's wondering what happened to these little guys.*

Seeing Mrs. Anderson's flowers, he picked them up. Since they'd wilt before next Sunday, he decided to take them back for the Andersons to enjoy.

When he knocked on their door, he heard a hard thump inside. He stepped into the living room and found Reverend Anderson tipped over in his wheelchair. He was braced against a doorway so he hadn't fallen out – but it was close. Grabbing the chair, Joe set him upright and turned to look for Mrs. Anderson.

She came running in from the bedroom. "I heard a noise..." she started to say, and then she saw Joe. "I don't know how on earth you always know when we need you," she said.

"I'm beginning to think its divine guidance," the Reverend said.

"You could be right, sir," Joe said.

Mrs. Anderson's face fell when she saw the flowers he'd set by the door. Reading her thoughts, he said quickly, "The congregation loved your flowers, Mrs. Anderson. They thought they were beautiful and said to thank you for thinking of them. I didn't want to leave them in the church to wilt. So I thought I'd bring them back and let you enjoy the rest of the blooms."

Obviously pleased by what he said, she put the flowers in their window. "They truly are beautiful and that was very kind of you to share them with us," Joe said, as he left.

Mrs. Anderson followed him outside and told him the Reverend spoke to the congregation for a few minutes in church today. She hadn't seen him that happy in weeks. The chair was a blessing. She thanked him and gave him a quick hug.

Back at the house, Joe smiled. It seems he'd found two new grandmas in one week. They were both remarkable ladies and, truth be told, he'd come to love them both.

As he changed into his basketball clothes, he wondered about Harry and Richard. Their dads were the vocal skeptics in church. It'd be interesting to see how the kids reacted to him.

Just beat them at hoops, he told himself. *They'll make their folks bring them back next week for a re-match.*

He locked up and jogged over to the lot.

They divided into three-man teams and played several lively matches. As soon as Harry and Richard started playing, they lost their reservations about Joe. They took their lead from Chris. By the time they quit, he was their *Preacher Man*, too.

When he got back to his house, he was beyond tired.

Man those kids are good, he thought, rubbing his legs. *They make me feel like a senior citizen. Thank God, I didn't jog this morning.* He was starting to understand why he hadn't seen any dads joining the boys. Of course, the kids hadn't been thwarting criminals at two a.m. either. With that thought, he collapsed on his bed and slept for a few hours.

He woke at eleven, changed to black and made his surveillance run. Then he sent Jack an e-mail.

I KNOW I'M PUSHING THE BAPTISTS WITH MY RELIGION AND RACE SPEECHES. BUT I HAVE TO BE ABLE TO CROSS ALL THE DIVIDING LINES IN THIS TOWN TO DO THE INVESTIGATION. AND I NEED THE TOWNS' TRUST, IF I'M GOING TO GET ANY POSSIBLE CLUES FROM THEM. THE SOONER THEY ACCEPT THE FACT THAT THE BAPTIST PREACHER CAN BE FOUND IN ALL PARTS OF TOWN, WITH ALL RELIGIONS AND RACES, THE SOONER I CAN FOCUS ON THE MISSION. SO FAR, I'VE SPENT MORE TIME ON THE CHURCH AND MY PREDECESSOR THAN THE REAL PURPOSE FOR MY PRESENCE.

ALSO, LET ME KNOW IF YOU GET ANY FEED BACK ON THE MEN ARRESTED LAST NIGHT, ESPECIALLY THE WOULD-BE KIDNAPPER-RAPISTS.

PLEASE CHECK ON GOLDIE. I'M WORRIED ABOUT HER.

CHAPTER NINE

MONDAY – SECOND WEEK

When he finished his morning jog and visit with Grandma, he locked the door to the parsonage and started searching for concealed compartments. He didn't find anything. Putting things back in place, he decided to go have lunch at the grocery store. He was anxious to see what Ben had heard about him. It wasn't just a personal interest. His mission depended on him being a part of this community.

After greeting Katherine, he sat down in the coffee shop to eat his usual lunch and chat with Alice. He was almost finished when Ben came in.

"Roger Scott called me this morning," he said

"I guess I expected that," Joe said.

"Well, I didn't," Ben said. "I was braced for a complaint about the position you took yesterday. But he just wanted to know if you could help their two kids apply for scholarships, too. He said anyone who could be his son's *Preacher Man* in one afternoon, was good enough for him." Joe nodded cautiously.

"Personally," Ben said, "I think Roger and Jesse were setting you up. Their kids have practically grown up with Hispanic and Catholic kids on the ranch. Of course, they'd never mention that to the rest of us. I knew because Chris told me." Seeing the relief on Joe's face, Ben slapped him on the back and said, "Looks like you're a keeper, Preacher Man."

"I never expected basketball to be my strong suit," Joe said. "Who would've guessed? I have Chris to thank for a lot of this. The kids look up to him. They trust anyone he trusts."

"Don't discount yourself in this deal," Ben said. "Kids have a sixth sense about people. They trust you, because they know they can. I'm glad they have you as a role model."

Humbled, Joe just said, "Thanks, Ben," and left.

Between lunch and his daily match with the boys, he went back to his notes. *What am I missing?* he asked himself. *In one week I've met everyone on the Anglo side of town and none of them have given me any reason to believe they'd be involved in anything illegal, except Phillips. If it hadn't been for his narrow-minded isolationism......*

Wait a minute! I'm counting on open communication lines to provide clues. If Phillips was involved in this scheme, it would serve his purpose to keep people separated and suspicious. Did he create this divisiveness to minimize exposing the operation? Obviously, he was effective, the town stayed divided a year after he left. Was that his mission? Does he go into towns and create so much hate that they become ideal spots for smuggling? Why did he leave? Where did he go? Is he setting up another town and, if so, where? It's a stretch, he thought, but he put it in his notes.

He wondered why Jack hadn't sent him any information on Phillips. He'd send this theory to Jack and ask him to rush the Phillips research – and he needed more scholarship forms.

He was back at the lot with the boys when he noticed a couple of Hispanic kids watching them play. When they took a break, he asked Chris who they were.

Chris looked at them and they backed away.

"Oh, that's Edwardo Salazar and Gabriela Perez," Chris said. "We call them Eddie and Gabbie."

"Do they play basketball?" Joe asked.

Chris looked shocked for a second, then grinned and said, "They sure do. Eddie's on our team at school and Gabbie's on the girl's team."

"Call them over," Joe said.

"Okay," Chris said. "But watch Gabbie, she'll kick your....uh, she's really good."

It took some persuasion, but Eddie and Gabbie finally joined them. As with the other kids, the reluctance disappeared once they started playing. And Chris was right, Gabbie was very good. When they quit for the day, Joe made a point of asking Gabbie and Eddie to join them at four tomorrow.

When they started to say, "Thank you, Reverend ....."

Chris said, "Naw, he's just Preacher Man to us."

They grinned and said, "Thank you, Preacher Man."

Walking home, he was very pleased with the afternoon. Sports had been the ice breaker, again.

When he ran his surveillance later that night, he noticed a semi back in the hotel parking lot. But it wasn't Simms' grocery truck. It was the truck he'd seen at the feed store last week. He'd have to check his notes for the date. What had Charley said? He couldn't loan the ladder on Tuesday because Bart's deliveries arrived then. This must be Bart's truck. He worked his way around to the back of the truck, wrote down the tag number and checked the trailer. It was padlocked shut.

He was moving back to the street when the light in Max's apartment came on and a man, probably Bart, stepped inside. Joe sat in the shadows and watched. A few minutes later Bart came out with a towel over his shoulder. He walked to the back door of the hotel, unlocked it and went inside.

Aha! Joe thought. *This may be what I'm looking for.* He waited, expecting to see more people emerge from the truck. But nothing happened. About half an hour later, Bart came out of the hotel, drying his hair as he walked back to the apartment. He handed the towel to Max and returned to his truck.

Joe sat there for another thirty minutes before he left. On the surface, it appeared that Bart had just used the hotel for a shower. *The hotel is closed to the public. So why would Bart have access?* he wondered. *Apparently he picked up the key from Max. So that's where I'll start tomorrow. I need to mark that parking space. It looks like the same one Simms used.*

Back at the house, he checked his notes. Simms had parked his grocery truck there last Tuesday night.

CHAPTER TEN

TUESDAY – SECOND WEEK

When he jogged around the feed store, the semi was already at the dock and Jerry was helping the driver unload the large bags of feed.

Seeing Joe, Jerry called out, "Hi, Preacher Man." So, Joe had a perfect opportunity to hop up on the dock to say hi to Jerry and introduce himself to Bart.

No last name was offered. While chatting with them, he asked a couple of questions about the seeds they were unloading. Bart obviously wasn't interested in a conversation with the preacher. Jerry volunteered the answers.

To engage Bart in the conversation, Joe asked, "How far do you have to go to pick these up, Bart?"

Again, Bart ignored Joe. "He drives down to Texas for most of this," Jerry said. "I forget the name of the town. What's the name again, Bart?"

"It's not a town," Bart said, "just a silo in south Texas that sells grain."

Noting Bart's hostility, Joe decided not to push for any more answers. He'd get Jack on it. They already suspected Bart was transporting drugs. He could be part of the other ring, too.

He walked into the truck and looked at the bags. He patted a couple and said, "I see you have a lot to unload. I'll get out of your way. See you later, Jerry. Nice to meet you, Bart."

From the cursory glance he had inside the truck, the bags looked legitimate. But he didn't like Bart and he had no doubt the feeling was mutual. He'd ask Jack to put a tracer on that truck. The electronics guys loved to do things like that.

He jogged on around to Grandma's yard. She was waiting for him. "Would you have time to go to the Andersons with me today?" she asked.

"Absolutely," he said. "The Reverend usually rests until noon, why don't we try to go over around one?" She agreed. He gave her a quick kiss on the cheek and said, "I'll pick you up."

After breakfast, he wandered over to the general store and was greeted by Lily and Petey and their parents.

He picked Petey up and said, "Cowboy, a couple of little lizards told me you want to help me with my sermons."

Petey wiggled away from the threatening looks he was getting from his parents.

Struggling to keep a straight face, Joe said, "So why don't you memorize John 3:16 for me and I'll let you come up to the podium and tell it to the congregation."

Not realizing the under currents of Joe's assignment, Lily said, "I want to do one, too."

"Okay," Joe said, "why don't you do, John 3:17."

Beaming with pride, Lily ran to the back room shouting, "Diane, help me learn John 3:17 for the preacher."

Petey was right behind her.

Joe glanced at Gene and Ginger and burst out laughing.

"It's nothing," he said. "I used to do the same thing. Why do you think I know about these tricks? Personally, I think it's good to get the kids involved. It makes the service less boring for them."

When Gene and Ginger finally relaxed, he wandered back to the feed store to be sure Bart had finished unloading. He didn't see the semi or Bart, so he walked up to the storage units to have a chat with Max.

Since he wasn't sweeping out any units, Joe walked up the same stairs he saw Bart use last night and knocked on the door. When he didn't get an answer, he remembered that Max didn't use his hearing aids. He knocked louder and Max finally answered. He was surprised to see Joe.

81

He casually brushed his hands off on the seat of his pants and waved Joe into his home. Over a cup of coffee and light conversation, Joe started asking Max about his job. Unlike Bart, Max was very relaxed talking about his work. As he'd said before, Cozen Oil built the storage units and uses them to store drilling equipment close to their wells.

Joe wandered over and looked out Max's window. "I've noticed a couple of trucks parked back here," he said, pointing to the space behind the hotel. "Is this where delivery trucks are supposed to park if the drivers need to rest?"

Max followed him to the window. Looking down where Joe pointed, he said, "Oh no, only Bart and Simms are allowed to park there. They have permission from Cozen to use the space for their semis."

"Really," Joe said. "Do they pay Cozen for the space?"

"I don't know anything about that," Max said. "All I know is it's only for those two and they get hot if anyone else parks in their space. In fact, I saw Bart get real tough with one trucker who tried to park there."

"So, if I wanted to park my van back here to make more space at the church, who would I need to contact?" Joe asked.

"I don't know, right off," Max said. "As far as I know Cozen doesn't want any other trucks back here."

"Well, its nice Bart and Simms get to stop here for the night," Joe said. "It must be tough on them since there isn't a hotel in town. It's hard enough to go days without a shower. At least they have a place they can pull off and sleep."

Taking the bait, Max said, "They get to shower here."

"They do?" Joe asked. "Where do they go, to some friend's house?"

"No," Max said. "I give them a towel and a key to the back of the hotel. They use a shower in there."

"Really," Joe said. "I thought the hotel was closed."

It is," Max said. "But Cozen lets them use it."

"Does Cozen own the hotel?" Joe asked.

"Yep, they built it before they built the storage units," Max said. "They had to have a place to put their workers. Of course, back then, the farmers still had some crops. So the town had more visitors."

"How many rooms are in the hotel?" Joe asked.

"I think it has about twelve, plus the lobby," Max said.

"That's about right for a town this size," Joe said. "It's a shame it had to close. I was lucky I had a house. Otherwise, I would've been out of luck for a place to stay here."

Max nodded.

"Have you been in any of the rooms lately?" Joe asked. Then he quickly added, "I was just wondering how much work it would take to re-open it, if this drought ever ends and the town starts to grow again."

"I haven't been in it for three or four years," Max said. "I guess we could go take a look at it now, if you want."

"Sure," Joe said. "Let's see what it'd take to restore it."

Max got the keys and let Joe in the back of the hotel. He pointed to the bathroom the truckers used. Then he unlocked an interior door that led to the rest of the hotel. Joe commented on architectural techniques and the floor plan to cover his disappointment.

None of the rooms appeared to have been used since the hotel closed. The layers of dust were consistent throughout the area. None of the plastic covers on the furniture had been removed or disturbed. Even if the building had concealed areas, they hadn't been used – at least not from this access, because the only footprints on the floor belonged to Max and Joe.

After some more comments about the hotel's potential, he thanked Max for the tour and, remembering he was a preacher, invited him to Sunday services.

Joe was not happy when he left. He hadn't realized how much he'd hoped he had a lead on the operation. He was balancing his gut reaction about Bart, against the obvious fact that the hotel wasn't being used for covert activities. Bart might just be a small time drug dealer, but Joe didn't think so. He decided to install a surveillance camera on the lot and see if it caught anything.

Based on his visit today, he was convinced Max wasn't involved. Or if he was, it was inadvertent. Max was too open and honest with Joe to be trying to hide anything.

He was so deep in thought, he almost missed Simms' truck at the grocery store. He turned and wandered over to the loading dock. He exchanged greetings with Ben and Chris.

Simms managed a polite, but cryptic conversation. Looking in the truck, Joe was surprised at the number of boxes.

"Is all this for your store, Ben?" he asked.

"No," Ben said. "We get half of it. The rest goes out to the Catholic Church."

"That makes a long day for you Simms," Joe said. "Where do you have to go to pick up this stuff?"

"The fresh food I get in Portales," Simms said. "The rest I pick up at a warehouse outside of town."

"And you do all that in one day?" Joe asked.

When Simms nodded, Joe said, "I'll let you get back to work." Turning to Ben, he asked, "Can I go through the back door? I think Alice has some egg salad for me."

"Sure," Ben said. "She's waiting for you. I'll join you in a minute."

After lunch, Joe said, "Gotta run. I can't keep a pretty lady waiting." At Ben's quizzical look, Joe said, "Apparently, the town gossip line is down today. I'm taking your mom over to visit the Andersons." Ben nodded and walked out with him.

Promptly at one, Joe and Grandma walked down the street to the Andersons. He could tell Grandma was nervous when he knocked on the door.

He squeezed her hand and said, "It'll be okay. Just relax and be yourself. Isn't that what you told me?"

She giggled and took a deep breath.

When Mrs. Anderson answered the door, she smiled at Joe, but looked perplexed at Mrs. Morrison. "Good afternoon, Mrs. Anderson," he said. "May we come in for a visit?"

She opened the door while Joe said, "I thought I'd visit with the Reverend for a few minutes. Mrs. Morrison thought you might like some company."

After a couple of tentative comments, Mrs. Anderson brought out a pitcher of lemonade and four glasses. Joe wandered into the bedroom to visit with Reverend Anderson. The two ladies sat down at the kitchen table.

When the Reverend discovered that Mrs. Morrison came with Joe, he insisted on being wheeled out to thank her for coming. He knew how much the visit would mean to Sherie – and he knew who had been instrumental in the meeting.

"Thank you, Joe," he said quietly. Joe just grinned.

By the time they said their farewells, *Grace* was promising *Sherie* another visit tomorrow. Grandma chattered about her visit with Sherie all the way back home. He suspected Sherie was doing the same with the Reverend.

Later, joining the kids on the lot, he was delighted to see that Eddie and Gabbie had come back. But something was different today. Both of them were more reserved around him.

When they took a break, he asked, "Have I done something to offend you two?" They shook their heads no. "Well, I know something's wrong," he said. "Can you tell me what it is?" They looked at Chris with a silent plea for help.

Chris said, "Someone called their priest and reported them playing ball with you. The priest called their folks and warned them about your influence over their kids."

Joe struggled to conceal his anger around the kids.

"Would it be better if I didn't shoot hoops with you anymore?" he asked.

All five kids said, "No," in unison.

"I don't want to cause trouble for you with your parents or your priest," Joe said.

This time Gabbie found her voice, "We told our parents you were just helping us get good at basketball. You weren't the El Diablo the priest said you were."

Covering the priest's insult and his own mounting anger, Joe laughed. "Thank you for your support, Gabbie," he said, as he mimicked horns with his hands. "I'll try to leave my horns at home when I come over here." When he had them laughing again, he said, "Now let's shoot some more hoops."

Mrs. Anderson stopped him when he walked home from the games. She thanked him for bringing Grace over for a visit. She hadn't realized how much she'd missed having another woman to talk to. Then she asked him for some help getting Raymond back into bed.

Inside, he tried to cover the Reverend's embarrassment, by telling him what the priest said.

"I assume, that was Father Romero," the Reverend said. "He won't even let his people speak to us as they come and go in our church. How did you get Eddie and Gabbie into the game?"

"Just invited them," Joe said, with a grin. "They love to play and they're good. In fact, all these kids are very good."

"I've tried for years to break the barriers in this town and you've done it in a week with basketball. I don't understand it," the Reverend said.

"Neither do I, sir," Joe said. "If it's beginner's luck, let's just hope it continues."

"You're going to have your hands full with Romero," the Reverend said. "Don't let him see weakness or he'll walk all over you."

"Thank you for that advice," Joe said. "I imagine I'll be meeting him soon. I might even drive out to see him."

"That would be good," the Reverend said. "But don't let him know you're coming. Catch him off guard. Otherwise, he'll have all his armor on." Joe laughed at the image of a priest in armor and waved goodbye.

Relaxing over a cup of coffee and a microwave dinner, Joe started his daily report to Jack.

Tonight he was venting his frustrations.

WHY DID YOU HAVE TO PUT ME IN THIS LITTLE TOWN AS A PREACHER? WHY DIDN'T YOU MAKE ME SOME TYPE OF BUSINESSMAN OR SOMEONE LESS IMPORTANT TO THE PEOPLE HERE? I HAVE A LOT OF PEOPLE TRUSTING ME AND I ADMIT I'M GROWING VERY FOND OF THEM. HOW WILL THEY FEEL ABOUT ME WHEN I FINISH THE MISSION AND AM EXPOSED AS NOT BEING THE MAN THEY THINK I AM?

DID ANYONE RESEARCH THE RELIGIOUS DIVISIONS IN THIS TOWN BEFORE THEY DEVELOPED THIS SCHEME? WHY AREN'T I GETTING ANY FEEDBACK ON THE DATA I'M SENDING? WHAT ABOUT THE LAB REPORTS, FINGERPRINTS, ETC? WHO IS PHILLIPS? WHERE WAS HE BEFORE HE CAME HERE AND WHERE IS HE NOW? WHAT ABOUT BART AND SIMMS AND THEIR TRUCKS? WHAT ARE THEIR NORMAL ROUTES? PUT TRACERS ON BOTH OF THOSE TRUCKS! WHERE'S THE RESEARCH ON COZEN OIL? IS ANYONE BACK THERE WORKING ON THIS BESIDES ME?

QUIT LEAVING ME HANGING ON A LIMB TRYING TO SECOND GUESS EVERYTHING! DO YOU HAVE ANY SUGGESTIONS ON HOW TO HANDLE A CATHOLIC PRIEST WHO HAS LABELED ME

A DEVIL – AND THE HISPANICS WHO BELIEVE HIM? I NEED
SUPPORT AND FEED BACK, ASAP. COVER MY BACK – JACK!!

He dressed in black, retrieved a couple of surveillance
cameras from the van and started his nightly rounds. He found
Simms' truck parked where Bart's had been last night. Simms
must have parked it after dark, because it wasn't there when they
played ball this afternoon. Not wanting to risk being seen, he
carried the cameras back to the house. He'd try again tomorrow.

CHAPTER ELEVEN

WEDNESDAY – SECOND WEEK IN EL PASO

Angelique arrived at Jack's office the same day he received Joe's frustrated e-mail. Before she could knock, she heard him raging over the phone at someone. Then he hit the hold button and started arguing with someone else. Obviously unhappy, he cursed freely as he slammed the phone down. Looking up, he was surprised to see her standing in his doorway. While he greeted her, he remembered what Joe had predicted. She'd lost weight and she'd taken a sabbatical from her concerts.

She, on the other hand, was asking for word about Joe. She was worried about him. As much as it pained him, he had to tell her that he had no news for her, except that Joe loved and missed her. And no, he couldn't tell her how much longer Joe would be gone. She paled at the news.

"Are you all right, honey?" he asked. "I'm sorry I don't have more news for you. I know how hard it is to wait this out."

"I'm okay," she said. "Just feeling a little lightheaded, I guess. May I have some water, please?"

"Of course," he said. "Sit still, I'll be right back."

"When was the last time you had a good meal?" he asked, handing her the water.

She shrugged and said, "It's been a while."

"Well, why don't you let me take you to dinner tonight and we'll catch up on the news from Boston," he said. "Then I'll put you on a flight back there tomorrow."

She gave him her hotel number and promised to go rest until he picked her up for dinner.

WEDNESDAY – SECOND WEEK IN EUTOPIAN SPRINGS

During his morning jog, Joe noticed Simms had already pulled his truck out of the lot. After a quick cup of coffee, he changed and went over to the feed store to see if Charley could spare the ladder for a day.

Much to his surprise, Jerry was waiting for him with the ladder in tow. When he reached for it, Jerry held on and said, "No, Preacher Man, I'll carry it. I'm going to help you with those windows today."

"That's nice of you to offer," Joe said, "but I can't take you away from the store. I'm sure your dad needs you here."

"Nope," Jerry said. "Dad said anyone nice enough to help our minister deserves our help in return. He told me not to come home until those windows shine all the way back here."

Joe poked his head inside the store and thanked Charley for Jerry's help. Charley waved it off and said, "We appreciate the help you've given the Andersons."

When Joe turned to leave, Charley added, "Just don't try to convert him while he's over there."

"You drive a hard bargain," Joe said, grinning at him. "It'll be tough, but I'll try not to."

He and Jerry carried the ladder back to the church. Cleaning the windows would not only make the church look better, it would give him an excuse to open those front shutters. If Phillips could use them for surveillance, so could he. Maybe he'd see something that he was missing on the ground.

After washing the front windows, they decided to remove the boards on the stained glass windows in the sanctuary.

By noon Chris and Danny had come over to help. With some good natured joking about Methodists and Baptists working together, they fell into the routine. They helped pass tools, wood and window cleaner back and forth to Joe on the ladder. He was pleased with the results of their work on the windows. But he was bursting with pride at the kids who voluntarily spent their time helping – and he told them so.

After their daily hoops game, he took the kids into the drug store for some ice cream.

"Hey," Danny said. "How come Eddie and Gabbie get ice cream? They didn't help with the windows."

Seeing the crushed look that crossed the kids' faces, Joe wanted to smack Danny. "Sure they did," he said quickly. "Didn't you see them? They were on the corner. It was their job to signal me when they could see El Diablo's face in the glass."

Danny blushed when he understood Joe's message. To his credit, he apologized. "Sorry guys," he said. "I forgot about the priest's warning." Then he picked up Joe's lead and said, "So that's why you made us wash them three times." Turning back to Eddie and Gabbie, he said, "I'll bet you just waited to signal him so we'd be too tired to beat you today."

That started the robust exchange that followed. Who beat who today and who was going to eat dust tomorrow, restored the balance as they walked out of the store.

Later that night, Joe carried the surveillance cameras with him. He placed one under the eave of the barber shop and aimed it at the hotel parking lot. He'd like to put another one on the side of the Kelly's house, but he was afraid they'd hear him. So he worked his way over to the storage unit stairs and hid the second one under the landing. Now he'd be able to monitor the conversations the truckers had with Max. Next, he slipped into the church and placed a camera outside the upstairs window.

Back at the house he wrote his nightly report to Jack. He told him about Simms' truck and the cameras he'd placed. Since he still had no supporting information from Jack, he just reported the events and signed off. Apparently, Jack couldn't or wouldn't help him. He was beginning to wonder why he was even writing reports. Did they just drop him off out here and forget him? He was feeling alone and betrayed.

CHAPTER TWELVE

THURSDAY – SECOND WEEK IN EUTOPIAN SPRINGS

Joe jogged his normal path, chatted with Grandma and headed home for a quick shower and breakfast.

When he locked his door, he saw Mrs. Anderson outside and stopped to talk to her. She told him Raymond had taken three more falls this week. He was getting weaker. Doc checked on him daily, but he didn't have any encouragement. Raymond didn't want to go to a hospital if they couldn't do anything for him. He'd rather stay home with her. Doc added oxygen and prescribed some more medication to keep him comfortable.

He gave Mrs. Anderson a hug and got in his van.

He left town, heading west.

Twenty five miles later, he pulled off on a heavily rutted side road leading to the Catholic Church. It was larger than he expected and appeared to have a sizeable amount of agricultural land attached to it. He saw several men working in one of the fields, but he couldn't identify the crop.

When he walked up to the church, a priest stepped outside. Joe asked to see Father Romero.

"Father Romero isn't available," the priest said piously. "Perhaps I can help."

"No thank you," Joe said. "How long will Father Romero be *indisposed?*"

Objecting to Joe's assumption, the priest corrected him. "Father Romero is not indisposed. He's in prayer and asked not to be disturbed."

91

Joe looked at his watch and said, "Apparently he prays slowly, if he's still in morning prayers. When he's finished, please tell him he has a visitor."

"May I tell him your name?" the priest asked.

"No," Joe said. "I'll introduce myself." He turned away from the priest and started looking around the grounds.

Indignant at his dismissal, the priest went back into the church. Joe grinned. He bet Father Romero would finish his *prayers* in the next five minutes.

Father Romero emerged from the church four minutes later and had to look around to find Joe. He'd wandered back to look in one of the side buildings.

Clearing his throat to get Joe's attention, he assumed a dignified air and said, "I'm Father Romero. I understand you asked to see me. Is there something I can do for you?"

He's saying the right things, Joe thought. *But his tone is definitely not conciliatory.* Giving the Father a long steady stare, he said, "Hello, Father Romero. It's nice to finally meet you. I'm Joseph Marsh, the new Baptist Preacher in Eutopian Springs. I understand you call me *El Diablo.*"

The Priest's eyes flared with anger before he could control them. "Why didn't you tell Father Tobias who you were?" he asked.

"Well," Joe said, "first, I don't introduce myself to people who aren't willing to offer their own names. And second, if you'd known who I was, I doubt you would've agreed to meet me." Shocked at his bluntness, Father Romero acknowledged the truth with a simple shrug of his shoulders.

Pushing his advantage, Joe said, "I drove out here today to find out why a Christian priest would defame another man of God, when he hadn't even met the person."

Father Romero regained his composure and stated regally, "You are not a member of our faith. You have no right to come into my parish and challenge me."

"Correction," Joe countered firmly. "I am a Christian. Therefore I *am* a member of your *faith.* I am not Catholic, which means I am not a member of your *religion.* However, as a man of God, I do have *a right* to challenge anyone who presumes to place *himself* above the scriptures – and I do mean the *Catholic* scriptures."

"You're a *Baptist*," Father Romero said. "You don't know anything about Catholic scriptures."

"I know more than you think," Joe said. "And I know that turning strangers into enemies is *not* what Christians do – *Catholic* or otherwise. No man of God is serving the Lord when he spreads fear and hate. And *nothing* in your *religion* allows you to *abuse* the sanctity of the priesthood to promote your *personal prejudices*. Your condemnation of me damaged *your* reputation more than mine. I did nothing to deserve your *El Diablo* attack – and you know it."

Father Romero was furious. He started to interrupt Joe with his own arguments, but his statements were hard to refute.

Joe watched Father Romero's face and saw the emotions change. He knew he'd made his point. He softened his voice and said, "Look, Father Romero, I didn't come out here to argue with you. I am well aware that my predecessor created a great deal of animosity between the different religions in Eutopian Springs. I don't condone his actions and I don't support the divisions he created. As long as I'm the Baptist Preacher in town, I will not ostracize anyone for their religion, origin or race. All I'm asking is that you show me and my congregation the same respect. I drove out here to meet you today and to ask you to give me a chance to make a difference in town. We're both men of God representing the Christian faith. We should be able to work together for the good of all of the people. I'm in town. You're twenty-five miles away. Everyone will benefit, if we can develop some basic respect between us."

He waited for Father Romero to digest what he'd just said. He could still see distrust on his face. But at least the hate was tempered. Trying to diffuse the situation, Joe said, "I can see I've said some things you need to think about."

Father Romero nodded.

"Can we at least declare a truce until I prove what I'm saying?" Joe asked, as he offered his hand.

"On one condition," Father Romero said, tentatively shaking his hand. "You tell me how you know so much about the Catholic religion."

"It's a long story, Father," Joe said. "But the truth is, I actually attended a year of seminary."

The shock on Father Romero's face was priceless.

93

"Look," Joe said, "I want to get to know the Hispanic families in town without causing recriminations from you. I'm not trying to make converts and I have no intentions of preaching against their religion. But you have to admit, you aren't always there when they need you. I'm in town and I'll help them any way I can in your absence. Now do you think you could rescind your El Diablo statements and give me a chance? Or do I have to challenge you to a game of hoops?"

For the first time in the entire meeting, Father Romero relaxed and said, "Oh, no! Edwardo and Gabriela have already told me you're very good."

"They're good kids and good players," Joe said seriously. "But they're worried that you're angry with them for joining us."

"I'll modify my statements when I come to town on Sunday," Father Romero said. "I'm ashamed to admit it, but you're right. I was willing to believe that you were just another version of the last preacher. I practiced the same prejudice I preach against. Please accept my apology."

"Apology accepted," Joe said. "I truly believe that we can both provide valuable support to the town and our worshipers without compromising either of our religions."

"It'll take a while for me to adjust to the change you're proposing," Father Romero said, "but I'm willing to try."

"Thank you, Father," Joe said. "I look forward to working with you. May I visit again sometime?"

"Certainly," Father Romero said. "I'd like to hear the story about a Baptist Preacher attending a Catholic Seminary."

Pleased with the outcome of his meeting, Joe said goodbye and left.

On his way back to the main road, he noticed a familiar pickup truck coming in from the field. He checked the license plate through his rear view mirror and kept driving.

Approaching the Scott Ranch a couple of miles away, he pulled over to jot down the license number. Since he was already there, he decided to go ahead and stop for a short visit. He knew he should've called first, but hopefully, they'd forgive him for just dropping by. As he drove up to the ranch house, Ellen Scott came out on the porch and waved.

"Reverend Marsh," she said, "how nice to see you. Come on in. We were just sitting down to lunch."

He looked at his watch and grimaced. "I'm sorry" he said. "I shouldn't have come at meal time. I'll come back later."

"Nonsense," she said. "Come on in and join us."

She took his arm and pulled him inside with her. "Roger," she called out, "Reverend Marsh has come to visit."

Roger came around the corner with half a sandwich in his hand and said, "Come on in Reverend Marsh, join us for lunch." Joe gave him a hesitant look and Roger blushed.

"I owe you an apology," Roger said. "Jessie and I weren't very nice to you on Sunday and apparently we embarrassed both our families. I shouldn't have criticized you for helping Reverend Anderson. In fact, I should've thanked you for caring. And we have a lot of very good friends who are both Catholic and Mex...uh Hispanic. We didn't mean to sound so prejudiced. But according to Sheila and Ellen, we came across as *royal hypocrites* – at least that's the only name they'll let me repeat to the preacher." Joe chuckled and tried to let him off the hook, but Ellen made him continue.

"The women were still fussing at us when our kids came back from their hoops game and started hammering us for giving their *Preacher Man* a hard time," Roger said. "And then they started talking about the *college scholarships* and we had everyone mad at us." Joe was laughing by the time he finished.

"Are we forgiven?" Roger asked.

"There's nothing to forgive," Joe said. "I'm sure a lot of other people wanted to ask the same questions. I know the entire congregation was waiting for my answers." Roger cut a look at Ellen. She nodded. Joe caught the exchange and grinned.

"Okay," Roger said. "Now that I'm out of the dog house, let's have some lunch."

Before he could be seated, Harry burst through the back door saying, "I saw Preacher Man's van outside. Is he here?"

"I'm here, Harry," Joe said. "How are you doing?"

"Great," Harry said, as he sat down and started making his sandwich. He cut a look at Roger.

"I've apologized, Harry," Roger said.

Harry nodded and started eating.

"Help yourself, Reverend," Roger said, "before the other four kids get in here and eat it all up." As if on cue, Will, Sandra, Laurie and Dale barreled through the door arguing over who won the race to the house.

"Welcome to the Scott home," Roger said. "There's never a dull moment with this crew around."

Joe laughed and said, "It's wonderful. You may have some track stars in your midst. By the way, I've sent for more scholarship applications. I'll let you know when I get them."

That led to a discussion about the information they'd have to collect. "Since Harry's a junior, I need to work on Chris' application first," Joe said. "His has to be submitted before the end of the month. Then I'll come out and help you get Harry's ready. Do the MacKennas want Richard to apply, too?"

"Yes," Harry said. "We both want to be vets and open a practice in town."

"Great," Joe said. "Keep your grades up and you'll be on your way to a good career." Harry groaned and Roger laughed.

When they finished lunch, Joe asked Roger about the size of his ranch. Obviously a pride point, Roger led him outside and showed him the different corrals, barns and sheds.

While they were talking Jesse rode up. He glanced at Roger. Roger nodded and said, "I apologized for both of us."

Jesse blushed and said, "Sorry, Reverend."

"It's forgotten," Joe said, staring at the horse. Jesse was obviously very comfortable on his horse, but this was as close as Joe had ever been to one. He was amazed at how large it was.

Seeing Joe's discomfort, Roger said, "That's right, Reverend, you're a city boy aren't you?"

When Joe nodded, Roger looked at Jesse and said, "Step down and let the Reverend ride your horse."

Joe's eyes must have popped, because Roger and Jesse both laughed at him. He tried to swallow his fear. Roger quit laughing and gave him some basic instructions. Joe followed his lead and tentatively patted the beast. A few minutes later, he was actually in the saddle. Joe knew he was trembling. He tried to laugh to cover it, but he couldn't.

"This is wonderful," Joe said nervously.

"Sit in that saddle twelve to fourteen hours a day," Jesse said, "and you'll discover how *wonderful* saddle sores can be."

Joe moved in the saddle and understood what he meant. Laughing with them, he dismounted.

"I'd love to learn how to ride a horse someday," he said.

"Come back at round up and we'll give you all the riding you want," Roger said.

"I just might do that," Joe said, backing away from the horse. "How large of a herd do you have?"

"Not as many as we used to have," Roger said. "We've had to trim it down a lot. We don't have enough grass to support very many on the land right now. We lose money when we have to buy feed to raise them."

Joe nodded and asked Jesse where he lived. Jesse pointed to another house about half a mile away. Joe asked about his family. Jesse said his wife and kids had gone to Portales to buy school clothes.

"Do your two families run this whole ranch?" Joe asked.

"Just about," Roger said. "Sometimes we hire a couple of hands to help Jesse, depending on our workload. The rest of the time they work for the Catholic Church."

While he drove back to town, he reviewed his two visits. The shared church and ranch workers might account for the additional Saturday traffic in town. He wanted to check on that pickup truck, too. Glancing at his watch, he realized he'd have to hurry to get changed in time to meet the kids at the lot.

When he jogged up, Chris grinned at him and said, "I hear you rode your first horse today, Preacher Man."

Joe looked at him and asked, "Who told you?"

"Harry called. He said you were terrified when Mr. MacKenna rode up," he said.

"He was right," Joe said. "I've never been that close to one before. I'd like to learn to ride one someday."

After some more taunts, the kids started playing.

How could anything get by the people in this little town? he wondered. *Every move I make is certainly public knowledge!*

He replaced the tapes in the three cameras during his nightly run. He added another one to the side of the Church of Christ that faced the bar parking lot and a fifth one on the side of the Baptist Church facing the empty houses by the school. Then

97

he went home and reviewed the first ones. He had nothing on the two in the lot and only Dave's patrols on the one from the church window.

Frustrated, he created a tape log on his laptop and sent Jack his daily report. He checked his earlier notes and confirmed that the pickup he saw today was one he'd seen at the bar last Saturday night.

THURSDAY – SECOND WEEK IN EL PASO

While Joe was visiting the Catholic Priest, Jack was taking Angelique back to the airport. He could tell she wasn't happy about his decision, but she finally agreed that it was probably best.

When he got back to his office, he picked up the phone and started making more calls. He threatened to make some people very unhappy if he didn't get some answers soon. He considered calling the Boston office to pull his other unit members back down here. But he was afraid it might blow Joe's cover if he started moving too many people around.

He didn't like waiting back here while Joe was out there alone. Joe was doing a great job infiltrating the community. In fact, he'd exceeded all their expectations. None of them had anticipated the divisiveness. They'd assumed he'd be able to walk in and take over Sunday services.

Jack smiled as he thought about Joe's personality and the way he was handling the town. *Maybe he's more of his father's son, than he realizes,* he thought. *He's taken to the ministry like a pro. And Joe was right, they'd have to develop a plan that wouldn't destroy the trust he was building with these people when the mission was over.*

But right now, he had to focus on getting some help for him. He read Joe's e-mail again and decided not to add to his worries by telling him about Angelique's visit.

CHAPTER THIRTEEN

FRIDAY – SECOND WEEK

Joe jogged around town trying to look at it from a different perspective. He'd changed his routes each day, jogged different directions and checked alleys and spaces between buildings. He was obviously missing something, but what? He'd always been good at reading people. He'd be willing to bet his paycheck that none of the townspeople he'd met were involved in the smuggling ring. Maybe the Agency misunderstood the informant. Maybe this wasn't the right town.

He stopped for his morning chat with Grandma and went home to work on his Sunday service. Since he hadn't asked for another meeting with Ben and Gene, he needed to plan the service and let them know what he'd need. He selected some songs from the hymnal and then outlined a short sermon based on the scriptures Petey and Lily would recite. Looking ahead, he planned next week's sermon. He'd have to watch his Bible around Petey. He realized he'd inadvertently given Petey the perfect opportunity to stash the lizards last week. He'd left Gene and his family in the church while he helped the Andersons.

He fixed a quick lunch and another pot of coffee. He spent the afternoon studying the little information he'd managed to gather. Discouraged and more than a little disappointed, he changed to go meet the kids at the lot.

He decided to drop the list of hymns off for Gene and see if any mail came in on the bus. Petey and Lily were ready for him when he walked into the store. They each had to say their verse to prove they were ready for church. They basked in his praise and raced back to tell Diane. Obviously, she was the helpful big sister who taught it to them. He gave Gene his list of hymns and in return, Gene gave him a large envelope.

After the games, he ran home to read his mail. He had three letters from Angelique written over a week ago. Unfortunately, they just added to his dark mood. The letters made him even more homesick for her. He could tell she was as lonely as he was.

"Why hasn't Jack helped support her?" he asked out loud. "Where the hell is Jack anyway? He's not answering my e-mails. He didn't even add a note in the envelope. If no one wants to give me some support over here, why shouldn't I just pack up and go home to Angelique?"

He microwaved a dinner and sat down to read her letters again. He looked around the parsonage and seriously considered packing up. He hadn't found a thing in this town to indicate it was involved in the crimes they were looking for.

Later he made his nightly run. The bar had a few more customers tonight. But they appeared to be the same regulars he'd seen before. He changed tapes in all five cameras and went home to review them. None of them had anything new. He sent a terse report to Jack and went to bed.

CHAPTER FOURTEEN

SATURDAY – SECOND WEEK

He woke up as tired as he was when he went to bed. The hollow-eyed images haunted him all night. He cursed and grumbled all the time he fixed his coffee and started jogging.

Shake this attitude, he told himself. *They're out there somewhere. They've had months to set up their operation. You haven't even been here two weeks. They're slick. That's why they haven't been caught. Stay focused. There are fifty women a week counting on us to rescue them. If the people in this town are the honest citizens you think they are — they're in danger, too — if the smugglers are running through here.*

Back at the house, he pulled out his notes and tried to create scenarios that the smugglers might use. There were plenty of empty buildings in town, but he couldn't see how they could transfer that many women without the townspeople noticing something. He shook his head as he crossed out ideas.

Since he expected to have another late night, he took a nap before he went over to meet the kids. Playing with them helped. He was even smiling when they finished. He heard some youngsters laughing and followed the sounds to a field across from the Hispanic homes. Eddie and Gabbie fell in step with him. He watched the kids play follow-the-leader and tag.

"It's good to hear children laughing and playing," Joe said. "I didn't realize so many little ones lived over here."

"Oh yeah," Gabbie said, "and we just added another one. Mrs. Sanchez had her fourth last month, a little girl named

Rosalie. That's her cousin playing with the kids. She came over to help with the baby because Mrs. Sanchez has been sick."

He looked at the kids and said, "I see Raul out there, I guess his arm's healed."

"How do you know Raul?" Gabbie asked.

"I met him and his mother, Mrs. Sena, in the Doctor's office last week," Joe said. "He fell off a chair." *If Father Romero keeps his word tomorrow,* he thought. *I may be able to get over here and meet a few more of these families.*

He said goodbye to Eddie and Gabbie and walked home. He noticed the traffic hadn't thinned out much from the earlier shopping crowd. It looked like it would to be another late night for Dave – and him.

Back out at eleven, he changed the tapes in the cameras by the church and the hotel. Waiting for a break in the dance crowd lingering outside, he changed the one by the Church of Christ. He sat in the brush outside the bar again and wrote down the tag numbers on tonight's vehicles. Luckily, the crowd didn't seem as rowdy this week. He suspected word about last Saturday's arrests probably slowed them down a bit. He watched until after midnight before he worked his way home. Again he reviewed the tapes, and again, they didn't give him any new clues.

CHAPTER FIFTEEN

SUNDAY – THIRD WEEK

Determined to be back at his church in time to greet his worshipers, he helped the Anderson's over to their church a little earlier this week. That gave him some time to relax and visit with his congregation. Ben and Gene arrived with their families and went inside to set up the communion service. Doc and Nancy walked up with the Kellys.

When Roger and Jesse drove up with their families, the younger kids piled out of the trucks and ran over to play with the town kids. Harry and Richard headed inside to sit with Katherine and Barbara. Joe grinned when he overheard Ellen and Sheila telling their men to behave themselves today.

Ellen winked at Joe and said, "If he gives you any more trouble, make him sing a solo." Roger's mouth flew open, but he closed it again when she said, "Don't you dare say what you're thinking in front of the Preacher." Roger grinned at Joe and nodded as they walked on into the church.

Several people commented about the restoration of the stained glass windows. Joe thanked Chris for his help and then told the congregation that Jerry Jasper and Danny Thompson had also helped with the project. He noticed their surprised looks when they realized the Methodist kids had worked on their church. He stifled a grin and nodded to Gene to lead a hymn.

Before he started his sermon, he asked Petey and Lily to come up front and announced that they had memorized verses for the congregation. He sat down on the step in front of the podium and waited for them. Lily walked right up to Joe. Petey had to stop and wave at everyone on his way. When Petey finally said his verse, the whole room chuckled and clapped. Lily said hers and got a round of applause, too. The two kids ran back to their seats giggling.

"I want to do that, too," he heard Dale Scott say.

His mother tried to shush him, but Joe said, "We'd love to have you say a verse for us next Sunday, Dale. I'll tell you which one before you leave today. Okay?"

Dale nodded. Sarah MacKenna raised her hand and asked, "Can I have one, too?"

"You certainly can," he said. "We'll look forward to both of you reciting our verses next week."

The congregation clapped for them and the kids grinned. He moved on up to the podium and delivered his sermon. The Deacons served communion and passed the offering plates. Joe said a closing prayer and hastily selected two verses for Dale and Sarah to memorize for next week's service.

As the congregation was leaving, Chris, Harry and Richard set up another game of hoops at three.

He was locking the church, when he saw Ralph Thompson wheeling Reverend Anderson back to the parsonage. He went over to help him back to bed.

Then he went home to have a quick lunch and check his e-mail. To his surprise, Jack had finally sent him some information: SEE ATTACHED ON THE VEHICLES YOU REPORTED. HAVE A TRACER ON BART'S TRUCK. WE SHOULD HAVE ONE ON SIMMS' SOON. NO RECORDS FOUND ON PHILLIPS SO FAR. NO MATCH YET ON THE PRINTS YOU SENT. DRUG IN SYRINGE WAS HEROIN. ALSO FOUND TRACES OF MARIJUANA IN THE TRASH. GREAT WORK WITH THE TOWNSPEOPLE AND THE RELIGIOUS DIVISIONS, HANG IN THERE. WE'RE WORKING IT OVER HERE. SPOKE TO GOLDIE, LONELY, BUT OKAY.

His mood was much better by the time he met the kids. It brightened even more when Eddie and Gabbie ran up to tell him their news.

"Father Romero said it was okay for us to play basketball with you," Gabbie said. "Then he said he'd been wrong to call you El Diablo. He said that he'd *met* you. He said he thought you were a person we could *trust* when he wasn't here to help."

"What did you do?" Eddie asked. "I've never heard him say anything like that about *anyone* who wasn't Catholic."

"Nothing much," Joe said. "I just drove out and met with him to assure him that I wasn't like the last preacher."

"That's for sure," Gabbie said. She tossed the ball into play while the guys were still absorbing the fact that Joe had visited Father Romero.

I guess I've made the local news again, Joe thought. To the boys, he said, "Look alive or she'll have your hides before you wake up."

After his nightly rounds, he put his tapes in the viewer and e-mailed Jack on the priest's statements. He told him he planned to start meeting some of the Hispanic families this week.

Looking at the tapes from the bar parking lot, he wondered about that one pickup that seemed to be in and out of town several times a week. It had been at the feed store both days Bart was unloading and was at the bar both Saturday nights. The tapes from last night showed the driver talking to a person in another pickup before going inside.

According to Jack, the truck was registered to the Catholic Church. But he doubted the bar trips were official church visits. The driver could have been buying seed on Tuesdays, but the church already had crops growing in their fields. So what were they seeding? He needed to know more about the person, or persons, driving that truck.

CHAPTER SIXTEEN

MONDAY – THIRD WEEK

Something's different this morning, he thought as he jogged behind the feed store. It took him a minute to realize he wasn't hearing fussy kids and crying babies in the Hispanic section. Since everything else appeared normal, he decided the kids must be giving their folks a break today. He jogged on around the next blocks, spoke to Grandma and headed home.

He stopped before he reached the parsonage.

Doc Stockwell was walking up to the Anderson's. He looked at Joe and just shook his head.

An hour later, Doc knocked on Joe's door. Over a cup of coffee, he said, "I've told Sherie to call their children and let them know Raymond's condition has reached a critical level."

Joe grimaced at that news. He listened quietly while Doc reminisced about the Andersons' earlier days in town. In the process, he talked about the families who'd had homes and businesses there.

"What happened to those businesses and houses?" Joe asked. "Do the families still own them?"

"Oh, no," Doc said. "They lost them to the banks that were holding their loans. Since the town is far from thriving, they're just sitting here, rotting away."

"What about the houses on the Hispanic side of town?" Joe asked. "Do those families own them or are they rentals?"

Doc's harrumph, said it all.

"No, they don't own them," he said. "They pay good money for those rundown places. The owner lives out of state. Cozen built them. They needed rent houses for their workers' families. When the oil company left, they sold them to the current owner. He rented them to the Spanish families who weren't welcome on this side of town."

Joe waited when Doc stopped to take a sip of coffee.

"It evolved into what the locals called ..." Doc shook his head and said, "Never mind. The polite version would be Mexican town. The houses are in deplorable shape. We haven't been able to get the landlord to make any repairs for years." He finished his coffee and thanked Joe for a chance to talk.

"They were good stories, I'm glad you shared them with me," Joe said. "I'm here for you and the Andersons, anytime."

"Thanks Reverend Marsh, I appreciate that," Doc said. "They aren't just patients. They're good friends I hate to lose."

After Doc left, he decided to try to meet some of the Spanish families. He changed and headed back across town. He could hear the kids playing outside when he walked up to the first door. He silently cursed. He hadn't arranged to have a translator with him. He was turning around to go home, when he heard a child's terrifying scream.

Racing around to the field, he froze. A rattlesnake was coiled and ready to strike one of the little girls. Holding a hand out flat to signal her to stand still, he picked up a large rock and prayed he could protect her while he hit the snake. One of the ladies slowly moved up behind the child. She signaled she'd get the girl. He nodded.

He threw the rock and she grabbed the child in the same heart stopping moment. Several women and children screamed. One of the women pointed to the snake. He'd only stunned it. It was trying to crawl away. He grabbed a shovel from the side of one of the houses and made sure it was dead this time.

When he turned to check on the little girl, he found what must have been every mother and child in the block staring at him. He scanned the crowd for someone who could translate.

Gabbie ran up the block to the field. She spotted the shovel and the snake. "Who did it bite?" she asked anxiously, as she searched the crowd. She asked the same question in Spanish and everyone pointed to the little girl in the lady's arms.

"It didn't get her, Gabbie," Joe said quietly. "But it was a very close call."

Gabbie and the lady both checked the little girl carefully. Then Gabbie gave her a big hug and soothed her. A few minutes later she handed the child to Joe and said, "This is Angie Sanchez. She thinks you're very brave. She wants to give you a hug for saving her."

Joe melted. He'd never had a more precious hug in his life. Asking Gabbie to translate, he said, "Please tell her I'm sorry I scared her."

Gabbie translated and said, "She said the snake scared her, but you didn't."

He gave Angie another hug and handed her back to the lady. Turning to Gabbie, he said, "Please thank this lady for grabbing Angie. She's the one who really saved her."

Gabbie gave the woman a hug and translated. Joe got a small smile from her. As the crowd began to disburse, he asked Gabbie if she would translate and help him meet the families.

"Sure," she said. "Where do you want to start?"

"I'll leave that up to you," he said.

"Okay," she said. "We might as well go to the end of the block and work our way around. Most of them already know who you are." He nodded and followed her lead.

"Wait until this gets back to Father Romero," she said. "He'll probably make you a Saint next Sunday."

He laughed out loud and said, "Gabbie you're priceless!"

When they knocked at the first house, he heard the lady refuse to meet him. Gabbie was his champion. She switched to Spanish and reminded the woman about Father Romero's statements. "How can he help you, if he doesn't even know who you are?" she asked.

He shook his head at Gabbie and said, "I don't want to cause any trouble."

Gabbie looked at the woman and said, "You're treating him the same way the gringos treat us. I'm ashamed of you."

She took Joe's arm and walked away.

"Wait," the lady said.

Gabbie turned around and introduced Joe to Carmen Montoya and her four children. Gabbie told him that Carmen's husband, Pedro worked at the feed store. He nodded and thanked Mrs. Montoya. She gave him a shaky smile.

"Let's don't push these families, Gabbie," he said. "I don't want to make them uncomfortable."

Gabbie swore in Spanish. He had to bite his cheek to keep from laughing. He understood exactly what she'd said. She was a little spitfire.

"They cause some of their own problems," she said, knocking on the next door. "They hate it when the gring.. ...uh...Anglos treat them this way. They're a bunch of hippos if they think its okay to do this to you."

"Hippos?" he asked.

"Yeah," she said, "people who say one thing and do another thing."

He chuckled and said, "I think you mean hypocrites."

"Yeah, that's it," she said, knocking again.

He grinned while he waited for Gabbie to introduce him to Sofia Chavez and her three children. "Her husband, Jorge, works at the feed store, too," Gabbie said.

The third house was the Sanchez home. Elena Sanchez had obviously left her bed to personally thank him for saving her three-year-old daughter, Angie. Gabbie sat down on the floor with the kids and translated. Elena introduced Joe to her other children, Christina, Francisco and her new baby, Rosalie. Her cousin, Dominique, was holding the baby. Elena insisted that he sit and visit for a few minutes.

He joined Gabbie with the kids on the floor. Elena explained that her husband, Miguel, would also want to thank him when he got home from work. She said Miguel worked at the utility building by the Baptist Church. Joe made sure Gabbie told Elena that Dominique was the one who really saved Angie.

Dominique shook her head and said, "He hit the snake. I couldn't grab her with the snake trying to bite."

Gabbie translated. He chuckled and said, "It took teamwork. Thank Dominique for her help and tell Elena that Angie's safety is all the thanks I need."

Gabbie translated again and he stood up to leave.

Nodding goodbye to the ladies, he waited while Gabbie translated something Dominique was saying.

"She said she's very grateful for your rescue today," Gabbie said. "And she asked if you know of any work in town."

"I don't know of any jobs right now," he said. "But I'll keep her in mind if I hear of anything. What kind of work can she do?"

"She says she can clean houses and work in stores," Gabbie said. "And she says she plays some piano, but that's mostly for fun."

"She can play a piano?" he asked.

"Yeah, she says she plays a little," Gabbie said.

"Then she may be the answer to my prayers," he said. "Tell her I'll do some checking and let her know."

They moved on to the next house. Gabbie introduced him to Nadia Martinez and her three children. He'd met her husband, Archibaldo. He worked at Ben's store.

Rounding the corner to the row that faced the back of the drug store and feed store, Gabbie introduced him to her mother, Consuelo Perez, her sister Ana, and her two brothers, Mario and Sergio. He already knew Gabbie's dad, Alberto. He worked at Ben's store, too.

The Senas lived next door to Gabbie. So Joe said hello again to Nadina Sena and met Raul's brother and his three sisters. Of course, he had to have a conversation with Raul to see if his arm was healed. Raul proudly showed it to him. Raul's dad, Manuel, worked at Gene's store.

At the next house, he met Margarita Salazar, Eddie's mother, and his two sisters and younger brother. Eddie's dad worked at Gene's store, too.

When they finished the two rows of houses, he thanked Gabbie for taking the time to help him. Then he said, "I have a good memory, but I have to admit I'm overwhelmed. Would you please make a list of these families and their kids for me?"

"Sure," she said, "and thanks again for saving Angie. Everyone really is grateful, but they don't trust many Anglos."

"Because they haven't known many they could trust," he said. She gave him a surprised look and nodded. "Thank you for being my translator – and my champion today," he said. "I

111

might not have understood the words, but I know you argued on my behalf and I appreciate it."

She blushed and ran up to her house.

He walked back around to look at the field again.

The tall grass was a natural haven for snakes. Broken pieces of glass and metal littered the area near the street. It was an awful place for children to play.

Picking up the shovel, he moved the dead snake across the field to a large flat rock. He'd heard that rattlesnakes could travel in pairs. If it was true, he wanted the mate to be far away from the children. He'd have to warn some of the men to watch the rock and kill any others that showed up.

He headed back to his house and walked across the back lot to the utility building. Inside, he went up to a Hispanic man and asked, "Are you Miguel Sanchez?"

"Yes," the man said. "Can I help you?"

After he introduced himself, he said, "I need to tell you something. But first, I want you to know that everyone is safe." Then he told Miguel what happened. Miguel was out of his chair and heading for the door. Joe managed to assure him that Angie was safely napping at home. When Miguel relaxed, he told him what he did with the snake and asked him to watch for a possible mate. He agreed. Still shaken, he thanked Joe again.

Walking back to his house, he saw Miguel lock the building and drive across town. He smiled. He knew he would've done the same thing. No reassurance is better than seeing your family for yourself.

His phone rang when he stepped inside his house. He answered hesitantly, expecting to hear Mrs. Anderson's voice. Instead he heard Father Romero on the other end saying, "I heard about your rescue of our little Angie today. I am truly grateful."

"Thank you, Father Romero," he said. "Quite honestly, today was just a matter of timing. I was in the area when Angie screamed. But I'm concerned about the field the children are playing in over there. If I can find the owner and arrange permission to mow that grass, would you have some equipment we could use?"

"Yes," Father Romero said. "Call me if you get the approval and I'll send one of my men in to mow it."

"That would make the field much safer for the kids," Joe said. "Let me see what I can find out, and I'll get back to you."

Father Romero agreed and said, "I'll wait for your call."

"Oh," Joe said, before they hung up. "What's your number out there?" Father Romero laughed and gave it to him.

He grabbed a quick sandwich at the house and changed to meet the hoops kids.

On the way over to the lot, he stopped at the town hall to ask Susan Nelson what they had to do to get the field mowed.

"The field is owned by Mr. Wellman, the same man who owns the Hispanic houses," she said. "Unfortunately, he lives out of state and refuses to communicate with anyone about his property here."

Joe asked for his name and address. Since it was a public record, she could release it. Then he asked if those were the only properties Wellman owned.

"Oh, no," Susan said. "He's bought most of the houses and businesses that closed. I can give you a list if you'd like."

"Yes, please," he said. "I can come back and get it when you have it ready."

"It shouldn't take very long," she said. "Why don't you pick it up on your way back from your hoops game?"

Obviously, his clothes told her where he was headed. And of course, the entire town knew about the games.

"I'll do that," he said. "One more thing, is that empty field in the town limits?"

"Yes," she said. "Why?"

"I was just wondering if there was an ordinance on keeping open fields mowed," he said. "If there is, we'd at least have the authority to mow it."

"True," she said, "but you'll never get him to pay for it."

"I may know someone who won't charge to mow it – if we can get the authority," he said. "Is there an ordinance?"

"Yes," she said. "I'll look it up and have a copy for you when you get back."

He thanked her and left to join the kids. When he walked up the kids were in a huddle around Gabbie.

Probably hearing about my day, he thought.

True enough, Chris looked at him and said, "Gosh, Preacher Man, you had a close call with Angie."

"That's true," Joe said. "I was terrified the snake would strike before I could get to her. It all happened so fast, most of it was pure reflex." To lighten the mood, he chuckled and said, "Maybe shooting all these hoops with you guys kept my reflexes sharp. Let's play ball."

On the way home, he stopped to get the paperwork from Susan. "You didn't tell me you saved Angie from a rattlesnake in that field today. No wonder you want it mowed. If these aren't enough," she said, handing him some papers. "Come back and we'll look up health and public safety ordinances."

"Thanks," he said. "I don't want a repeat of today's situation with the kids."

Stepping back outside, he leaned against the corner of the building and read the ordinance she gave him. He folded up the property records and headed for the grocery store. Since, Chris had already told Ben about the incident with Angie, Joe got right to the point.

"We have to mow that field, Ben," he said. "I checked with Susan and I understand that the owner is out of state and not responsive. What I need to know is whether or not we have the legal authority to mow it based on this town ordinance?"

He handed Ben the ordinance.

"Yes, we do," Ben said. "But we'll never get the owner to pay for the services."

"If I told you the Catholic Church will mow it free of charge, will you give them the authority to do it?" Joe asked.

Ben's mouth dropped open. "Are you telling me that Father Romero is going to mow that field, if I grant the authority?" he asked.

Joe grinned and said, "I have his word on it. He called to thank me for saving Angie and I asked him to help us mow that field. He has the equipment. He said he'd send a man in to mow it, as soon as I get the legal authority to let him do it."

Shaking his head, Ben said, "I don't believe this. Two weeks ago none of us were even speaking to each other. Now you have us working together to fix things. I think I'm witnessing a small miracle in this town. If my authorization is all you need, you have it."

"Thanks," Joe said. "I'll let Father Romero know as soon as I get home. Also, I need to know if we have any money in the church fund for a pianist."

"I haven't looked at the account lately," Ben said, "but we probably have some. Why? Did you find a pianist?"

"I may have," Joe said. "Elena's cousin is helping her with the children, but she's also looking for a job. She says she plays some piano. I didn't want to build her hopes up if we couldn't pay her. I'll ask her to come by the church and see if she can read the music well enough to play for us. If she can't, I'll help her look for another job."

"Okay," Ben said. "You see if she can play. I'll check the account and see what we can pay. It won't be much for just one day a week, but maybe it will help."

"Thanks," Joe said. "I've got to go call Father Romero before it gets too late. See you tomorrow."

Back home, he called Father Romero and explained the situation with the out of state owner and the ordinance violation the Mayor used as authorization for them to mow the field – as long as the mowing service was free.

"I'll have the mower in there tomorrow," Father Romero said. "And thank you again, Reverend Marsh."

Then he called Ben to tell him what they'd arranged.

"Can you spare Chris tomorrow?" he asked.

"Sure," Ben said. "What do you need?"

"I thought I'd ask Chris to call some of the other kids to meet me at the lot with some rakes," Joe said. "We'll clean up the broken glass, metal, and other junk the mower won't get."

"I'll take care of it," Ben said. "They'll be there."

"Okay," Joe said. "Oh, Ben?"

"Yes," Ben said.

"Can I borrow a rake?" Joe asked. "I don't think it'd look very good, if I showed up without one."

"I think we can manage that," Ben said laughing. "I'll send a spare with Chris."

He started a pot of coffee and sat down to look at the list of properties this man, Wellman, owned. Susan was right. He'd bought every vacant property in town. Apparently he waited for the foreclosures and picked them up at the public auctions.

Joe marked the locations on his map of the town.

Why would anyone want to own all the properties in a little town that was barely surviving? he wondered.

Looking closer, he noticed the purchase dates started in 1990 for the old acreages and ended in 1995 when Wellman bought the Church of Christ. He made some notes and got ready for his surveillance run.

Since Bart's truck was back in the lot, he couldn't change the tape in the camera under Max's stairs. He changed the other four and reviewed them at home.

Then he sent his daily report to Jack and requested all available information on Homer Wellman at the P O Box Susan gave him – ASAP.

CHAPTER SEVENTEEN

TUESDAY – THIRD WEEK

He was surprised to see the mower already pulling into the field when he jogged that side of town. He ran home to change and ran back to meet the driver, Domingo. He watched him work across the area and wondered where Chris and the other kids were. To his surprise, Ben, Gene, Ralph and Charley marched side by side onto the field. Behind them was probably every Hispanic man in town. All of them were carrying rakes, hoes and shovels.

"This sounded like a man size job," Ben said, "so we decided to let the wives and kids take care of the stores while we cleaned up this place." Then in an aside to Joe, he said, "Our workers are getting paid to work over here instead of the stores. They wanted to help clean up this hazard. Besides, we figured if our priest and preacher could work together, so could we."

Joe was speechless. Ben grinned and handed him a rake. The men spread out and scoured the field for anything that could hurt the kids – especially any more snakes. When Domingo finished mowing, he loaded the equipment back on the truck. Then he pulled out a rake and joined them. By three o'clock, they had twelve trash bags full of debris. The field was cut and clean. They were all proud of their work.

"This looks great," Joe told Ben. "Please thank all of the men for me."

Ben did. Then he said, "We need to thank you for making this happen. It really does look nice – but something's still missing." He whistled. Alberto and Archibaldo grinned and walked around the block. Joe watched as they drove the grocery truck around to the field. They hopped out, pushed the back door up on its rollers and started dragging out a swing set.

At Joe's surprised look, Ben said, "It's been sitting in the back of the store since our kids grew up. We decided it would get more use over here."

When the men had it positioned on a level spot, Charley sent one of his guys over to his store for a couple of bags of concrete. Together they dug anchor holes, filled them with concrete and bolts to attach to the swing set. Then they recruited a couple of the moms to keep the kids off the swings until the men could anchor them later tonight. In a mass exchange of handshakes and thanks, the men drifted back to their jobs.

Joe ran after Domingo and thanked him for the mowing – and the extra help with the raking. He also sent a special thank you out to Father Romero.

Running back to join the other men, he saw Dominique holding Angie. He asked Ben to translate. He asked about Angie and was assured that she was okay. Next, he asked Dominique if she could come to the church and play the piano for him. She said she could after Miguel came home, probably between six-thirty and seven. Joe agreed. He thanked Ben and they walked back to join the other men.

"That may be our new pianist," Joe said.

"Great," Ben said. "If you're happy with her playing, we could probably pay her twenty-five to thirty dollars a week to play on Sundays. We might be able to pay more once we get the church going again, but that's all we can do right now."

"I'll let her decide," Joe said, "if she can play our music. It probably isn't the kind of music she's played before."

Walking home, he saw two strange cars parked in front of the Anderson's house. Sadly, he knew, their children had come home for one last visit. He started to knock, then looked at his dirty clothes and decided to call a little later.

He made a quick call to thank Father Romero again and then changed to run back down the street to meet the kids.

He knew it wasn't going to be much of a game today. He was exhausted.

He found the kids around the block looking at the field. "What do you think?" he asked.

Turning at his voice, Chris said, "It looks, great." Danny and Jerry agreed.

"Well, I don't know," Gabbie said.

"I guess it'll do," Eddie said.

"What?" Joe asked. "What do you mean, it'll do? It looks wonderful."

Grinning at Eddie, Gabbie reached around one of the houses and said, "Yeah, but it'll look a lot better with these." They held up a pint-size hoop and ball.

"How are we going to grow a new team if they can't practice?" Gabbie asked.

"We started to put the hoop out there," Eddie said, "but we wanted to ask you if it should be in concrete like the swings."

He hugged both of them and said, "I'll take care of that part. You two start coaching our junior squad."

They grinned and nodded.

"Now let's see what this team can do," he said, as he batted the ball out of Chris' arm and dribbled it back to the lot.

When they finished playing, he could barely hobble home. *I should've made those kids help on the field today,* he thought. *Then they'd be as tired and sore as I am.* He grinned. He had to admit he was proud of the men in the community. They'd stepped up to the challenge and worked together.

"All I want to do is sleep for a week," he grumbled, as he walked through his door. But he knew he couldn't. He had to take a quick shower and get over to the church to audition Dominique. And he should call on the Andersons afterward, if it wasn't too late.

He tried to revive his spirits with a cup of morning coffee, fresh from the microwave. It tasted so bad he tossed it down the drain. The shower did help his aching muscles.

A quick sandwich and glass of milk had him feeling almost human again by the time he opened the church door. He was turning on the lights and pulling the piano out of the corner when Dominique knocked timidly at the entry.

"Come in," he said, as he motioned her toward the piano. Then he groaned mentally. He should have arranged for a translator. *Oh well,* he thought. *Music is supposed to be an international language, this is definitely going to test that theory.*

He picked up a hymnal and handed it to her. She leafed through it and gave him a puzzled look. He took it back, opened it to a familiar hymn and gestured for her to try to play it. She rolled a couple of scales to test the keys, then leaned forward and studied the music carefully.

She managed to play it quite well, even with the piano out of tune. With a little practice, he was convinced she'd do fine. Frustrated by the language barrier, he said, "Gracias," and then signed that he would get Gabriela to translate for him, "mañana." She nodded, and said, "Gracias," and left.

Seeing the living room lights still on at the Andersons, he locked the church and walked over to pay a visit. He wasn't sure the family would approve, but he wanted to see Mrs. Anderson. When she answered the door, he knew he'd made the right decision. She greeted him warmly and took him through the round of family introductions.

He asked about the Reverend. She shook her head and stepped outside. He followed her over to the privacy of the garden she loved. Saddened beyond words, he held her in a gentle hug while she cried.

She looked up at him and managed a teary-eyed smile. "He's had a good life and we've had a good life together," she said. "I don't guess we can ask for more than that."

"No ma'am, I don't guess we can," he said, still fumbling for the right words... and realizing there were none.

"Thank you for not reciting scriptures and platitudes to me right now," she said. "That's all I've been hearing. I'm not in the mood to hear any more."

"No ma'am, I wouldn't do that to you," he said. "I know your pain is as personal as the love you two have shared all these years. I'm just here to hold a beautiful lady as long as she needs me." He felt her relax in his arms and gain strength for the days ahead. She gave him a gentle kiss on the cheek and walked back inside – carrying a chunk of his heart with her.

Later, as he ran his surveillance, he realized he'd forgotten to change the tapes on the camera under Max's stairs.

Now Simms' truck was on the lot. He changed the other tapes and continued on his run. The pickup was back in front of the bar. He needed to find a way to get the name of that driver.

When he returned home, the bedroom candle, that Mrs. Anderson had kept burning this week, was out. He knew the Reverend had passed away.

With a heavy heart, he reviewed the tapes and wrote his report to Jack. THE CATHOLIC CHURCH MOWED THE FIELD TODAY. THEN THE METHODIST, BAPTIST AND CATHOLIC MEN ARRIVED IN UNISON TO HELP HUNT SNAKES AND CLEAR DANGEROUS DEBRIS OUT OF THE FIELD.
REVEREND ANDERSON PASSED AWAY TONIGHT.

CHAPTER EIGHTEEN

WEDNESDAY – THIRD WEEK

He started jogging at five-thirty and discovered the town already stirring. News of Reverend Anderson's death had traveled fast. Since Simms' truck was gone, he took a calculated risk and made a quick daytime switch on the camera under the stairs. With the Reverend's funeral pending, he wanted a record of any additional vehicles or visitors in the back parking lot.

Rounding the corner of the Hispanic block, he stopped to enjoy the scene. The field really did look nice. The Morrison swing set was anchored and ready for the kids. He needed to come back and anchor the junior hoop set for them.

He jogged up to say hello to Grandma. He knew this loss was going to be hard on her, too. She and Sherie had become close these last few days. It was a shame they'd missed so many of the earlier years together.

Mrs. Anderson was waiting for him when he jogged home. She'd brought the wheelchair back to him. She wanted to be sure it went to someone else who needed it.

"Raymond's funeral will be at ten tomorrow at the church," she said. "Our son-in-law, who is also a Methodist minister, will conduct the service. My children have convinced me that I should move back with them. It'll be different for me up there. But I'll enjoy being closer to my children and grandchildren, especially with Raymond gone. They're already packing my things. Normally, they wouldn't move quite this fast. But they have to get their kids back for school next week and they don't want to leave me behind. After all, the parsonage

122

isn't my house. I'd have to move out of it anyway, so the next minister could live there."

Joe's head was spinning with all the details she was sharing. He was sure she was too numb to think about these things right now. As much as he'd love to have her stay, he knew her children were right. He gave her a hug and walked her back to her house.

He went home, picked up the junior basketball set and headed back to the field. He swung by the feed store to get some more concrete and saw the pickup back in the parking lot. Inside, he extended condolences to Charley on the loss of his minister. Then he took some good natured ribbing about the pint-size hoop set he was carrying. After getting some concrete and borrowing a shovel, Joe looked for the driver of the pickup. He didn't see anyone else in the store.

When Charley saw him looking around, Joe said, "I saw the truck outside. I thought you had another customer."

"Oh that's Sampson's truck," Charley said. "It quit on him last night. He pushed it over here from the bar. He left me a note saying he'd pick it up today."

"Sampson," Joe said. "I don't think I've met him yet."

"Sorry, I forgot how new you are," Charley said. "Sampson is the Field Foreman at the Catholic Church. He's in and out of here a lot. He usually comes in on Tuesday to see his cousin, Bart, the man who delivers my seeds. If they're not too busy at the church, he hangs out with him at the bar."

Joe nodded and asked, "What are their last names?"

Charley thought for a minute and said, "Sampson is a nickname for Samuel and his last name is...Gonzales. Bart is Bartholomew Gallegos."

Joe shook his head and said, "I'm still trying to get used to the Spanish names. I'm worried I'll mispronounce them and offend someone."

"They have the same problems with our language," Charley said, "so, the insults balance out."

Joe agreed and waved out. He carried the supplies over to the field and was delighted to see a group of kids already swinging and sliding. Others were playing tag in the open area. The kids came over to watch him set the basketball hoop.

Since they knew about the concrete with the swing set, they understood that they needed to let this concrete harden before they could play with the toys. He was thinking about a tether ball and t-ball set while he watched the kids play.

Before he stood back up, two little arms swung over his back and locked around his neck in a big hug.

"Is that my Angie?" he asked.

"Si, Preaker Maan," she tried to say.

He swung her around and gave her a hug.

"So, I'm Preacher Man to you, too," he said laughing. "You're right, Angie. I'm your Preacher Man and I like all the big hugs you give me." He growled and pretended to give her a monster hug. When he put her down all the other kids ran over to get hugs, too. He heard every conceivable pronunciation of Preacher Man and loved them all.

After everyone got a bear hug, he picked up his things and noticed Dominique watching them. Looking around for a translator, he found Mrs. Chavez. With her help, he told Dominique they wanted to hire her to play for the church, if she wanted the job. He suggested she come over and practice the songs they were going to sing Sunday. She appeared anxious to play and they agreed she'd come back again between six-thirty and seven to practice.

He decided to return Charley's shovel and see if he could find an egg salad sandwich and maybe a slice of Grandma's pie at Ben's.

Sitting down with Alice, he actually relaxed for a few minutes. Ben came in while he was eating. They compared sore muscles from their efforts yesterday.

Joe had him beat. "You didn't hang around and shoot hoops for another two hours," he said.

Ben laughed and yielded the point. Joe told him about the addition Eddie and Gabbie made to the field. He also said he was going to hire Dominique. He thought she'd be pretty good once she became familiar with their hymns.

Then the discussion moved to the loss of Reverend Anderson and the funeral tomorrow. Joe told them about Mrs.

Anderson's plans to move north with her children, which was probably best for her. But he was worried about Grandma.

"I just brought the two ladies together and now Sherie's moving away," he said.

"You're right," Alice said. "We need to keep her busy."

"Maybe she can make more pies," Ben said, rubbing his hands together. That brought the humor back to the conversation.

At home, he reviewed the storage unit tape. It picked up Max's conversation with Bart on Monday night and Simms on Tuesday night. Both were just general comments as they picked up and returned the key and towels – consistent with what Max had told him.

He did notice a faint scraping noise both nights. And both times it occurred while the drivers were showering in the hotel. The camera was aimed at the parked trucks. No one was near them, including the drivers. He didn't remember the hotel door making that noise and Max's door was already closed. He'd have to check the area tomorrow to see if he could identify the source of that sound.

After his hoops game, he microwaved a dinner and cleaned up to meet Dominique. When she arrived, he showed her the hymns he picked for Sunday and decided to work in the office while she practiced. He could hear her faltering the first time she played them. But it wasn't long before she was playing them quite well – except for the sour notes that needed tuning.

He leafed through the office files and decided to look for any records on Phillips that might help Jack find him. He found a baptismal document in the file for Gene's daughter, Diane, and another one for Roy's daughter, Jeanette. Both were signed by H. Phillips. Hoping they contained Phillips' fingerprints, he carefully placed them in an envelope to mail to Jack.

Apparently Phillips didn't worry about the church's administrative issues, because the most recent documents he found were signed by Reverend William Whitsworth. Judging from the dates, Whitsworth was Phillips' predecessor.

In the UTILITY folder, he found some handwritten notes from Whitsworth requesting tests on the parsonage water. He believed it had been poisoned and cited several severe abdominal attacks he'd experienced after drinking it. There were other documents indicating that Miguel had tested the water, but he couldn't identify any foreign substances in it. Miguel also ran a test on the residual contents of a glass of water Whitsworth drank before an attack. It contained normal minerals consistent with the contents of the town's water supply and a miniscule trace of cephaelis ipecacuanha considered harmless. The last tests were run in November 1994. Phillips had arrived in the spring of 1995. He wondered if illness was the reason Whitsworth left.

He was replacing the files when he heard a loud thud in the sanctuary. Rounding the corner, he found Dominique trying to loosen the front panel of the old piano. The top cover, which must have made the noise, was lying on the floor. Embarrassed, she let Joe help her remove the awkward panel. Looking inside the piano, he wondered how the thing played at all. It was covered with dirt and cobwebs. Signaling her to wait there, he ran next door to get the vacuum. Together, they cleaned the wires and hammers.

Then to his surprise, she tapped the sour keys and started adjusting the screws and tuning the piano. Seeing his shocked look, she said, "Mi Tio." Which he knew meant, her uncle. Apparently he'd taught her how to do it.

Once they reassembled the piano, she sat down and played one of the hymns he'd given her. It sounded wonderful and he tried to tell her that with his facial expressions and his one word of Spanish, "Gracias."

When she left, he carried the envelope and vacuum back to the house. He was pleased with her playing. He knew it would make a big difference in Sunday's service.

He ran his night surveillance, changed the tapes in the other four cameras and wrote his report to Jack – including the full names of Samuel Gonzales and Bartholomew Gallegos. He advised Jack that he'd be mailing an envelope to Reverend Brownstone that needed to be opened by the fingerprint lab.

CHAPTER NINETEEN

THURSDAY – THIRD WEEK

When he awoke, the hearse was already parked in front of the Methodist Church. Out of respect for the mourners, he didn't go jogging. Instead, he fixed a pot of coffee and checked his e-mail. Jack had sent registration information on the other license plates. Then he added: FOUND SOME INFORMATION ON HOMER WELLMAN. HE OWNS SEVERAL BUSINESSES IN SMALL TEXAS AND NEW MEXICO TOWNS, INCLUDING INSURANCE COMPANIES, REAL ESTATE OFFICES, HEAVY EQUIPMENT COMPANIES AND WAREHOUSES. WELLMAN ALSO HAS SOME STOCK HOLDINGS THAT WE'RE RESEARCHING. He included a picture of Wellman they found in one of his offices. Joe printed it and hurried to shower and dress for the funeral.

At the church, he spoke to the Anderson's son-in-law, Reverend Stevens, who was conducting the service. Then he took a seat in an open pew near the back of the sanctuary. Within minutes, the Morrisons and Reeds joined him. Father Romero arrived with Father Tobias and sat in the pew behind him. The church members were obviously surprised by the Baptist and Catholic representation. Joe was personally very proud of the significance.

When the church door was closed, indicating the start of the service, Reverend Stevens seated the family and then walked back up the aisle to Joe. Leaning over, he whispered, "Mother asked if you would be her strength today and sit beside her."

127

Joe rose and followed Reverend Stevens to the front of the church where he was gestured into the seat beside Mrs. Anderson. He held her through the service and escorted her to the cemetery for the burial.

After the service, he changed clothes and went back to the Andersons to help load boxes. They'd pulled a moving truck up to the door and were obviously rushing to meet the deadlines Mrs. Anderson mentioned. Together they loaded the treasures that had made the little house a home.

He walked into the empty house and saw Mrs. Anderson staring out the back door at her flowers. He ran out front and asked her daughter if she'd help him dig up some of her mother's flowers to have at her new home. She loved the idea and grabbed a shovel and some buckets off the truck. She told her husband to keep her mom busy so she wouldn't see them. Together, they packed some surprise blossoms for her.

When the family was ready to leave, he tried to brighten Mrs. Anderson's day by asking if she'd grant him one last request before she left.

"Of course," she said. "What is it?"

"Tell me how you make your lemonade," he said.

With probably the only chuckle she'd had in days, she told him she always used half a cup of sugar, the juice of two lemons and one orange in a pitcher of water. Then, as if forgetting something important, she walked to the refrigerator and handed him two gallon containers of water. At his puzzled look, she said, "We only use spring water from the Samuels Farm for consumption." Joe nodded, but he was still puzzled.

"Oh dear," she said, "I didn't think to warn you when you arrived. Raymond and Reverend Whitsworth were both stricken repeatedly with terrible abdominal distress after drinking tap water. It happened almost like clockwork every Saturday night when Raymond stayed up late to work on his sermon. Miguel tested our water several times, but he could never find the problem. Doctor Stockwell spent practically every Saturday night walking between our two houses. I guess I was spared because I drink a lot of hot tea. Boiling the water must have protected me. Reverend Whitsworth gave up and left. We probably would've left too, except one of our members,

Billy Samuels, started bringing us some of his artesian well water. Raymond never had another attack."

"Without being too indiscrete," Joe said, "can you tell me how the attacks hit?"

"To be blunt," she said, "they'd throw up for an hour or so. Then their stomachs doubled them up with cramps. Doctor Stockwell had to sedate them to get it to stop. I don't know how many Sunday services they both missed because they were too exhausted from the ordeal. Then they'd get better during the week and it would happen again the next Saturday."

Looking at the two gallons in her hands, she said, "Here, I won't need these any more. You might want to start using the Samuels water to avoid the problem. Their farm is out Third Street on the south side. Raymond and Reverend Whitsworth were convinced someone was tampering with the parsonage water, but they couldn't figure out who or why." Joe nodded and they said their final farewells. He helped her into the family car. With promises to write, they waved goodbye.

It was seven o'clock before he walked through his door and started a pot of coffee. Looking at the gallons of well water he wondered if he had escaped the problem by drinking coffee. He rarely drank water from the tap. He needed to look at Whitsworth's notes again – and he'd have to find a way to test his water. Jack would have to arrange something. He couldn't just walk over to Miguel with glasses of water to test. While he waited for the coffee, someone knocked on his door.

Answering it, he found Chris holding another plate of food. "Grandma said you look too thin," he said. "Actually, she was very proud of you today. But she figured you probably hadn't eaten since morning. She was worried about you. We all were." Joe thanked him and turned to set the plate on the table.

"Oh, *please* tell me you aren't going to frame that picture and put it in the church," Chris said.

Looking up, he realized Chris was looking at the picture he'd printed of Homer Wellman. Trying to understand Chris' reaction, he hesitated to say anything.

Chris looked at him and said, "I'm sorry. I know he's a preacher, but I don't ever want to see Phillips again, in person or in photograph."

Swallowing his surprise, Joe swept the picture off the table and said, "No Chris, I wouldn't think of giving him any position of honor in the church. I found this picture in one of the files. I was going to ask your dad who it was. Now that I know, you won't see it again. I promise."

Chris took a deep breath and said, "I didn't think. You never met the man, so you couldn't have known who he was."

"No problem, Chris," Joe said, as he put a hand on his shoulder. "I'm sorry it gave you such a start. I'm sure it's not what you expected to see tonight." Then to change the subject, he said, "By the way, I was very proud of you and your family for attending the funeral today. Mrs. Anderson noticed and said to thank all of you. And she sent a special thanks to you for mowing her yard. Please tell Katherine that she packed the poetry book in her overnight case. She said she reads it every night." Chris nodded, still visibly shaken by the picture.

"Have you eaten, or do you want to share some of this with me?" Joe asked, pointing to the plate. "It looks like enough food for three or four of us."

"No thanks," Chris said. "My plate's waiting for me at home, so I'd better go. See you tomorrow, Preacher Man."

"Thank your grandma and mom for the dinner," Joe shouted, as Chris cut across the yard and ran home.

Closing the door again, he sat down and enjoyed a plate of pork chops, mashed potatoes and green beans.

He stared at the picture of Wellman and tried to understand what he'd just learned. *Wellman and Phillips are the same person. Why was Wellman here as Phillips?*

He changed his clothes and ran surveillance. He was still wondering about the man's motive. He switched tapes on the outside cameras and then went into the church to change the one on the second floor. While inside, he went back to the office and used a flashlight to pull the UTILITY folder.

Back home, he reviewed the tapes. Everything looked normal. Then he looked up cephaelis ipecacuanha on the internet. Its common name was ipecac, a chemical well known for its ability to make people vomit. In fact, it was often kept in medicine cabinets as an emergency treatment for accidental poisoning.

Did someone deliberately add that to the parsonage waterlines? he wondered. *Was it only on Saturdays to make the ministers too sick to preach? If so, why? The obvious answer, where Whitsworth was concerned, was to make him leave. If the Anderson's hadn't had the Samuels water, Mrs. Anderson said they probably would have left, too. If Wellman-Phillips was behind this, did he do it so he could get more property?*

If that was his plan, it only worked on one preacher. Since the Andersons didn't leave, did Phillips come in as the Baptist Preacher to keep the town from hiring another one – and then leave once he knew Reverend Anderson was dying? He probably assumed the town wouldn't or couldn't replace him. I'd better watch my back. I've not only replaced him, I've reversed a lot of the hate he obviously tried to create here. If the different religions weren't talking to each other, I wonder if they traded with each other, probably not. Phillips may have stirred up all this hate to make the businesses fail.

Pulling out his map, it was easy to see that only four businesses – the grocery store, general store, drug store and feed store – were keeping this town together. If they fell, the Hispanic men would lose their jobs at those stores and their families would have to move.

Why does Wellman want this entire town? he wondered. *It's in the middle of nowhere, but that could make it a good place for their drugs and smuggling. Maybe he intended to populate it with his own men when the townspeople left. If I've messed up his plans, he isn't going to sit still very long. Now that Reverend Anderson is gone. I guess I'm the only one standing in his way.*

He put his discoveries and theories into an e-mail to Jack. He stressed the need for faster data and told him to think about having backup forces available. I'M CONVINCED THE TWO TRUCKS ARE THE CONVEYANCES FOR THE HUMAN SMUGGLING. I WANT ALL TRACE DATA THAT'S BEEN COLLECTED. HAVE WE FOUND THE SILO BART USES? WHERE DOES SIMMS GO WHEN HE LEAVES TOWN? WHERE DOES HE PARK AND WHO OWNS THAT PROPERTY? NEED TO CHECK COZEN OIL CLOSER. WELLMAN MAY OWN IT UNDER ANOTHER ASSUMED NAME.

I'M GOING TO ARRANGE TO GET SAMUELS WATER ASAP. ASK THE LAB IF THERE'S ANY WAY I CAN TEST MY WATER FOR IPECAC – IF NOT, WE'LL NEED TO SET UP A WAY TO TEST IT WITHOUT USING MIGUEL. I NEED FASTER DATA – PUSH THE GUYS FOR ME. PLEASE CHECK ON GOLDIE – I'M WORRIED ABOUT HER.

CHAPTER TWENTY

FRIDAY – THIRD WEEK

Since he wanted to check the truck space for that scraping sound, he jogged directly over to the lot. Standing where the trucks had been, he couldn't find the source of the sound. He'd checked the visible parts of the hotel. Without a warrant, he'd have a hard time checking all the storage units. But he didn't believe they were being used. Basically, because Max would have to be involved and he didn't believe he was. If anything, Max was the perfect straight man people liked to use to front their operations.

Behind him, the peanut station was still locked. He couldn't find any foot prints or other clues around the gate to indicate any traffic. He was baffled. He knew he couldn't stand there much longer, someone would wonder what he was doing.

Turning to leave, his sneaker caught on a piece of paving. Cursing silently, he bent down to rub his toe. That's when he noticed a notch in the asphalt. Then he saw the line beside it. It formed a rectangle that appeared to be one of many patches in the parking lot. *If that's a trapdoor,* he thought. *They could be dropping people from the trucks into a tunnel. I need to get this information back to Jack ASAP.*

When he jogged away from the lot, he saw Doc coming out of the Hispanic section. "Good Morning, Doc," he said, slowing down. "I don't like that worried look I see on your face. What's wrong?"

"Morning, Reverend," Doc said. "I can't tell you the specifics – patient privacy, you know. But I can tell you this.

Elena Sanchez had complications having Rosalie. She needs surgery to fix the situation. We could lose her if she doesn't have it soon."

Shocked, Joe asked, "Why isn't she in the hospital?"

"Well," Doc said, "Miguel's insurance with the town will pay for part of it, but their share is a thousand dollars. They don't have that kind of money."

"How much time do we have if she doesn't get the surgery?" Joe asked.

"At the rate she's hemorrhaging, probably no more than a week," Doc said.

"She'd have to go to Portales right?" Joe asked.

When Doc nodded, Joe asked, "How long would she need to be in the hospital?"

"It can be done as outpatient surgery," Doc said. "She could be home the same day, since she has her cousin with her."

"Well, we have to do something," Joe said. "Let me see what I can do. I'll talk to you later, Doc. And thanks for telling me about her." He shortened his jog, stopped to speak to Grandma and ran home to shower.

He pulled into the Catholic Church parking lot at exactly seven-thirty. Seeing Father Tobias outside, he ran up to him and said, "Father Tobias, I have an urgent need to see Father Romero. Can you take that message to him, please?" He saw a flash of defiance on Father Tobias' face, but the serious look on Joe's face must have convinced him to be more contrite.

"I'll tell him, Reverend Marsh," Father Tobias said piously. "Please wait here."

Fifteen minutes later, he was ready to ring the church bells with Father Tobias' feet. He knew the little mouse was exacting payment for his last visit. Just because he tried to respect other religions didn't mean he couldn't find his way through every room in this church, if they didn't want to respond to his request. Ten minutes later, he was ready to do exactly that.

Then he saw Father Romero rushing out to meet him.

"I'm sorry, Reverend Marsh," Father Romero said. "I just noticed you when I glanced out the window. Did you ask someone to find me?"

"Yes," Joe said, through clenched teeth. "At exactly seven-thirty, I asked Father Tobias to tell you I had an urgent need to see you. I asked him to give you that message. I'm *very* disappointed that he takes his mission so lightly. I rarely use the word *urgent*. I assumed I'd be taken seriously."

"I can assure you I will speak to Father Tobias. This will not happen again," Father Romero said. "What is the urgent matter you wish to discuss?"

Joe explained Elena's serious condition and the need for immediate surgery. "They need a thousand dollars to save her life," he said. "I don't know if your church has that much or if you need to contact your superiors for the funds. But we have to get the money fast, or we're going to have another funeral neither of us wants to attend. I'll drive to Albuquerque, Santa Fe or wherever I need to go to get the funds they need."

Father Romero nodded and said, "Our church has that much money available for this type of emergency. I'll write you a check immediately."

"We'll need to call Doctor Stockwell to find out what hospital he plans to use," Joe said. "If you write the check directly to the hospital, it should eliminate any processing delays. Do you want the family to know the church paid for the surgery? Or do you want this to be anonymous?"

"It might be better if the source remains anonymous," Father Romero said, "so they won't feel obligated to repay it."

Joe smiled and said, "That's very kind of you, Father. They've worked hard for the little they have. I'd hate for them to try to repay a debt this size. I'll ask Doctor Stockwell to tell them it was funded through a philanthropic grant that doesn't have to be repaid. Is that honest enough to keep both of us out of trouble with the Lord?"

Father Romero laughed out loud and said, "You are a classic, Reverend Marsh. Yes, I believe that will keep both of us out of trouble. Now let's go call the doctor and get that check for Elena."

By ten o'clock, Doc had a check in his hand.

Joe went over to the utility building to tell Miguel that Doc had some grant money to pay for the surgery. "You need to go home and get Elena to the hospital today," Joe said.

Miguel was so relieved, he didn't ask any questions. Joe watched him lock up and drive home. Then he went to the grocery store to tell the Mayor what was happening.

Ben was surprised. "I didn't even know Elena was sick," he said. "I just thought the cousin was helping because of the other children. Tell Miguel to take whatever time he needs and keep us informed on Elena's progress, please."

Joe agreed and went back to the Hispanic section. Once Doc had Elena and Miguel in his car, Joe checked on Dominique and the four children. Mrs. Chavez said she'd help Dominique until Elena came back. After bear hugs for Angie and more sedate ones for Christina and Francisco, he gave Dominique and Mrs. Chavez his phone number to call if they needed him.

Back home, he sent a lengthy e-mail to Jack.

I THINK I'VE FOUND A 'TRAPDOOR OR HATCH' IN THE PAVEMENT THAT WOULD OPEN UNDER THE TRUCKS, PROBABLY TO A TUNNEL. THE TRUCKS MUST HAVE MOBILE PANELS IN THE TRAILER BEDS. IF MY THEORY IS CORRECT, THESE ARE THE REST OF MY THOUGHTS:

IN TOWN:

- BART IS BRINGING THE WOMEN INTO TOWN IN FEEDBAGS. I REMEMBER SEEING A STACK OF EMPTY BAGS IN BART'S TRUCK LAST WEEK. IF HE JUST PICKED UP A LOAD, WHERE WOULD HE HAVE EMPTIED THOSE BAGS? THE WOMEN ARE APPARENTLY UNLOADED INTO THE TUNNEL MONDAY NIGHT. THEN BART MAKES HIS DELIVERIES TO THE FEED STORE AND LEAVES.
- WHEN SIMMS COMES TO TOWN ON TUESDAY, HE DELIVERS HIS PRODUCTS TO THE GROCERY STORE AND THE CATHOLIC CHURCH. THEN HE PARKS IN THE LOT SO THE WOMEN CAN BE LOADED INTO HIS EMPTY TRUCK TUESDAY NIGHT. HE DRIVES THEM OUT OF TOWN WEDNESDAY MORNING.

OUT OF TOWN:

- BART MUST BE PICKING THE WOMEN UP AT THE SILO – WE HAVE TO TRACK THE SUPPLY SIDE OF THAT SILO BEFORE WE SPOOK THEM BY ARRESTING BART. UNLESS BART MAKES OTHER STOPS, HE MUST BE GETTING THE DRUGS FROM THE SILO, TOO.
- WE HAVE TO KNOW WHERE SIMMS UNLOADS THEM – WHO OWNS THE PROPERTY WHERE SIMMS PARKS WHEN HE LEAVES HERE?
- DOES ANOTHER TRUCK PARK IN HIS EXACT SPACE THE NEXT NIGHT? WHERE DOES THAT NEXT TRUCK GO?

OPEN ISSUES WE HAVE TO RESOLVE:
- THERE HAVE TO BE WORKERS IN THE TUNNEL –
I HAVE TO FIND OUT WHERE THEY ARE ENTERING AND
EXITING – AND HOW MANY ARE INVOLVED – AND HOW
WELL ARMED THEY ARE.
- WE HAVE TO HAVE MANPOWER TO COVER THE TUNNEL
EXITS – WHEN I FIND THEM.
- SINCE WE DON'T KNOW THE SPECIFICS ABOUT THE
TUNNEL, WE DON'T DARE MAKE A MOVE WITH THE
WOMEN INSIDE. THEY'D BECOME HOSTAGES AND WE'D
HAVE A STANDOFF.
- WE MUST HAVE BACKUP READY IF THIS THING POPS.
I CAN'T PROVE IT, BUT I KNOW WELLMAN-PHILLIPS IS
RIGHT IN THE MIDDLE OF THIS WHOLE THING. I THINK HE OWNS
THE PROPERTIES THE TRUCKS ARE USING. ALSO, THEY MAY BE
PROPERTIES WHERE COZEN DRILLED – AND CONVENIENTLY LEFT
'TUNNELS' HALF DUG.
JACK – WE NEED THESE PIECES, ASAP! DO YOU HAVE
PEOPLE ON THIS OR DO I NEED TO TRY TO FOLLOW THE TRUCKS?
THEY'LL BE COMING BACK INTO TOWN MONDAY AND TUESDAY.
I KNOW IT'S FRIDAY AFTERNOON – BUT LET'S BURN SOME
OVERTIME – AND GET THESE GUYS. WE'RE GOING TO HAVE TO
TIME THIS SO WE CAN GET THE WHOLE RING AT ONCE.
OTHERWISE, I'M AFRAID THEY'LL KILL ANY WOMEN IN TRANSIT
TO AVOID BEING CAUGHT WITH THEM. I DON'T WANT ANY
COLLATERAL DAMAGE – IF WE CAN AVOID IT.

Changing to go meet the kids for hoops, he decided to
check on the Sanchez family first. Dominique and Mrs. Chavez
were relieved when they saw him. Rosalie had been fussing all
afternoon. They'd been so busy with her, they hadn't been able
to take the other kids out to play.

Joe tossed Angie on his shoulder and said, "Come on
kids. Let's go play." He looked like a pied piper as he led the
five Sanchez and Chavez kids across the street to play. They fell
into a modified follow-the-leader game with Joe hopping on one
foot, then the other, then zigzagging, walking backwards,
sideways and pigeon-toed. They collapsed in a pile of laughter
back at the swing set.

That should take care of some of their energy, he
thought, as he started to put Angie down. She held on to a hank
of his hair and bounced up and down on his shoulder. She
wanted more. Since Mrs. Montoya had come out with her kids,

he asked her to watch the others while he gave Angie another ride. Bouncing across the field he relished the sheer joy of her laughter. He crossed the road to jog over to the lot to tell the hoops kids where he was.

As he bounced closer, Angie pulled hard on his hair and the giggles changed to, "No, No, Noooooooo, Preaker Man, Noooooo!"

Shocked, Joe stopped and pulled her down to see what was wrong. The hoops kids heard her and came running. Joe was totally bewildered. Angie ran to Gabbie, talking with a terrifying sense of urgency.

"What's wrong?" Joe asked. "Did I scare her? She didn't fall. I was holding her."

"No," Gabbie said. "We forgot to tell you that Angie is afraid of this area over here. She thinks it's ..." she looked to Chris for the word.

He said "haunted."

"Yeah, that's it," Gabbie said.

"Haunted," Joe said, "why does she think that?"

"I'm not sure," Gabbie said. "She wandered off last winter and had all of us searching most of the night. When we found her, she was hiding behind the trash cans by the hotel. She was lost, cold and scared. She kept telling us she heard ghosts crying over here. It was a windy night. We've all tried to convince her that she just heard the wind whistling through the buildings, but you can see she's still afraid."

"Tell her I'm sorry, I didn't know about the ghosts," Joe said. "See if she wants to ride back to the playground."

Gabbie translated. Angie let go of Gabbie and hugged Joe. Then she crawled up on his shoulder for a jog back to the other kids. Joe told Mrs. Chavez what happened, so she could promise Angie that he wouldn't take her back there again. Since Rosalie had finally gone to sleep, she was free to watch the little ones, so he went back to the kids at the lot.

Elena's surgery was over at three. Doc brought her home at seven. He got her settled with the family and gave Dominique and Miguel instructions about her care. Then he drove over to see Joe.

Sitting at the table with a fresh cup of coffee, Doc asked, "How did you manage to get that check from the Catholic Church today?"

"I just drove out to the church and let Father Romero know about the situation," Joe said. "You know you're sworn to secrecy about that check, right? We don't want Miguel and Elena trying to repay it."

"I understand," Doc said. "That makes it even more remarkable. I'm just amazed. Every time I've tried to see Father Romero, Father Tobias tells me he's too busy."

Another strike against Father Tobias, Joe thought. To Doc, he said, "I've had the same treatment from Father Tobias. I guess I just got lucky today."

"Well, I'm glad you did," Doc said. "The surgery was successful, but it was close. Elena was almost too weak to survive it. I'll watch her for the next couple of weeks. I think she'll have a full recovery."

"Thank God," Joe said.

"Yes," Doc said. "And thank you for intervening in time to make the difference." Glancing around the room, he noticed the two gallons of water on the counter and asked, "Are you having trouble with the parsonage water, too?"

"Not yet," Joe said. "But Mrs. Anderson warned me about the Saturday night attacks before she left. She gave me her last two jugs of well water in case I needed it. I understand you spent several Saturdays taking care of two sick preachers."

"That I did," Doc said. "It was the strangest thing. Regardless what they ate or did, they came down with identical attacks. I had to sedate them to give them any relief. Both of them swore it was in the tap water. They said they could taste something in it. We tested it, but couldn't find anything. Reverend Whitsworth was so distressed he packed up and left. Of course, he'd missed so many services, the congregation was ready to ask him to leave. As soon as the Andersons switched to the Samuels spring water, the attacks stopped." Joe nodded.

"Come to think of it," Doc said. "It's strange that Reverend Phillips never had any attacks while he was here."

"Why did Reverend Phillips leave?" Joe asked.

"I'm not sure," Doc said. "He wasn't exactly friendly with any of us. Of course, the fact that I continued to care for the *Methodists* and *Catholics* made me a target of several of his tirades." Joe shook his head in disgust.

"As I recall," Doc said, "Reverend Phillips said he'd been called to serve another community. One that was more receptive to his teachings – according to him."

They both chuckled at that thought.

"Did he mention where that church was?" Joe asked.

"I don't think he named the church," Doc said. "But it was near a small town in Texas. I may have the address at home, if you want it. He left town owing me some money for a leg injury. I kept billing him until he finally sent me a check."

"Good for you," Joe said. "Yes, I'd like to have that address to add to the church records. I don't think he left a forwarding address." Doc nodded.

"What kind of leg injury?" Joe asked.

"Oh, he said he cut his leg on a piece of pipe in the yard over here," Doc said. "But judging from the oil in the wound, he must have been out around one of the rigs. I had to clean it up and stitch it back together." Then Doc laughed and said, "I remember how uncomfortable he was, having to come to a man he'd *damned,* for help. He didn't even say thanks. He just grumbled about *inadequate* medical facilities in small towns. I was ready to pour iodine over the cut just to prove his point."

Joe laughed with him and said, "Speaking of the oil rigs, do you get many injuries from their operations?"

"I used to," Doc said. "When they were drilling around town, they couldn't seem to keep their hands and feet out of the way. Nancy and I were talking about finding a larger building just to be able to take care of all of them. I'm glad we didn't, since they pulled out over night."

"Really, that fast?" Joe asked.

"Yep," Doc said. "One day they were digging craters everywhere and the next day they stopped. Within a week they had filled up the holes, stuffed their equipment in the storage units and left town. We were all in a state of shock."

"When did they leave?" Joe asked.

"Summer of '93," Doc said.

"Did they pay their bills or did you have to chase them down, too?" Joe asked.

"They paid most of them," Doc said. "I think we had to follow them back to Texas for some of it."

"Texas?" Joe questioned. "I thought Cozen was a New Mexico company."

"Well, that's a curious thing," Doc said. "Cozen has New Mexico printed on the side of their trucks, but their bills were paid by a warehouse place in Texas. Apparently, Cozen is some sort of a subsidiary of that company."

"Do you still get injuries from the men they left here?" Joe asked. "Or do they know how to handle the equipment?"

"I hadn't seen any of them for months," Doc said. "Then I got two of them a couple of weeks ago, with head injuries. They said they were hit in the head with trash can lids, but as drunk as they were, they probably fell into the trash cans."

"I haven't met any of them," Joe said. "Do they come to town often, or should I try to go meet them in the field?"

"You can usually find them at Clive's bar on Saturday nights, but I don't suppose you'd want to meet them there," Doc said. "Six of them were in Dave's jail the night of the trash can attack. The other two were probably in Portales." Joe nodded.

"They're rough men," Doc warned. "Not the kind I want as neighbors, if you know what I mean. They have so much hardware strapped to them they should jangle when they walk."

When he saw Joe's puzzled look, Doc added, "I'll bet Dave took eight knives and a couple of guns off my trash can victims." Joe grimaced.

Looking at the time, Doc said, "I'm sorry. I didn't realize how long I've been bending your ear."

"No problem," Joe said, as Doc walked to the door. "I enjoyed the visit. Come back anytime. Let me know if Elena needs anything over there."

"I'll do that," Doc said. "I think she'll be fine – thanks to you. See you later and thanks again."

Changing into black, Joe gave Doc time to drive away before he started his surveillance run. He took his last camera and binoculars with him. He switched tapes as he worked around town. He moved the camera from the eave of the barber shop to the north side of the hotel. He placed it at ground level. He hoped he'd catch the *hatch* opening under the trucks. He knew the ideal spot for the camera would be by the back steps to the hotel. But he couldn't risk having the drivers see it when they went in and out to shower.

He wondered about the timing of the transfers. The scraping noises had occurred while the drivers were showering. *Was it possible that the drivers didn't know about the women in their trucks? Could they unload, lock their trailers, shower, sleep and drive away, thinking their trucks were empty? If the women were bound, gagged and/or drugged, they wouldn't be able to make any noise. Interesting thought.*

Moving on, he placed his last camera near the location of Angie's ghosts. It's possible she did hear crying. She was a smart little girl and something had obviously terrified her. He rubbed the top of his head. He could vouch for that. He probably had two bald spots up there.

After changing the other tapes, he went to the side of the church and moved that camera to focus on the back of his parsonage. He wanted to watch his water line. Then he entered the church and went upstairs. He pulled up a chair and focused his binoculars out past the town to the oil rig nearest the storage units. He could see a Cozen truck parked by the shack and a light on inside. He watched for an hour. Then the light went out, but the truck didn't move. Apparently someone was staying in the shack. If they were part of the smuggling group, they could use their location for surveillance purposes. Working with the camera on the church window, he raised it to the top of the casing to see if he could get some tapes on the activity out there.

Back home, he sent Jack another e-mail. THE COZEN BILLS WERE PAID BY A WAREHOUSING CO IN TEXAS. ADDRESS FROM DOC TO FOLLOW. WONDER WHY COZEN WORKERS ARE DRIVING TRUCKS NOT REGISTERED TO COZEN OIL. DOES HOMER WELLMAN OWN THE COMPANIES ON THEIR REGISTRATIONS? NEED MORE INFORMATION ON THE 'GARBAGE CAN' ARRESTS. I NEED A SHORT RANGE SCOPE SO I CAN GET MORE DETAILS AND I NEED MORE SURVEILLANCE CAMERAS.

Then he told Jack about Elena Sanchez. He described his encounter with Romero and Tobias. He added Doc's comments about Tobias. LET'S ADD TOBIAS TO OUR LIST OF POSSIBLE SUSPECTS. HE'S DEFINITELY RUNNING INTERFERENCE BETWEEN FATHER ROMERO AND HIS PARISH IN TOWN.

CHAPTER TWENTY-ONE

SATURDAY – THIRD WEEK

Joe was relaxed while he jogged through town. He was comfortable with the area and the people. Somehow it had become *his* home town – at least for a while. He spoke to Charley while he was opening the feed store and recognized Rosalie's cry in the Hispanic section.

He intentionally ran past the camera at the hotel, to help establish the range and time on the tape. Cutting across the front of the storage units, he was surprised to see five men pulling equipment out of one of the units.

They turned in unison and almost bristled when they saw him. Max looked up and waved. He said something to the other four in Spanish. It was hard to hear, but Joe thought he told them he was a preacher. That didn't make them relax their stance at all. They still looked braced for action. Wondering why, he decided to press his luck.

"Good morning, Max," he called out. "Looks like you're busy this morning."

"Yeah," Max said. "The guys want some more pipes and one of their pumps has to be replaced."

Walking through the open gate, Joe wandered closer to the unit and ignored the hostile looks he was getting. He thrust his hand out and introduced himself to the closest man. Dumbstruck at Joe's audacity or stupidity, the man shook hands with him while Max translated the amenities. He continued around the group. He met Chad, Ernesto, Arturo and Bernardo.

Arturo and Bernardo had band-aids on their foreheads. He suspected he'd already met them.

He asked Max to tell the men that he was a city boy. Since he'd never seen equipment like this before, he found it very interesting. He pointed to different items and asked how they were used. The men started volunteering information. When he left, he couldn't say things were friendly, but at least he hadn't backed away from their attempts to intimidate him.

Better learn that lesson now boys, he thought, grinning to himself. *The classes get tougher the more you try.*

He jogged on over to see Grandma and took time to relax for a minute or two. She asked about Elena and was pleased when he told her the good news. Then she offered to bring a vase of her flowers for the Sunday service. He was delighted and told her so. He gave her a quick kiss on the cheek and finished his jog.

She hadn't fooled him. She was lonely with Sherie gone. He had to think of something to put that glow back in her cheeks. He'd go have lunch at the grocery store later and see what Ben and Alice thought.

At home, he took time to look at his sermon for tomorrow. Some day, if he ever told his father about this assignment, he guessed he'd have to thank him for the use of all his sermons. Jack was right. He could recite them from memory. He planned next week's text and selected two more verses for the children to recite. Who would've guessed that his *punishment* for Petey had become a hit with the kids and their parents? Tomorrow would be Dominique's first day to play. He'd have to be sure he made her feel welcome. He was looking forward to having piano music in church again.

Thinking about Petey, he decided to shower and go see how the Reeds were doing. When he walked into the store, it was full of customers. He hadn't considered mingling with the shoppers on Saturday, but it would definitely be another way to meet people in the area. He browsed through the store and listened while Ginger helped a lady select an electric skillet. When she saw him, she introduced him to Arlene Samuels.

"I believe I have a couple of gallons of your well water in my kitchen," he said. "Mrs. Anderson told me it's the best water in the county."

Arlene blushed at the compliment and invited him to come get more any time he needed it. He thanked her and wandered away to let Ginger complete her sale. On the other side of the store, Gene introduced him to Billy Samuels. Their three children, Carrie, Jolene and Paul were running around with Gene's kids.

When Gene finished his sale with Billy, he went to the back and gave Joe a box that had come in the mail. Since the bus came yesterday, he realized he was supposed to stop by and check the mail. Otherwise, it would sit in the store. Obviously, he didn't expect someone to deliver it to him. He just hadn't thought about it. Thanking Gene, he took the box back to the house and walked up to the grocery for lunch.

Like the general store, it was bustling with shoppers. Katherine's fingers were flying on the cash register as she rang up the purchases. But she still managed to wave and say, "Hi Reverend Marsh," when he walked in. He worked his way back to the coffee shop. Alice already had a cup of coffee waiting for him and was almost finished with his egg salad sandwich.

"You're something else," he said. "How did you hear Katherine over all that noise out there?"

"Motherhood training," Alice quipped back with a smile. "A mother always hears her child's voice over all the others."

"Are you always this busy on Saturdays?" he asked.

"Saturdays have always been our busiest days," she said. "But we've noticed a significant increase in business these last two weeks." Looking directly at him, she added, "*Someone* came to town and dropped the religious barriers with his kindness. Now we're back to talking and trading with each other again."

"Really?" he asked. "What did they do before?"

"They'd drive to Portales to make their purchases before they'd cross the religious lines over here," she said, shaking her head. "It sounds ridiculous now. But we did it, too. We were starving each other out over religions. How foolish was that? I'll bet some stores in Portales are regretting this. But it's the best thing that could've happened to our town. Go look in the store. We have Methodists, Catholics and Baptists talking to each other. It's wonderful!"

He grinned and went back to his sandwich.

"Thank you, *Preacher Man*," she said. "We needed you here, more than we realized." He blushed and she giggled.

On a serious note she asked, "How is Elena doing?" He gave her an update and she was relieved to hear the good news.

"I really feel bad that we didn't know she was so sick," Alice said. "Is there anything we can do to help now?"

"Not that I know of," Joe said. "Doc says she'll be fine as long as she rests for a couple of weeks. Don't feel bad about this. I went over to the house to meet her and didn't realize she was so sick. I just thought she was in normal recovery from Rosalie's birth. If I hadn't seen Doc, yesterday morning, I wouldn't have known about it either."

She nodded and turned to refill coffee for a customer.

"Now," Joe said when she came back, "what can we do to help Grandma over this lonely time? She's saying all the right things. But the sparkle is gone."

"I don't know," Alice said. "We've noticed it, too. We've tried to think of something, but obviously, we haven't found anything yet. It may just take time."

"If you think of something, let me know," he said. "I'll help any way I can."

He went home to see what *Reverend Brownstone* sent him. The box contained more surveillance cameras and tapes mixed with religious literature and two letters from Angelique.

Although the letters were dated two weeks earlier, he was anxious to know that she was all right. He read them and shook his head. Her loneliness was even more pronounced in these letters. He'd have to get Jack on that, too. He'd promised to look after her for him. On the bottom of the box, he found an envelope with an athletic scholarship application for the university in Portales.

Later, when he changed to go meet the kids, he walked over to check on Elena first. Dominique answered the door with Miguel close behind. Elena was sitting in a chair, smiling. After a brief conversation about her recovery, Dominique asked

Miguel to find out what time Joe wanted her to be at the church. Joe said services started at eleven. He suggested she might want to get there around ten forty-five to give herself time to get settled at the piano.

Then she asked Miguel something else that he didn't want to translate. "It's all right, Miguel," Joe said. "Let her ask me whatever she wants to know."

Embarrassed, Miguel said, "She wants to know if there is anyone who could teach English to the children and her."

"I don't know," Joe said, heading out the door. "Let me think about it for a while."

Of course, the kids need to learn English, he thought as he walked over to the hoops lot. *Look at the disadvantage I have trying to communicate. Although I know more Spanish than I can reveal, I have a terrible time speaking it. It's a great idea. I just need to find a way to make it happen.*

When Chris showed up for their game, he told him the scholarship application had arrived. "Check with your folks," he said, "and let me know when they can get together to fill it out. It needs to be as soon as possible to meet the deadline."

"Why don't you come to dinner tomorrow," Chris said. "We'll work on it then."

"That's fine with me," Joe said. "But don't you think you should ask your mom before you invite someone to dinner?"

"Naw," Chris said grinning. "Grandma said to invite you, before I left the house."

"Did she mention baking any pies?" Joe asked.

"I think she said something about it, but I told her I get them," Chris taunted.

"Not if I get there first," Joe said, as they started shooting free throws while they waited for the others.

After the game, he took a short nap. Then he filled his coffee pot with well water, as a precaution, and microwaved a dinner. While he ate, he sent Jack an e-mail. THANKS FOR THE BOX OF SUPPLIES. I'M VERY CONCERNED ABOUT GOLDIE. CHECK ON HER PLEASE. I'M TAKING WATER PRECAUTIONS – IN CASE THE SATURDAY NIGHT ATTACKS BEGIN AGAIN. SINCE I HAVE THE TOWN TALKING AND TRADING AGAIN, I'M SURE WELLMAN IS VERY UNHAPPY WITH ME. I EXPECT HIM TO MAKE A MOVE SOON. I'M CARRYING NOW – ESPECIALLY AT NIGHT.

He dressed in black, added his firearms and slipped out of his house at eleven. Most of the homes were dark. But the bar had a lively group. He worked his way around the other parts of town, switching tapes as he went. Then he eased over to the Church of Christ to change that one. Moving into the brush, he logged license plates and listened to the crowd around the bar.

He recognized the four men he'd met earlier at the storage unit. He assumed the other four were the rest of the Cozen crew that Doc mentioned. They seemed to be content to harass some of the women inside tonight.

He was about to move on when he saw another familiar face in the window. Father Tobias, in street clothes was dancing lecherously close to one of the beauties in the bar. Watching a while longer, he saw Tobias pay a man for a white packet, then turn and lead his lady friend upstairs.

So much for that vow, Joe thought. Halfway up the stairs, Tobias stopped and said something else to the man and gave him some more money. A few minutes later the man came out and drove away in the truck Charley said was Sampson's.

The truck was a block away before he realized it was turning down his street. The driver pulled into the Methodist Church and headed for Joe's house.

Joe slipped through the shadows and watched him sneak around back. He saw him remove a panel of siding by the kitchen sink, unscrew a cap and inject a syringe full of liquid into the water line. Joe hoped the camera was taping all of this. When he finished, the man tossed the syringe in the bushes and walked back to his truck.

So that's how they've been doing it, he thought. *The water pressure probably holds the liquid close to the surface, so only the first glass is potent enough to sicken someone. By the time the water's tested, the amount is miniscule. I think I have a glass of water I want Miguel to test.*

He worked his way back to the bar. He heard the man bragging to some of the Cozen men that the new preacher probably wouldn't be around much longer. They obviously knew each other and clearly understood what he meant. He had a frightening thought, as he listened to the men talk.

If Wellman had made attempts on the health, if not lives, of the ministers in town, wouldn't Father Romero be a target, too? They were already trying to isolate him from the townspeople. Since Joe had broken that barrier – twice – had he put Father Romero's life at risk, literally? Was Tobias the next in line at that church, if Father Romero was gone?

Since the crowd at the bar seemed relatively tame, He worked his way back to the house. He grabbed a pair of rubber gloves and a plastic bag and went out back to retrieve the syringe the man tossed in the bushes.

Then he dumped the contents of his peanut butter jar in the trash, washed it carefully with the well water and filled it with the contaminated tap water. Next, he washed out a small spice bottle and poured a little contaminated water in it.

Then he wrote Jack an URGENT e-mail. I SAW FATHER TOBIAS AND ANOTHER MAN AT THE BAR TONIGHT. I THINK THE OTHER MAN IS SAMPSON, BART'S COUSIN AND THE CATHOLIC CHURCH FIELD FOREMAN. I'M CONVINCED THEY'RE BOTH ON WELLMAN'S PAYROLL AND TOBIAS IS IMPERSONATING A PRIEST TO ISOLATE FATHER ROMERO AND KEEP HIM OUT OF TOWN. TOBIAS WENT UPSTAIRS WITH A PROSTITUTE, BOUGHT DRUGS FROM SAMPSON AND PAID HIM TO POISON MY WATER. I SHOULD HAVE THAT ON TAPE. I'VE SAVED THE WATER FOR TESTING.

I THINK THEY WANT ALL THE PREACHERS OUT OF TOWN SO THE CHURCHES WILL FAIL AND THEY CAN BUY THE PROPERTIES. SINCE I HAVE FATHER ROMERO INVOLVED IN THE TOWN AGAIN, I MAY HAVE MADE HIM A TARGET AND ENDANGERED HIM. I NEED PERMISSION TO COMPROMISE MY COVER WITH FATHER ROMERO – TO EXPOSE THESE TWO AND POSSIBLY SAVE HIS LIFE. I THINK I CAN MINIMIZE MY EXPOSURE, BUT I HAVE TO LET FATHER ROMERO KNOW WHAT'S HAPPENING.

IF MY SUSPICIONS ARE CORRECT, TOBIAS AND SAMPSON COULD BE POISONING FATHER ROMERO OUT AT THE CHURCH WHERE NO ONE CAN HELP HIM. THE PROOF WILL BE IF FATHER ROMERO IS TOO "ILL" TO PREACH IN TOWN TOMORROW. IF THAT'S THE CASE, I'LL NEED TO TAKE THE DOCTOR AND POSSIBLY THE CONSTABLE OUT TO THE CATHOLIC CHURCH.

ANOTHER QUESTION – IF I SIGN A COMPLAINT AGAINST THESE TWO, WILL "JOSEPH MARSH" STAND UP IN COURT OR WILL I NEED TO SIGN IT JOSEPH MORRIS? ANSWERS NEEDED, ASAP.

CHAPTER TWENTY-TWO

SUNDAY – FOURTH WEEK

Rising early, he grabbed some gloves and plastic bags and took a closer look at the back of the parsonage. He found the panel Sampson removed the night before. Inside the wall, he found a water cutoff valve and a tee on the cold water line. Apparently, Sampson turned off the water supply, removed the cap on the open end of the tee, injected the solution, replaced the cap and turned the valve back on.

Joe used the surveillance camera behind the parsonage to tape the open section and the plumbing configuration, before he replaced the panel. When he stepped aside, he felt something under his foot. Moving the bushes over, he found more syringes half buried in the dirt. After taping that area, he dug up sixteen more syringes that he placed in another plastic bag.

Since it was still very early, he walked over to the Methodist parsonage and found a similar panel behind their kitchen pipes. Opening it, he taped that set of pipes and retrieved eleven more syringes in the dirt around those bushes.

He changed the tape in the camera and put it back behind his house. After he stored the contaminated water and the bags of syringes, he cleaned up for church.

He checked his e-mail and had an answer from Jack. PROCEED WITH CAUTION, REVEAL AS LITTLE AS NECESSARY TO REMOVE THE RISK TO FATHER ROMERO AND OTHER INNOCENTS. YES, JOSEPH MARSH WILL STAND UP IN COURT. WE'LL SEE TO IT. STAY SAFE.

While he played the surveillance tape, he watched out his window to see if Father Romero arrived for the early service at the Methodist Church. Surprised, he saw Tobias and Sampson help an obviously ailing Father Romero out of the car.

He's tougher than you thought, isn't he Tobias? Joe thought. *Good for you Father Romero. Hang in there. We'll get rid of your problem very soon.* He stepped outside to smile and wave at Father Romero – and his shocked helpers.

Since Father Romero managed to make it to town, Joe revised his plans. He called Doc, Dave and Ben and asked them to meet him at the church immediately. "But act like you're just walking over to an early meeting, please," he said.

He reset the tape player to Sampson's arrival behind the parsonage and carried it, the UTILITY folder and the small spice bottle of water with him.

He unlocked the church and waited. All three men arrived within ten minutes. Looking at his watch, Joe said, "Time is too critical to answer your questions right now, but I swear I can support everything I'm about to say."

The men looked at his serious face and nodded.

"Remember the Saturday night illnesses your other preachers had?" he asked.

"Yes," Ben said. "We never could find the cause."

"Well," Joe said. "I taped a man poisoning my water last night. I found proof this morning that the same thing had been done to the Andersons' water."

"What," Ben said. "That's not possible. We tested that water. It was clear."

"I'll explain how they did it later," Joe said. "We don't have time now." Ben was stunned, but he just nodded.

"Doc and I have both noticed the way Father Tobias has kept Father Romero isolated from any issues in town," Joe said.

Doc nodded agreement to the others.

"But, I think I inadvertently made him another target," Joe said, "because, I've pushed past Father Tobias twice and managed to get Father Romero involved again. When Father Romero arrived this morning, he could barely climb out of his car. I think they've poisoned him, too."

"Oh my God," Ben said. "We have to help him."

"I agree," Joe said. "I want to set a trap for them, but I don't have time to do it before church."

"Tell us what you want us to do," Ben said.

"Doc," Joe said, "I need you and Constable Nelson to just *happen* to be walking by the Methodist Church when they bring Father Romero out to his car. You have to be *very concerned* about his condition and *insist* that he come back to your office for medical attention. Check him out. See if he has the 'preacher' symptoms. I think they're feeding us ipecac."

Doc was surprised, but he agreed ipecac could create the problems he'd seen.

"Constable," Joe said, "I need you to support Doc and *not* let Tobias or Sampson intervene. I have reason to believe Tobias and Sampson are also involved in drugs, but I'll have to give you that information later. Right now we need to keep Tobias and Sampson in town – but away from Father Romero."

"Ben, I need to ask you to ask Miguel to run a quick test on this," Joe said, as he handed him the spice bottle. "It's some of the water I collected from my faucet last night. I know its Sunday, but we have to identify the poison they used on me."

"No problem," Ben said. "Consider it done."

"Constable," Joe said, "I don't want to confront Tobias and Sampson about any of this until we have preliminary results from Miguel. I don't know why they're poisoning preachers. Maybe together we can get them to tell us. Can you use delay tactics until I get back to you?" Dave nodded, as Joe added, "I'll sign a complaint against Sampson, but I'd like to catch both of them in the poisonings if we can." Dave agreed.

"Their church service will end in about twenty minutes," Joe said. "I've got to hold my service to keep them from achieving their goal. As soon as I finish, I'll check with Miguel to see if he has any test results for us. Then I'll go to Doc's office. Father Romero doesn't know anything about the ipecac or the rest of what I've told you. Please keep him in the dark until I get a chance to talk to him." Dave and the others agreed.

"I know you all have questions. I promise I'll answer them later," Joe said. "The most important thing is to get Father Romero to Doc's to find out if he's been poisoned. And we have to keep Tobias and Sampson here until we can sort this out."

He watched the men fan out on the street. He prayed they could pull this off.

Dominique arrived moments later.

He took a deep breath and started greeting the congregation at the door. He watched Doc and Dave corner Father Romero. He saw Tobias and Sampson arguing, as expected. True to his word, Dave backed Doc up and they escorted all three men over to Doc's office. Ben rounded the corner as Joe was closing the door.

"Miguel's on it," Ben said. Joe nodded. Then he remembered the family dinner. "I think we'll have it later tonight," Ben said. "Will that work?"

Joe agreed and walked up to the podium. He noticed the large vase of flowers and realized Ben must have brought them. He made a point of recognizing Dominique and the flowers before he began the service. The piano accompaniment made a world of difference in the music. Dale and Sarah proudly recited their verses. Petey and Lily wanted another set for next week.

Reciting his father's sermon based on the verses, Joe decided once again, he was going to have to thank him for his indirect help.

When the service was over, he promised Chris he'd see him tonight, but said he wouldn't be able to join the guys for hoops today. Before Dominique left, he noticed Grandma talking to her. Walking closer, he heard a very comprehensive Spanish conversation. *Grandma is bilingual and a teacher!* He'd have to pursue that thought a little later.

He picked up his tape player and the UTILITY file and locked the church. He walked over to the utility building. Miguel had the results he needed. The preliminary test showed high concentrations of *cephaelis ipecacuanha* – ipecac.

He could see Miguel was puzzled.

"I promise to come back tomorrow and tell you what's happening," Joe said. "But I can't take the time now. Thank you for running the test. This is the critical information we needed." Miguel nodded and locked up.

Joe rushed back to his house to change and retrieve the water in the peanut butter jar. He dropped his firearms in place and grabbed a new tape. He picked up his camera behind the parsonage and stuffed it under his shirt before he walked over to Doc's office.

When he opened the door, he ignored Tobias and Sampson and waved Dave outside. He showed him the report from Miguel. Ben walked up and read it, too.

"Doc has confirmed that Father Romero's symptoms are very similar to the other preacher attacks," Dave said. "He's given the Father a mild sedative. It should be wearing off soon."

"Good hunch, Reverend," Ben said. "Let's go catch some crooks and then you can tell us how you figured this out."

"First," Joe said, "I have to talk to Father Romero. He'll probably be our best ally once he knows what's going on. Have Tobias and Sampson given you any trouble?"

"No," Dave said. "It was like you said, they didn't want Doc interfering. But once we *insisted*, they've just been sitting quietly in the waiting room. They're probably afraid Doc will discover something."

"I knew it would take your presence to keep them from overruling Doc," Joe said. "Thanks for backing him up."

"No problem," Dave said. "They really argued with us."

"I'm going to see if Father Romero is able to talk to me," Joe said. "I need you two to hang loose with Tobias and Sampson until I finish. Let them squirm a while longer – just don't let them leave. If they need to use the bathroom, make them do it in a bottle. That should shake them up. They're suspects. Let's treat them like they are." The guys agreed.

Joe walked back into Doc's office and knocked on the exam room door. Tobias started to step up and protest. Dave laid a *very* firm hand on his shoulder. He decided to stay seated.

When Doc let him in, Joe asked about Father Romero's condition. It was obvious he was still resting.

"You were right," Doc said. "It appears to be the same kind of attack."

"Has he vomited since he arrived?" Joe asked.

"A little," Doc said, motioning to a small pan.

"Can we have it tested for ipecac?" Joe asked.

"Sure," Doc said. "But it'll take a day or two to get the results back from the lab."

"That's okay," Joe said. "Miguel confirmed the ipecac in my water. Your lab work will just back it up. Did Father Romero say when his attack started?"

"About an hour after breakfast," Doc said, looking at his notes. "He said he had his usual morning tea and toast, but he thought the tea tasted different. When he mentioned it to Father Tobias, he was told they'd purchased a different brand."

"Yeah," Joe said, "one with *ipecac* on the label."

When Father Romero began to stir, Doc went over to check on him. After speaking a few words, Father Romero started to sit up. Seeing Joe in the room, he gave him a weak smile and asked, "Are we in trouble with the Lord again?"

"No, Father," Joe said, "but I suspect some others are."

Looking at Doc for approval and getting a nod, he asked Doc to let him have some time to talk to Father Romero.

When Doc left, Father Romero looked at Joe and said, "This is more than a stomach attack. Isn't it?"

"Yes, Father it is," Joe said. "I have some shocking things to tell you. But before I do, I need you to trust what I'm going to say. I have no ulterior motives in any of this."

Father Romero gave him a long look and nodded.

"Someone, I don't know who, wants all the religious leaders out of this town," Joe said. "I don't know if it's because they're atheists or if they want the property. Nonetheless, I have proof that Reverend Whitsworth, the Baptist Preacher before Phillips, was poisoned weekly to keep him from preaching his Sunday services. I found his notes about the poisonings in the church files and copies of town water tests."

Joe handed him a copy of one of the water reports.

"Also," Joe said, "Reverend Anderson suffered identical attacks. Doc can verify that he spent most Saturday nights caring for both of them. Both preachers swore they'd tasted something in the water. But no tests could confirm any unusual substance. The attacks drove Whitsworth out of town. The Andersons would have left, too, if the Samuels family hadn't shared their artesian well water with them."

Father Romero gave him a puzzled look and waited.

"Before the Andersons left," Joe said, "Mrs. Anderson gave me her last two gallons of the well water and warned me against the Saturday night preacher attacks. Since I had already read Reverend Whitsworth's notes, I picked up some equipment in Portales last week and put a surveillance camera behind my parsonage. This is the tape I recorded last night." He played the tape. Father Romero's face went from white to red.

"That's my foreman, Sampson," he said. Turning to Joe, he started offering assurances that he did not have any knowledge of the poisonings – obviously afraid that Joe thought he'd ordered the action. Joe stopped him.

"Father Romero, if I thought you had any knowledge of this," he said, "I wouldn't be talking to you right now. I trusted you the first day we met. Unfortunately, I believe our mutual trust may have led to your poisoning this morning. Let me continue and I think you'll understand."

Father Romero looked back at the tape and just nodded.

"When the first round of poisoning didn't drive both preachers out," Joe said, "I believe Phillips was an impostor who arrived as a Baptist Preacher to keep the town from hiring another real preacher. I can't find any record of Phillips in the Baptist registry and we both know how divisive and harmful he was to the town. The fact that Phillips never had a Saturday preacher's attack is another indication that he was probably working with the people who want the churches gone. Again, I can't prove it, but I believe Phillips left, because he assumed the town couldn't find anyone who'd want to take on such a small church. His divisions were causing the businesses to fail and it was common knowledge that Reverend Anderson was dying. So the people behind this scheme thought they'd succeeded."

Father Romero shook his head in disgust.

"Obviously, they hadn't expected a new Baptist Preacher to arrive. Especially not one with my attitude," Joe said. "I've, categorically reversed Phillips' edicts and crossed *forbidden* religious barriers. Whoever's behind this plot is probably very angry with me right now."

Father Romero gave him a bewildered look.

"Now, I have to ask you how well you know Father Tobias," Joe said gently.

"Not very well," Father Romero said. "He arrived about two years ago to replace a dear friend of mine, Father Lopez, who passed away." Joe nodded.

"In fact, now that I think about it, I believe Father Lopez suffered numerous vomiting attacks before his heart weakened and failed. Do you think they caused his death?" Father Romero asked, as his mind began to work on the facts he'd just heard.

"I honestly don't know," Joe said. "I pray not, but I'm not sure this group didn't do it. Frankly, you've made me wonder if all the attacks weakened Reverend Anderson's heart the same way. It's something we'll want the follow up on, once we take care of the immediate problem."

"Definitely," Father Romero said.

"Did you check Father Tobias' credentials?" Joe asked.

"Not personally," Father Romero said. "He arrived with what appeared to be proper paperwork from the church."

"Is he second in line, in your church?" Joe asked. "I mean, if something happens to you, would he have control?"

Father Romero winced and nodded yes.

"Was Father Lopez involved with your parish that's here in town?" Joe asked.

"Yes, very much so," Father Romero said. "He knew every family down to the newest members. He frequently came to town during the week to check on them. How did you know?"

"It was an educated guess," Joe said, "because, without your knowledge, Father Tobias has turned away people from town who have tried to visit you."

At Father Romero's surprised look, Joe said, "Doc has driven out to try to talk to you and Father Tobias has told him you were too busy to be bothered. You already know Father Tobias left me standing in the driveway for twenty five minutes the day I came with urgent news about Elena. He had no intentions of telling you I was there. He just didn't realize that I wasn't going to leave like the others did."

Father Romero shook his head and said, "I didn't know what he was doing."

"I know," Joe said, "and that was probably safer for you. From what I can tell, my insistence on seeing you and our subsequent friendship is what put you at risk. You've become involved in this town again and that isn't what they want. To put it bluntly Father, I believe Father Tobias is another impostor who was sent to your church to undermine your involvement in this town." Father Romero was shocked, but Joe could see he was starting to accept the possibility.

"Now I need to tell you something in strictest confidence, because other lives may still be involved," Joe said. "Do I have your word?"

"Yes," Father Romero said.

"A couple of weeks ago six men caused some problems in town," Joe said. "Rumor has it that they were trying to rob one of our Hispanic families. Since then I've tried to walk around town on Saturday nights to watch the neighborhoods. No one knows I'm out there and I don't want them to know."

Father Romero nodded and waited.

"Last night, the bar was noisy," Joe said, "so I walked over to that area. Father Tobias was inside, dressed in street clothes, dancing very close with a redheaded lady. While I watched, Tobias handed Sampson some money for a white packet. Then he led the redhead upstairs to what I assume are private rooms. Halfway up the stairs, he gave Sampson some more money which is when Sampson left the bar and drove to my house to poison the water." Father Romero was shocked.

The problem we have," Joe said, "is that we can't tell them what I saw or we'll lose what little protection I'm trying to provide. If we say someone else saw them, they could randomly decide on that other person and make an innocent person a target." Father Romero winced and agreed.

"We'll work on the drug issues later," Joe said. "But I want to try to trick them into telling us what they've done to you. My thought is a little deceptive, but it might work. I propose that you lie back down and let them think your attack was very serious – which it actually was until Doc intervened. Let's see what they tell us."

"I want them gone by nightfall," Father Romero said angrily. "Where are they?"

"Ben Morrison and Constable Nelson have been keeping them company in the waiting room while we got you stabilized," Joe said. "I guess we've left them squirming long enough, I'll go get Doc." Halfway to the door, he stopped to turn on his camera. Then he said, "There's one more thing, Father."

Father Romero watched him pull the peanut butter jar out from under his shirt and pour some of the contents into two small paper cups from Doc's dispenser.

He carried them over to Father Romero and said, "Will you bless this water for me? It came out of my faucet this morning. We know Tobias served it to you and we can prove Sampson served it to me. I may want to offer those two some of the *Holy Water* they keep delivering to preachers."

Chucking, Father Romero actually blessed the cups, looked upward and said, "Father forgive me – but a small dose seems only fair."

Joe went to the door and asked Doc to come back in the room. Again Tobias tried to press forward and again Dave's heavy hand settled him back in his chair. Once they had Doc comfortable with their story, Joe warned Doc about the two cups on the counter. Doc grinned at Joe and said, "I guess I need to find a couple of buckets."

"They might come in handy," Joe said. On the way to the door, he turned and said, "Lie down and look sick, Father."

Joe was grave when he opened the door and signaled the two men to come in to see Father Romero. On cue, Ben and Dave pulled some extra chairs in from the waiting room. The room was small and they definitely crowded it.

Good, Joe thought, *it'll make them thirsty.*

Doc was great. He described Father Romero's actual condition, but he used *cephaelis ipecacuanha* and a couple of other impressive medical terms that obviously confused Tobias and Sampson. Joe asked them if they had any idea what might have caused the illness. When neither of them offered an answer, he nodded to Doc.

"When did the Father become ill?" Doc asked.

"This morning after breakfast," Tobias said.

"What did he eat for breakfast?" Doc asked.

"Just his regular tea and toast," Tobias said.

"Did you prepare it for him?" Joe asked Tobias.

"The cook makes the toast," Tobias said, "but I always make his tea."

"What kind of tea do you use?" Doc asked.

"Just regular black tea," Tobias said.

"What were his first symptoms?" Doc asked.

"He turned pale, clutched his stomach and started vomiting," Tobias said.

"How many times did he vomit?" Joe asked.

"I'm not sure," Tobias said. "I called one of the women to come take care of him. I don't have much of a stomach for that sort of thing."

Joe silently seethed at that irony and said, "I'm sure."

"I don't understand why I'm in here," Sampson said, becoming uncomfortable with the questions. "I wasn't with him until he got in the car."

"Did you notice anything different about him when he got in the car?" Joe asked.

"Just that he was sick," Sampson said. "We tried to get him to stay home."

"Who do you have out there who could have taken care of him?" Joe asked.

"We could've had the women take care of him," Sampson said.

"Oh, I see," Joe said, glaring at Sampson. "You were going to leave the leader of your church – who was vomiting incessantly – with a couple of women. Are they medically qualified to care for a seriously ill person?"

Sampson shook his head.

"What were they supposed to do? Besides clean up what you didn't have the *stomach for?"* Joe asked.

When neither man answered, he pressed harder.

"What were you going to do? Just leave him out there? This is your leader! He's a Holy Father in the Roman Catholic Church! He cares for all those under his wings and you weren't even going to take care of him?"

Both men visibly slumped in their chairs. "Why weren't you rushing him to the doctor?" Joe demanded.

Sampson looked at Tobias.

Tobias shook his head and both men stopped talking.

Joe was so angry he turned away and walked over to the sink. He took a cup out of Doc's rack and got a drink from the faucet. Watching him, Sampson asked for a cup. Tobias wanted one, too. Joe carried the two cups over to them.

"Here you go," he said. "Two cups fresh out of my faucet this morning."

Sampson had the cup up to his lips before he realized what Joe said. "Don't drink that," he told Tobias.

Tobias spit out the sip he took and cursed.

Joe grinned at them and asked, "What's wrong? I thought you were thirsty."

"Not any more," Sampson said, putting the cup down.

Joe cut a look at Dave and nodded.

Dave placed Sampson under arrest for poisoning the parsonage water and read him his rights.

"You can't arrest me," Sampson said. "I didn't do anything wrong."

"If you didn't do anything wrong, why won't you drink that water?" Joe asked. "What did you put in my water, Sampson? Was it the same thing you gave the Father?"

"I didn't give anything to Father Romero," Sampson said, as Dave cuffed him.

"Then who did?" Joe demanded.

Sampson looked at Tobias.

"Shut up, Sampson," Tobias growled.

"Sure, Sampson," Joe said, "go ahead and take the rap for Tobias. We'll just wait for the lab tests. If the contents of Father Romero's stomach contain the same poison you put in my water, we'll have you on two counts of poisoning. There are a lot of prison inmates who aren't going to be very nice to someone who tried to poison a priest." Joe nodded to Dave.

Dave signaled Ben to take Sampson out of the room. "Tell them Tobias," Sampson said over his shoulder, "or I will."

"Tell us what, Tobias?" Joe asked, as Ben shut the door. Tobias shook his head. Joe grinned and said, "You're starting to sweat, Tobias. What's wrong? Is your last fix wearing off?"

Tobias' eyes flared at him. Joe laughed and turned back to Doc. "How is Father Romero doing?" he asked.

"I think he's going to pull through," Doc said, checking on the Father.

"You'd better thank God for that, Tobias," Joe said. "Otherwise you'd be facing murder charges for that tea you served the Father this morning."

Dave took the cue and arrested Tobias for the poisoning and read him his rights. Tobias swore.

"Careful, Tobias," Joe said. "Real priests don't use words like that." Tobias swore again.

Joe grinned and said, "You're not even a priest are you?"

"No," he said. "I was just supposed to keep Father Romero out of town. It was an easy job until you came. You're the reason we had to make him sick."

"Oh, I see," Joe sneered. "It's my fault that you're an *evil little worm* who sold your soul and betrayed a man of God! Check your scriptures, Tobias – especially the chapters on *Judas*!" Tobias glowered at Joe while Dave cuffed him.

"What did you give Father Romero to make him sick, Tobias? You might as well tell us now," Joe said. "You know we'll find out as soon as we get the lab reports back."

"It's called ipecac," Tobias finally said. "It's harmless. It's just supposed to makes people vomit."

"Constable," Joe said. "Do you have a big rock these two can slither back under?"

"I certainly do," Dave said. Looking around the room, he added, "All of you are witnesses to the confessions we heard. I'll need you to testify when the Judge arrives." The men agreed.

"He paid me to do it," Sampson said, when Dave opened the door with Tobias.

"Why, Tobias?" Joe snarled behind him. "Why did you pay Sampson to poison innocent people?"

"I...I," Tobias stammered. "I was hired to get the preachers out of town."

"Who paid you to do this?" Joe demanded, as he pulled Tobias back around to face him. "What kind of an ogre do you work for?"

Cowering away from Joe, Tobias said, "His name is Peter Philman."

"Where does he live?" Dave asked.

"I...I don't know," Tobias said. "I only met him once. He just calls when he wants something done."

"Why does he want the preachers gone?" Joe asked, still glaring at Tobias.

"I don't know," Tobias sniveled. "I just know he wants them out of town."

Turning back to Father Romero, Joe asked, "Have you heard enough, Father?"

Father Romero sat up and said, "I certainly have!"

Tobias and Sampson both looked at the floor when Father Romero stared at them.

"You told us he was seriously ill," Tobias said, cutting a look at Joe. "You lied."

"No, I didn't," Joe said. "He was – and he's still too weak to deal with your betrayal. Get out of here before the sight of you makes him sick again." Joe shook his head in disgust, as Dave and Ben led the men off to jail.

He collected his camera, tape player, peanut butter jar and UTILITY folder. Then he helped Father Romero out of the room. When they stepped into the waiting room, Nancy looked up and shook her head.

"What happened in there?" she asked, as Ben and Dave walked back in.

"Nothing we can talk about right now," Joe said, sending a warning look to the others.

She nodded and handed him a sheet of paper.

"Henry said you wanted this," she said. Looking down, he saw Wellman's address at a Warehouse Company in Texas.

"Thanks," he said, as he put it in his pocket.

He thanked Doc for his help and walked outside just in time to hear Ben say, "Man! If I'm ever in a jam, I want him on my team." The others agreed.

Dave took a deep breath and said, "Right now, I have more questions than answers. I've got Susan at the jail with the prisoners until I get back. Reverend, can we go over to your place and try to sort this thing out?"

Joe nodded and ran ahead to start some coffee. Dave and Ben walked slowly with Father Romero. The men sat around his table, drinking coffee and asking questions. He answered them and Dave took notes for his report. Joe gave Dave the new tape from Doc's office, the Sampson tape, Miguel's report, the UTILITY file folder and his jar of contaminated water.

"I don't understand why they left me alone all this time," Father Romero said.

"Because they had you isolated twenty-five miles away," Joe said. "My persistence in getting past Tobias to you, inadvertently put you at risk – because you became involved in the town again."

"I don't understand why someone wants the preachers gone," Ben said.

"Well, they definitely influence the town," Joe said. "As a newcomer, I guess the divisions were more obvious to me. I was amazed at all of them when I arrived." Then he laughed and said, "I don't guess being here three weeks makes me an old timer yet." The guys shook their heads and chuckled.

"But really," Joe said, "look at the damage Phillips and Tobias did through religion. The town did nothing as a unit. Religions and races were totally divided. That's not a recipe for success in any town, but it spells disaster for a town this size. I just don't understand why someone wants that division."

"Well," Father Romero said, "the Tobias era is over and I can guarantee that my group is going to be much more involved than we have been in the past." Looking at Joe, he added, "I can't imagine a force strong enough to keep you from being involved. In three weeks you've tossed this town on its ear and set it back down the right way. I haven't taken a moment to thank you for sensing my danger and the rest of you for responding so quickly. How did you pull this together so fast?"

"Reverend Marsh called Doc, Dave and me," Ben said simply, "and we came."

"Did he tell you what he needed?" Father Romero asked.

Dave and Ben looked at each other and shook their heads. "He just said he needed us immediately," Ben said.

"And you trusted him that much?" Father Romero asked.

"Absolutely," Ben said.

Father Romero turned to Joe and said, "Then so do I. If you need me, just let me know. I'll be there for you. And thank you again for saving me today."

Joe nodded and said, "It was a team effort, Father. I'm glad you're okay."

Father Romero thanked all of them again. Looking out the window, he said, "I think that's my ride pulling up outside. I need to go get my parish back in order."

Joe walked the Father out to the car. Before he opened the door, he cautioned Father Romero to watch his workers for drug withdrawals. "It's possible these two men were supplying others at the church or in the fields," he said. Shocked by that thought, Father Romero thanked him again and drove off.

Ben and Joe offered to watch the prisoners so Dave and Susan could have lunch. "Thanks," Dave said. "I could use a break before I start writing these reports."

Joe locked up and they walked down the block with him.

"Thank God they didn't drink that water before I locked them up," Dave said.

"I'm almost sorry they didn't," Joe said. "They deserved it, and more, for all the suffering they've caused."

"Yeah," Dave said. "I hope your camera was on their faces when they realized what you said. Did Father Romero know you were going to do that?"

"Yep," Joe said. "He even blessed it so I could give them a taste of some of the *Holy Water* they kept giving the preachers." Ben and Dave laughed out loud.

"Oh, by the way, Constable," Joe said, getting serious again. "When Father Romero recovers a little more, you may want to talk to him about Father Lopez's death. Apparently, he had a series of these attacks that eventually weakened his heart and caused his death. That sounds similar to the Anderson situation. These poisonings may have directly or indirectly caused two deaths. Since Tobias replaced Lopez, he may have been involved in that one – possibly Sampson, too."

"How long have you been here?" Dave asked.

"Three weeks," Joe said. "Why?"

"How have you found out about all of this in such a short time?" Dave asked.

"I don't know," Joe said. "Just lucky, I guess."

Dave stepped inside the jail to get Susan. Ben and Joe took over the watch. Tobias and Sampson were each blaming the other one for their situation. Joe looked at Ben and grinned. They ignored both men.

When Dave returned, he sat down and looked at his notes. "I still can't figure out how you found all of this," he said.

"Just a series of coincidences," Joe said.

Dave shook his head and started writing.

Joe turned to Ben and said, "Let's go see if your kid left any pie for us." To Dave, he said, "Bye Constable, thanks for your trust and help today."

"Any time," Dave said. "Thanks for figuring this out in time to save the Father."

Ben and Joe went back to the parsonage to get the scholarship application for Chris. They were still discussing the day as they walked up to Ben's house.

"I couldn't have done it without the three of you," Joe said. "Thanks for dropping everything when I called. I expected Father Romero to be too sick to preach today. I thought I was going to have to storm his church to get him out. But he was stronger than they thought. He insisted on coming to town. That meant next time they would've used more on him. And that dose could've been fatal without sedation. I think we had a very close call. I just wish I knew who was doing this and why."

"What about the name Tobias gave us?" Ben asked. "Peter Philman, wasn't it?"

"I'm sure Dave will check it out," Joe said. "But I can almost bet you it's bogus. If you were running a scheme like this would you let your flunkies know your real name?"

"No, I guess not," Ben said, obviously disappointed.

"By the way," Joe said, changing the subject. "What did you think of Dominique's playing today?"

"I thought she was great," Ben said. "She looked a little nervous, but that's to be expected the first day."

"I discovered something about your mother today," Joe said. "I heard her talking to Dominique. I didn't know she was bilingual. That's very interesting."

"She's quite fluent in Spanish," Ben said. "Why?"

"Well, the other day Dominique asked me, through Miguel's translation, if there was anyone who could help the kids, and her, learn English," Joe said. "Your mom's bilingual and a teacher. And she just happens to be a lady who seems to need a new purpose since Sherie left. Do you think we can make that combination work? And what about the Wilsons, they're both retired teachers who don't seem to have a lot to do? Could the three of them form some type of team and work with the Spanish kids?"

Ben stood in the middle of the street with his mouth wide open. "I don't believe you," he said. "I'm just now digesting the fact that we saved a priest's life and caught two people who have been terrorizing our preachers for the last five years – and here you are planning a small school on the way to lunch. How do you do it? It's a great idea! I love it! I just don't know if I can keep up with you. Have pity on an old man. Let me have some lunch before we open...a...a...*Kindergarten*."

Joe laughed out loud at Ben's antics. He was flapping his arms and bouncing all over the street venting his fake frustrations at him

"Come on old man," he said, as he took Ben's arm. "I'll have pity on you and help you up the street. But when we get to Grandma's pie, you're on your own."

They walked arm in arm into the house and were barraged with questions as soon as they closed the door. Apparently rumors had been flying around town. Everyone was speculating about the sick priest and the Constable at Doc's office this afternoon. Ben deferred to Joe for the explanations and noticed how he skimmed over most of the specifics.

"Father Romero was ill," Joe said. "We think the other men caused the problem, but we won't know for sure until the Constable completes his investigation."

After some coffee and food – and a mock battle over Grandma's pie – the family sat down with Joe and the scholarship application. Ben and Alice had most of the information ready, so it didn't take very long to complete it. Chris was trying to be nonchalant. But it was easy to see how excited he was. He was a great athlete and he had good grades. Joe just hoped they could get him into a scholarship space.

When they finished, Ben poured another round of coffee and broached the Kindergarten idea with Alice. After his melodrama earlier, Joe was surprised he was even discussing it. Apparently he really did like the idea and so did Alice.

"The biggest problem I see," Ben said, "is finding a location for them."

"They could use the church during the week," Joe said. "But the kids would have to come across town to attend. That would be hard for their mothers."

"There's one empty house at the end of the Hispanic block," Ben said. "But we'd have to pay Wellman six hundred dollars a month to use it."

"Are you serious?" Joe asked. "That's a staggering amount for those families."

"I know," Ben said. "It wouldn't be so bad if they were nice houses. But they're in deplorable shape and we can't get Wellman to fix a thing."

"Well, where there's a will, there's a way," Joe said, quoting the old idiom. "Let's think about this for a day or two."

He said goodbye and headed for the door when he heard Ben and Alice chime, "Good night, Reverend."

Turning back around, he looked at them and said, "I hadn't even noticed – and I should have days ago. Between friends like us, it's just Joe. Let's save 'Reverend' for the front door of the church. Good night you two and thanks for dinner – it was delicious." To his delight he heard, "Good night, Joe," as he closed the door.

Since it was already dark, he walked the quieter parts of town on his way back to his house. Inside, he changed to black and went out to switch tapes. He still had to review the other ones from last night and e-mail Jack about today. Slipping around the buildings, he was happy to see everything quiet again. He changed all the tapes in town and the one in the church.

Back home, he made coffee – with well water. He wasn't going to use the tap water until Miguel tested it again. Then he started playing the surveillance tapes while he composed an e-mail to Jack:

I DID NOT HAVE TO EXPOSE MY COVER. THE ONLY INFO I GAVE OUT CONCERNED MY WALKS AROUND TOWN ON SATURDAY NIGHTS TO TRY TO HELP THE COMMUNITY – AND THAT WAS TOLD ONLY TO FATHER ROMERO IN CONFIDENCE.

TOBIAS AND SAMPSON ARE IN JAIL. THEY ALMOST GOT A TASTE OF THE 'HOLY WATER' COCKTAIL THEY'D BEEN SERVING ALL OF US. I REALLY WANTED TO LET THEM TRY IT – BUT I FIGURED YOU'D KILL ME IF I DID – SO I GAVE THEM A CLUE BEFORE THEY DRANK ANY OF IT.

TOBIAS SAID HE WAS PAID BY A PETER PHILMAN. I THOUGHT PHILMAN MIGHT BE ANOTHER MUTATION OF PHILLIPS AND WELLMAN, BUT TOBIAS WOULD HAVE SEEN PHILLIPS IN TOWN AND KNOWN IT WAS A BOGUS NAME. SO THERE MUST BE ANOTHER PERSON IN THE MIX. SEE ATTACHED MEMO FOR FULL DETAILS OF THE DAY.

DAVE NELSON MAY SUSPECT SOME LAW ENFORCEMENT BACKGROUND AFTER TODAY. BE SURE YOU HAVE A JOSEPH MARSH ON THE BOSTON PD RECORDS. I CAN FALL BACK ON MY SHORT STINT THERE, IF I NEED A COVER.

THANKS FOR THE BOX OF MATERIAL AND LETTERS. WE FINISHED CHRIS' SCHOLARSHIP APPLICATION TONIGHT.

ANY WORD FROM GOLDIE? HAVE YOU TALKED TO HER LATELY? LET ME KNOW, PLEASE!

CHAPTER TWENTY-THREE

MONDAY – FOURTH WEEK

The morning was peacefully quiet when Joe jogged through town. After yesterday, he appreciated the tranquility. He waved at Charley opening the feed store and smiled when he realized even little Rosalie was sleeping today.

Running up Grandma's street he found her digging in her flower bed. "Good morning, Grandma," he said brightly. "How are you this morning?"

"Good morning, Reverend," she said.

"Just Joe, Grandma," he said. "I'm sorry I didn't correct that earlier, but let's drop the Reverend until we're in church."

Smiling, she modified her greeting and said, "Good morning, Joe."

"What are you digging up in your flower bed?" he asked, pointing to her spade.

"Oh," she said, "my begonias didn't do very well. So, I decided to dig them up."

"Did Mrs. Anderson have begonias?" he asked.

"Oh yes," she said, "hers were beautiful."

"Well, I think she'd love for you to have hers," he said. "In fact, I think she'd want you to have anything you wanted out of her garden. She left in such a state of shock, she didn't have time to think about her flowers. She loved her garden as much as you do yours. Why don't you get Chris to help you bring some of her plants over here?"

"Do you think it would be okay?" she asked.

"I don't know why not," he said. "A couple more weeks in this heat without water and they'll all be gone. Then no one will enjoy them. Let me know when you and Chris go over and I'll help, too. I'd love to see her flowers find a new home."

"Ben told me about the Kindergarten," she said. "I think it's a wonderful idea."

"It was really Dominique's idea," he said, "at least the part about teaching the kids English. I'm not sure they're technically Kindergarten age, but I've heard younger kids learn languages better than the rest of us. And you gave me a surprise when I heard you speaking Spanish to Dominique, I didn't know you were bilingual." She grinned and answered him in Spanish.

He wiggled his eyebrows and said, "You've been keeping secrets from me."

Giggling at his antics, she said, "Every lady needs a few secrets in her life."

"What about the Wilsons?" he asked. "Do you think they'd be interested? I thought maybe the three of you could set up some sort of rotation, so it wouldn't be too tiring for you."

"They would probably jump at the chance," she said. "They've missed teaching, too. Even though the kids are rascals, the challenge gets in your blood. It's hard to give it up."

He grinned at her excitement while she talked.

"I told Ben we could probably get some education funds from the state to help with the costs," she said. "He'll check on the requirements for us."

"That would be great," Joe said. "Apparently, the only thing we need is a place. I told Ben we could use the church, but it's too far away for the Hispanic families. We'll keep looking." He gave her a quick hug and jogged home.

After a shower and some well water coffee, he walked over to the utility building to tell Miguel what happened.

"Good Morning, Miguel," he said. "I'm sorry I was so blunt yesterday, but I'm back today to fill in all the blanks."

"I heard you saved our priest," Miguel said. "I assume my work helped with that."

"Yes it did," Joe said. "We had to verify the chemical. You actually gave it to me in your earlier analysis of the water in Reverend Whitsworth's glass. It had a trace of ipecac in it."

"How did you get that report?" Miguel asked. "I did it years ago."

"Reverend Whitsworth left the information in the church utility folder along with some notes about his attacks. I found them when I was sorting the files," Joe said. "Then Mrs. Anderson told me about her husband's attacks. They seemed to go together." Miguel gave him a puzzled look and nodded.

"The sample I brought you was from my parsonage," Joe said. "But we were pretty certain they used the same chemical on Father Romero. It was a gamble, but it was all we had to go on – and it worked. Your test results helped Doctor Stockwell treat Father Romero. Thanks again for your fast action."

"Your parsonage?" Miguel asked. "Did you have an attack, too?"

"No, I'm okay," Joe said quickly. "Mrs. Anderson warned me about the Saturday night attacks and left me some of the Samuels well water. I used it as a precaution, so I didn't drink any of my tap water."

"Oh, thank God," Miguel said.

"Amen to that," Joe said. "I brought another cup of water I collected this morning. I don't want to drink anything from that tap until you tell me it's clear. This time there isn't any rush. Just let me know when you have time to check it."

"What I don't understand," Miguel said, "is how they put it in your water, without putting it in the town's water?"

"If you have a minute to walk over to the parsonage, I'll show you," Joe said.

Miguel walked over with him. He was puzzled at first and then angry when he saw the setup on the pipes. Joe showed him the same arrangement at the Methodist parsonage.

"Someone had to modify these pipes to add that tee," Miguel said. "Plumbers are supposed to register with us before they do work in town. Of course, they probably weren't worried about our rules, but let's go check our records."

Back at the utility office, Miguel pulled the file on Joe's parsonage. "The last work we show on your parsonage – that was registered with us," he said, "was done by a Cozen pipe worker. He was fixing *leaks* in the kitchen pipes."

Digging a little longer, Miguel found the file on the Methodist parsonage.

"The same pipe worker did the same work on the Methodist parsonage," he said. Joe read the paperwork with him. Peter Philman signed both forms.

"I'd like a copy of these," Joe said. "And I have another favor to ask. Can we keep the information on these reports just between us? I don't want people blaming Cozen for one employee's possible involvement in the poisonings."

When Miguel raised a skeptical eyebrow, Joe said, "Although these make one of their employees look suspicious, we can't prove he installed the tees. And even if he did, we can't prove Cozen authorized him to do it. Like you said earlier, someone else may have done it and not filed a report with you. So it wouldn't be fair for people to use these against Cozen. We've had enough hate in this town, we don't need any more."

Miguel was still angry about the poisonings, but he could see the logic in what Joe said. He finally agreed not to say anything about their research.

Joe left the building cautiously comfortable with Miguel's agreement. If Cozen, or some of its workers, were involved in trying to close down this town, it was very possible they found more oil than they reported – and men have killed for a lot less. He didn't want Miguel targeted because he disclosed their connection.

Back at the house, he e-mailed Jack: A COZEN 'PIPE WORKER' NAMED PETER PHILMAN REGISTERED WITH THE TOWN TO FIX 'LEAKS IN THE KITCHEN PIPES' AT BOTH PARSONAGES. WE HAVE ANOTHER PROBABLE CONNECTION WITH THE PREACHER POISONINGS. CHECK GEOLOGICAL REPORTS ON THE AREA. I SUSPECT THE TOWN IS SITTING ON MORE OIL THAN COZEN REPORTED. HAVE YOU FOUND ANYTHING ON COZEN? IT HAS TO EXIST SOMEWHERE. THEY DRILLED HERE AND STILL HAVE RIGS AND WORKERS HERE. NEED TO KNOW ASAP.

He locked up and headed down to the drug store. He doubted that Sampson bought the ipecac from the Thompsons, but he thought he'd drop in and see what they had to say. Claiming blisters from the basketball games, he picked up some band-aids and chatted with Ralph and Doris.

"I heard you had a close call with Father Romero yesterday," Ralph said.

"Yes," Joe said, "but he's okay now."

"That's good to hear," Ralph said, going back to work.

"You seem preoccupied today, Ralph," Joe said. "Is something wrong?"

"No just trying to keep my head above water," he said.

"Is business that slow?" Joe asked.

"Not really, given the size of the town, but things are tight," Ralph said. Then he stopped and added, "Danny's been talking about college since Chris applied. We're not sure we can handle the costs." Joe looked surprised, then he realized what had happened.

"I'm sorry, Ralph," he said. "With everything that's been happening, I haven't come in to see you as much as I should've. I'm encouraging the kids to get good grades so they can try to get scholarships, too. It's almost a daily subject during our games. But I tell them not to expect their parents to pay for their college. I push them to do well and earn scholarships, if they want successful careers. I guess my pep talks inadvertently caused more worries for you and Doris. I'm sorry."

"That's okay," Ralph said, taking a deep breath. "I think it's good to encourage the kids. Danny's already talking about degree careers, so I guess he's been listening. He has two years of high school left. If he makes better grades than he has so far, he might get a scholarship."

"Don't tell Danny," Joe said, "because I want him to get serious about his studies and his future – but he plays as well as Chris. If he continues playing like that, he'll have a good chance at a sports scholarship, too."

"Really?" Ralph asked. "I thought hoops were just a fun thing for him. In fact, I hate to admit it, but I grumble about the time he spends out there."

"Well they are fun," Joe said, "which makes it even better. He loves it and he's good at it. That's a winning combination in my book."

"Thanks for telling me that, Reverend," Ralph said. "It gives me a different perspective on things."

"No problem," Joe said. "Now if I can just find a Kindergarten, I'll be happy."

"A what?" Ralph asked.

"A Kindergarten," Joe said, laughing at the look on Ralph's face. "You don't happen to have one in your pocket do you?" Then he explained the idea they had.

"Our retired teachers could help teach English to the Hispanic children so they wouldn't be so disadvantaged when they start school," he said. "The teachers love the idea, but we haven't found a good location for it, yet."

"I think it's a great idea," Ralph said. "I know some place that might work, but I need to check a couple of things first. I'll let you know tomorrow."

"Really?" Joe asked. "Are you serious?"

"Yes, I am," Ralph said. "Give me some time and I'll get back to you." He grinned when Joe literally hopped out of the store like a little kid.

Joe's phone rang at two o'clock. Ralph asked if he and Ben could come over to the store for a few minutes. Joe locked up and went after Ben. While they walked over to the drug store, Joe told him that Ralph thought he had an idea for the Kindergarten.

Ben was laughing at Joe's excitement when they walked into the store. He looked at Ralph and said, "This guy's gonna need a sedative in about five minutes. He's too excited to stand still. It's like having another Chris in town."

Joe took the teasing in stride. In fact, he proved Ben's point by mimicking both Chris and Danny for their dads.

"Enough," Ben said, as he and Ralph laughed at his antics. "You've convinced us." He turned to Ralph and said, "When you catch your breath, you'd better tell us your idea before you and I have to have those sedatives."

Ralph nodded and led them into the back storage area. It was full of shelves stacked with boxes of supplies. Joe and Ben were puzzled. Then Ralph opened another door at the back of the room. Expecting it to go outside, they were surprised to find themselves standing in a large empty room with a sink and small bathroom at one end. They looked at each other and back at Ralph. He just stood there grinning at them.

Finally Ralph said, "Doris and I lived back here until we saved enough to build our house. We were going to cut a door through here and rent the space to Doc when he had so many oil worker patients. As you can see, we didn't do that, because they left town and Doc didn't need the space. If you think this would work for your Kindergarten you're welcome to it. The side door opens onto Luna, so the kids could just walk across the street. The teachers trade here all the time, so it should be convenient for them, too."

Joe's mouth was still hanging open when Ralph finished.

Ben laughed and shut it for him. "This is perfect." Joe said. "I had no idea you had this space back here."

"Don't feel bad," Ben said. "I've lived here a lot longer than you have and I didn't know about it either." He turned to Ralph and said, "I've contacted the state to see if we can get some education funds, at least for the Kindergarten age kids. I don't know how much, if any, we'll be able to get. Whatever it is, we'll give it to you for the space."

"No," Ralph said, "pay it to the teachers. We'll watch the utility bills. If they go up too high, I'll come see you about some money for them. Otherwise, it won't cost us any more to have someone back here than it does to have it sitting empty."

He walked around the room with Ben and said, "If you can find some kids with a couple of cans of paint and some rollers, this place could be ready for class in a week or two – or an hour or two if they all have Joe's energy."

Joe was still trying to absorb the generosity. Three hours ago Ralph was worried about paying his bills and now he was practically donating space for a Kindergarten.

"Who would have guessed?" he asked Ben, as they walked back to the grocery store. "I went in there mouthing off about finding a Kindergarten and three hours later he produces one – almost out of thin air."

Ben swung an arm around Joe's shoulder and laughed.

"I know, it's crazy," Ben said. "It's almost too much to believe. Of course, you know we have you to thank for this, too. Before you arrived, the Baptists, Methodists and Hispanics weren't even speaking to each other – let alone helping each other. Thank you. We needed you more than any of us knew."

Joe was too humbled to say anything.

To lighten the mood again, Ben said, "Let's go tell Ma she has a school room."

They walked around the store to Grandma's house. She was almost as excited as they were. She was also amazed that the Thompsons had an apartment behind the store. It was wonderful watching her enthusiasm. They put her in charge of the project. She and the Wilsons could pick the color of paint they wanted and give them a list of the supplies they'd need.

"She's so happy she could hardly wait for us to leave so she could go see the Wilsons," Ben said, as they stepped outside.

"Get ready to order desks, chairs, scissors, paste and lots of paper," Joe said. Ben rolled his eyes and groaned playfully.

"This town's going to have to find a new source of funds," he said, "just to keep up with you and your projects."

When he went home to change for the hoops game, he saw Grandma sitting with the Wilsons in their back yard. Even from the street, he could see they were having a lively conversation.

Totally relaxed, he put his whole heart into the game with the kids. *Sometimes, life is good,* he thought. *It's nice to enjoy those moments.*

He walked back to the Hispanic section with Eddie and Gabbie after the game. He wanted to check on Elena and asked Gabbie to translate a practice schedule for Dominique. Elena was well on her way to a full recovery and Dominique agreed to come over tomorrow night to practice. Angie got a shoulder ride before he headed home.

He found a note on his door from Miguel. It said, "H_2O OK." Relieved, he went inside and started a pot of coffee – with tap water. He had to remember to buy a hammer and some nails so he could seal the siding panels shut. Looking in his cabinet and refrigerator, he decided he needed to shop for some more food, too. He didn't even have peanut butter any more.

He sat down with his last microwave dinner and a cup of coffee. Since he'd been thinking about Father Romero all day, he decided to call him.

As expected, Father Romero said he was still weak, but definitely better than yesterday. He'd spent the day assigning a new man to the Field Foreman position and contacting his superiors for a real priest to replace Tobias. Joe smiled when he noticed Father Romero had dropped Tobias' title. When he finished, he asked Joe about his day.

Joe told him about the Kindergarten. "The teachers are energized," he said. "And the kids will have an easier time when they start real school."

Father Romero was silent for a long minute, before he asked, "Are you aware that part of our church is a school?"

Grimacing, Joe said, "No. I'm sorry. Did I step on some parochial toes doing this? If I did, it wasn't intentional."

Father Romero laughed out loud.

"I'm not sure I've ever seen parochial toes," he said. "But no, you didn't step on them – if they exist. I'm sorry if my question left the wrong impression. I should have said that we *used* to have a school out here and we still have four rooms full of furniture and equipment stored in the back of the church. Once you know how many kids will be attending, why don't you bring your teachers out here and look at what we have? If they can use any of the furniture, blackboards and other things back there, we'll put them on long-term loan to the town."

"Can you do that?" Joe asked. "I mean, will the church let you do that?"

"Members of my parish are attending, are they not?" Father Romero asked.

"Well, yes," Joe said.

"Then, as you said yesterday, I care for all those under my wings," he said. "The furniture will help my parish more in your Kindergarten than it will sitting in empty rooms out here."

"Thank you, Father," Joe said. "That's very kind of you. I'll let Ben and the teachers know. It'll probably be another week or two before we have the room ready for furniture. I'll call and arrange a time with you before we visit."

As soon as he hung up with Father Romero, he called Ben. He laughed when Ben snarled into the phone.

"Oops," he said. "Sorry I interrupted dinner. I didn't check the time before I called. But if you're eating my piece of pie, I called at the right time."

"No, I'm not eating *your* piece of pie, Joe," he said. "Now what's on your mind?"

"Have you swallowed your food?" Joe asked. "I don't want you to choke when I tell you my news."

"I've swallowed, now what is it?" Ben growled.

"The Catholic Church is going to loan us desks, chairs, blackboards and any other furniture they have, for our Kindergarten," Joe said.

"What!" Ben sputtered into the phone. "How did you manage that?" Obviously turning to the family at the table, he said, "The Catholic Church is going to loan us all the furniture we need for the Kindergarten. I don't know how he did it. Heaven only knows what he can do. I need more vitamins to keep up with him." To Joe, he said, "I know I'm not going to believe the answer, but tell me anyway. How did you do that?"

"See why I told you to swallow?" Joe teased. Ben mumbled something Joe probably didn't want to hear.

Joe laughed and said, "I just called Father Romero to see how he was feeling. When he asked about my day, I told him about our Kindergarten. I didn't know his church used to have a school attached to it. They have four rooms of desks, blackboards, and other stuff in storage. He said he's willing to loan it to the town for the Kindergarten. When we get the room painted and ready for furniture, he said to bring the teachers out and let them decide what they can use."

"I knew I wasn't going to believe it," Ben said. "Only you could make these things sound so easy. This was just an idea yesterday afternoon and today it's a reality."

He apparently turned to answer a question for Grandma and then came back to Joe. "Don't tell me about your next project," Ben said. "I need to rest first."

Joe heard the family laughing at Ben's exasperation.

Then Ben said, "Seriously, Joe that's great news and thank you. Now I'm going to go eat the last piece of Ma's pie, just so I have enough energy to keep up with you." When Joe sputtered a reply, Ben chimed, "Byeeeeee, Joe," and hung up.

If you only knew what my next project is, Ben, he thought, as he sat at his table. Bart's truck would be back in the lot tonight. If his scenario was right, more women were being moved into sex slavery. He prayed his camera caught the activity. At least they'd know they were on the right track.

178

Instead of running his nightly surveillance, he decided to watch the oil rig across the road from the storage units. If Bart was transporting – and if his cargo was being dropped into a tunnel – they had to have some workers to make the transfers.

Although there was still a little light outside, he tucked his binoculars under his shirt and walked over to the church. Once he was locked inside and seated, he focused on the rig. He recognized all five pickup trucks clustered around it. He couldn't see faces from this distance, but he could see size and shirt colors, two tall black shirts, two medium height red shirts and one tall green shirt.

One man was standing on top of the rig with his own set of binoculars. When he signaled the others, all five walked into the shed beside the rig. That shed was so small it couldn't possibly hold more than two men at a time. They had to be going into a tunnel.

He logged the time, seven forty-five, and waited. At nine o'clock the men came back out of the shed and stood under the rig light talking. Two of the men that went in, the two tall black shirts, didn't come back out. But two that were not in the original group, two shorter black shirts, came out at nine.

If he was on the right track, that meant two men stayed in the tunnel to guard the women – and possibly travel to the next stop with them. Apparently, the men who were staying in the tunnel wore black, for obvious reasons. He'd watch again tomorrow night and see if the process was repeated.

He sat in the chair clenching his fists and grinding his teeth. He knew he couldn't move yet, but he wanted to. It killed him to know there were women in there that he couldn't help. Finally resolved to the situation, he took a deep breath, locked up and went back to the parsonage.

One thing he knew – he was going to get in that tunnel. He'd e-mail Jack and see if Tommy could meet him Saturday night, since that was the night the oil men went to the bars.

Pulling out his notes, he tried to make sense out of the information he had on the people involved in the various crimes.

Peter Philman:

- Is the Cozen pipe worker who apparently put the tees on the parsonages.
- Paid Tobias to poison the water and isolate Father Romero from the town. Tobias paid Sampson.

Homer Wellman:

- Is the Imposter Preacher who divided the town.
- Owns the Hispanic houses and the lot behind them.
- Owns the land Cozen is on.
- Owns all the vacant buildings in town.
- Bart delivered drugs to Wellman and Tobias.
- Bart brings women to town in his truck.

Cozen Oil:

- Employs the men who work in the tunnel.
- Employs Peter Philman.
- Leases the land from Wellman.

He looked at the list. It was obvious there were at least three criminal elements using this little town as a pawn – drugs, human smuggling and underlying oil interests.

Is it just a coincidence that all three are here? he asked himself. *Or are they interlinked and if so, how? Are Philman and Wellman related or the same? Wellman could have used a disguise. Two men trying to isolate and destroy the same town have to be connected. But how?*

He sent Jack his daily report: SEE THE ATTACHED LIST OF MY FRAGMENTED, FRUSTRATING DATA. THERE HAS TO BE A CONNECTION. WHAT HAVE YOU FOUND?

CAN YOU GET TOMMY TO GIVE ME SOME COVER SATURDAY NIGHT WHILE I INVESTIGATE THE TUNNEL?

HOW IS GOLDIE?

I HAVEN'T HAD ANY MORE MAIL. I'M WORRIED.

CHAPTER TWENTY-FOUR

TUESDAY – FOURTH WEEK

He had a sleepless night. He knew he would. The nightmares wouldn't go away until those women were safe. He made a pot of coffee, drank a quick cup and jogged over to the feed store with a new tape.

He stopped again to talk to Jerry while they were unloading Bart's truck. Walking into the truck to try to lift a bag and *struggling* with the weight, he saw another stack of empty bags near the back of the trailer. All the grain they were unloading was conveniently placed near the trailer door – opposite the way most truckers want their loads distributed. Stopping to tie his shoe, he counted about fifteen empty bags. At an average of a hundred pounds, the women would've balanced the load during the drive. Handing another bag to Bart, he feigned exhaustion trying to lift them.

"I'll leave the weightlifting to you two," he said. "I'm going back to jogging." To Jerry, he added, "I'm going to come over some day and let you teach me what all these grains are."

Jerry laughed and said, "Sure, any time."

Since Bart was busy at the store, he jogged over to the truck lot and stopped to tie that shoe again. With his back to Max's steps, he changed tapes in his camera on the side of the hotel. He'd wait for the one under Max's steps until tomorrow.

Jogging around to Grandma's, he enjoyed her excitement. She was as bubbly as he was last night and it was

181

contagious. She had Joe laughing with her. She even promised him a whole pie for himself, if he wouldn't tell Ben and Chris.

"Naw," he said grinning, "I'd rather fight them for it. It's more fun that way. But thanks for the offer." She giggled and he jogged off. She was happy again and he loved it.

Back at the parsonage, he dropped the tape in the player. He should've felt some sense of satisfaction at being right, but he didn't. It made him furious. He had clear pictures of the truck bed opening – the sliding noise – and the paving section opening. He counted fifteen women, obviously drugged. They were handed down to the workers he'd seen at the rig. He even had face shots of three of the men, Chad, Ernesto and Bernardo.

All three were Cozen men who drove unmarked company trucks. The angle of the camera shots showed him the tunnel's direction. "It's under the peanut silo," he said, swearing to himself. "That gives them a nice big area to use."

He timed the entire operation. It started when Bart went into the hotel and ended before he came back out. The tape clearly identified the key sounds in the door.

He reached for his laptop, logged on and sent Jack a FOUND IT e-mail. THEY'RE USING A DROP FROM THE TRUCKS TO A TUNNEL LEADING TO THE PEANUT SILO. I HAVE THEIR DEPOSIT ON LAST NIGHT'S TAPE. TONIGHT'S TAPE SHOULD GIVE US THE TRANSFER TO SIMMS' TRUCK. I WANT ALL AVAILABLE UPDATES ON THIS RING – NOW! I WILL NOT AND CAN NOT JUST SIT HERE AND WATCH THESE TRUCKS COME AND GO – NOW THAT I KNOW THEY HAVE HUMAN CARGO. GIVE ME THE WORD AND I'LL BLOW THIS OPERATION TOMORROW – ALONE IF I HAVE TO!

The longer he thought about the situation, the angrier he became. Resigned to the fact that he had to wait for the entire operation to be covered, he showered and walked up to the grocery store.

He was supposed to be happy about the Kindergarten. *Get with the program*, he told himself. After an early lunch and a lot of banter with the Morrisons, he picked up a hammer and some nails and a few more groceries for the house. *Peanut butter will never look the same,* he thought, as he replaced the jar he emptied Sunday.

He carried his purchases home and put the groceries away. Then he took the tools outside and nailed both parsonage panels shut. *Too little, too late,* he thought, *but they're shut now.*

He changed into his basketball clothes and decided to work in the church office until it was time to go to the hoops lot.

Opening the file drawer that contained the congregation records, he leafed through them and tried to become more familiar with the individuals. Of course, there were a lot of files on previous members, too. He found two families from the Archer Farm and one from the Thatcher Farm. He hadn't heard those names before. He made a note to ask Ben about them.

Halfway through the drawer, he decided to divide the current members' files from the prior ones. As he sorted the names, he found one that stunned him, Peter Philman. Philman had been a member of this church.

Inside the folder, he found his date of birth, baptismal certificate and marriage certificate. On Oct.12, 1988, Peter Philman married Roberta Wellman. Reverend Whitsworth performed the service.

A newspaper announcement of the wedding said Roberta was the daughter of Homer and Sylvia Wellman from Lubbock, Texas. It said Peter was a geological contractor who provided independent surveys for several major oil companies. The picture in the article was badly faded, but he wondered if any of the old timers might recognize him. Since Doc had already heard the name, he'd be a good one to ask. The picture might jog his memory. He cut the picture away from the article. He didn't want to expose Philman's connection to Wellman.

Looking at his watch, he closed the church, put the Philman file in his house and carried the picture over to Doc.

Doc didn't recognize him, but Nancy did. She said Peter was the son of one of the families that worked on the Archer farm back in the '70s.

"He was a sullen boy," she said. "He never could get along with the other kids, especially the two Archer boys. I'd see him when he needed a cut or scrape patched up. His folks were always nice to us. They had two girls, too. I think they still live around Portales somewhere."

"Do you remember when they left the area?" Joe asked.

"They left when the Archer and Thatcher farms failed," she said. "Remember Henry, when their wells went bad?"

"I'd forgotten that," Doc said. "I remember the boy, too, now that you mention it."

"What happened to the wells?" Joe asked.

"It was the strangest thing," Doc said. "Those two farms had the best grade of peanuts in the county. Then one spring, right after they fertilized their fields, their irrigation wells hit a pocket of salt water. It tainted the soil and ruined their crops. They lost their farms right after that."

"Where were the farms?" Joe asked.

"They were just north of town," Doc said, "on the land Cozen leases now."

"Is that why the peanut station closed?" Joe asked.

"Yes," Doc said. "Those two farms were a major part of the business. The drought ruined several of the crops on the smaller farms. It was a sad time. We've lost a lot of good people over the last few years."

"Well let's hope we get some rain soon and times get better," Joe said. Changing the subject he asked if they'd heard about the Kindergarten. Both of them had, of course, and were happy about it.

"Get ready for some noise on that back wall," he said. "I'm sure they'll be a rambunctious group. It's good we have you two next door to take care of the bumps and bruises they're bound get." Doc and Nancy chuckled and agreed.

"Thanks for the information," Joe said, as he glanced at the clock. "I guess I'd better go beat some kids at hoops."

He took a second to ask Doc to keep their conversation about Philman quiet. "I don't want the name getting around town," he said, "while Dave's investigation is still open."

Doc agreed and said he'd tell Nancy.

When the kids showed up they had a lot of jokes about Joe's Kindergarten obviously being more his speed. But after they had their fun, every one of them said they thought it was a great idea and offered to help with the painting. *Good kids*, he thought as he gave them hugs and stole the ball for a quick dunk – just to prove he was up to their speed, too.

Still chuckling about the kids, he ran home to clean up before Dominique arrived to practice. Over a peanut butter sandwich and a cup of coffee, he sent a quick e-mail to Jack. PETER PHILMAN MARRIED ROBERTA WELLMAN OCT 88. NEED TO TRACK HIS TWO SISTERS IN PORTALES, TOO. RESEARCH THE MARRIAGE RECORDS. THEIR HUSBANDS COULD BE INVOLVED AND WE WOULDN'T RECOGNIZE THEIR LAST NAMES.

Then he tucked his binoculars under his shirt and went over to the church. While Dominique practiced the hymns for Sunday, he went back to the files in the office. He sorted the congregation files and moved to the Administrative drawer where he'd found the utility folder. He went through every folder and was disappointed when he didn't find anything else.

When Dominique left, he locked the door and went upstairs to watch the oil rig again. The same trucks pulled into the field, but there were six men tonight. *They probably need extra hands to lift the women into Simms' truck,* he thought.

As before, two in black shirts went into the shed – but didn't come back out. And two others in black shirts, who were not part of the original group, came out. Apparently, two men stayed on the truck with the women. *That accounts for the eight men Doc mentioned,* he thought. He waited for them to drive off before he went back to the office.

Four down and four to go, he told himself as he opened the next file drawer. It was full of church bulletins and booklets dating back to the 1980s. He pulled the waste basket over and discarded the old stuff. He found a couple of bulletins that mentioned current members and put those in a separate stack. He also found some references to the three families from the Archer and Thatcher farms. One mentioned Philman's baptism and provided the names of his parents and sisters.

We can use these, he thought, and set them aside. He discarded the rest of the outdated literature, moved to the next drawer and did the same. When the third and fourth drawers didn't provide any more information, he bagged the trash.

At least I've cleaned out the files, he thought, as he hauled the bags out the back door to the trash can.

Returning, he locked the back door, picked up his binoculars and the Philman data. When he started to turn out the light, he noticed the lower file drawer still ajar. He kicked it with his toe and turned back to the light. It rolled out again. Putting his things down, he sat on the floor and pulled the drawer out of the cabinet.

No wonder the drawer didn't close, he thought when he looked at the dirt. He cleaned the track and put the drawer back – it still wouldn't close. He pulled the drawer out again and flipped it over to check the rollers. The rollers were fine, but a large manila envelope taped to the bottom was loose. It had kept the drawer from closing.

He locked the church and went home for some rubber gloves and a box of plastic bags. When he returned, he locked himself in again. He put the gloves on and carefully opened the envelope. He didn't recognize the handwriting on the outside, but it was addressed to Reverend Whitsworth.

Inside he found a handwritten letter from Reverend Whitsworth clipped to a stack of official looking documents – apparently copies of the originals. Removing the clips and staples, he placed each sheet in a separate bag, being careful to keep subsequent sheets of correspondence together. Once he had all of them protected, he took off his gloves and sat down at the desk to read the material.

Whitsworth's letter, dated, June 25, 1994, began like a last will and testament.

In case of my death or incapacitation, I believe the attached sheets will identify the parties who will be responsible. They are not aware of the material I have attached to this letter. But they have been very vocal against me and all religions in Eutopian Springs. Someone has been poisoning the water in my parsonage. I don't know who is doing it, but I know I've had so many violent abdominal attacks that I fear for my life. So they have achieved their objective. I must leave to survive.

Many of the attached documents were passed to me by Peter Philman's sister, Patricia, when she and her husband, Chad Orson, were in town. She said she collected several of them while she was caring for Peter's wife, Roberta (Homer Wellman's daughter) in their home. Patricia believes her husband is involved, since he's the Foreman for the Cozen operations north of town. She said she was going to leave him. Unfortunately, she was killed in a house fire before she could. It was very suspicious to me. But I can't prove Chad did it. If he knew she had these papers, he could have set the fire to destroy her and them.

Patricia said she didn't think Roberta knew what the men were doing. She thinks someone is keeping Roberta on drugs, because she rarely gets out of bed any more. They have a Nanny raising their two children.

Also, Patricia said her sister, Pauline Philman, is married to Thomas Tyson, the Strataroc Contracting Officer who signed the subcontract agreement with Cozen. We don't know if he's involved or not, but it looks suspicious.

I don't know who to trust with these documents. I know Cozen has people working for them in town. I've seen their men paying everyone from seasonal workers to a Catholic Priest. I don't think Dave Nelson can handle this alone and I don't want to put him in danger. He's been very kind to me.

I pray the reader of this letter has the will and the strength to stop these people. They are ruthless. They're not going to stop until they own this town and the oil under it.

Praying for God's Mercy and Intervention,
William Whitsworth

Joe took a deep breath when he finished reading the letter. Reverend Whitsworth was obviously terrified when he wrote it. He picked up the attachments and started to understand why. Whitsworth had proof that Philman intentionally salted the Archer and Thatcher wells to kill their crops.

The first four attachments contained:

- A water analysis report dated, April 20, 1990, on the well the Archer farm used for human consumption showing a normal range of minerals.

- A water analysis report, dated April, 20 1990, on the wells the Archer farm used for irrigation. The report showed an unusually high alkalinity in the water. Whitsworth noted – *the Archers and Thatchers had just fertilized their peanut crops.*

- An agricultural report with a paragraph underlined – stating that <u>excessive salt in the soil could ruin peanut crops.</u>

- A receipt from a store in Portales, dated, March 15, 1990, for a large amount of sodium nitrate – *salt* – Whitsworth noted. Sold to <u>Peter Philman</u>. *Three weeks prior to the well tainting,* Whitsworth added.

The next four attachments proved that Philman and Thomas Tyson had manipulated Strataroc Oil into financing the exploratory drilling in town with Cozen Oil as their subcontractor. Then Philman convinced Strataroc to sell their oil leases to Cozen Oil. *There's the Wellman connection,* Joe thought, as he read through the attachments.

He had a copy of:

- An article in the Portales paper dated February 27, 1990, reporting that Strataroc Oil was starting to explore the east side of the state.

- A Geological Analysis Report dated March 12, 1991, from Peter Philman to Strataroc Oil, stating, in his professional opinion, that the potential for oil in and around Eutopian Springs warranted additional exploration. However, the amount indicated by his readings, did not appear to require a large operation. He recommended that Strataroc subcontract the exploration to Cozen Oil, a small drilling company located outside of Lubbock, Texas. The document continued with a list of geological readings by latitude and longitude.

- A subcontract between Strataroc and Cozen, stipulating that Cozen would provide the labor and Strataroc would provide the materials. Homer Wellman signed the agreement as the President of Cozen Oil and Thomas Tyson signed it as the Contracting Officer for Strataroc.

- A Geological Analysis Report, dated, June 30, 1993, from Peter Philman to Strataroc stating, in his professional opinion, that the exploration efforts in and around Eutopian Springs, were yielding a grade of oil too inferior for their continued investment in the region. He recommended Strataroc sell their lease interests to Cozen and let Cozen continue operating the existing wells. Again the document provided a list of readings.

If Joe had any doubt about the intent of the first eight attachments, the next one made it perfectly clear. It was a copy of a handwritten note from Peter Philman to Homer Wellman also dated, June 30, 1993. Joe swore when he read it.

Homer:

We did it. Eutopian Springs is sitting on one of the richest grades of oil in the area. I've recommended Strataroc sell Cozen the lease rights because the wells were 'yielding a grade of oil too inferior for their continued investment in the region.' They should be contacting you soon. I recommended a $5,000-$7,000 sales price. Once we shut down the rest of the town, we'll 'discover' a new pocket of rich crude.

I understand the Archers and Thatchers are still trying to find the source of all that sodium nitrate. I'd love to tell them I did it to get even for all the hell they gave me when I lived there. But I'll keep quiet. Getting rich off their oil rights will be revenge enough.

Let me know when you hear from Strataroc. Be sure to get back in Lubbock in time to drive over here.

Peter

PS: Burn this after you read it.

Someone, possibly Patricia, had added a handwritten note on the copy indicating that the letter was sent to:

H.P.Wellmanson
RR 9
Pueblo, Colorado

The last attachment was a copy of the sales agreement between Strataroc and Cozen Oil dated, July 5, 1993. Cozen Oil purchased the operations from Strataroc for $7,000. Homer Wellman signed the document as the President of Cozen Oil and Thomas Tyson signed it as the Contracting Officer for Strataroc.

"Dear Lord have mercy," Joe said out loud, as he leaned back in the desk chair and tried to absorb the material he'd just read. "No wonder the poor man left town in such a hurry." Looking back at the letter he said, "Yes, Reverend Whitsworth, the reader of this letter does have the will and the strength to stop these people. And when this is over, I'm going to find you and let you know that we did."

He carefully stacked the documents back behind Reverend Whitsworth's letter and put all of them inside a plastic trash bag. Once he had them flattened, he tucked the bag inside his shirt. He replaced the file drawer, locked up and went home.

CHAPTER TWENTY-FIVE

WEDNESDAY – FOURTH WEEK

It was two a.m. when he entered his house. He locked the bag of documents in a metal tool box he had in the closet and fell back on his bed. He couldn't stop thinking about everything he found at the church.

A few minutes later, he thought he heard footsteps outside. Then he caught the unmistakable odor of gasoline. Grabbing his pistol, he eased out his front door. He saw a man's shadow behind the church. The smell of gas was definitely getting stronger. He waited a minute to see if he could hear a second person. Then he worked his way around the church in the same direction the man had taken. He picked up a piece of broken concrete in the field and edged up behind the man as he stooped over to pour more gas. Joe had the advantage – he took it. A moment later, the man was face down in a puddle of his own gasoline. Joe rolled him over and recognized Bernardo.

Disgusted, he pulled Bernardo's unconscious body across the yard to the parsonage door. He kept him covered while he reached inside for his phone.

When Dave answered, Joe said, "Sorry to bother you, Constable. But I have an arsonist on my doorstep that I need you to pick up." Dave was obviously trying to wake up and comprehend what Joe said.

"You have a what?" he asked. "Did you say arsonist?"

"I'm afraid so," Joe said. "Complete with a gas can and I assume matches in his pocket. I don't guess he liked my sermon last week."

"Are you okay?" Dave asked, genuinely concerned.

"I'm okay," Joe said, "but your prisoner's going to have a bad headache when he wakes up. I'd like to have him in cuffs before then."

"I'll be there in five," Dave said and hung up.

Joe concealed his firearm while he watched Dave run to his patrol car and roll up the block.

Either he slept in his clothes or he's going to have pajama bottoms dragging below his pants, he thought.

When Dave walked up, he looked down at Bernardo and shook his head. "He hasn't been out of jail more than a week. He just won't learn," he said, as he cuffed him. Then sniffing the air he asked, "What was he trying to burn? Your house?"

"No," Joe said. "He thought he'd torch a church tonight. He made it around three sides before he ran into a piece of concrete in my hand. I predicted I was making some people angry with my actions around town. But I didn't think they'd try to burn the church." Dave swore.

"His gas can and the concrete block are on the other side of the church," Joe said.

"How did you catch him in time?" Dave asked.

"I was working in the church office tonight and lost track of the time," Joe said. "I didn't come back here until about two, so I wasn't asleep yet. I heard footsteps and then smelled the gas. He was rounding the back of the church when I came out. The piece of concrete was on the ground out back. It looked easier than trying to tackle the guy – so I used it."

Dave nodded and pulled out his camera, flashlight and a trash bag. He walked around the church and photographed the scene. Then he picked up the gas can and the rock. Joe helped him find the cap to seal off the rest of the gas in the can. Dave put the bag of evidence in his trunk.

"I hate to say this, you being a preacher and all," Dave said, "but have you considered getting a firearm?"

Joe looked concerned and said, "I hadn't given it much thought."

"Well, these guys are definitely trying to get to you," Dave said. "I'd hate to see you get hurt. If you want my advice, I'd consider getting a gun for your own protection – maybe a small revolver."

"I'll give it some serious thought, Constable," Joe said. "I appreciate your concern. And you're probably right about these guys. Thanks for coming over so fast. I hated to wake you up, but this couldn't wait until morning."

"No problem," Dave said. "I'm just sorry these men are causing so much trouble."

Bernardo started moaning about his head while Joe and Dave were stuffing him into the patrol car.

"Oh shut up," Dave said. "Anyone who tries to burn down a church deserves a headache – and more."

"I didn't want to do it," Bernardo whined.

"Then why did you do it?" Dave asked.

"They told me I had to," Bernardo said.

"Who told you that you had to?" Dave asked.

Bernardo looked at Dave and Joe and shut his mouth.

"That's okay," Dave said. "You don't have to tell us. We'll just tell people you told us. Those guys will get to you before the Judge gets in town."

Good move, Dave, Joe thought, as he watched real fear wash over Bernardo's bloody face.

"It was Chad," Bernardo said. "But don't tell him I told you, he'll kill me. *Really* kill me."

"Okay," Dave said, "let's go wake Doc up and get your head stitched." Back to Joe, he asked again, "Are you sure you're all right?"

"Yes I am," Joe said. "I think I'd better try to dilute some of this gasoline before something accidentally ignites it – if that's okay with you. Do you have all the evidence you need?"

"Yeah, I've got plenty. Go ahead and water it down," Dave said and drove off with Bernardo.

Joe stepped back inside his house and sent Jack a quick e-mail: JACK! GET YOURSELF TO PORTALES ASAP! I HAVE SOME THINGS THAT ARE TOO HOT TO DISCUSS ON LINE. BRING EVERYTHING YOU HAVE, NO MATTER HOW SMALL. LET ME KNOW AS SOON AS YOU ARRIVE.

P.S. WE CAUGHT AN ARSONIST TRYING TO BURN THE CHURCH DOWN TONIGHT. HE'S IN JAIL.

It was four a.m. when he finished washing the gasoline off the church and grass. He fixed a pot of coffee, sat down at his table and contemplated the night. If he hadn't had such a strong feeling that something else was in the office – and if Bernardo had succeeded – Reverend Whitsworth's packet would've burned up. No one would've ever known about it.

He looked upward and said sincerely, "Thank you Lord for saving me and the church tonight. And thank you for leading me to Whitsworth's envelope. Now please help me find the right way to use it to catch this gang of murdering...scumbags."

He thought of a couple of other names he wanted to use, but he didn't think the Lord would like them. Then chuckling to himself, he said, "Like He doesn't know what I'm thinking."

He was asleep as soon as he stretched out on the bed.

Incessant pounding on his door woke him up at nine. When he opened it, Ben almost put a fist in his face.

Pulling back quickly, he said, "Sorry, I've been pounding on your door for five minutes. Are you okay? I just heard about the arson attempt over here."

He waved Ben inside while he poured some coffee from the pot he made at four. "I'm okay," he said. "Give me a minute to wake up and get human again."

Ben persisted. He was still worried about Joe. "Are you hurt?" he asked. "Do you need to see Doc? Are you sure?"

Joe held up both hands and said, "I surrender."

"What do you mean, you surrender?" Ben asked.

"Do you have any idea how hard you interrogate a person?" Joe asked. "I know the news scared you. It would scare anyone, but I promise I'm okay – just sleep deprived. Another cup of this reheated coffee will spike my caffeine level into wide awake."

Finally relaxing, Ben wanted to hear every detail of the night. Joe told him the same story he told Dave.

"Thank God you stayed at the church so late," Ben said. "I shudder to think what could've happened if you'd been asleep over here."

"Yeah," Joe said. "The what-ifs always get to you after a close call. I think we just have to focus on the positive and stay alert. You've befriended me since the first day I arrived in town. Don't assume they'll stop with me. I'm the prime target, but you could be in their path, too. Dave suggested that I get a firearm for protection. You might consider the same."

"I've got a double barrel shotgun hanging over my bedroom door, locked and loaded," Ben said. "I thought I might need it if someone broke into the store. But you're right. We're going to have to be very careful until we get all these guys."

If you only knew, Joe thought, as he agreed with him.

"I've got a revolver," Ben said. "I'll clean it up and put it in the night stand."

"Do the kids know how to shoot?" Joe asked.

"Yeah," Ben said. "They've both gone hunting with me, but I don't think they've ever shot the revolver. I'll take them out today and let them get used to it."

"That's good," Joe said. "Be sure they know where you're going to keep it, so they don't have an accidental firing."

"Will do," Ben said. Then he looked at Joe and said, "You know a lot about firearm safety for a preacher."

"I'm a city boy, remember," Joe said. "Do you honestly believe families can survive in big cities without protection?"

"No, I guess not," Ben said. "It's just different for us out here."

"I know," Joe said. "I'm sorry it's become necessary. I just want us protected."

"Okay," Ben said. "Why don't you hit the shower and come up to the house with me. Ma said she'd fix you some eggs and bacon if you didn't take all day." Then he said, "She has to lay eyes on you before she'll believe you're okay."

"Give me about ten minutes and I'll be ready," Joe said. Turning back at the bedroom door, he asked, "Could you do me a favor while I shower?"

"Name it," Ben said.

"Would you go over and open the church doors for a few minutes to air out the gas smells?" Joe asked. "I watered the grass and foundation right after Dave left. But I didn't try to air out the inside. I was afraid I'd pull more in than I'd take out."

"Sure," Ben said. "Meet you outside in a few."

Showered and shaved, Joe locked up the house while Ben locked the church. Looking at all the dry grass around the church and parsonage, both of them knew how serious last night could have been.

Shaking off the gloomy thoughts, they started bantering over the Kindergarten and who was going to have to push the paint rollers. They walked in the house laughing.

Grandma's face was pinched with worry.

Joe walked over and gave her a hug. "I'm okay, Grandma, I promise," he said. "My aftershave may smell like gasoline for a day or two. But otherwise, I'm all right."

She held his face in her hands for a long minute and said, "You're very precious to us. We couldn't bear to have anything happen to you."

Stunned speechless, Joe just hugged her.

"I'm sorry this worried you," he finally said. "Thank you for caring so much. I feel the same way about you and your family." To lighten the mood, he said, "But don't tell the men I said that, I still have a reputation to protect with them."

Picking up Joe's cue, Ben said, "Yeah, Joe just said he's going to do all the painting at the Kindergarten tomorrow."

"Excuse me," Joe bantered back. "I believe you lost the coin toss on that chore."

They glanced over at Grandma, she was smiling – she had her boys back. Before they finished their mock fight, she had bacon, eggs and biscuits on the table in front of them.

Alternately, Alice, Katherine and Chris ran over from the store to be sure he was okay. After quick hugs, they rushed back to cover for Ben.

Ben's phone rang four times during breakfast. Joe heard him reassuring Gene, Charley, Ralph and Doc, that he was okay.

Good people, he thought, *who have no idea what criminal elements are doing to them. They deserve better – and they'll get it – if I have my way.*

Since he grabbed another tape on his way to breakfast, he wandered over to the truck lot when he left Grandma's. Stopping to *shake a rock out* of his shoe, he switched the one in the camera for a new one. He'd get the others later tonight.

Wandering around town, he stopped to enjoy the kids playing in the field. He gave Angie a shoulder ride and checked on Elena. She looked much better. He spoke, through Elena, to

Dominique. He noticed that Dominique was trying more English words on her own. They'd heard about the Kindergarten and were as excited as he was. He told them they were going to start painting it tomorrow so it wouldn't be much longer before it was ready. He waved at Charley and Jerry at the feed store and then swung by Doc's office.

He stuck his head inside and asked Nancy, "Am I sending you enough patients? Or do I need to find some more?"

She laughed and shook her head.

"I heard you had another close call last night," she said. "I'm glad you're okay."

"Thanks," he said. "Did I give that guy a good headache?"

"Oh yeah," Doc said, coming out of the exam room. "He was whining all the way to jail this morning."

"Sorry we had to get you up in the middle of the night," Joe said. "I really wasn't trying to hit him any harder than I had to, but I couldn't let him start that fire."

"You did fine," Doc said. "He didn't have any fractures. I put a few stitches in him and packed him off with Dave. We were more worried about you."

"I'm fine," Joe said. "I caught him off guard. He had his head down pouring the gas when I hit him. He didn't have a chance to do anything – except take a nap until Dave arrived."

Doc nodded and pointed to his exam room. Nancy giggled and shut the door. Henry wasn't going to be satisfied until he checked Joe himself. Joe walked back out with six band-aids on his arms and three suckers in his hand. Nancy laughed and Doc rolled his eyes as Joe waved out the door.

He stopped in the drug store to be sure Ralph and Doris didn't mind them painting tomorrow. They didn't. After he assured them that he was okay, he went across to the general store to be sure Gene had the paint and equipment ready. The teachers had given Gene their order and all of it arrived yesterday. Joe answered more questions about last night and arranged to pick up the equipment in the morning.

Back home, he made a fresh pot of coffee and put the tape in the player. He was right, but it didn't give him any satisfaction. He watched the same men plus one more, load fifteen women into Simms' truck.

He grinned at one shot and said, "Sorry guys, you'll have to do without Bernardo for a while. Why don't the rest of you come over here and try your luck with me – instead of defenseless women?"

Nightmares or not, he had to get some sleep. He took a nap and woke up at three, feeling much better. He checked his e-mail. He had one from Jack. ARE YOU OKAY? DID YOU HAVE A FIRE? I'LL ARRIVE IN PORTALES LATE THURSDAY NIGHT. CAN MEET WITH YOU FRIDAY. WHERE? DO YOU WANT TOMMY, TOO?

Joe sent a message back. I'M OKAY, NO FIRE. ARSONIST IS NURSING HEADACHE IN JAIL. TRY TO FIND A MOTEL WITH ADJOINING ROOMS, NEAR A RESTAURANT, IF POSSIBLE, SO WE CAN BRING IN FOOD. I'LL ARRANGE TO BE GONE OVERNIGHT FRIDAY. I'LL NEED TO PARK MY VAN IN BACK. TOO MANY PEOPLE CAN RECOGNIZE IT. OR MAYBE TOMMY CAN GET SOME MAGNETIC SIGNS I CAN PUT ON IT. NO TOMMY – UNTIL YOU AND I HAVE SEVERAL HOURS TO COORDINATE OUR INFORMATION.

I NEED YOU TO BRING ME A SMALL REVOLVER –THAT WILL FIRE THIRTY EIGHT SPECIALS. IF YOU'VE FOUND A SHORT RANGE SCOPE, PLEASE BRING IT. SEE YOU THEN, STAY SAFE. BRING MAIL FROM GOLDIE!

He forced himself to shift his focus while he walked over to meet the kids. Chris, Jerry and Danny had already seen him. But Eddie and Gabbie had to be assured that he was all right. He gave them an abbreviated version of the events last night and then took a few minutes to talk to all of them about self-defense. Using his example of the concrete he found last night, he had the kids look around the lot and find things they might be able to use to defend themselves. In a matter of minutes they identified large and small rocks, sticks, bricks, trash, trash cans and trash can lids...which brought giggles about the men who were arrested a few weeks ago.

Joe joined them in the jokes, but on a serious note he said, "The best defense you can have for yourselves and your families is to always stay focused on finding something you can use. If you panic, the scumbags win. If you act, you can catch them off guard and that could make a big difference. It's a lot like the defensive and offensive moves we make in basketball. You have to stay focused and have a strategy."

Then he reminded them about the painting project tomorrow and they fell into a more relaxed banter, which rolled into the game.

On his way home, he stopped by Dave's office. He looked at Tobias, Sampson and Bernardo sitting in the cells.

"Hi guys," he said, waving at them. They grumbled something he probably didn't want to hear.

Back to Dave he said, "Not very friendly are they?" Dave laughed. "Can you step outside for a minute?" Joe asked.

Dave nodded and followed him.

"I'm going to follow your advice and get a revolver," Joe said, "but I didn't want to tell you in front of the prisoners. I was already planning to go to Portales on Friday. I'll try to pick one up then. I probably won't be home until Saturday. Could you keep an eye on the church for me?"

At Dave's quizzical look, Joe shrugged and said, "I just want to take a break. Things have been a little hectic lately."

Dave laughed and asked, "Are you trying to master understatements? A *little* hectic? I don't want to see your idea of really hectic! I'll keep an eye on things here. Go have a good dinner, catch a movie and relax."

"I'm going to keep my overnight plans quiet, so the thugs don't take advantage of it," Joe said. "I'll tell Ben, but I'll let everyone else assume it's a day trip."

"Go and enjoy, Reverend," Dave said.

"Can we just make it Dave and Joe when we're not officiating?" Joe asked.

"Dave and Joe it is," Dave said. "I've got to get back to those rats in my jail."

"Okay," Joe said, grinning at him. "If I find any more I'll send them over to you."

"Not until I ship these out, *p l e a s e!*" Dave begged.

As Joe waved off, Ralph called his name and walked across the street. "Reverend," he said, "could you meet with Charley and me later tonight?"

"Sure," Joe said. "Is there a problem?"

"Yeah, a pretty big one," Ralph said. "Charley and I went over the church books last night. We don't see any way we can afford to keep the building open financially. And frankly, we aren't doing a very good job trying to act like preachers – and the few members we still have know it." Joe nodded and waited.

"We want to discuss the possibility of using your church for our services, too," Ralph said. "Then we can pool the funds we have to keep at least one church open."

Joe was surprised at the proposal, but it made sense.

"What about the Catholic services?" Joe asked. "They'd have to move, too."

"I don't know," Ralph admitted. "We didn't want to talk to anyone else until we met with you to see what you thought."

"Let me call Ben and Gene and see if they can join us," Joe said. "They'd have to agree to this, too. I need time to change and grab a bite of dinner. Would seven-thirty at the church work for you?"

"We'll be there," Ralph said, "and thanks. I'll let Charley know."

"Don't you think we should call Father Romero?" Joe asked. "I'd hate to hold a meeting that affected his parish without having him involved."

"Yeah, you're right. Do you want to call him?" Ralph asked, obviously hesitant about making the call.

"Sure," Joe said, "I'll let you know if I can get us all together." He detoured up to the grocery store and told Ben what Ralph had said.

"I'll call Gene for you," Ben said. "You go see if you can get Father Romero."

Joe ran home and called Father Romero. He explained the situation and asked if he could come in for the meeting.

Father Romero was quiet for a minute, then he said, "We have Mass tonight, but I guess one of the younger priests can handle it. They've been trying to wrangle a way into more experience with the actual services. It might as well be tonight. I'll see you at seven-thirty."

"Great," Joe said. "But don't intimidate that new priest before you leave or he'll stutter all through the Mass."

"How would you know about that?" Romero asked.

"Been there and done that," Joe said laughing. "See you tonight, Father."

Rushing through a shower and a microwave dinner, Joe tried to adjust to the presence of three services in the little church. *We'll make it happen*, he thought. *At least they're trying to keep a church open instead of folding like Wellman wants.*

At seven-thirty, the Baptist Deacons, Methodist Elders and the Senior Catholic Priest were sitting together with a Baptist Preacher in a Baptist Church. *Wherever Wellman-Phillips is tonight, he's turning purple,* Joe thought.

Ralph explained the financial situation at the Methodist Church and their desire to continue having services in town. Since they knew Joe's background was inter-denominational, they wondered if they could combine services in the Baptist Church. They asked Joe to handle their services and offered to pay him what they'd paid Reverend Anderson. Joe waived off the extra pay and suggested they just split his current salary with the Baptist Church – then both congregations would pay less.

Turning to Father Romero, who had been silent during the meeting, Joe asked, "Do you think your parish will agree to the change?"

"I think they'd jump at the chance to go to the Preacher Man's church," he said, with a rare twinkle in his eye. "Between the playground and the Kindergarten, you've become a candidate for sainthood with them."

"I'm not trying to steal them," Joe said carefully. "I'm just trying to take care of them, when you're not in town."

"I know," Father Romero said, "and I do appreciate it. My only real question about the change is how we're going to handle it logistically?"

"That will be a challenge," Joe said. "Your parish meets at ten, and both of the others meet at eleven. The only way I see this working, is to back the services up an hour. If your parish met at nine, would that give you enough time to get to town?"

"We can make that work," Father Romero said. "We have Mass from eight to nine, right now. But we can move it thirty minutes earlier."

"Instead of that," Ralph said, "why don't we move the Methodists to a nine o'clock service and leave the Catholics at ten and the Baptists at eleven. That would give Reverend Marsh a short break between the services, too."

They all agreed on that schedule.

Since the Catholics required a different altar configuration than the Methodists and Baptists, they decided to renovate the rooms upstairs for their services. Father Romero looked at them and agreed that the space would be more than adequate, if they removed the walls between the rooms and opened the space up to the original balcony design. By nine o'clock the group had reached an amicable agreement on the move. *Amazing,* Joe thought, as he watched them work together.

"Father Romero, would you say a prayer and bless this decision before we leave?" Joe asked. He laughed at the surprised looks on the other faces and said, "Don't worry, it's painless. If we're going to make this work, we'll need all the blessings we can get." They bowed their heads while Father Romero said a prayer and blessed their work.

After the priest left, Joe told the others, "Father Romero's blessings will go a long way toward the parish's acceptance of this change. Also, if any of the scumbags we're fighting are Catholic, they might think twice before attacking a *blessed* church."

The guys nodded and agreed. Before they left, Joe told all of them he'd like to drop the Reverend title except on Sundays. The rest of the time he was just Joe.

He locked the church and went home to change for his surveillance run. While he waited for the men to go home, he tried to remember the differences in the two services.

Great! Now I'm in a real jam. Dad didn't preach any Methodist sermons. I'll have to do some research when I get back to town on Saturday. Their ministers wear robes and stoles, too. He groaned at that thought. *I'll have to go over to the Methodist Church and see what I can find.*

"Reverend Anderson, if you can hear me," he said, looking upward, "I hope you left some sermon outlines in your office." He chuckled and slipped out his door.

He completed his surveillance run and changed the tapes. Since the Catholics were going to use the balcony, he removed the camera over the second floor window.

It wasn't able to pick up anything from that distance, anyway, he thought. *I need to place it closer to the action. Maybe Saturday night I could plant it near the shed. But how would I get back and forth to change the tapes? Something else to think about.*

In his nightly e-mail, he told Jack about the church changes and asked him to bring any Methodist sermons and service bulletins he might have lying around. The tapes were normal, so he logged them in his file and went to bed.

CHAPTER TWENTY-SIX

THURSDAY – FOURTH WEEK

Waking early, he jogged around town and stopped to move the camera at the Church of Christ to a post in the weeds across the street from the bar. Vehicles would block some of the view, but it should still get most of the main window. Now that Sampson was in jail, he wanted to see if anyone else was selling drugs in there.

He made quick work of the other blocks and stopped to see Grandma. She was watering her flowers, as usual, but instead of a demure dress, she was wearing paint stained jeans and a shirt. Obviously, she planned to join the painting party at the Kindergarten today.

Showered and appropriately attired in his old clothes, Joe grabbed a cup of coffee and a quick bowl of cereal. Then he ran over to Gene's to pick up the paint and supplies.

When he walked in, he heard Petey and Lily playing in the back, so he joined them. As soon as Petey saw Joe, he put his head down and walked away.

"Hey, Cowboy," Joe said. "Where's my hug?"

Petey looked back at him with big tears in his eyes. Joe was stunned. Getting down on the floor in front of Petey, he asked, "What's wrong partner? Why won't you talk to me?"

Lily provided the answer. "He's mad at you 'cause you fixed a Kindergarten for the Mex... uh ... Spanish kids and didn't fix one for him."

Joe could kick himself for the impression he'd left with Petey. In his excitement about having a place where the kids could learn English, by inference, he'd left out kids who could already speak it.

"Well I didn't fix one for him because I needed him to help the teachers show the Spanish kids how to say things," he said. "He's supposed to be a special teacher's helper."

As Petey listened to Joe, his face went from tears, to doubt, to a grin, to a big lunging hug. They rolled on the floor in a growling, snarling, tumble of horse play. They were still wrestling when Gene and Ginger walked in. Joe knew they were trying to identify the child. Laughing, he sat up.

Petey squirmed out of his arms and shouted, "I'm gonna help teach the kids in the *Kindergarten.*"

Gene and Ginger both showed relief at that announcement. Joe looked straight at Gene and asked, "Why didn't you tell me?"

"I wasn't sure how to bring it up," Gene said.

"Just walk up and say, Joe you've done something dumb and you need to fix it," he said. Gene laughed. Joe didn't.

"Seriously," Joe said. "Don't ever hesitate to tell me. I'd never intentionally hurt anyone, especially not a child."

After a few more assurances, Joe picked up the paint supplies and carried them over to the drug store.

He unlocked the back door to the Kindergarten and went back for the paint. The basketball kids met him coming across the street. Grabbing a can each, they followed him inside. What they lacked in technique, they made up for with enthusiasm. The banter started as soon as they popped the paint cans.

When Grandma walked through the door two hours later, they had the ceiling, three walls and themselves painted. The room looked great. The painters looked ridiculous. She tried to keep a straight face, but she couldn't. She burst out laughing at them. By noon, the room was finished. Joe sent the kids home to clean up. Grandma called the Wilsons to come over and help decide on the furniture they'd need.

Before he left, he told Grandma about his discussion with Petey and asked her to play along with the *special helper* story, at least until she had to sit on him for his mischief. She agreed, as long as he left his lizards at home.

He cleaned up and went over to have lunch at the grocery store with Ben and Alice. They were laughing about the paint on Chris when he came home.

"He looked like a can of paint in sneakers when he walked into our shower a few minutes ago," Alice said. "Did the kids get any paint on the walls?"

"Yep," Joe said grinning, "the walls and the ceiling, too. They really did do a good job – but we had a little fun, too."

The conversation switched to a discussion of the merged church services. They thought it would work. But they knew some people wouldn't be happy about it.

"We'll just have to work on them," Joe said. "Hopefully, when they see the rest of us accept the situation, they'll come around."

Since the painting went so fast, Joe decided to go over to the Methodist Church and see what he could find to use on Sunday. He picked up the keys from Ralph and went inside.

Looking around, he realized the church was in a total state of disrepair. Sadly, he walked through the sanctuary and stepped up to the podium.

When he picked up the preacher's stole, he thought about Reverend Anderson and his struggle to keep this church together. He gave his life here. And, as he predicted, the church was no longer able to support itself. He collected the two service candlesticks, the snuffers and a box of new candles under the podium. He'd have to ask Ralph who the candle lighters were. He emptied the baptismal bowl and added it to the stack.

He stepped into the office, sat down behind the desk and started glancing at the paperwork. Obviously, Ralph and Charley had been over there looking at the finances. The bills and bank statements were on top of the stacks.

Their bank balance was $300. Their utilities were $45 and their mortgage payment was $450. He looked at the miscellaneous papers underneath. Then he stopped and came back to the mortgage payment.

This building has to be at least forty years old, he thought. *And it was probably built by townspeople. How could it still have a mortgage?*

Going over to the file drawers, he found a filing system similar to the one at his church. He moved past the congregation files and pulled the *ADMINISTRATIVE* drawer open. He found one labeled *MORTGAGE*. He took it to the desk and began reading the specifics. Apparently, in June 1995, the church borrowed $15,000 for *renovations* and used the building as collateral.

Since it was obvious that no renovations had been done, he wondered what happened to the money. He searched the rest of the files, but he didn't find any labeled *RENOVATIONS* or *CONTRACTS*.

There has to be a contract somewhere, he thought. *Surely they didn't just hand the money to someone and trust them to do the work.* Starting at the top drawer, he opened each file folder looking for the answer. He scanned the names on the tags in the congregation files. Since he didn't even know the current members, he was lost trying to make much sense out of them. He found a folder of sermon outlines, in the third drawer.

"Thank you, Reverend Anderson," he said out loud, as he set it aside to take home. The next few folders had old pamphlets and bulletins similar to the ones he'd found at his church. In the fourth drawer, he found more church publications. Closing the last drawer he opened them all again and checked the bottoms for any more hidden envelopes.

No such luck, he thought.

Going back to the desk, he sorted through the papers. He set the bills and bank statements on top of the file cabinets so Ralph and Charley could find them again. Then he created stacks of church publications, correspondence from the Methodist Conference, and apparent junk mail. Since he didn't feel comfortable reading and discarding items in this church, he left them for Ralph.

He opened the desk drawers and added some more material to all three stacks. Again, he checked the bottoms of the drawers. He didn't find anything but cobwebs.

What happened to the $15,000? he wondered. *I wish I'd known about this while Reverend Anderson was alive. I don't want to ask Ralph, but I might have to, if I can't find the answer.*

He leaned back in the desk chair and tried figure it out. That was a lot of money. Reverend Anderson wouldn't have agreed to that expense lightly. Turning around to the bookshelf, he saw a white envelope lying on top of a row of books. Opening it, he found a contract, dated May 30, 1996, for a $15,000 water purification system for the church water supply. Attached to the contract was a water report, dated May 15, 1996, showing high concentrations of arsenic in the water at this address, signed by Peter Philman. "Son of a ..." he said.

Going back to the *MORTGAGE* folder, he wrote down the name and address of the bank in Albuquerque, the account number, and the current mortgage balance of $11,500. Leafing through the stack of papers in the folder, he found the original bank note, signed by Raymond Anderson and Pauline Tyson, the bank loan officer. He carefully removed the bank note from the folder and added it to the contract envelope.

He looked at his watch. It was three o'clock. He had just enough time to catch Miguel at the utility office. He called Ben and asked him to tell Chris he'd be a few minutes late to the game. He put the paperwork back on the desk in the same order he'd found it, locked the church and went over to see Miguel.

After a quick chat about Elena, Angie and the rest of the family, Joe asked Miguel if he could look at the water folder on the Methodist Church. Miguel cut a puzzled look at him.

"I'm just following up on the poisonings," Joe said. Miguel nodded and Joe sat down with the folder. He leafed back to June 1996 and found Peter Philman's registration to put a water filter on the Methodist Church's water system. He asked Miguel for a copy of the document.

Miguel read the page and swore.

"I'm still working on this," Joe warned. "It may just be a coincidence." Miguel's face said he didn't think so.

Joe asked to see the parsonage water folder again.

Going back to May and June 1996, he found four water tests that Miguel ran for Reverend Anderson, due to his abdominal illnesses. All four tests showed the water in the normal range – safe to drink.

"Is the water in the Methodist Church on the same pipeline as the parsonage?" Joe asked.

When Miguel said yes, Joe asked for copies of all four tests. "We're both angry about this situation," he told Miguel. "But these are just a few pieces of a larger puzzle. We have to be very careful. We're dealing with ruthless people who don't care who they hurt – and we don't know who all of them are yet. Promise me you'll keep everything you and I have found and discussed confidential. I don't want you or your family – or any other innocent people hurt – because this information got out to the wrong people. They've already targeted me, so let me take the risks. Help me keep you and the rest of the town safe, by keeping this quiet."

Miguel expressed concern for Joe, but agreed to keep quiet. Joe thanked him and took the papers and the contract home to add to the tool box. He grabbed the extra surveillance camera on his way out and took pictures of the large filter attached to the water pipes behind the Methodist Church. He took pictures of any model numbers he could find. He locked the camera inside the church and joined the kids.

When they finished their games, he told the kids he was going to Portales tomorrow and wouldn't be back in time for their game. Then he went back to the Methodist Church and took the camera home. He made a second trip and carried the other items over to his church. Running back to return the keys, Joe stopped to get one of the Methodist hymnals. He gave it to Ralph and asked him to select the hymns for Sunday. He also told Ralph that he was going to Portales tomorrow.

Back home, he put on a pot of coffee, fixed a peanut butter sandwich and threw a load of laundry in the machine.

Then he ran his surveillance and changed the tapes.

He reviewed the new tapes while he waited for the clothes to dry. Then he checked his e-mail. Jack had sent him a phone number to call when he arrived in Portales. He sent a reply saying he was on schedule for tomorrow.

He packed an overnight bag and grabbed his suit and some other things he needed dry cleaned. He put his laptop, tape player and derringer in his overnight bag. He decided to carry his other hand guns on him. He added the Methodist Church mortgage, water reports and filter tape to his earlier collection in the tool box and put a padlock on it before he finally fell into bed for a few hours of sleep.

CHAPTER TWENTY-SEVEN

FRIDAY – FOURTH WEEK

He bypassed his morning jog, loaded his van, locked his door and checked both church doors. He drove to Grandma's to wait for her to come out to water her flowers.

He told her he was going to Portales to get his dry cleaning done and run some errands. "I think I'll book a room somewhere tonight and try to get some rest," he said.

"I'm glad," she said. "You need a break. Things have been crazy around here."

"Please tell Ben where I'm going," he said. "I forgot to tell him yesterday. But you two and Dave are the only ones who know I'm going to stay overnight. I'm trying to keep it quiet so the thugs won't try to do more damage while I'm gone."

She gave him a quick hug and said, "Go and relax. We'll watch things here." He thanked her and drove off.

Once he was out of town, he released the choke and drove quietly into Portales. He dropped his cleaning off, went to two ATMs and called Jack.

They met at a motel Tommy found for them. Joe put two large magnetic signs on his van and unloaded his things into the room. Once inside, they relaxed.

He hadn't realized how much he'd missed Jack until they sat down to eat their fast food breakfast and catch up on things. Jack gave him two letters from Angelique. Those brightened his spirits significantly.

In the first letter she told him she was taking a sabbatical from the tedium of the concerts. She was tired and wanted a break. The second letter said she'd spent a week in the Poconos and felt better. After Joe read the personal parts of the letters, Jack told him about her visit to El Paso and return to Boston. They were both glad she'd gone back home and agreed it would be good for her to take some time for herself.

Then they cleared the table and started working. Jack gave him the reports they'd collected on the smuggling trucks. They'd tracked them from the border to Chicago. They had agents watching the distribution center and final destinations.

"They'll move in and make the arrests as soon as they hear from us," Jack said. He read the Whitsworth documents and shook his head at Joe. "I can see why you wanted me over here ASAP. This is hot."

Joe nodded and handed him the Methodist Church mortgage, contract and conflicting water reports.

Jack looked at him in disbelief.

"They're ruthless," Joe said. "I think they poisoned Reverend Anderson and Father Lopez until their hearts failed – and they definitely want me gone."

Finally, they discussed their official case and Jack looked at the smuggling tapes. Joe gave him some time to absorb that information. Later, they were going to have to try to develop a plan that would catch the thugs involved in the other issues, without hurting the innocent people in town – at least, not any more than they'd already been hurt.

Jack was amazed at the material Joe had found in four short weeks. He could also tell how personally attached he'd become to several of the families in town.

They set up their laptops and Jack's printer-fax machine. Spreading the paperwork out, they started working on the smuggling ring. They drew a rough map of the route the smugglers were using to transport the women from the border to Chicago. They estimated the entire trip took between three and four days, depending on weather conditions.

"The semis have two drivers," Jack said, "so they drive straight through to Chicago when they leave the warehouse in Portales. They don't make any more transfers. But they stop in secluded areas and change the logos on the sides of their trucks several times to confuse anyone trying to track them. So far, the truckers appear to be independents, but Wellman is the owner of the warehouse. So we have him on smuggling charges."

Joe nodded and made some more notes.

"Bart makes a second run to the silo on Wednesdays," Jack said. "He drives a flat bed load of hay back to a feed lot near the warehouse. We suspect he has a false bottom in that trailer for voluntary illegals. But we don't want to stop him until we have the women out of danger." Joe agreed.

"Since there's another pair of drivers that leave the warehouse for Chicago on Thursday night," Jack said, "we think they're transporting the voluntary group. We're tracking those drivers. I'm waiting for a call from Chicago this weekend to tell me if they unloaded any illegals."

"Do they use the same two semis for all these runs?" Joe asked, looking at the reports.

"They have for the two weeks we've been tailing them," Jack said. "Of course, they keep changing the logos. But it's been the same two rigs, so far." Joe nodded.

"Where do you want to take them down?" Jack asked.

"When I get in the tunnel, tomorrow night, I'll know more about it," Joe said. "I suspect they're using the open area inside the peanut silo. We don't want to take them in there, unless we want a standoff with a lot of tear gas." Jack agreed.

"All eight of them go into the tunnel on Tuesday night," Joe said. "Apparently, they need extra help lifting the women out of the tunnel. I think that's the best night to hit them. They'll be one man short this week. So they may have a new guy in their group. I'd like to get Tommy in the hotel behind Simms to cuff him and get the truck keys. I'll probably need to bait Max outside on some pretense, to keep him from making any phone calls. We can cuff him in the hotel with Simms."

Jack listened and made several notes.

"If Tommy follows the same timing we have on the tapes," Joe said, "he can come out of the hotel and replace Simms in the cab. I want us in the trailer, before they open the door from the tunnel. We can pick the lock on the back and slip in that way. We'll knock out the two men who hop up and replace them in the relay."

"I like that idea," Jack said. "We'd have all the women in our custody."

Joe nodded and said, "When the others finish handing the women up to us, we'll let them close up and head out the rig exit. You and I can drive over and help our guys take them down while Tommy watches the semi and our prisoners in there. Whoever is waiting at the oil rig needs to disable their trucks while we're loading the women. We don't want to give any of them a chance to run. These men are roughnecks. They'll put up a fight." Jack winced and agreed.

"When we get all the men rounded up," Joe said, "we'll call in backups to take them to detention. I hate to say it, but you'd better put our guys in that group. Wellman may have some of the locals on his payroll."

Jack agreed and sent an encoded e-mail to Boston ordering the six men in his unit to: PROCEED TO AMARILLO, TX, ASAP. BE THERE NO LATER THAN SUNDAY. PACK UNIFORMS AND FIREARMS, DRESS IN CIVILIAN CLOTHES. TRAVEL IN UNMARKED VEHICLES. DO NOT DISCUSS WITH ANYONE. CONSIDER TOP SECRET. CONTACT ME BY CELL PHONE WHEN YOU ARRIVE.

He forwarded a copy of the message to his superior.

Good idea, Joe thought. *If anyone does pick up on their departure, they won't know where the real assignment is located.*

Going back to the plan, Joe said, "I think Tommy should drive the semi to the Portales hospital. We can leave the women there with a couple of our guys. Then he can drive the rest of us over to the warehouse to sweep it out."

"I like the plan," Jack said. "But that's going to take more than our six men."

"Well, the Artesia trainees always want to see some real action," Joe said. "Why don't we grab some of their top achievers to help at the warehouse?"

Jack agreed and sent an e-mail to Artesia. NEED TEN TOP TRAINEES AND ONE INSTRUCTOR TO PARTICIPATE IN FIELD EXERCISES AROUND TUCUMCARI ON MONDAY. PACK UNIFORMS AND FIREARMS, DRESS IN CIVILIAN CLOTHES, TRAVEL IN UNMARKED VEHICLES. PLAN TO BE GONE THREE DAYS. DO NOT DISCUSS MISSION OR ASSOCIATION WITH TRAINING FACILITY WITH ANYONE. TREAT AS TOP SECRET. CONTACT ME BY CELL PHONE WHEN YOU ARRIVE.

"I assume you're staying in the area for a while," Joe said, when he finished typing.

"Yeah, I had to come get my *kid* out of trouble," Jack teased. "I can't turn my back on you for a minute. Every time I do, I have another mess to clean up."

"That's true," Joe said. "It's a good thing I'm the Boss' favorite." Jack chuckled and poured some more coffee.

They went back to their plan. They replayed the two truck tapes and timed the sequence of events. On the second tape, Jack stopped it, backed it up and stopped it again.

"Listen," he said. "Do you hear that buzzing sound?"

"Yes," Joe said. "But I can't place the source."

"I think they have a sensor in the hotel carpet that buzzes them in the tunnel," Jack said. "That way they know when the driver steps inside and when he comes back out. Your speculation about the driver's involvement could be right. They may not know about their extra cargo. We'll still pick them up for questioning. But right now, it doesn't look like they know what's going on."

"Good ear, Boss," Joe said. "If you hadn't picked that up on the tape, I would've sent Tommy in to get Simms and the men in the tunnel would've been alerted. We'll have to get Simms after he comes back out of the shower. And we'll need to tie Max up under the stairs." Jack agreed and changed his notes.

"We're going to have to let Dave Nelson in on this," Joe said. "He's been a straight arrow so far with me. He's thorough with his night patrols. If he catches Max tied up or sees one of us moving around, we could be on the wrong end of his revolver before we have a chance to get these guys. He could keep Simms and Max in his jail for us until we get the known smugglers." Jack took a moment to think about that option.

"I just teased Dave about finding some more prisoners for him when he got rid of Tobias, Sampson and Bernardo," Joe said, grinning at Jack. "And Doc wouldn't know what to do if I didn't send some more thugs his way. So, we have to try to wound a couple of these guys."

Jack laughed and then asked seriously, "You've become very close to these people, haven't you?"

Answering honestly, Joe said, "Yes. They're the kind of good, warm-hearted people we all hope to meet in our lifetime. They've been wonderful to me and they had no reason to be – especially, after their experience with Phillips."

"You have a natural way with people," Jack said. "You're open and friendly, but you don't compromise your integrity. Look at the way the kids trust you."

Embarrassed, Joe turned to refill their coffee.

"I wonder," Jack said, "where your loyalties are going to be when this mission is over – in Boston with Angelique and your families – or in Eutopian Springs with your new friends?"

"I honestly don't know," Joe said. "I want to stay focused on the assignment right now. Either way I go, I know I'm going to leave part of my heart in the other place. I don't need my judgment clouded with that emotional dilemma right now. I do know that I won't be able to leave here until these injustices have been rectified and the right people are in jail."

"You're right," Jack said. "I should've thought before I brought it up right now. We'll worry about that after we have these thugs put away. Why don't I run get some lunch and let you shift gears for a few minutes." Joe nodded.

"Dumb move!" Jack told himself, when he walked outside. "Throw an emotional question at a guy who's up to his neck in criminals. That was stupid! Shape up! The man can't take much more right now." Determined to do better, he walked in with hamburgers and said, "If we're firm on our plans for Tuesday night, let's see what we can do to smoke out the rest of the skunks in this wood pile."

Munching on his burger, Joe pulled up the spreadsheet he'd created and said, "Here are some of my preliminary notes."

Jack looked over his shoulder. He was impressed.

Joe had the Wellman and Philman families outlined and their known activities identified. Jack used his Agency access codes and found Wellmanson in Pueblo, Colorado.

"No wonder we couldn't find him in Lubbock," he said.

"We have to find a way to flush him out," Joe said. "The way I see it, after our arrests Tuesday, we can seize Cozen Oil. But we don't know where it is, do we?"

Jack shook his head no.

"It has to exist somewhere," Joe said. "Maybe we can find some paychecks or other information when we seize their trucks." Jack agreed.

"I wonder," Joe said, "if Pauline Tyson handles the Cozen accounts through the Albuquerque bank. Do you have any way to see if it's in their account records?"

"Not without tipping our hand right now," Jack said. "We'll check on that after Tuesday."

Joe nodded and added it to his notes.

"Anyway," Joe said, "Wellman is going to be livid after Tuesday, because we're going to be able to seize, Cozen Oil, the Archer farm, the Thatcher farm, the peanut station, the storage units, the hotel, the warehouse outside Portales and at least one semi, maybe two. Of course, we'll be arresting a lot of his workers, too."

Jack looked at Joe's notes and whistled at the list.

"This is going to take a lot of manpower," he said. "Even if we just take the operation at the silo in town and the warehouse, we'll be cutting it close."

Joe nodded and said, "I agree, but I'm worried about blowing our operation if we get many more people involved. We can't afford a leak with all those women at risk."

Jack studied the situation and had to agree.

"Since all the property fraud in town is related to Cozen Oil and we're seizing the company, do we have jurisdiction over it?" Joe asked. "Or does that go to another Agency?"

"I think we have it," Jack said. "But I'll check with our legal office after Tuesday."

"Whoever gets it," Joe said, "I'd like to put an agent in the Albuquerque Bank as an examiner. We need someone to look for other loans made to families or businesses in town – without alerting Pauline. As soon as I get back, I want to check the empty houses and buildings for water filters like the one I found on the Methodist Church. If I find them, I'll bet they all had $15,000 loans from Pauline."

"Why would they agree to a loan that large?" Jack asked.

"At the time the loans were made, the town was thriving," Joe said. "They had no reason to believe they couldn't pay them off. Of course, when Cozen pulled out in one short week, according to Doc, they were all left holding the bag. If that scenario is true, Wellman picked up most of these properties for $15,000 or less." Jack winced and nodded.

215

Come to think of it," Joe said, "we can seize the Spanish section, too. Those are Cozen houses originally built for the oil workers." Jack added them to his notes.

"We don't have to make the families vacate do we?" Joe asked, visibly concerned.

"I don't think so," Jack said. "If we seize any money from all of this, maybe we can give some of it back to the families for all the delinquent repairs." Joe liked that idea.

"Moving on," Joe said, "after Tuesday, we need to find the president of Strataroc and figure out if his company is involved. Judging from the paperwork we have, he and his company were victims of this fraud, too. Of course, since he leased land from Wellman that was fraudulently acquired from the original owners, I'm not sure Strataroc has any rights. But they'll want to know about Peter Philman, in case they relied on his reports in other transactions. And they'll definitely want to look at Thomas Tyson's involvement."

Looking at his two pages of notes, Jack said, "I think we're going to keep attorneys busy for ten years on the information you've managed to collect this month."

Joe looked at his own notes and agreed.

"Let's take a break," Jack said, stretching. "I'll go get some dinner for us. You start another pot of coffee and let's talk about anything but this case for an hour or so. If I try to process any more while I'm eating, I'll have indigestion all night."

"I have one more thing to discuss with you, before we take a break," Joe said seriously. "Reverend Anderson lost his life trying to save his church and the town. I don't want Wellman to own that building for a single minute. The current church account balance is $300. They owe $45 to utilities and $450 on the mortgage – which is why they think they'll lose the church. Here's the account number for the mortgage at the Albuquerque bank and here's $450 for this month's payment. These are my personal funds, so the Agency isn't involved. I just need someone to make the payment and get a receipt. Will you do that for me, please?"

Jack looked at the emotions on Joe's face while he talked. He saw the pain in his eyes and suddenly realized just how deeply those SOBs had hurt him and the people he cared about in Eutopian Springs. To Joe, he said, "I'll take care of it."

"Thanks," Joe said, looking back at his notes.

"I'll be back with dinner in a bit," Jack said. "We both need a break." Joe agreed.

After dinner, Jack called Tommy to join them. They limited his briefing to the exploration of the tunnel tomorrow night and the plans for Tuesday night.

"We'll need a lot of handcuffs," Joe said.

"I'll take care of those," Tommy said. He handed Jack the revolver and scope Joe requested.

"That's quite a scope," Joe said, looking at it.

"It has a camera attached," Tommy said, showing him how to operate it.

"That's great," Joe said. "Thanks."

He drew a map to the oil rig he wanted to explore. Once they agreed to meet at nine tomorrow night, Tommy left.

"How do you expect to get in and out of a town the size of Eutopian Springs without a cover identity?" Joe asked.

Jack gave him a puzzled look.

"Well, you're not planning to show up in town on Wednesday as an INS officer, are you?" Joe asked. "If you do, you'll blow both of our covers before we smoke out Wellman."

"Honestly, I hadn't thought that far ahead," Jack said. "I've just focused on getting through Tuesday."

"Well, as you told me a month ago," Joe said, "there aren't many ways to get a stranger into a town this size. So, I'd suggest you get acquainted with the Gideon in your room. Because the only way you and I can be seen together in Eutopian Springs is for you to be my friend and mentor, Reverend Brownstone." Jack sputtered and Joe laughed out loud.

By the time they said goodnight Jack was resigned to the fact that Joe was right. He didn't like admitting it – especially since Joe was feeding his own words back to him.

"At least he's in a better mood," Jack grumbled to himself. "But I'm not."

CHAPTER TWENTY EIGHT

SATURDAY – FOURTH WEEK

They rose early and shared a quick breakfast in the room before Joe packed up and left. He picked up his cleaning and drove back to Eutopian Springs.

When he pulled up to his house, he saw red paint smeared across his door and the front of the church. He parked the van and walked closer. He read *'Go Home or Die'* on his door and *'Closed'* across the front of the church.

He drove down the block to Dave's office. Dave wasn't there, but Susan and the three prisoners were. He started to leave a message when Dave drove up. Joe pointed down the street and Dave rolled forward. He was trying not to curse in front of Joe, but he was obviously furious.

"This wasn't here when I made rounds last night," he said. "I was coming back down this street when you drove up. I'd like to get my hands on the people doing this."

"So would I, Dave," Joe said. "So would I."

When they didn't find any obvious fingerprints or other evidence, Dave said, "Let's go inside the buildings and see if they did any damage there."

Joe walked into the parsonage and checked the rooms. He didn't find any broken windows or visible signs of damage. But when he opened the refrigerator, he bit his own tongue to keep from cursing. "Judging from the spoiled food in my refrigerator," he said, "I think someone turned off my power."

Dave called Miguel to see if he could get it restored.

Then Joe called Gene and asked him to shake up three gallons of white paint for him.

"I'll be over to pick it up shortly," he said and hung up.

He grabbed the church keys and they walked through all of the rooms. Nothing had been disturbed.

"Apparently, the painter was content to stay outside or didn't have time to do more," Joe said, as he locked both doors. They walked behind the parsonage and found the cut power line.

"Someone was lucky they didn't get fried doing this," Dave said. "Then again, it would've served them right if they did. It's a clean cut. They knew what they were doing."

They checked the panel behind the kitchen plumbing to be sure it was still nailed shut.

Dave took some pictures and wrote his report.

Joe unloaded his van, locked his house and walked over to Gene's to get the paint.

Miguel met him as he came out of the store. He helped carry the supplies back to the church. Seeing the damage, Miguel swore in Spanish, assuming Joe wouldn't understand. Joe had a hard time keeping a straight face, since he clearly understood Miguel's colorful description of the fate he wished on the perpetrators.

He showed Miguel the cut line. Miguel walked a few feet away to a power pole, strapped on his belt, and climbed about eight feet up. Reaching overhead, he disconnected the line. Back on the ground, he repaired the line and reversed his actions on the pole. In less than twenty minutes, Joe had lights and a functioning refrigerator.

"Thank you," Joe said. "And thanks for coming over so fast. I'm sorry I managed to disturb another of your weekends with your family."

"No problem," Miguel said. "I'm sorry these idiots are bothering you."

"By the way," Joe said, "I meant to ask you who your landlord is. He needs to put a new roof on your house and several of the others."

Miguel snorted indignantly and said, "Yeah, we know. He takes our money, but he won't do a thing for us."

"What's his name?" Joe asked. "Maybe we need to pressure him a little more."

219

"Homer Wellman," Miguel said, "but he doesn't live around here. He lives in another state."

"That's the same man who owns the lot we had to mow," Joe said.

"Yeah, that's him," Miguel said.

"Who collects the rent for him?" Joe asked.

"No one," Miguel said. "We buy a money order at the drug store and mail it to a bank in Albuquerque."

Joe dumped his spoiled food in a garbage bag and made a mental note of the things he needed to pick up again. When he walked back outside with the trash, Miguel asked to use his phone. Waving him inside, Joe put his suitcase and dry cleaning away in the bedroom. Then he changed into the clothes he wore to paint the Kindergarten. When Miguel finished his call, he went outside with Joe.

Joe opened the first can of paint, poured some in a tray, picked up a roller, and started trying to cover the red paint.

At the sound of footsteps, he turned around to see Miguel, Eddie, Jorge and Archibaldo. They stopped to look at the mess and shook their heads in disgust. Pulling brushes out of their hip pockets, they grabbed the other cans of paint and started on the church walls. Joe was speechless.

Eddie laughed and said, "You better close your mouth, Preacher Man, or you'll be spitting flies."

Joe shut his mouth and shook his head.

"Why are you so surprised?" Eddie asked. "You're the one who told us we all have to work together. You fixed the field and Kindergarten for us. And now you're sharing your church with us. Do you really think we'd let you clean up this mess by yourself?"

He gave Eddie a big hug and said thank you and *gracias*, to the men who appeared to speak only Spanish.

To Miguel, he said, "That's what you needed the phone for, isn't it?" Miguel nodded and grinned. Joe thanked him again. Then they got busy. By ten a.m. the red paint was gone.

Waving goodbye, the men left as quickly as they arrived.

He cleaned up and went after some more groceries. Confronted with the Saturday morning crowd at the grocery store, he sought refuge in the coffee shop before he tackled his list. Having waved hello to Katherine, he knew Alice would have a cup ready for him before he got to a chair. He was right.

"Heard you came home to more problems at the church this morning," she said.

"It's history," he said, loud enough for other listeners to hear. "When you have more good people than bad, it doesn't take very long for the good to win." Then quietly he told her about Miguel, Eddie, Archibaldo and Jorge.

"As soon as I replace the food in my refrigerator, I'll be back to normal," he said. "Thanks for the coffee. I needed it."

Walking home with his groceries, he decided he needed more defense in the grocery store than he did on the battle field. He obviously hadn't refined the skill required to play *bumper carts* in a busy market. *Those women are vicious,* he thought. *But I'll bet Ben loves the business.*

At the house, he got busy on the things he'd planned to do when he drove up at eight. He opened his laptop and sent Jack a quick note on the greeting he found and the Hispanic helpers. Then he grabbed a couple of tapes, locked up and set off for the drug store to get the keys to the Methodist Church. He walked around the Church of Christ and noticed a water filter similar to the one at the Methodist Church.

Stopping to shake an imaginary rock out of his shoe, he bent down and changed tapes in the camera outside the bar. He wanted to see if anyone bragged about the church damage last night. When he straightened back up, he decided he'd have to ask Jack for a raise, if this job was going to require all this acting. Grinning at trapping Jack into being another preacher, he walked into the drug store.

"I heard your church was defaced," Ralph said.

"Yep," Joe said, "but Archibaldo, Miguel, Eddie and Jorge came over and helped me clean it up."

Ralph's face registered surprise and then pride.

"How's the Kindergarten looking?" Joe asked. "Do you mind if I go peek?"

Ralph walked him through the storeroom, opened the door and let him see for himself. The walls they'd painted soft blue were pleasantly covered with various Kindergarten cutouts. An alphabet strip was hanging above the space the teachers had obviously identified for the black board. Toys were piled in one corner of the room and cute little towels were already hanging in the bathroom.

"This looks great," Joe said. "The teachers didn't waste any time putting this together did they?"

"No," Ralph said, "I think they're more excited than the kids – if that's possible."

"Well none of this would've happened without your generosity," Joe said. "I hope you know how much we all appreciate it."

"Yeah," Ralph said, "but you're the one who asked me to pull one out of my pocket. Remember?"

"Sure I remember," Joe said. "I mouthed off at you and you made it happen. Actually, Dominique is the one who originally suggested it. See what happens when we all work together?" Ralph nodded.

"Just remember that," Joe said grinning, "when the noise back here has your pills jiggling off the racks."

Ralph rolled his eyes and chuckled.

"Speaking of Dominique," Joe said, "do you have anyone playing the piano for your congregation?"

"Not since the piano got damaged," Ralph said.

"Well, if you have the hymns picked out for tomorrow, I'll see if Dominique can go over and practice them this afternoon," Joe said. "If not, we'll try to have her ready to play next week. We're paying her twenty-five a week to play for us. If you can add a little to that I'm sure she'd be grateful." Ralph nodded and handed him the hymnal with his selections.

Joe walked over to the Sanchez house to see if Dominique could practice for a few minutes. Knocking on the door, he heard the kids squealing at each other. Then Christina looked out the window and started shouting her version of Preacher Man. Elena answered the door a minute later. Before he could ask for Dominique, Angie flew into his arms and crawled up as far as she could go. Elena scolded Angie, but she knew it wouldn't do any good.

Joe chuckled and put her on his shoulder.

He asked Elena to see if Dominique would like to play for the Methodist service tomorrow. If so, could she go over to the church and practice for a few minutes today? Elena went to the back of the house and asked her. Dominique returned saying she could go over now if that would work with his schedule.

"That'd be great," he said. He gave Angie a quick shoulder jog and hugged Christina and Francisco. Then he asked Elena if Father Romero had music for his service.

"At the church," she said, "but not in town."

"Would you ask Father Romero to bring some of his music with him tomorrow?" Joe asked. "Maybe Dominique could play for your service, too."

Elena loved that idea. She hadn't thought about Dominique playing for them. She said she'd find out and let her know. He thanked her and walked Dominique back across town.

He stopped at the Methodist Church to pack up a box of their hymnals for tomorrow. Dominique wandered over to the piano in the sanctuary. She sat down and the bench leg fell off. She giggled and put it back on. Then she tried to play a song. The face she made said it all. Joe agreed. It was badly out of tune and literally falling apart. One side panel was leaning against the wall and the front panel was tilting toward the bench.

She stopped giggling and became pensive. Carefully walking around the piano, she checked the strings and hammers. Then she asked, in broken English, "Kindergarten?"

It took Joe a minute to understand what she was saying.

"Do you think you can fix it up enough to use it at the Kindergarten?" he asked. She nodded yes.

"That's a great idea," he said. "Let me see what I can do." They locked up and carried the hymnals over to his church. She practiced the Methodist songs for an hour or so and left. He arranged the hymnals while she practiced.

Then he went home to play the tape from the bar. He watched it closely to see how much he could see through the window. Since this was a Friday night tape, Clive didn't have as much activity. *A good time to test the camera,* he thought.

He watched people come and go. He saw Tobias' redhead put some money down her dress and go upstairs with a man – who was obviously not Tobias. *We might have evidence of prostitution on this tape,* he thought.

Then he watched a tall man he recognized from the oil rig, drive up and go inside for a beer. When he paid for his drink, he slipped an envelope to Clive. Clive opened it, pulled out a couple of white packets and tested the contents on his tongue. Then he went to the cash register and handed some money back to the man.

We have drugs tied to Cozen, Joe thought, *Good!* A few minutes later the man walked outside into the voice range of the camera. He stopped to talk to a couple of men standing around their trucks. They were mad about Joe still being in town.

"What's it going to take to get rid of that guy?" one of them asked.

"He'll leave when we get through with him," another one bragged.

"Yeah, if he doesn't get the message soon, we'll take him out on a country road and convince him," the third one said.

You and what army? Joe thought.

A fourth man walked up from the west side of the bar. "Hey, Chad," he said to the tall one. "You should see what I just did to that church. I guess the preacher's gone tonight, so I did his door, too."

"Good for you," Chad said. "There'll be a little extra in your paycheck for that. I'll tell Pauline."

"Hey, Arturo," another man said. "You got red paint on your new boots." Arturo cursed profusely and tried to rub it off on his jeans. It didn't work.

"It'll wear off in a day or two," another one said.

Arturo cursed again.

When Joe finished watching the rest of the tape, he packed it away in the tool box and walked down to Dave's office. He was doing paperwork on his three whining prisoners when Joe walked in. Giving Joe an evil eye, he growled and said, "This is all your fault."

"That's right," Joe said. "And I'm about to give you another stack. Step outside and I'll tell you who painted my church last night."

"Who?" Dave asked. He glanced at the prisoners and followed Joe out the door.

"I can't tell you my source," Joe said. "But I understand there's a fella named Arturo who has some fresh red paint on his brand new boots."

"I'll check that out tonight," Dave said. "Chad and his crew always come to town on Saturday nights, unless there's something going on in Portales that looks better. I'll let you know what I find."

Joe thanked him and walked down the block to meet the kids for hoops. As usual, they were already bantering when he walked up. Today they were teasing Gabbie about the way she always jerked her head back before she took her free throws. They threatened to start calling her Jerk. She countered with some nicknames for them and they reconsidered.

She's a spunky kid, Joe thought proudly. *She knows how to hold her own with these guys.* After giving Eddie some peer recognition for his help with the church this morning, they started their game.

When he got back home, he grabbed some coffee and a peanut butter sandwich while he reviewed Reverend Anderson's sermon outlines. Selecting a moderate one, he tried to memorize the key points for tomorrow's service.

Then he changed into his black clothes and concealed all three firearms. He packed some rubber gloves and plastic bags in his pockets, along with a flashlight and some extra tapes for the camera he was carrying.

He locked his door, slipped behind the church and skirted the back of the utility building and the school, so he could cross First Street in a less populated area. He worked his way across a portion of the Thatcher Farm and crossed the north extension of Main Street into the Archer fields. He watched the area around the rig for a few minutes before moving closer.

He spotted a dark car parked on the side of the road about half a mile east of the shed and waited for Jack and Tommy to join him. Within minutes, the three were together in the shadows.

Tommy, carrying binoculars, would stay in the shadows and watch the *hatch* in the parking lot and the other approaches.

Jack was going into the shed to be available for Joe.

They had their first surprise when they opened the door. It wasn't a pump house. This was a fake oil rig. Inside, they found a ladder leading down to a four foot round pipe. Joe grabbed his flashlight and followed it for approximately a hundred feet until he found another ladder which led him back up to ground level. He was standing in a large round area. It was obviously the interior of the peanut silo. Some torn pieces of clothing and other remnants from previous occupants were littered around the edges. A box on the floor contained some food, water and miscellaneous medical supplies.

Working across the space, he searched for the access to the trucks. He found concrete steps leading back down ten or twelve feet into a concrete room. At the bottom of the steps there was a switch attached to a hydraulic system. Following the line, Joe found the hatch that opened under the trucks. Looking at the room a little closer, he realized it was a storm shelter, apparently built to protect the peanut workers. All the smugglers had done was install the hatch and put a step ladder under it.

He taped everything in the shelter and the silo. Then he went back to the ladder. The *tunnel* from the shed was obviously a run off drain designed for the peanut operation. The smugglers had simply built a shed over the outflow end of the pipe and used it for their access. He retraced his steps through the drain and up the ladder to Jack. He gave Jack the tape of the tunnel and briefed him on what he'd found.

"The latest bar tape shows prostitution, Chad selling drugs and a man named, Arturo, bragging about painting the church," Joe said. "I have Dave working on that. The tape also has Chad telling Arturo that he'd tell Pauline to increase his pay for painting the church. So, Cozen's accounts are apparently in the Albuquerque bank." Jack nodded.

"Oh," Joe said, "Miguel said they send their rent to a bank in Albuquerque. Pauline's probably handling that account, too." Jack shook his head in disgust.

"I want to wait until Tuesday afternoon to tell Dave about our plans," Joe said, "to minimize any inadvertent slips."

Jack agreed and said, "We'll synchronize our times for Tuesday by e-mail." He and Tommy slipped back to their car.

Joe worked his way back home – just in time to see two men step through his bathroom window with their guns drawn.

He dropped to the ground behind the north side of the church, and put his flashlight, camera and other gear down. He glanced at his clothes and pulled off his black shirt. Then he ran to the jail, knocked on the window and signaled Dave outside.

"I have two men ransacking my house," he said.

Dave nodded and ran in to call Susan over with the prisoners. He followed Joe back to the parsonage.

Joe waved him to the bathroom window to listen. They could hear the men tossing things inside his house and cursing because he wasn't there.

Then they heard one of the men say, "Crawl back out the window and see if you can hear the preacher in the church."

They faded into the shadows and waited for that one.

"What the hell," he said when he met Dave's revolver.

"Call your friend out, Hernando," Dave said, "before someone gets hurt – and you know it won't be me."

Hernando shook his head.

Dave nodded at Joe to take Hernando.

Joe shook his head and whispered, "Tell the other one to come out. I'll go cover the front door."

Dave nodded and waited until Joe waved.

"This is Constable Nelson," Dave boomed through the window. "You're under arrest. Come out with your hands up."

The man inside swore and threw something at the window. Then he bolted out the front door and ran right into Joe's fist. Dave walked Hernando around front. The second man was on his knees, holding his stomach and gasping for air.

"You never listen, do you, Felipe?" Dave asked.

Joe stepped over with Hernando while Dave cuffed Felipe and searched both men. Then they walked them over to the jail. Dave came back with his camera and took pictures of the mess in the house and the broken window. Then he photographed the guns and knives he took off of them.

"Those two don't come to town very often," he said. "They prefer Portales. They should've gone there tonight."

Joe nodded and agreed.

"I just picked up their buddy Arturo, for his paint job last night," Dave said.

"They really want me out of town, don't they," Joe said.

"Yep," Dave said. "Instead they're becoming permanent residents of my jail. I've already told the Judge to book some extra time when he comes to town on Tuesday."

"Who's the Judge?" Joe asked.

"Steve Orson," Dave said, with obvious contempt.

"It doesn't sound like you have much respect for him," Joe said. "What's the problem with him?"

"Well, he's Chad Orson's brother," Dave said. "Chad's the Cozen Foreman. So, Steve is always *very lenient* on these oil workers, which is why they cause so much trouble. They know he's going to let them off with 'time served.' He always does."

Great, Joe thought. *The four men in Dave's jail will probably be back on the street Tuesday. Oh well, if we catch them in the tunnel, they'll have a harder time getting 'time served' on Federal smuggling charges. Dave's jail will seem like a four star hotel compared to Federal prison.*

Dave looked at the house and asked, "How did you hear them this time?"

"I thought I heard someone at the church," Joe said, "so I was over to check on it. I came around back, just in time to see them going through the window. That's when I came after you."

Dave nodded and said, "Thank God you weren't hurt."

Joe agreed and thanked him for his help.

After Dave left, Joe went back around the church to get his gear. Then he locked the door, swept up the broken glass in the bathroom, taped a piece of cardboard over the window and went to bed.

CHAPTER TWENTY-NINE

SUNDAY – FIFTH WEEK

Joe swore he'd just put his head on the pillow when his alarm clock buzzed. He crawled out of bed, started a pot of coffee and started picking up the mess the men made.

He set up his laptop and sent a quick e-mail to Jack. HAD TWO NIGHT PROWLERS CRAWLING THROUGH MY WINDOW WHEN I CAME HOME. GOT DAVE TO HELP CAPTURE THEM – TO STAY IN COVER ROLE. THEY'RE IN JAIL NOW. PER DAVE, THE JUDGE, STEVE ORSON, IS CHAD ORSON'S BROTHER. CHAD'S THE COZEN FOREMAN. ORSON USUALLY LETS THE COZEN MEN OFF WITH TIME SERVED. COURT IS TUESDAY. IF DAVE'S RIGHT, THE MEN IN JAIL WILL BE OUT IN TIME FOR THE NIGHT ACTION.

Showered and dressed for church, he slipped his revolver in his ankle holster. Church or not, he had to be ready. These guys were out for blood and he didn't want it to belong to any of the congregation.

He grabbed Reverend Anderson's notes and his Bible, locked his house and opened the church at eight. He placed the Methodist baptismal bowl and candles by the podium. Then he donned Reverend Anderson's robe and stole. Dominique arrived at eight-thirty and played soft hymns. The music had a calming effect on the church and him. He needed that this morning.

As the Methodists began arriving, Joe welcomed them at the door. He stopped Ralph and Charley and asked who normally led the singing and lit the candles. Ralph led the singing. They said they'd been lighting the candles themselves before the service. Joe asked them to light the candles the way

229

they normally did and then take their seats, as Elders, in the Deacon's seats behind the podium. The Methodist congregation consisted of Ralph and Charley's two families and the Samuels family that he'd met in the general store.

Dave and Susan rushed over as he was about to close the door. He gave Dave a quizzical look. "Ben's watching the jailbirds for us this morning," Dave said.

Joe nodded and walked up to the podium.

He opened with a short prayer and a hymn led by Ralph. He delivered a brief sermon, similar to his first sermon with the Baptists. After the communion service, offering and another hymn, Joe ended the service with a prayer.

Then he gave the congregation time to get to know him better. They asked about his background and he honestly told them it was inter-denominational with a greater emphasis on the Baptist religion.

"However, with your help," he said, "I hope to be able to adapt to the nuances of your religion and serve both congregations. Nothing I will ever say or do during your services will be an intentional affront. But, until I refresh myself on the Methodist doctrines, I could inadvertently misstate a significant point in your religion. Please tell me if I do and I'll correct it. If we work together, I think we can have a comfortable worship service."

The families nodded and seemed satisfied.

Father Romero and his new assistant, Father Herman, arrived as the Methodists were leaving. Joe slipped out of Reverend Anderson's robe and stole, and helped them carry their statuary upstairs. Since the walls hadn't been removed yet, they were going to be crowded. Father Romero waved off Joe's concerns and said they'd manage. When Father Herman went back downstairs, Father Romero asked Joe about the paint on the church and the armed attempt last night.

Joe gave him a surprised look.

Father Romero laughed and said, "Thanks to you, I'm involved in this town again. So I hear a lot more news."

Joe confirmed the events and asked Father Romero to recognize Miguel, Eddie, Archibaldo and Jorge for their help. He agreed and Joe left, so the parishioners could be seated.

Downstairs, he heard Dominique continue playing. He started to tell her she didn't need to play for this service, then he stopped and listened. She'd switched to appropriate music for the Catholic service. Smiling at her, he walked into his office to wait for the next group. *Of course, she knows the Catholic music,* he thought. *It's her church music.*

He selected some verses for the kids to memorize next week. Petey and Lily were doing the recitations this week.

He heard a noise in the sanctuary while he was preparing the communion trays. Looking around the corner, he saw two lizards running across the floor to freedom.

Petey's here, he thought. *And judging from the lizards, I guess I'm back in his good graces.*

Petey crawled out from under one of the pews, obviously trying to catch his lost reptiles. He was shocked to see Joe already in the church.

"Surprise, Petey," Joe said. "I caught you this time you little scoundrel." He laughed when Petey ran for the door.

Father Herman stuck his head around the stairs and shushed Joe. Joe apologetically hushed his antics with Petey.

Have to remember to be quiet, he admonished himself.

He glanced at Dominique. She was trying to stifle her own giggles. Tiptoeing out the door, Joe joined Gene's family waiting outside.

When the Catholic families filed out, Angie broke away from Elena, shouted, "Preaker man," and flew into Joe's arms. Elena and Miguel were mortified.

Joe just laughed and put her on his shoulder. The rest of the kids ran over to join her.

When Father Romero and Father Herman stepped out of the church, they stopped to watch. Father Romero smiled at the scene. Then he noticed Father Herman's frown. Turning sternly to his new assistant, he said, "You are witnessing one of the most unselfish displays of love that you'll ever experience. If you can't see the purity in this scene, you will leave my church before sundown."

Shocked, Father Herman turned and said, "But he's...he's a *Baptist*! How can you sanction this?"

"Because, as he told all of us when he arrived in town, we're all Christians," Father Romero said firmly. "Look at him. He loves those children deeply and they love him. Instead of criticizing him, we should strive to be more like him. I'd love to be able to instill that kind of pure love in people."

Unknown to Father Romero, Joe heard his comments. *Something to work on,* he thought.

He walked over to the two Fathers and asked if he could bring the teachers out to the church tomorrow to select the furniture for the Kindergarten. Father Herman started to protest.

Father Romero silenced him with a stern look and said, "Tomorrow will be fine Reverend Marsh. Would one o'clock work with your schedule?"

"That would be great," Joe said, "and thank you again."

He turned to greet the Scott family walking up.

"Still don't know which church you serve, do you Preacher Man?" Roger Scott said, with a big grin on his face.

Then he stepped past Joe, extended his hand to Father Romero and said, "I'm Roger Scott. I own the Scott Ranch down from your church. It's a shame we've let our religions keep us strangers all these years. It took Reverend Marsh to show me how foolish I've been. I hope we can be more neighborly in the future."

Father Romero accepted his handshake and the offer.

"I'd like that very much," he said. "I know we share several of our farm workers. They speak highly of your ranch and your kindness to them."

"I'm glad to hear they feel that way," Roger said. "The Santiago and Gallegos families are wonderful people. We've practically raised our kids together."

Father Herman was bewildered as he watched them.

Joe wandered over to him and said, "Don't worry, Father, human fellowship with other religions doesn't weaken our beliefs. It strengthens them." Father Herman just nodded.

Joe walked back inside for his second service. He noticed the baptismal bowl, candles and Reverend Andersons' robe and stole had been moved to his office. Looking at Dominique, he mouthed a thank you. She smiled and nodded.

This service was a little easier because he knew the people and he had his dad's sermons backing him up. Petey and Lily were great. And Sarah and Dale wanted more verses for next week. Dominique seemed to pick up the tempo of his mood and her playing affected the congregation. He allowed a few minutes after his sermon for them to discuss the combined services in their church. The only comments he received were positive ones. After communion and the offering, they closed with a hymn and prayer.

Standing outside with his members, he answered questions about the attacks on the church and parsonage.

When Dominique walked out, several people spoke to her. He asked Grandma to thank her and tell her that he really enjoyed her playing.

Then he asked Grandma if she and the Wilsons could go to the Catholic Church to select the furniture tomorrow at twelve-thirty. Grandma was delighted. She said they'd be ready. She invited him up to the house for Sunday dinner and fresh apple pie.

He locked the church, checked his parsonage door again and skipped back over to her like a little kid. They laughed and joked all the way up the street. When they walked past her house, she showed him her *Sherie Anderson* flowerbed. Chris had helped her transplant the flowers while he was in Portales.

"They're beautiful," Joe said. "Mrs. Anderson will be pleased to know you have them. Why don't you take a picture of the garden and send it to her, I know she'd love to see it."

"I'll do that," Grandma said. "Ralph's going to give me her address."

The relaxed family atmosphere at the dinner table gave Joe a break from his stress, but Chris was a nervous wreck. School was starting Wednesday and he still hadn't heard about the scholarship.

"Give it time," Joe said. "We know you're the best choice. They'll figure it out."

"Ohhhhh pleeeeese," Katherine moaned. "Don't tell him that, he's hard enough to live with now!"

"When you become a Poet Laureate, he'll have to pay homage to you," Joe said.

233

"Oh all right," she said, faking resignation. "I guess I can suffer a little longer."

"Our drama queen," Chris said, mimicking her.

When the threats and retaliatory challenges escalated, Ben sent them into the living room to settle their dispute.

He refilled their coffee and asked Joe for more details about last night's attack.

"I don't like this armed break-in stuff at all," Ben said. "I'm worried about your safety over there. The area around the church is more isolated now that the Andersons have left. Dave and Susan are your closest neighbors. Of course, that's probably convenient, since you're giving them so much business."

Joe laughed and agreed. "I've made some people mad," he said. "They want me out of town. They aren't going to give up easily. We just have to stay ahead of them." Ben nodded.

"By the way," Joe said, "what do you know about Judge Steve Orson?" Ben's grimace told him he agreed with Dave.

"I've put four Cozen men in jail this week," Joe said. "Dave thinks the Judge will just let them go with time served. I don't know what he'll do with Tobias and Sampson, but I don't like the idea of any of them just getting a one week jail term."

"We've complained about him before," Ben said. "But he has connections somewhere. We can't get him removed from our jurisdiction – even with his relationship to Chad."

Joe walked home thinking about the Judge and his effect on justice in this town. He'd get Jack to work on that. When he unlocked his door, a folded piece of paper fell out of the jamb. He hadn't seen it when he walked up. Someone had worked to conceal it.

Opening it he read, MAKANAK BENG FOLOED.

Inside, Joe laid it on the table and started a pot of coffee. Reading it as written, it didn't make any sense, but if someone wrote it phonetically, it said, mechanic being followed. Apparently, someone was trying to warn him. Who and why would have to wait. He needed to tell Jack. If Tommy was being followed, he may have led someone to them.

Pulling out his laptop, he sent Jack an URGENT e-mail. FOUND THE FOLLOWING NOTE IN MY DOOR: "MAKANAK BENG FOLOED." TOMMY MAY HAVE BEEN TAILED TO OUR MEETING ON

FRIDAY. HAVE TOMMY CHECK HIS TRUCK FOR A TRACER. IF NONE FOUND, HAVE HIM DRIVE SOMEWHERE AND SEE IF HE HAS A TAIL. CHECK OUT OF YOUR HOTEL AND GET ANOTHER CAR, IN CASE THEY'RE FOLLOWING YOUR CAR, TOO. WAS THAT YOUR CAR YOU DROVE OUT HERE? IF TOMMY FINDS A TRACER, HE CAN DRIVE HIS TRUCK OUT OF TOWN AND HOP A RIDE BACK WITH YOU. IF THE THREE OF US HAVE BEEN TAILED, MISSION MAY HAVE BEEN COMPROMISED. LET ME KNOW ASAP.

Joe's phone rang as he was finishing the message. Chris and the kids wanted a game of hoops. He looked at the mess in his house and decided it could wait. He changed, jogged over to the lot and played until dark.

Finally back home, he started cleaning up the mess Hernando and Felipe made. He locked his tapes and extra camera in the tool box and decided to move it into the cabinet under the bathroom sink. *They didn't have time to find this stuff last night*, he thought. *But they might next time.*

"Better get used to this," he told himself, as he picked up a broken cup. "They're going to be twice as mad after Tuesday."

He threw some clothes in the washer, fixed a microwave dinner and wondered what they had planned for him tonight.

He checked his e-mail. Jack had responded: TOMMY FOUND TRACER ON TRUCK. NO APPARENT TAIL. NO TRACER ON MINE. I BORROWED A CAR SATURDAY. THANKS FOR THE HEADS UP. WONDER WHO SENT THE NOTE AND WHAT THEY KNOW.

Joe answered: THANKS FOR THE INFO. I WONDER THE SAME THING. BUT I'M GRATEFUL FOR IT – SINCE IT PROVED ACCURATE. ARE WE STILL ON?

Jack was apparently still working on his laptop, because he sent an answer right back. YES. WHOEVER SENT IT SEEMS TO BE ON OUR SIDE.

Joe tossed the clothes in the dryer and took a short nap. When he woke, he changed into his black clothes, grabbed a stack of replacement tapes and slipped his own revolver and pistol under his clothes. He unloaded his new revolver and left it in his night stand. He hadn't had a chance to fire it yet, so he didn't trust it the way he did his old one.

He locked his door and circled the church first, to be sure he didn't have any more visitors. Then he worked his way around town, collecting and changing the tapes as he went. He was even able to change the one under Max's steps, which he was sure had run out. The bar was quiet so he sat down in the weeds to change that tape.

Hearing a click, he drew his pistol and flattened on the camera in a single move. He watched the bar's side door open and heard at least two men talking. He eased the camera out from under him and started taping. Once the men seemed satisfied that the street was clear, they stepped outside.

There were three of them. The last one was holding the door open, apparently to keep it from locking behind them.

Clive slapped one of the men on the back and asked, "Does that take care of everything you need for Tuesday?"

"Yep," the man said. "That's a tidy little bonus you gave me. I wondered what was going on when the Constable called to schedule more time this week."

Clive swore and said, "He keeps thinking you're going to actually hear the cases."

That has to be Judge Orson, Joe thought, as he listened and prayed he was getting this on tape.

"So why haven't you been able to get rid of that pesky preacher?" Orson asked. "Chad's having a fit and Homer's threatening to come take the town by force."

"I don't know," the third man said. "He's either very lucky or our men are clumsy. I lost Tobias and Sampson when he caught them trying to poison him and the Priest. Then he caught four of Chad's men. Those are the six you have to release Tuesday."

"Well, Pete, you better think of something soon," Orson said. "I don't know how much longer I can get by with this charade. It's amazing how easy it was to fool these country bumpkins around here. They bought the credentials Pauline made for me and I have to admit I like the salary they insist on paying me – to let your guys out of jail. But I can't afford to get assigned to a complicated case. A good lawyer will get suspicious the first time he expects me to understand his brief."

Pete nodded and said, "We're working on the preacher. We'll get him soon."

"You'd better," Orson said. "I need to get off the bench soon. The town has already sent Evermundy a couple of complaints about me."

"Tell me who did that and we'll make sure they keep quiet," Pete said.

"I'll get their names when I go back to my office," Orson said. "But it was a while ago and he didn't believe them. If you do something now, it'll just put me under suspicion again. As long as I keep his daughter happy in bed, she'll tell him how wonderful I am. She's starting to plan a wedding, can you believe that?" The men laughed as Orson walked to his car.

Joe took a picture of the car and the tag.

Orson waved and said, "Bye guys, thanks for the bonus."

After he left, the other two stood on the street talking.

"What are we going to do about the preacher, Pete?" Clive asked. "With Sampson in jail, my supply of H and weed are running low. Chad can't be seen running the stuff and he doesn't know who to trust right now. Bart just carried Sampson a box from the Catholic Charities. He had no idea what was in it – or that my bar was the charity. Of course, with Tobias in jail with Sampson, the Church demand is down right now."

"It sounds like he needs to have a bad accident," Pete said. "Do you know how to cut a brake line on a car?"

"Me!" Clive said. "Oh no, I'm not going to get involved in murder. Find someone else for that job."

"Okay," Pete said. "It's a ten grand job. I thought you'd want it. I can get someone else to do it."

"Ten grand?" Clive asked. "Are you really going to pay that much to get rid of him?"

"Yep," Pete said, grinning at him. "Want it?"

"Yeah, I'll take it," Clive said.

"Good, go do it tonight while everyone's asleep," Pete said. "The new Father at the Catholic Church told me Marsh is going to take the town teachers out there to get some furniture for their *Kindergarten* tomorrow. If we're lucky, we can get rid of all four people – and the school at the same time."

"Why would the new Father talk to you?" Clive asked.

"Because I sent him out there," Pete said. "I intercept all the mail Romero sends to the church."

"Where will you be tomorrow?" Clive asked.

"Out at the Samuels farm, their well water is about to go bad," Pete said, laughing as he got in his car and drove away.

237

Joe taped his car and license. He kept taping until Clive closed the door and turned out the light.

He went home, put the tape in the player and reviewed it to be sure he got the whole conversation. While he listened, he loaded his new revolver and put a new tape in the camera.

Then he slipped into a pair of jeans, locked his door, positioned the camera beside his step and sat on the side of his house to wait for Clive.

It didn't take long before he saw him inching his way around the Methodist parsonage. He was apparently debating which way to cross the dry grassy area. He finally decided to skirt around the edge of the parsonage. He crossed within five feet of Joe and didn't see him.

Joe waited until Clive was halfway under his van and reaching into his hip pocket for his cutters, before he let his new revolver make the distinctive cocking noise that every crook knows too well. Clive froze with his hand still on his pocket.

"Touch one thing on my van and I'll blow off your kneecaps and work up from there," Joe said, in a cold, lethal voice. He was thinking about the three teachers Clive was willing to kill along with him, when Clive tried to pull the cutters out. Joe fired a round so close to the intersection of Clive's legs that he wet himself.

"Move again and my shot goes an inch higher," Joe said.

No need to go inside to call Dave, he thought, as he saw three houses light up. *Someone has already called him – or he heard the shot from the jail.*

Dave ran to his patrol car and hit the siren – on an empty street in the middle of the night. He skidded to a stop at Joe's house with the headlights at full tilt, spotlight on and gun drawn.

"Joe, are you all right?" he shouted.

"Yeah, Dave," he said. "I've got another skunk for you. He's under my van."

"Under your van?" Dave asked.

"Yep," Joe said. "I caught him trying to cut my brake line. Since several people heard me offer to take the teachers to the Catholic Church to get the Kindergarten furniture tomorrow, we need to book this one on four counts of attempted murder."

"You can't prove that," Clive said, as Dave pulled him out from under the van. Dave cuffed him and confiscated the cutters and two knives.

Joe swung around with the revolver still in his hand.

"I'm not in any mood for your games tonight, Clive," he said. "You and I both know you intended to cut my brake line and kill me and three teachers tomorrow. Now, tell the Constable who paid you to do this, before I really get angry."

Joe spoke with such intensity, Dave was afraid he was going to have to take him into custody until he cooled off.

Joe caught the look on Dave's face, took a deep breath and lowered the gun. He heard Dave exhale beside him.

"You're facing four counts of attempted murder," Joe told Clive. "How many years will he get Constable?"

"Probably about thirty," Dave said.

"Are you going to spend thirty years of your life in jail and let your partner go free?" Joe asked.

He could see Clive thinking about it.

"Take this snake to jail, Constable. I'll tell people he named his partner," Joe said, as he turned back to his house.

"Wait," Clive said. "If you do that, I'll be dead by morning."

"Yep," Joe said, with a wicked grin. "That's about the same time you expected three elderly teachers to die with me." He walked on up to his door.

"Wait," Clive said. "I'll tell you, but you have to protect me from him."

"Who paid you, Clive?" Joe roared back at him.

"P...P...Peter Philman," Clive stuttered.

"I didn't hear you," Joe said. "Say it louder!"

"Peter Philman," Clive shouted.

"How much was he going to pay you?" Joe asked.

"Ten thousand dollars," Clive said.

"So each of our lives was only worth $2,500? Is that what you're telling me?" Joe asked, walking back to face Clive.

"I didn't think of it that way," Clive said.

"Spoken like a true killer," Joe sneered in disgust. "Where can the Constable find Peter Philman?"

"He's going to the Samuels farm tomorrow," Clive said.

"What's he doing out there?" Dave asked.

"He's going to check their well," Clive said.

"Take him to jail," Joe said. "He's lying. We'll let Philman take care of him."

"Wait," Clive said.

"Nope," Joe said. "I'm through with you. Save your lies for Philman." Dave pulled Clive over to the patrol car.

"He's going to salt their well the same way he salted the Thatcher and Archer wells," Clive blurted out.

"What!" Dave said, in disbelief. "He salted the Thatcher and Archer wells?"

"Yeah," Joe said. "It's a long story, Constable."

"Where can we find Philman tonight?" Joe asked Clive.

"I don't know," Clive said.

"Wrong answer," Joe said, waving to Dave.

"He stays in the Archer farm house," Clive said, as Dave opened the car door.

"Who else is with him?" Joe asked.

"No one," Clive said. Joe shook his head at Dave.

"That's the truth," Clive said. "Honest. He swore one day he'd live in that house. And now that he has it, he won't let anyone else inside."

"Where are the other Cozen men?" Joe asked.

"Home with their families until tomorrow," Clive said.

"Constable, do you have another cell in your jail for this murderer?" Joe asked.

"I sure do," Dave said.

"Good," Joe said, pulling his revolver. "We'll meet you there. I'll walk him over, so he doesn't *soil* your car."

He walked Clive up the street with his revolver pointed at his back. He hoped everyone with windows saw this low down scum. When Dave pulled up, he relinquished the prisoner.

Once Clive was securely locked behind bars, he signaled Dave to step outside.

"Are you up to a ride to the Archer's farm tonight?" Joe asked. "I'd like to get Philman before he knows we have Clive."

"I agree," Dave said. "I was going to ask if you wanted to go with me. Obviously, you do. Let me get Susan over here and I'll pick you up in ten minutes."

"We've put seven men in your jail this week," Joe said. "I'm worried about Susan staying alone with them while we're

240

gone. Let's call Ben to stay with her until we get back. I'm sure he'll do it for us."

"You're right," Dave said. "She's good, but I'd feel better having Ben here, too."

"I'll call him from my house. Come get me when he joins her," Joe said. "And you'd better make me a deputy for an hour or so – just in case." Dave nodded cautiously.

"I'm qualified," Joe said. "I was member of the Boston Police Department before I went into the ministry."

Dave's face went from shock to a narrow eyed stare.

"I'll explain later," Joe said. "Let's get Philman behind bars first." Dave shook his head and agreed.

Joe went home and called Ben.

"We caught another thug tonight," he said. "And we have one more we need to pick up. Can you stay with Susan at the jail until Dave and I get back? I'm not comfortable leaving her alone with seven prisoners."

"Certainly," Ben said. "I'll be there in ten."

"Bring your shotgun and some extra shells," Joe said. "That should convince them to behave while we're gone."

CHAPTER THIRTY

MONDAY – FIFTH WEEK

Joe slipped his pistol in the back of his waistband and his revolver in his ankle holster. He reloaded the one empty chamber in his new revolver and tucked it into his belt. Then he locked his door and waited for Dave.

When he rolled up, he swore Joe in and handed him a badge. Joe hopped in and they headed out to the Archer Farm.

"I have a lot of questions that I think you can answer," Dave said. "But I want to stay focused on Philman. What do you expect out here?"

"I expect an extremely ruthless man who wouldn't hesitate to kill either or both of us," Joe said honestly. "Since his kind are always cowards, I'm not counting on him being alone. I'd suggest going in dark, stopping about half a mile away and walking in."

Following what Joe said, Dave parked his patrol car, checked his revolver, pulled his rifle out of the trunk, stuffed some extra ammunition in his pocket and threw a set of cuffs over to Joe. "You might need a set of these, yourself," he whispered. Joe nodded.

Carefully, the two of them worked their way up to the house. When they didn't find any guards, Joe suggested that Dave get in the bushes near the front door and let him roust Philman. Dave argued but Joe insisted.

"He doesn't know me," he whispered. "I might be able to bait him out." Dave reluctantly agreed and took his position in the bushes.

Joe walked up to the front door and banged on it.

He pounded incessantly until he heard a man's voice cursing as it came nearer. When the door opened, a sleepy eyed man peered out at him.

"Peter Philman?" he asked.

"Yes, what..." Philman said.

"You're under arrest," Joe said.

"Like hell..." Philman said, trying to close the door.

Joe pushed back and punched him so hard his head snapped. Taking full advantage of that first punch, Joe grabbed him by his pajama top and tossed him into the yard.

Dave cuffed him while Joe went inside.

Turning on the lights, Joe looked at the opulence and wanted to hit the greedy monster again.

These things will go back to their rightful owners, he promised himself. Once he was certain no one else was in there, he went out and let Dave check the house.

When Philman woke up, he was sitting in a jail cell in his pajamas. "What the hell..." he started to say.

He stopped when he saw the fury in Joe's eyes.

"Come on, Philman, give me a reason to shut you up," Joe said, glaring at him.

"What did I do?" Philman whined – just the way Joe knew he would.

"You offered a man ten thousand dollars to kill me and three elderly teachers in this town," Joe snarled.

Dave forgot about Ben when he walked up with Joe.

"He did what?" Ben bellowed. "He paid someone to kill my mother? Go outside, Dave. Give me five minutes with this man and you can flush what's left of him down the toilet."

It took both Joe and Dave to pull him away from Philman. Joe took him outside and told him what had happened.

Ben exploded again. "If I'd known that was why Clive was in there," he said, "I would've killed him."

"Neither one of them is worth going to jail for," Joe said. "Everyone's okay, so let the law handle this."

"The law," Ben sneered. "If it's Steve Orson's court, it won't be the law."

"They've been arrested on four counts of attempted murder, Ben," Joe said. "Orson won't be able to let them walk." He finally convinced Ben to cool down and let Dave handle it.

He went home and sent another e-mail to Jack. URGENT – MUST HAVE JUDGE EVERMUNDY IN MY HOUSE NO LATER THAN 8 AM TUESDAY. WE ARRESTED PHILMAN AND CLIVE OSBORN (BAR OWNER) ON FOUR COUNTS OF ATTEMPTED MURDER. HAVE PROOF STEPHEN ORSON IS TAKING BRIBES – HE MAY NOT BE QUALIFIED TO BE A JUDGE. HAVE TO HAVE EVERMUNDY HERE TO REMOVE ORSON FROM THE BENCH BEFORE HE RULES ON ANY CASES IN TOWN. DON'T DISCUSS THIS WITH THE JUDGE – OR HE'LL REFUSE TO COME – BECAUSE HE BELIEVES ORSON IS OKAY. DO WHATEVER YOU NEED TO DO TO GET HIM HERE. DON'T LET HIM MAKE ANY CALLS – MAKE HIM COME HERE TOP SECRET

He locked the bar tape in his tool box and watched the other surveillance tapes. The Saturday night tape from the bar showed some drug sales and more apparent prostitution, but that was mild compared to the last one he collected. The tape under Max's stairs contained conversations similar to the earlier ones between him and the truck drivers. He turned off the lights and tried to get a few hours of sleep.

He rolled out of bed at six-thirty and forced himself into his jogging clothes. He started a pot of coffee, grabbed his revolver and locked up his other handguns before he headed out.

As he ran, he thought about the last month in this town. A lot had happened and there was a lot more to come. He waved at Charley and spoke to the Hispanic men as they left for work.

Swinging behind the closed stores, he found more water filters. There was one on the second grocery, the theater and the appliance store.

He jogged over to see Grandma and found her heading into the house. "Good morning, Grandma," he said.

She brightened when she heard his voice.

"Good morning, Joe," she said. "I was about to give up on you. I heard you had another bad night at the parsonage."

He prayed she didn't know the details.

"Yes ma'am," he said. "I'll wear them out eventually."

Then to change the subject, he asked, "Are you ready to go get the furniture for the Kindergarten?"

"Oh yes," she said. "We'll be ready at twelve-thirty."

"I'll be here to pick you up," he said. Looking around, he asked, "Is Ben still at home or at the store?"

"I think I saw him go over to the store," she said.

"Thanks," Joe said. "I need to ask him a question. See you at twelve-thirty."

He caught Ben opening the door on the dock.

"Can you go with us to the Catholic Church today?" he asked. "Father Romero has two more insiders I need to tell him about – and hopefully turn over to Dave. I'd rather have the teachers ride with you, until I'm certain my van is still okay."

"I'll arrange to go with them," Ben said. "I'll feel better being out there with Ma, after last night."

Joe agreed and jogged home. He sat down with his coffee and a bowl of cereal while he checked his e-mail.

Jack had replied. WILL DO WHAT IT TAKES TO GET HIM THERE. WILL I NEED TO STAY OR JUST DELIVER? MY TIME ON TUESDAY WILL BE TIGHT. LET ME KNOW.

Joe answered, JUST DELIVER – AND THANKS.

He thought about the trip to the Catholic Church. He hoped Father Romero would trust his word, because he couldn't risk carrying the tape around with him. There were at least two people he needed to get out of there – the new Father Herman and whoever handled the mail for the church. He wondered if he should call first, but decided not to, in case Herman was nearby.

He showered, and dressed for the trip. Then he added his revolver and pistol. When he checked his pockets, he found the badge and extra set of handcuffs Dave gave him last night. He decided to keep them an extra day. He locked his door and headed for his van. He was shocked when he checked his watch and realized he was two hours early.

For some reason, he felt he needed to go on out to the church. So he decided to go handle the problems before Ben took the teachers out. Arriving unexpected might give him an advantage with Father Romero and Herman.

He drove over to the store and told Ben about the strong feeling he had. "I'm going to go on out to the church now," he said. "If things are okay out there, I'll call you at twelve-thirty and you can bring the teachers out. If I don't call at twelve-thirty ask Dave to go check on things." Ben agreed and Joe drove off.

He parked the van and walked up to a priest who'd just stepped outside. "I'm Joseph Marsh," he said. "I need to speak with Father Romero."

"I'm sorry," the priest said. "Father Romero is in a meeting right now."

"Is Father Herman available?" Joe asked.

The priest shook his head and said, "No, he's in the same meeting."

"May I ask your name?" Joe asked.

"I'm Father Gordon," he said. "I'm sorry, I should've introduced myself."

Joe nodded and said, "I've heard Father Romero speak of you often. He thinks you have great potential with the church. Are you the priest who performed the services when he was in town last week?" Blushing, Father Gordon nodded.

"How did you do?" Joe asked.

"Fairly well," Father Gordon said.

"It's intimidating, isn't it?" Joe asked. "The first time I held a service, I stuttered over every word. And my legs shook so hard, I thought I was going to fall."

"Exactly," Father Gordon said. "I know every word of that Mass, but I was so nervous, I couldn't remember parts of it."

"Well, the worst is over," Joe said. "The first one is the hardest one."

Father Gordon smiled and said, "I hope you're right."

Looking at his watch, Joe said, "I really need to talk to Father Romero. Do you think we could interrupt their meeting for a minute?"

"Father Herman said not to disturb them," Father Gordon said. "But I'm sure Father Romero won't mind a short interruption."

"If I may," Joe said, "I'll walk in with you. That way Father Romero will only have to step out of the room for a minute, instead of having to come out here."

"That's fine," Father Gordon said.

Joe followed him to Father Romero's quarters.

"Are they having a meeting in his quarters?" Joe asked.

"It does seem peculiar, doesn't it," Father Gordon said, as he knocked on the door.

Father Herman answered it and held the door tightly cracked. When he saw Joe, he was surprised and angry.

"What are you doing here?" he asked. To Father Gordon he demanded, "Why did you bring him up here? He's a *Baptist*! He doesn't belong here."

While Father Gordon was reeling from the criticism, Joe kicked the door open and grabbed Father Herman's arm. Looking across the room he saw Father Romero tied and gagged in a chair. He checked for other occupants.

When he didn't find any, he said, "Father Gordon, untie Father Romero quickly."

As soon as the gag was removed, Father Romero said, "Thank God you came when you did. He was going to haul me out in a laundry cart and kill me."

Joe was still holding Father Herman. He'd been trying to wiggle loose. Joe slugged him – hard. When he sank to the floor, Joe pulled the priest robes off of him.

Father Gordon was shocked.

"He isn't a priest," Joe said. "He's another imposter sent here to harm Father Romero. I came to warn the Father, but I was almost too late. We both have you to thank for trusting me enough to bring me up here."

Father Romero agreed and thanked Father Gordon, too.

"Who was going to bring the laundry cart?" Joe asked.

"Juanita," Father Romero said. "But I'm not sure she knew about his plan."

Turning to Father Gordon, Joe asked, "Can you go outside and tap lightly when she arrives, please?"

Father Gordon nodded and stepped into the hall.

Joe tied Herman up with his rope sash and went over to check on Father Romero.

"Are you all right?" he asked. "Did he hurt you, or make you swallow anything?"

"No, Joe, I'm all right," Father Romero said. "Father Herman…"

"Don't call him that," Joe said. "He's not a priest. That's what I came to tell you. We've arrested the man who hired both Tobias and Herman to pose as priests. He's been able to do that because he has another person who's sending him all your correspondence with the church. I need to know who handles your mail."

"I do," a voice behind him said.

Joe and Father Romero turned in unison. They saw the priest and the gun.

"Father William....you're the one?" Father Romero asked, visibly shocked.

"Yes," Father William said. "Now you can untie Father Herman and both of you can leave in the laundry cart."

"Where is Father Gordon?" Joe asked.

"Napping in a closet," Father William said. "I'll take care of him later."

"But I don't understand," Father Romero said. "You're not an imposter. You've served this church faithfully for years. Why would you do this?"

Joe looked at Father William and said, "For your next fix, right Father William?"

Shocked, Father Romero asked, "Is that true Father William, are you on drugs?"

Father William didn't answer. He just kept his gun pointed at Father Romero.

"Yeah, he's a user, Father Romero," Joe said, as he moved over and pretended to untie Herman. "We locked up Tobias and Sampson so he's hurting for a fix. What are you on Father William, heroin? How much did they offer you to kill the leader of your church? What price did you put on the life of your friend and mentor? Judas got thirty pieces of silver."

Father William didn't answer.

"What did you sell your soul for," Joe sneered, "a fix?"

Infuriated by Joe's taunting, Father William swung his body toward Joe. When his gun moved off Father Romero, Joe took his shot. Father William sagged to the floor holding his shoulder. Grabbing Father William's gun, Joe hauled him over to the chair Father Romero just vacated.

"Watch Herman, Father," Joe said, "while I get this one ready for the Constable." He looked at William's shoulder and was relieved it was only grazed. He'd tried not to make it a fatal shot. Father Romero handed him a towel to pad the wound.

Once he had both men secured, Joe looked for Father Gordon. He found him in a closet down the hall. He'd been knocked out. Joe pulled him into the room and watched him until he woke up. Then he called Dave.

Dave answered, "Where and how many?"

"Catholic Church – two," Joe said. "One has a shoulder wound. It's only a graze, but Doc may want to send him to Portales. Can you let him know, in case he wants to get an ambulance rolling?"

"I'll bring him with me," Dave said, hanging up.

Dave just shook his head at Joe when he arrived. Doc bandaged Father William's wound while Dave photographed the crime scene. Joe helped get the prisoners in the patrol car.

"I'll book them on two counts of attempted murder," Dave said. "I'll need both of you in court tomorrow to testify."

They agreed.

"Watch them for withdrawals," Joe said. "Father William is definitely hooked." Dave nodded and drove off.

Joe looked at his watch. It was twelve noon.

Turning to Father Romero, he asked, "Are you up to a visit from the teachers this afternoon? Or do you want me to postpone their trip?"

"No," Father Romero said, "I don't want to postpone it. Let them come out. I'll get some of my workers to bring a truck around and help load the things they need."

"Okay, if you're sure," Joe said, "I'll call Ben and tell him its okay."

Puzzled, Father Romero asked, "You have Ben waiting for a call?"

"Yes," Joe said. "I found out about the imposter late last night and woke up with a strange feeling about your safety this morning. That's why I came out early."

"Thank God you did," Father Romero said. "Herman said I'd be dead by noon."

Joe winced. If he'd stayed on schedule, he would've still been in town at noon. Shaking off the implications of that thought, he said, "I told Ben about my feeling and asked him to wait for my call before bringing the teachers out."

"I didn't know Ben was bringing them," Father Romero said. "I thought you were."

Obviously, Father Romero hadn't heard about Clive.

"Let me call Ben," Joe said. "Then let's find a sandwich and a cup of coffee. I need to tell you about my adventures last night." Father Romero rolled his eyes and led him to the kitchen.

They met Ben and the teachers when they drove up. Grandma and the Wilsons had their lists of hopeful items and were anxious to see what they could find.

Father Gordon joined them as they entered the church.

Knowing this was probably the first time the members of his congregation had been inside a Catholic Church, Joe asked Father Gordon to provide a brief explanation of the rituals and symbols in the sanctuary. Surprised, Father Gordon looked to Father Romero. When he received a nod of approval, he began.

Within minutes, the teachers were engrossed in the symbolism and the beauty of the things they saw.

While they talked to Father Gordon, Father Romero moved behind Joe and said, "Looks like some fresh converts to me." Joe laughed out loud.

When the teachers saw all the furniture in the back of the church, they were in teacher heaven. They walked down aisles of stacked desks, looked at blackboards, teacher's desks, school supplies on the shelves and rows of books.

Watching the teachers *shop*, Joe walked behind Father Romero and said, "I think they've found just about everything they need to open a *Baptist School* back here."

Father Romero's mouth flew open before he saw the gleam in Joe's eyes. It was his turn to laugh out loud.

Ben wandered over to Joe and said, "I assume those men in Dave's car were from your visit this morning."

"Yes," Father Romero said. "My new imposter priest, Father Herman, had me ready for a one-way trip on a lonely road. Joe changed my travel plans."

"I'm glad you're okay, Father," Ben said.

To Joe, Ben said, "I don't know about those feelings you get, but I'm grateful for them."

"Yeah," Joe said. "So am I."

While the men were loading the furniture on the truck, Joe turned to Father Romero and asked, "Why don't you come to town with us and enjoy the excitement of the new Kindergarten?"

When Father Romero started to decline, Joe grinned and said, "Otherwise, you won't get a chance to remove all the *Baptist* stuff I've planted in there."

Father Romero chuckled and agreed to go with them.

"Are you planning to officiate in town?" Joe asked.

"No," Father Romero said, puzzled at the question.

"Then why don't you shed the *official* you and let your parish see the man behind the office," Joe said. "You do have some street clothes, don't you?"

Looking at his robe, Father Romero was obviously considering what Joe said.

Apparently, he liked the idea, because he looked up and said, "Of course, I do. Are bell bottoms still in style?"

The look on Joe's face gave him his second laugh for the day as he walked away to change. When he returned, Joe was amazed at the difference and said so.

"Do you have five dollars in your pocket?" Joe asked.

"Yes," Father Romero said cautiously. "Why?"

"Because," Joe said, "I'm going to bet you five dollars that your own parish won't recognize you in street clothes."

"We can't bet," Father Romero said.

"Sure we can," Joe said, grinning at him. "When I win your money, it'll go in our collection plate."

Father Romero gave him a skeptical look.

"If you manage to hedge your bet and win," Joe teased, "my money will go in your collection plate. Either way, we're just helping our churches."

"We'll see," Father Romero said, shaking his head at Joe's twisted justification.

In town, the truck barely rolled to a stop before a crowd gathered. All the kids and most of their parents were waiting to see the furniture for the Kindergarten.

Joe heard the familiar "Preaker Man" just in time to catch Angie in flight. She scrambled up to his shoulder and had the best seat in town.

He scanned the crowd and realized Petey was missing. He went through the back door to the drug store and called Gene to bring his Cowboy over to see the furniture. He met Petey at the door and walked him through to the Kindergarten.

Petey looked at Angie and asked, "How'd she do that?"

"I don't know," Joe said. "You'll have to ask her after you teach her English."

Most of the furniture had already been unloaded by the time Joe, Angie and Petey walked back in the room. Obviously, the men had a lot of help. While the teachers were showing them where to mount the blackboard, the kids were standing in a corner, looking at the strange man in a chair.

Joe grinned. He walked up to Father Romero and held out his hand. Faking disgust, Father Romero pulled five dollars out of his pocket and shook his head.

Then Joe whispered something to Angie. She shook her head. He whispered something else and she scrambled off of Joe's shoulder and threw herself into Father Romero's arms. The shock on his face was priceless – and so was the bliss.

Joe watched him relish the joy of a child's hug.

Once the other kids saw Angie, the rest of they crowded around for a hug. Pretty soon, Joe and Father Romero were on the floor playing with them.

Miracles do happen, Joe thought. The parents were still standing along the wall. They hadn't identified the stranger.

When one of the kids asked the man what his name was, the room fell silent.

"Papa Romo," Angie said.

The parent's were shocked and then embarrassed that they hadn't recognized him. Father Romero reassured them in Spanish and soon all of them were getting comfortable with the man behind the robe.

Joe was delighted. Father Romero was, too. Glancing around the room, he saw Dominique smiling at the transition in the group. Even the teachers had turned to watch.

Seizing the moment, Joe asked Father Romero to bless the new Kindergarten.

Without the normal formalities of his office, he looked at Joe for a long moment. Then he blessed the Kindergarten, the teachers, the children, Dominique for the idea, Ralph for the room and Ben and Joe for the ability to make it happen.

At the end, Joe added, "And Lord, bless Father Romero for his generosity."

As if on cue, Ralph and Doris came through the back door with two large boxes of ice cream cups for everyone.

"We have to have some ice cream so we can celebrate the first clean up," Doris said, as the kids lined up.

Before everyone left, Joe asked the teachers if they were ready to officially open the Kindergarten. When they said yes, Joe formally introduced the teachers and their helper, Petey. They agreed that the Kindergarten would open on Wednesday, the same day the *big* schools started.

When the crowd disbursed, the teachers walked home together – still talking about their plans for the kids.

Joe, Ben and Father Romero stood in the room and enjoyed the moment.

"What a day," Joe said. "Started rough but it ended great, right *Papa Romo?*" He chuckled and patted Father Romero on the back.

Father Romero looked back at Joe and Ben and said sincerely, "I never would have guessed the difference in my parish's response when I shed the formal robes. Thank you, Joe. I'm glad you pushed me into this trip to town and introduced me to my *real* parish. And thank you, Ben, for all the support you and your family have given us."

"You're welcome, Father," Ben said. "Thank you for your support and trust."

"I hate to bring us back to less pleasant subjects," Joe said. "But I need to know what time court starts tomorrow and where it's held."

"It starts at ten o'clock sharp," Ben said. "The Judge uses Dave's office. Since we have so many cases for him to hear tomorrow and so many witnesses, we may need to pull the fire truck out of the station and open up that section."

Joe thought about that and asked, "The doors in the back of the jail open into the Fire Station?"

"Right," Ben said. "Why don't we plan to meet outside Dave's office at nine forty-five? We'll let Dave tell us where he wants us to sit." Joe and Father Romero agreed.

Ben and Joe thanked the workers again and watched them help Father Romero into the truck.

"I'll bet that's the first time Father Romero has ever ridden with his workers," Joe said. "I could've had another five dollars if I'd thought about it."

"I think Father Romero had a lot of firsts today and you instigated most of them," Ben said. "Did you see his face when Angie hugged him?"

"Yes, it was beautiful," Joe said. Looking back at the Kindergarten, he said, "We did it, Ben."

"Yes we did," Ben said. "It's a small room. But it's a big beginning for the town."

Together they walked over to Dave's office to see if he needed some help with all the prisoners.

Dave looked up and asked, "Where and how many?"

"No place and none this time," Joe said. "We just came by to see if you needed some help over here."

"No," Dave said. "But I'm ready to put you two in a cell so I can get a good night's sleep again."

"Me!" Ben said. "What did I do? I'm sleeping in my clothes so I can save Joe every time he calls."

"Save me," Joe sputtered. "By the time you get out of your pajamas, Dave and I are mopping up."

The banter worked, Dave actually laughed. They could see the stress was getting to him. It would get to anyone. They were stressed, too.

I still need to talk to him tonight, Joe thought. *When I tell him the rest of the story, he probably will lock me up.*

"Ben," he said, "why don't we cover the jail and let Dave have some dinner?"

"Sounds good to me," Ben said. "Go ahead Dave, I'll watch Joe and make sure he doesn't sneak another goon or two into the cells." Dave looked at his watch and nodded.

"Thanks, guys," he said. "It would probably do me some good to get away from this place for a few minutes."

On the way to the door, he turned and handed Joe his revolver, in case he needed it.

"Thanks," Ben said. "What do I get?"

"The double barrel behind my desk," Dave said. "It's loaded so be careful. Don't blow a foot off before I get back."

Dave left laughing while Ben sputtered indignantly.

Ben picked up a law enforcement magazine and Joe sat down at Dave's desk. Through some unspoken agreement, neither of them talked while they were on duty. Joe looked around Dave's desk and felt sorry for the poor guy. Not only did he have to arrest and process all these men, he literally had to fill out mountains of paperwork on each one.

He's probably being extra careful, since he expects a fight with Judge Orson tomorrow, Joe thought.

When Dave came back he looked much better. Joe and Ben returned the firearms and stepped outside with Dave long enough to tell him they'd be there at nine forty-five for court.

Then they stepped back inside. Dave went over to his desk. Ben showed Joe the Fire Station side of the building. He knew Joe wanted to see that the building was secure.

Ben looked at Joe when they finished and said, "Unless you have a hot plate of pot roast, veggies, mashed potatoes and gravy at your house, why don't you come have dinner with us?"

Joe laughed and said, "No I don't remember seeing a plate like that in my fridge. Thanks, Ben, it sounds too tempting to refuse. Are you sure it's okay with Alice?"

"Sure," he said. "She told me not to come home without you, when I left."

"She's something else," Joe said. "You have a wonderful family. Thanks for sharing them with me."

"Some day you'll have your own," Ben said, "and you can share them with us."

"Sounds like a deal," Joe said, as they walked through Ben's door.

Caught totally off guard, Chris tackled Joe to the floor before he had a chance to react.

"What the…" Ben said.

"I got it, Preacher Man, I got it!" Chris shouted.

"Got what?" Ben demanded.

"The scholarship!" Chris said, hopping around the room.

"How do you know?" Ben asked. "The mail doesn't come until tomorrow."

"They called," he said. "I left a number off my soc. They needed it to enroll me."

"I got it!" he shouted again, as he bounced in place.

Alice stuck her head around the corner from the kitchen and said, "I don't know what dinner is going to taste like tonight. He's been dancing me around ever since he got the call."

"Yeah," Katherine said, grinning at them. "He's even being nice to me. So you know he's not normal."

Chris picked her up and swung her around the room. When he set her back down, she looked at her dad and Joe and said, "See what I mean!"

Dinner was wonderful and full of excitement for Chris and Grandma. Before he left, Joe asked Ben if he'd cover the jail for another hour so he could answer some questions for Dave. He agreed and they walked back down the street together.

"Tomorrow is going to be a tough day," Joe warned. "We've got a lot of people in jail, but we still have some on the loose. We're going to have to stay alert." Ben agreed.

Ben relieved Dave and Joe took him over to the parsonage. When he unlocked his door, another note fell on the ground. Joe picked it up and read, FILP BAK + 11 MO. He checked the other rooms to be sure he didn't have any unwanted guests. Then he waved Dave to the table and started a pot of coffee.

He sat down with Dave and said, "I need to tell you some things. But before I do, I need to swear you to secrecy."

Dave's face said, *O Lord, what now*, but he agreed.

Joe laid his badge on the table.

Dave's eyes went from the badge to Joe and back. Then his eyes narrowed as he started adding up all the *coincidences* that had happened lately.

"Before you put me in the same category with Tobias and Herman," Joe said, "let me assure you that I am a qualified preacher."

"That's obvious," Dave said. "You're a natural"

"Thanks," Joe said. "Now, I need you to understand that I've received special permission to break my top secret cover with you, and only you, because of the trust we share."

"Now it's my turn to say thanks," Dave said. "Your secret's safe with me."

"Okay, let me give you a brief summary of the situation," Joe said, as he poured some coffee and sat down. "Then we'll do questions." Dave nodded.

"I was sent here," Joe said, "because Eutopian Springs was named as a town involved in smuggling women into the country and forcing them into sex slavery." Dave's jaw dropped.

"That was my first reaction," Joe said. "But it's happening here. They come in on Bart's truck Monday night, get unloaded and held in the Peanut Silo until they're reloaded into Simms' truck on Tuesday night. I'm not sure Bart and Simms even know about the exchange, because it happens while they're showering in the hotel. Max gives them the key and clean towels, but he may not know about it either. We'll have to hold them until we sort this out. We're planning to move in on them tomorrow night, hopefully, without putting the women in any more danger than they're in now." Dave was stunned.

"When we planned this," Joe said, "I told my boss I knew the town Constable too well to believe he wouldn't see us or something suspicious during our raid. And I didn't want to be on the wrong end of your revolver. I've seen you in action."

At his puzzled look, Joe said, "I threw the beer cans and cracked some skulls with trash can lids." Dave shook his head.

"I couldn't break my cover," Joe said, "but I couldn't let them get away with their plans. I've been watching the town at night on foot." Dave just nodded and waited.

"Now," Joe said, as he took a sip of coffee. "The smuggling was the assignment that brought me here. The attacks on the preachers were not in my initial orders, but they are inter-related. I can't explain all the other details tonight, but Philman, Wellman and Cozen Oil are up to their necks in this. Philman did ruin the farm wells to get the land. Wellman and Reverend Phillips are one and the same. Wellman and Philman want to own this town. We're not going to let them, but we'll deal with that after tomorrow night."

Dave gave him a confused look, but let him continue.

"Back to the smuggling," Joe said, "the Cozen men are operating the activities in the peanut silo. They enter through the fake oil rig shed just north of the silo. Yes, it's fake. They don't have a pump in the shed. It just covers the storm drain they use to get into the silo. When they get inside, they hit a hydraulic switch under the trucks that opens a hatch in the pavement. They enter and exit the trucks through a mobile panel in the belly of the trailer. They're slick. None of this is visible from the street, so don't go home and blame yourself for missing it."

"Then how did you find it in a month?" Dave asked, obviously disturbed that he hadn't found it. This was his town and Joe was telling him about a major crime happening right under his nose.

"I honestly don't know," Joe said. "How did I know I needed to be in the field the day the snake was there? Or how did I know Father Romero needed me today? A sixth sense, a feeling, divine guidance, luck, I really don't know. But I follow it. I literally stubbed my toe on a small piece of asphalt in the truck lot. When I bent down to rub my toe, I noticed an outline of a possible opening. After that, I just kept digging."

"What do you want me to do tomorrow night," he asked.

"Just stay alert – and don't shoot the good guys." Joe said. "Cell phones don't work here. Do two-way radios work?"

"Yeah," Dave said. "I have a set I can give you."

"Give me one and keep the other one," Joe said, "after court tomorrow." Dave nodded and stared at his coffee cup.

"Someone in town is trying to help me," Joe said, as he put the note on the table. "I don't think they know my official identity. I think they're trying to help because of the attacks I've had. Apparently, we've jailed so many key players this week that Wellman-Phillips has come to town with eleven extra men. My first guess is they're going to try to get their men out of jail. If they can't do that, they'll have to use the new men to replace the workers in the tunnel." Dave looked at the note and nodded.

"I need you to focus on court tomorrow," Joe said. "Then we'll shift to the action tomorrow night. I almost waited until court was over, to brief you. But I was afraid the day might get too involved to be able to pull you aside for a talk. If you see Wellman-Phillips let me know. I've only seen one picture of him. You can arrest him on sight and I'll provide enough proof to put him away for a long time. I don't know the other eleven he's bringing – so don't hesitate to give me a heads up."

When Dave agreed, Joe added, "Call me if you need anything. I can usually hold my own."

Dave choked on his last sip of coffee and said, "I think I've seen proof of that. I'll save my questions for a quieter time. But I've got your back, never doubt it."

"I know," Joe said. "You've proven that several times. That's why I'm telling you about this."

"It bothers me that this happened on my watch," Dave said. "But I'll take your word on the fact that there was no way for me to find it. At least, it makes me feel better."

"It's true," Joe said. "Believe it. I'll walk back with you and see Ben home. I'm edgy tonight."

"Yeah, so am I," Dave said, as they went back to the jail.

After he walked Ben home, he went back to the house and sent Jack a quick e-mail on the note he had in his door. Jack had sent one: THE JUDGE AND I WILL BE THERE AT EIGHT A.M.

He couldn't sit still. He knew he needed to go to bed. He had an early morning meeting with a Judge, but he couldn't relax. He dressed in black, loaded and carried his handguns, put a blank tape in his camera and grabbed some spares. He turned out his lights and waited a few minutes before he slipped outside.

He made his rounds and changed his tapes. Since Clive was in jail, the bar was closed. The rest of the town was quiet. Even Dave's jail was relatively quiet. He could hear the men whining and Dave telling them to shut up. He sat down outside the fire station and listened. Then he heard it – footsteps working down the far side of Main.

Moving over to get Ben, he watched the streets. He tapped lightly and faced the business end of Ben's shotgun when the door opened. Fully dressed in dark clothes, Ben was ready. Joe told him he thought Wellman had come to town to break the men out of jail. He sent Ben over to have Susan call Dave.

"Tell him the thugs are outside," Joe said.

When Ben returned, they waited. Eventually, the group clustered outside the door to the jail. Joe told Ben to shoot anything that moved in his direction. He circled around to Main and came up on the far side of the thugs. Sliding into Dave's patrol car, he reached for the keys he knew Dave kept under the driver's seat. He switched on the spotlight and reds in one move. He grabbed the bullhorn in the next.

"This is the Police. Drop your weapons and put your hands in the air," he ordered. All but one man was too startled to do anything else. Joe guessed that one was Wellman. Dave opened the door to the jail and had his shotgun backing up Ben's in the rear. Susan brought her shotgun around to back Joe up.

"Mr. Wellman, I presume," Joe said, still on the bullhorn. The surprised look on the man's face said Joe guessed right. "You have five seconds to drop your firearm before I take it away from you." Wellman just stared at him.

"Drop it before you make me angry," Joe roared.

Wellman looked at the rest of his men on the ground.

Ben and Dave moved up with their shotguns.

Wellman dropped his gun and swore profusely.

Joe and Ben kept the group covered while Dave disarmed them. Susan went inside to get a box of nylon cuffs. Joe used Dave's borrowed set on Wellman.

"Hello *Phillips*," Joe said. "My name is Joseph Marsh. I'm the new Baptist Preacher in town."

Wellman's eyes flared and Joe laughed.

Dave moved up to Joe and said, "I only have three cells and they're full. How am I supposed to hold all of these men?"

"Well," Joe said, "they arrived together, so they obviously like each other. We'll let them share a cell for the rest of the night." He walked inside and helped Dave move the prisoners. He was pleased to see that Max wasn't in the group.

"Looks like a sardine can in here," Joe said, laughing at the cursing prisoners. "Good night, guys."

He walked Ben and Susan home. Then he ran to his house and sent Jack another e-mail. CAUGHT WELLMAN-PHILLIPS AND ELEVEN MEN TRYING TO BREAK THE OTHERS OUT OF JAIL. TWENTY TWO NOW IN TOWN'S THREE CELL JAIL.

He grabbed his alarm clock and a blanket off his bed and went back to spend the night at the jail with Dave.

Dave was surprised, but visibly relieved to see him.

CHAPTER THIRTY-ONE

TUESDAY – FIFTH WEEK

Joe didn't need his alarm clock. The prisoners fussed and whined until midnight and started up again at five. He folded his blanket and told Dave he had to leave for a while. He suggested he call Susan for backup. He did.

At home, Joe started a fresh pot of coffee, washed the cups and cleared the table. He showered, shaved and put on a dress shirt and slacks. He added his pistol and revolver.

Pulling out his tool box, he set up his tape player and inserted the Sunday tape. He set it to start playing at Orson's conversation. He put the rest of his equipment away and waited for Jack and Judge Evermundy.

He was on his second cup of coffee when he saw a car pull up to the church. A man with a long beard, Jack, emerged from the driver's side and a middle aged man got out of the passenger side. Joe opened his door and let Jack make the introductions.

"Reverend Marsh?" Jack asked.

"Yes," Joe said.

"I'm Reverend Maxwell and this is the honorable Judge Evermundy. I was asked to escort him to your home," Jack said.

"Thank you, Reverend Maxwell. I appreciate your assistance," Joe said. Then he turned to meet Judge Evermundy and invited him inside. He waited to see if Jack would join them. He didn't. He went back to his car and drove away.

Turning to the Judge, he asked him to sit down at the table and offered him a cup of coffee. He accepted. Joe could see his skepticism, so he decided to be direct.

"I appreciate you coming today, sir," Joe said. "I think the easiest way to explain why I needed you here so desperately, is to let you watch a short tape. I will tell you that I personally heard this conversation and I was the one who taped it - and I will swear to both facts under oath."

The Judge nodded and Joe hit the play button.

Evermundy leaned forward and stared at the video.

"That's Steve Orson," he said, stopping the tape. "Who is the man he's talking to?"

"Clive Osborn, the owner of the town bar," Joe said.

"Are you the preacher they're talking about?" he asked.

"Yes, sir," Joe said.

"They paid him to release the prisoners?" he asked.

"That's what they said, sir," Joe said.

Evermundy looked at him and started the tape again.

"Charade!" he said, stopping the tape. "Is he saying his credentials are false?"

"I believe so, sir," Joe said. "But that's something you'll have to confirm."

Evermundy nodded and started the tape again. He slumped when he heard them talking about the complaints.

"I ignored those complaints," he muttered to himself. "People tried to warn me." Joe sat still and waited.

When the Judge heard Orson's comments about his daughter, he cleared his chair and stepped outside. Joe waited quietly while the Judge regained his composure.

"Sir," Joe said, when the Judge returned, "you and I are the only people who have heard this tape. I have no desire to cause you or your family any grief. However, I am *very* concerned about the justice this town is going to receive from a bribed Judge. Constable Nelson has twenty two prisoners in his jail this morning. Nine have been arrested on attempted murder charges. Twelve were arrested last night trying to break the first group out of jail. The last one defaced my church and parsonage. All twenty two prisoners are covered under the bribe Orson accepted. We can't let a crooked Judge release this group." Evermundy nodded.

"I have two questions for you, sir," Joe said. "The first and most important question is – based on the bribe he took, can you remove him from the bench this morning before he has a chance to release the prisoners who are trying to kill us?"

"Absolutely!" Evermundy said.

"Thank you, sir," Joe said. "My second question is – can you arrange to have these twenty-two prisoners transported to a county facility until their trials? Constable Nelson only has three cells in his jail, so the eleven he arrested last night have him severely over-crowded."

"Yes, I'll order them transported today, but I'll order twenty-three cells. Orson will be joining the rest of them," Evermundy said. "Where does he hold court?"

"I understand he holds his court in Constable Nelson's jail," Joe said. "But he rarely has this many to hear."

"He won't hear any today," Evermundy said. "I'll see that bas..." He caught himself. Remembering he was talking to a preacher, he said, "I'll personally handcuff him and throw him in a cell with his friends."

Looking at his watch, Joe said, "It's only nine o'clock, sir. Why don't you have another cup of coffee while we wait?"

Evermundy just nodded his head yes.

Joe refilled their cups and said, "I am truly sorry that I'm the one who had to make you aware of this problem. But I cannot and will not apologize for exposing fraud – especially in our judicial system."

Evermundy only took a few sips of his second cup before he stood up and said, "I want to go to the court now. I'd like to be there when he walks through the door." He stopped at the door and asked, "Is Constable Nelson part of the problem?"

"No sir," Joe said. "He's a very good lawman. You can count on him."

"Thank you for that information," he said. "And thank you for having the courage to show me that tape. It's definitely something I needed to know about."

"You're welcome, sir," Joe said. "I really am sorry for the pain it caused you."

"I appreciate that, Reverend Marsh," Evermundy said. "Now let's go put one more criminal in the Constable's jail."

Dave gave Joe a curious look when he and the Judge walked in. Joe introduced Judge Evermundy, and told Dave that the Judge was here to visit Judge Orson's court. Evermundy noticed and appreciated Joe's discretion. He nodded at Joe.

Dave offered the Judge his chair at the desk. He thanked Dave and sat down. Joe could see the Judge working on his composure and admired him for it. He had just given the man a big shock. But Evermundy was staying strong.

Joe intentionally positioned himself in the corner by the door, so he would be behind Orson when he came in.

At nine fifty-five Orson walked through the door talking to another man. They heard him say, "Sure, I'll join you for a beer. Let me release these guys and I'll be right there..."

He froze when he saw Evermundy.

"Just run in and release these guys on your way to a beer?" Evermundy asked. "Is that the type of justice you've been giving this town? What are the charges against these prisoners?"

"The usual Saturday night mischief," Orson said. "They're just a bunch of good old boys who come to town to have a little fun. What brings you to town today, sir?"

"A judicial review of my subordinates," Evermundy said. "What do you consider *a little fun in town*?"

"Drunk and disorderly, that kind of thing," Orson said, regaining his confidence.

"So you've already decided that all the prisoners in this jail are ready to be released?" Evermundy persisted.

"Yeah, that's all it ever is in these little towns," Orson said. "Martha and I were talking about that the other night."

Dropping the name card, Joe thought. *If that's the Judge's daughter, you just fried your ass.* Looking at the Judge's face, Joe knew he was right.

"You are in *my* courtroom, Orson. Answer me appropriately," Evermundy said. "This is *not* a family chat!"

"Yes sir," Orson said. "Sorry, sir."

Joe was watching the man who walked in with Orson. He suspected this was the guy named Chad. He'd been inching his way back to Wellman's cell.

"Excuse me, Judge," Joe said, obviously speaking to Evermundy. "We seem to have an unauthorized visitor moving very close to the prisoners."

"Move away from the prisoners!" Evermundy ordered. He turned to Dave and said, "Escort that man out of the jail."

"Yes sir," Dave said, taking the man's arm. "Come on, Chad, you heard the Judge."

Orson turned on Joe. "Who the hell are you?" he demanded. "How dare you interrupt the Judge."

Joe deferred to Evermundy. When he got an affirmative nod, he said, "My name is Joseph Marsh. I'm the new Baptist Preacher." He watched Orson's face pale as the name registered.

"And most of the men in these cells have tried unsuccessfully, obviously, to kill him and other members of this community," Evermundy said.

"Oh, I doubt that," Orson said. "They just like to play tricks on people, especially if they're new."

Evermundy looked at the list of charges Dave had given him. "May I have your car keys, Steve?' Evermundy asked.

Steve gave them to Evermundy. Evermundy tossed them to Joe and said, "Go cut his brake line."

"What!" Orson said. "Don't you dare, I could be killed!"

"Oh, it's just a little trick, Steve. You said so yourself," Evermundy said. "Reverend, do you still have some of that poison they fed you? I'd like for Steve to have some of it, too."

"I'll go get the bottle," Joe said. "I'll be right back."

"Wait a minute!" Orson said, grabbing Joe's arm.

Joe glared at him and Orson pulled his hand back.

"What is this all about?" Orson demanded.

"I'm just following your *standards of justice* for this town," Evermundy said. "You know, it's easy to fool *us country bumpkins* with your false credentials and the salary we pay you to let these boys loose." Orson was shocked when he heard the Judge quoting his own words.

Before he could respond, Evermundy said, "Constable, search this man and arrest him for impersonating a judge, accepting bribes and multiple counts of miscarriage of justice against this town." Dave stepped forward.

"What!" Orson said, backing away from Dave. "Wait a minute. You can't do this to me. What about Martha?"

Evermundy stared at Orson and shook his head.

Dave closed in on Orson.

Orson spun on Evermundy and said, "You're crazy if you think I'm going to let him lock me up. Martha and I are going to get married and you can't do a damn thing about it."

Evermundy didn't say a word.

"Damn you," Orson said. "We would already be married, if you hadn't refused to release her inheritance."

Evermundy took a deep breath and smiled – an icy cold smile – back at him. Orson swore at him.

Dave grabbed Orson's arm. Orson swung away and barreled over the desk at the Judge. Dave's fist caught his side, Joe's caught his stomach and Evermundy's caught his mouth.

Dave and Joe pulled a bloody Orson down on the floor and cuffed him.

"Are you okay, Judge?" Joe asked Evermundy.

"Mmomomm," Orson said.

"Not *you*," Joe said. "I was asking Judge Evermundy."

Dave put Orson in a cell with the others and called Doc.

Evermundy asked Dave some questions about the pending cases. Dave went over the list with him and indicated the other witnesses waiting outside.

"Where are their attorneys?" Evermundy asked.

"The prisoners waived their rights to representation and jury trial," Dave said. "Until today, they've always been released with *time served*." Evermundy winced and shook his head. He asked Dave to call the witnesses inside.

When Ben and Father Romero walked in, Dave introduced them. Evermundy told them Orson had been removed from the bench and he would be the presiding judge in the pending cases. Although he knew it would be an inconvenience, he asked if they could come back next week to testify. They both agreed.

When the Judge realized Ben was the town Mayor, he personally apologized for ignoring earlier complaints he'd received from Ben's office.

"I hate to admit it," Evermundy said. "But he had me fooled. I'm sorry." Ben graciously accepted his apology and walked back outside with Father Romero.

When Joe started to leave with them, Evermundy asked him to stay. Then he turned to Dave and said, "I see no reason for you to have to handle this many prisoners. Therefore, I'm ordering them to the County Detention Center until I put their cases on my docket. We'll transport them back here for their trials. Does that meet with your approval?"

"Yes, sir," Dave said. "Thank you, sir."

Evermundy nodded and signaled Joe to follow him out.

Apparently, while he was making notes about the cases, he'd written a note for Joe. He handed it to him and said, "This is my personal phone number. Anytime, day or night, if anything else happens in this town concerning the judicial process, call me and I'll be here for you. I sincerely thank you for exposing that …"

"Scumbag," Joe supplied.

"That'll do," the Judge said, grinning at the substitution.

Looking down at the phone number, Joe asked, "Where do you live, sir? I don't recognize this area code, but I'm still new to the state."

"In Clovis," Evermundy said.

"I believe you need a ride home, sir," Joe said. "I'd be happy to drive you back."

"No, thank you," Evermundy said. "If you still have the keys to Steve's car, I'll drive it home."

Joe handed him the keys.

"Apparently we'll need to seize it and his other property as part of his case," Evermundy said.

Joe nodded and agreed with him.

"Anyway, I've always wanted to drive one of these snazzy things, so why not now?" Evermundy said.

"One more thing, sir," Joe said, as the Judge got into the car. "The men bribing Orson also have some drug connections around here. You may want to have the car searched when you order the seizure. If they find anything, could you let Constable Nelson know? It might help him track things over here."

"Will do, Reverend Marsh, and thank you again," Evermundy said. He grinned and revved the engine loud enough for Orson to shout, "My car!" through the cell window.

Evermundy laughed and drove off.

Susan came around the corner to relieve Dave.

Dave grabbed Joe's arm and pulled him out to a vacant lot where no one could hear them.

"How the hell did you pull that off?" Dave asked. "Why didn't you warn me? I was dumbstruck when he walked in and threw Orson off the bench. We've been trying to get that crook for year. I'm so happy I could shout. And then you got the prisoners moved. I want to know what you did – and then I don't. Just let me say, Thank you! Thank you! Thank you!"

Joe was laughing so hard he couldn't talk. He'd never seen Dave this excited. He was talking so fast, Joe couldn't keep up with the questions, let alone answer them.

When Dave wound down, he grinned and said, "Thanks, Joe, you've worked a small miracle for justice in this town."

"You're welcome, Dave," Joe said. "I'm glad it worked out the way it did. I couldn't say anything because I wasn't sure what he would do – if anything. Wasn't he terrific? And he's going to hear all the pending cases. I'll bet your prisoners will worry a lot more now."

"From what you told me last night," Dave said. "I hope the county picks up this trash today, so I'll have some open space again."

"Yeah," Joe said. "So do I. I'm going to go over to Ben's and grab a bite of lunch. Want to go?"

"No thanks," Dave said. "Susan left mine on the table. I guess I'd better go eat it and get back with her."

"I'll sit with her until you come back," Joe said. "I don't like her in there alone."

"Thanks," Dave said. "I won't be long."

When Dave returned, Joe went up to the grocery store. He spoke to Katherine and enjoyed the coffee and egg salad sandwich Alice had waiting for him. When Ben heard Katherine announce Joe, he came running through the store.

Joe grinned. He knew Ben was dying to know what happened while he and Father Romero were outside. After blackmailing him out of half of his next piece of Grandma's pie, he told Ben he'd found some evidence against Orson and Judge Evermundy took it from there. He asked Ben to keep that information quiet, because the case was pending along with all the others. Ben agreed. He was just happy Orson was off the bench. He liked Evermundy and thought they'd get fair hearings from him. Joe agreed.

"Watch your back until we get the rest of these scumbags," Joe said. "The Judge apologized in front of the prisoners. They aren't happy about losing their Judge and he's Chad's brother, right?"

"You're right," Ben said. "This isn't over yet."

If you only knew, Joe thought.

After lunch he went home, locked the evidence back in the tool box and changed clothes. He sent Jack an e-mail. STEVE ORSON JAILED, ALL OTHER CASES DEFERRED TO NEXT WEEK. TWENTY THREE PRISONERS TO BE TRANSFERRED TO COUNTY FACILITY TODAY. THANKS FOR THE HELP. WHAT'S THE SCHEDULE FOR TONIGHT?

Jack responded. MEN WILL BE IN PLACE BY SEVEN. I'LL JOIN YOU AT SEVEN. WE'LL WORK IT FROM THERE.

Joe answered. OK. I BRIEFED DAVE LAST NIGHT – HE'LL SUPPORT AS NEEDED.

Jack answered. GOOD, SEE YOU AT SEVEN.

Joe logged off, locked his door and took a nap.

When he joined the kids at four they were talking about the county paddy wagon that had cleaned out the jail this afternoon. They'd never seen that many prisoners in town before. They wondered if they had a crime wave.

"Just some scumbags that needed a new home," Joe said casually, as he dribbled the ball and started shooting to distract the kids. Chris was still excited over his scholarship and he had the rest of them energized. Stressing good grades, Joe told the others they could get one, too.

While they played, he glanced at the truck lot. Then he looked again. There was a truck there. But it wasn't parked in the normal space – and it wasn't Simms' truck.

Turning back to the game, he said, "Hey Chris, did Simms come down today?"

"No, he's sick. Another guy brought his stuff," Chris said. "What do you need?"

"Did he bring any more watermelons?" Joe asked, as they played.

"No, he just brought a few canned goods. The truck was half empty," Chris said. "He didn't know he was supposed to bring the fresh stuff, too. We should have some next week."

Joe nodded and concentrated on the game for a few minutes. Then he deliberately bounced a wild ball up to the truck lot. Chasing after it, he looked closer. The truck was parked a good four feet off the hatch. He clutched his calf, as if in pain, and hopped to the corner of the hotel to sit down. Still rubbing his leg, he reached behind him and popped the tape out of the camera. Concealing it in his back waistband, he hopped the ball back to the kids. Using the cramp as an excuse, he left the game and hobbled home.

When he opened the door, he had another note: MNY MN WIT MAX CAM N TRUK. He locked his door, grabbed the player and started the tape. He sent an URGENT e-mail to Jack. HOLD EVERYTHING, WRONG TRUCK IN LOT. HAVE A NOTE SAYING MNY MN WIT MAX CAM N TRUK. I'M REVIEWING MY TAPE NOW.

Jack responded. OK LET ME KNOW AS SOON AS YOU CAN. TIMING IS CLOSE.

Fast forwarding the tape to the arrival of the truck, Joe watched and listened intently.

The driver that stepped out was not Simms. Cursing as he hit the ground, he turned to the men coming out of the back and said, "Hole up until dark. Then we'll spring Homer and the rest of the guys so we can get this operation back on track."

Joe watched the men walk toward the storage units. He heard them climb the steps to Max's apartment.

At the door, he could barely hear Max's surprise and one man saying, "We're from Cozen. We need a place to stay for a while. We're going to use your place." Max gave some kind of protest, but was overruled because a minute later Joe heard the door close. Playing on through the tape, he didn't hear the men leave. Apparently, they didn't know Homer had been moved.

Joe sent another e-mail to Jack. ABORT MISSION FOR TONIGHT. TAPE SHOWS THEY HAVE INTERRUPTED 'REGULAR RUNS' TO GET HOMER AND OTHERS OUT OF JAIL. ABOUT FIFTEEN MEN FORCED THEMSELVES INTO MAX'S APARTMENT ABOVE STORAGE UNIT. THEY'RE WAITING FOR DARK TO 'SPRING' HOMER. APPARENTLY, THEY DON'T KNOW WE MOVED THE PRISONERS. MISSION DOES NOT APPEAR TO BE COMPROMISED. OTHER ACTIONS IN TOWN APPARENTLY CAUSED THE INTERRUPTION. I'VE GOT TO GO LET DAVE KNOW SO WE CAN GET THESE GUYS BEFORE THEY TEAR UP THE TOWN.

Jack answered. OKAY. MISSION IS OFF FOR TONIGHT. WE'LL TRY AGAIN NEXT WEEK. STAY SAFE.

Joe locked up the tape and changed to body armor and black clothes. He checked all four of his handguns, concealed three and stuffed some extra ammunition in his pockets. He locked his house and walked over to the jail.

"Trouble?" Dave asked, looking at Joe's clothes and the revolver in his belt.

"Not yet, but soon," Joe said, as he checked to be sure the jail was empty. Then he showed him the note and told him about the different truck.

"What do you want to do?" Dave asked.

"Well, our other mission is canceled for tonight," Joe said. "But we need to catch these guys before they tear up the town or hurt someone. If the note is right, they're with Max. Since we haven't seen them yet, they're probably waiting until dark. Apparently, no one told them the prisoners were moved."

"How do you want to set the trap?" Dave asked.

"That's what I've been thinking about," Joe said, looking at the cells. "Since they apparently think the guys are still in jail, maybe we can set the trap right here. If we stuffed some shirts and propped them inside the cells and put a dummy in your chair, we could let them bust themselves into jail – instead of busting the others out. We could close in behind them and just walk them into the cells." Dave grinned at the irony.

"We'll have to hurry, if we're going to make this work." Joe said, walking into the first cell. "Do you know anyone who has some old clothes we can use?"

"There's some in a box in the fire station. They're leftovers from the last garage sale," Dave said, as he walked through the doors to the station. "I don't know how many shirts are in it, though."

"We can use the other clothes for stuffing," Joe said. "I'll call Ben."

When Dave came back with the box, Joe went to work.

"Are there any of the other men that we can call to back us up?" Joe asked.

"Yeah," Dave said. "I'll call Charley and Ralph. Gene's a lousy shot. I took him hunting once – never again."

271

He chuckled at Dave and kept working.

Between blankets and old shirts, he arranged a credible jail scene. He stuffed Dave's jacket and propped a canteen on top of it for his head. Then he grabbed the hat off Dave's head for the final touch.

"Hey," Dave said. "That's my favorite hat. We don't have to be that realistic."

"Do you know any of these men?" Joe asked. "Have you ever arrested any of them? Your hat is your trademark. Without it, they'll get suspicious before they open the door."

Dave grumbled, but he had to admit Joe was right.

Looking around Joe asked, "Do you have a radio anywhere?" Dave pulled an old one out of his desk drawer.

Joe took it to the middle cell, tuned it to a talk show and turned up the volume.

Dave watched and nodded at the effect. "That sounds about right for the group we had last night," he said.

When Ben walked in, they had the place ready to go. He liked the idea. He even said he thought that was Dave at the desk. Joe grinned at Dave. Dave grumbled. He was still feeling strange without his hat.

Charley and Ralph arrived a few minutes later carrying their hunting rifles. Susan followed with her revolver and shotgun. Joe was glad to see they were all armed. He quickly told them the plan and they moved into position.

Susan and Charley would stay behind the locked fire station doors, in case someone tried to break through them. Joe and Ben took the space between the grocery and the appliance stores to watch for their approach and follow behind them. Dave and Ralph went across the street and hid in the shadows of the Methodist Church.

At nine o'clock, Joe and Ben saw the shadows. This group split up. Joe counted five who walked down Main, turned on Second and approached the front of the jail. Another five crossed between the appliance store and theater in front of Joe and Ben. They flattened against the fire station wall. Four more moved to the far side of the jail. Joe waved Ben over to follow them. He covered the five at the fire station and left the other five for Dave. But he was puzzled, he'd counted fifteen men.

Did one stay behind with Max? he wondered.

When the first five burst through the jail door with weapons drawn, Joe watched Dave move forward to close in on them. Ralph apparently stayed behind to cover Dave.

Good move, Joe thought.

The five at the fire station moved up to trap Dave. Joe pistol whipped the back two before the others turned around. Shots were fired. Joe wounded three. He was reloading when he heard Ben challenge the men on his side.

Dave came out and covered Joe's five so he could help Ben. Two of Ben's had surrendered. The other two took cover on the side of Dave's house. Joe slipped behind them and wounded two more when they took aim at Ben.

Dave and Ralph were coming around to pick up those four when a pistol shot rang out over Joe's head. Spinning, he watched a man fall off of Dave's roof.

Close call, Joe thought. *There were fifteen. The other one was up there. Apparently, he was waiting for me. He had easy shots at Ben, Dave and Ralph.*

He checked the man who fell. He didn't recognize him, but either the bullet or the fall killed him. The bullet caught the man in the right shoulder, so the fall must have finished him off.

Turning back to Dave, Joe said, "Thanks Dave, you saved my life."

Dave looked surprised. "Me," he said. "I didn't shoot him, I thought you did."

"No," Joe said. "I hadn't seen him. He had me cold. I know I heard a pistol shot. Everyone else has shotguns and rifles. I thought you hit him."

"I would've, if I'd seen him," Dave said, "but I didn't."

Joe looked around. He was bewildered, but grateful.

"Whoever took that shot saved my life," he said. "I wish I could thank him."

Dave turned and said, "Ralph, go call Doc and tell him we have five gunshot wounds for him – courtesy of Joe."

"Thanks a lot!" Joe said, as the others laughed. "Doc's already down on me for the patients I sent him last week."

"He shouldn't be angry," Dave said. "He should put you on the payroll."

Dave asked Ralph if he could stay with Doc tonight in case he had problems with any of the prisoners. Ralph agreed.

"Good work, guys and gal," Joe said, as they replaced their dummies with real prisoners. "Dave, are you going to arrange a reunion with their buddies?"

"Yeah," Dave said. "I'll call the Judge in the morning." Then to the group, he said, "Thanks guys, I really appreciate the help. I hope we either catch all of them or wear them out soon. But until then, I may have to call on you again. Susan and I have this under control here, so why don't you go on home and get some rest. Thanks again."

Joe hung back after the other's left. "Are you taking the early or late shift?" he asked Dave.

"I'm going to stay here and start the paperwork," Dave said. "I sent Susan home to get some sleep."

"Okay," Joe said. "Call me, when you call her. I don't want her left alone with any of these men. I'll bring my *blankie* over and stay with her."

Dave grinned at the blankie comment. He remembered how uncomfortable Joe was last night. But he agreed and thanked him for helping her.

Joe went home to clean and reload his firearms. He was puzzled by the shot that saved his life, he wondered who helped him. "Obviously someone who wants to stay anonymous," he told himself. He thought about the different notes he'd received. They'd all been accurate – and because of them – he'd been able to act rather than react to the threats this week.

He sent Jack another e-mail before he went to bed. FIFTEEN MEN ARRIVED AND TRIED TO BREAK INTO JAIL TO FREE PRISONERS. APPARENTLY, THEY DIDN'T KNOW THE JAIL WAS EMPTY. NINE IN CELLS, FIVE AT DOC'S WOUNDED – OOPS. ONE DEAD BY UNKNOWN SHOT THAT SAVED MY LIFE. I MUST HAVE A GUARDIAN ANGEL OVER HERE THAT SENDS NOTES – AND SHOOTS PRETTY GOOD, TOO.

CHAPTER THIRTY- TWO

WEDNESDAY – FIFTH WEEK

Dave called at two a.m.

Joe finished the night on the jail floor. When he woke up, he swore he was going to drag his mattress with him, if he had to spend many more nights like this. He folded up his blanket, and stayed with Susan until Dave came back at six.

After some much needed coffee, he decided to get back into his routine and go for his morning jog – with his revolver in a shoulder holster. He didn't plan to be unarmed again. This group wanted him dead and almost succeeded last night. Remembering his empty camera behind the hotel, he grabbed another tape.

School starts today, he reminded himself, as he jogged past houses and heard more families moving around. The truck belonging to the prisoners was still parked behind the hotel – because they weren't free to move it.

It'll be interesting to see who comes after it, he thought. He dropped a new tape in the camera and wondered about Max.

He jogged to the front of the storage units and found him slowly sweeping out an end unit. Moving in front of him, Joe waved and waited for Max to turn on his hearing aids.

"Good morning, Max," he said. Then he turned Max's face to the light. He had a cut lip, cut cheek and a big bruise on his right eye. "What happened to you?" Joe asked.

"It's nothing," Max said, trying to turn away.

Joe held on gently, but firmly.

"Yes it is something," Joe said. "Who did this to you?"

Max seemed surprised at Joe's concern.

"A bunch of Cozen bums from Lubbock barged into my place yesterday," he said. "They beat me up and trashed my place. I didn't do anything, but try to keep them out."

"How many were there?" Joe asked.

"I counted fifteen," Max said. "When they left, I hid down here so they wouldn't hit me any more."

"They're in jail," Joe said. "They were arrested last night. Go lock your apartment, I'm taking you over to see Doc."

"Naw, I don't wanna be a bother," Max said.

"It's not a bother, Max," Joe said. "You need stitches and some medicine for the pain. I'm sure it hurts to talk."

"Yeah, it does," Max finally admitted. "Do you mind waiting for me?"

"Not at all," Joe said. "I'll wait. Take your time."

When he came back, Joe helped him walk down the street to Doc's office. On the way, he asked, "Do you know the names of the men who hit you?"

"There were two of them. Big men," Max said. "I don't know their real names they just called them Bruno and Bruiser."

Nancy rushed around her desk to help when they walked in. The poor man could hardly stand up. Joe guessed he probably had some broken ribs he hadn't mentioned.

Doc had the five prisoners in his exam room, so he came out to the waiting room to check Max.

"Hello, Max," he said, "we haven't seen you in months."

"Hi, Doc," Max said, between shallow breaths. "I don't get out much anymore."

"Let me see your face," Doc said, as Nancy slipped into the exam room to get some medicine.

Waiting for her, Doc and Max chatted.

When she didn't return, Doc cut a look at Joe. Joe signaled him to call Dave about Max and keep talking. He did.

While Doc was on the phone, Joe slipped around to the back door. He hoped it was still open. He'd seen Nancy taking some trash out when they walked up.

He pulled his revolver, eased the knob open and slipped inside. One of the prisoners was awake and holding a syringe against Nancy's throat behind the exam room door. Apparently, he was waiting for Doc to come back. Joe watched the patient. He knew he was too weak to stand very long. His hand was already shaking. When his arm slumped away from her throat, Nancy shoved away and Joe fired. Nancy screamed.

Not knowing Joe was in the room, she was almost hysterical, thinking someone was shooting at her. Joe and Doc reached her at the same time. Doc grabbed Nancy. Joe checked the man he shot. The other four appeared to still be sedated.

When he went over to Doc and Nancy, Doc had finally convinced her that Joe was the shooter. She gave him a big hug, sobbing and saying thank you all in one breath.

Max looked around the door and then down on the floor.

"That's Bruiser," he said. "Is he dead?"

"I believe so," Joe said. "Doc will have to make it official." To Doc and Nancy, he said, "Bruiser is one of the two men who beat Max up."

Doc checked Bruiser and pronounced him dead. He told Joe to call Dave while he covered the body with a sheet.

"Man," Joe said, "you and Dave are going to hate me before we get these guys out of this town."

Dave answered, "Where and how many?"

"One dead at Doc's," Joe said. "No need to hurry."

Since Max was already in the room, Joe asked him to look at the other men and see if he recognized them. Max named all four. Doc reminded Joe that he had one more in the back waiting for the morgue. Max said that one was Bruno.

"Well," Joe said, "you don't have to worry about these two anymore." While Doc had the body out, Joe asked him if he'd removed the bullet.

"Yep," Doc said, "a 38 special, why?"

"Just wanted to know what my guardian angel was shooting these days," Joe said.

When Dave arrived, he listened to Nancy's story and then Joe's. Doc turned around and said, "I didn't know our preacher carried a firearm."

"Oh," Dave said, "I told him to get one when those men kept trying to kill him."

"He's a pretty good shot for a beginner," Doc said, looking straight at Joe.

Joe laughed and said, "I'm not a beginner, Doc. I've been shooting most of my life. I just don't publicize that fact. People usually react the way you just did."

"Well, we're glad you had one today," Doc said. "You probably saved both our lives."

Joe told Dave that Max could name the other men.

Then he had Dave look at Max.

"Max said the two dead ones are the men who beat him up," Joe said, "but the others are accessories to the crime. They didn't do anything to stop the attack. I know it means more paperwork, but I don't think they should get away with this."

"I don't either," Dave said. "I'll write it up. I've got to get back to relieve Susan."

"Wait, I'll walk with you," Joe said. "I need to go home and clean up." He waved at the others and said, "See you later, Max. You let Doc and Nancy take care of you, okay?"

Max nodded, and winced. He was obviously feeling worse that he wanted to admit.

Back home, Joe reloaded his revolver, showered, shaved, and sent Jack an e-mail. ANOTHER PRISONER IS DEAD. HE TOOK NURSE HOSTAGE – I TOOK HIM DOWN. PRISONERS' TRUCK IS STILL IN TRUCK LOT. I'M WAITING TO SEE WHO MOVES IT. A COUPLE OF THE FIFTEEN MEN BEAT MAX UP. TAKING HIM TO DOC'S OFFICE IS WHY I WAS THERE WHEN THE OTHER SITUATION OCCURRED. MAX SAID ALL FIFTEEN CAME IN FROM THE COZEN FIELDS NEAR LUBBOCK.

SINCE WE HAVE TO WAIT FOR THEM TO RESUME THEIR TRUCKING BUSINESS, CAN WE GET A BANK EXAMINER INTO THE ALBUQUERQUE BANK WHERE PAULINE WORKS? IF WE CAN GET A LIST OF CURRENT EMPLOYEES, WE'D AT LEAST KNOW HOW MANY MORE TO EXPECT. THEY SEEM TO BE PULLING OUT ALL THE STOPS RIGHT NOW.

ALSO, WE NEED TO DISCUSS JURISDICTIONS AND PROSECUTORS ON THE OTHER ISSUES. CLIVE MENTIONED PHILMAN SALTING THE FARM WELLS, SO I'M SURE IT WILL SURFACE SOON.

I'VE FOUND 'WATER FILTERS' ON THE CLOSED BUSINESS BUILDINGS. WE NEED COPIES OF ALL THE LOANS PAULINE ISSUED BASED ON THE FRAUDULENT WATER REPORTS. WE'LL NEED TO GET AN EXPERT TO LOOK AT THE EQUIPMENT TO SEE IF

IT'S WORTH $15,000 AND WHETHER IT'S CAPABLE OF FILTERING OUT THE POISON – IF IT EVER DID ACTUALLY SHOW UP IN THE WATER. IN FACT, THE FILTER COMPANY MAY BE ANOTHER BOGUS COMPANY.

PHILMAN AND WELLMAN ARE GOING TO TRY TO BAIL OUT ON THE CURRENT CHARGES. WHO DO WE NEED AND WHAT DO WE NEED TO DO TO KEEP THEM IN JAIL? JUST WANTED TO BE SURE YOU STAYED BUSY WHILE YOU WAIT. HA! TAKE CARE.

He locked up and walked over to the general store to check the mail. The store was too quiet. He could hear Gene and Ginger whispering in the back.

"Hey who evacuated the store?" he asked.

"One word," Gene said, "school."

"Petey was so excited, he had us up at four to be sure he was ready," Ginger said. "Thank you for including him in the Kindergarten."

"And thank you for making the Kindergarten happen," Gene said. "It's going to help all our kids."

"It's a win-win situation," Joe said. "The kids learn and our retired teachers have a new purpose. You should see them. They're as excited as the kids."

Gene laughed and said, "I'm not sure anyone could be more excited than Petey."

"There's still one problem," Joe said. "We'll probably have to help Ralph and Doris for the first few days."

They gave him a puzzled look and waited.

He grinned and said, "It's going to take some time for them to adjust to the new noise level over there."

They laughed and agreed.

Joe asked Gene to call him with the songs for next week so Dominique could practice them tomorrow. Gene agreed.

He didn't have any mail, so he wandered over to the drug store. The noise wasn't too bad, but he had to admit it was more than they were used to hearing.

Walking back to Ralph, he asked, "Are you ready to have the grand opening and closing on the same day?"

"Not yet," Ralph said, chuckling, "but it's close."

"I don't guess this is a good time to ask you about putting a piano back there, huh?" Joe asked.

"What piano?" Ralph asked.

"The one in the Methodist Church," Joe said.

"That old thing," Ralph said, shaking his head. "It just needs to go to the dump. It's falling apart."

"I know," Joe said, "but Dominique thinks she can bring it back to life for the Kindergarten. She definitely knows how to tune them. Ours was awful. She popped it open, twisted some screws and it was much better. Since the one at your church has no value to the congregation, I'd like to let her see what she can do. If it works the kids would have some music back there."

"It's okay with me," Ralph said. "I'll check with Charley, but I'm sure he won't mind. I just don't want to get her hopes up. She does a nice job playing. We enjoyed her music Sunday." Joe agreed with him.

"Speaking of the church," Ralph said, "we had a small blessing of our own in the mail today."

"What was that?" Joe asked.

"Someone paid our mortgage payment on the church this month," Ralph said.

"Great," Joe said. "Do you know who did it?"

"No," he said, "but it made us feel better. We love that old church. It's going to be hard to let it go."

"I know," Joe said. "It's not *just a building* when you've grown up with it. We'll pray you find a way to save it."

He asked Ralph to call him later with the songs for Dominique to play on Sunday. He walked around to the Kindergarten and listened, but didn't go in and disturb the group. Outside, he noticed the truck had been moved out of the lot. He wondered if Chad came back for it and where he took it.

He wandered into the grocery store and caught Alice off guard. Katherine wasn't announcing him out front – she was in school – but the coffee and egg salad sandwich were as good as always. He knew he was going to miss a lot of pie, now that Grandma had the Kindergarten. He went out to the stockroom to thank Ben for his help.

"There are days I swear I'm going to hold you down and make you tell me the rest of the story about you," Ben said. "And then I realize you're doing what you need to for a purpose. Whether it's a divine purpose or a mortal one, you're protecting all of us and that's good enough for me. I just know I'm grateful you came to town, when you did. We had no idea how much we needed you." Joe nodded and changed the subject.

"You know we talked ourselves out of a lot of good pies dreaming up that Kindergarten idea," he said.

"Yeah, Ben said. "How am I going to get Ma back in the kitchen when she's got a room full of kids to teach?"

"I was over there earlier. It sounds like they're in full swing," Joe said.

Ben laughed and said, "I can't wait to hear the stories from Ma when she gets home."

"Oh, by the way," Joe said, "did you hear I shot one of the prisoners at Doc's?"

"You did what?" Ben asked. "Why? What happened?"

"He came out of his sedative and held a syringe at Nancy's throat," Joe said. "Apparently, he was waiting for Doc to come back into the exam room. I went through the back door and took him out. Nancy was terrified. She thought someone was shooting at her, but she's okay now."

"How do you manage to be in the right place at the right time?" Ben asked.

"I don't know," Joe said. "I honestly don't know. I was at Doc's, because I took Max over there to get fixed up. Two of those thugs we arrested last night, beat him up. His face is a mess and I think they broke a couple of his ribs."

"How did you find out about Max?" Ben asked.

"I stopped to talk to him while I was jogging this morning," Joe said.

"You talked to Max?" Ben asked.

"I've talked to him a couple of times," Joe said. "Why?"

"He hasn't talked to anyone in this town since his wife died," Ben said. "He doesn't even shop. He leaves his grocery list on my door and Chris takes the box of stuff up to his porch. We've never seen him leave the storage units. I can't believe you got him over to Doc's."

"Well, I did," Joe said. "I guess he was hurting too bad to refuse. Has he always lived over there?"

"No," Ben said. "He and Ellie used to live in that house on the south side of the church. He moved out when she died. Somehow, he got that job with Cozen."

"Where did he work before?" Joe asked.

"He was the school janitor for years," Ben said.

"While he was at Doc's, he identified the dead men as the guys who beat him up," Joe said. "I talked to Dave about charging the others as accessories to the crime since they obviously didn't stop them. Max said all fifteen were Cozen men from Texas." Ben nodded.

"Is there something special that Max orders?" Joe asked. "I'd like to take some food over to him while he's recovering?"

"Yes," Ben said. "He loves frozen strawberries and vanilla ice cream."

"Good," Joe said. "I'll take some over to him tomorrow. I want to be sure he's okay. That was a brutal beating, especially for a man his age."

He picked up the strawberries and ice cream and then shopped for himself. He didn't want to fight that Saturday crowd again, if he could help it.

He took the groceries home and started to change for hoops. He wondered if they'd play anymore, now that school had started. He went ahead and changed and decided to wait for them at the bus stop, wherever that was.

He locked up and walked over to the empty house south of the church. He hadn't really paid much attention to it. It was a small house, about the same size as the Hispanic homes.

Looking through the windows, he saw a fully furnished home. There was a set of china displayed in the china cabinet and a tablecloth and centerpiece on a little round table with two matching chairs. A stack of logs sat beside a small fireplace with two rocking chairs angled toward it. A large framed picture hung over the mantle. He could see a bedspread on the bed and a crocheted scarf on the dresser in the bedroom. The house was spotless. There wasn't any dust or cobwebs anywhere.

Is someone living here? he wondered. *Do I have a neighbor I haven't met? Could this be my guardian angel's house? Wellman owns this house like all the other vacant ones. But this one's too pretty to be occupied by the thugs I've been arresting. I need to put a camera over here and see what's going on.*

Then he saw the water filter on the back of the house and wanted to get his hands on Philman again. Since the filter was the same size as the one on the Methodist Church, he guessed it cost fifteen thousand dollars, too.

How could a school janitor possibly pay off a loan that size? he thought. *When and how did Ellie die? Did Max reject the rest of the town, or the rest of the town's water? I wonder if they convinced him the storage unit water was safe. More questions than answers, as usual.*

He walked up to the empty houses on the north side of the church. All of them were stripped of their furnishings – and every one of them had water filters – so did the closed school. Apparently, they'd bankrupted all these people with their bogus water story and special filters.

He looked at his watch and headed over to the hoops lot. He saw the school bus stop in front of the drug store. The same place the commercial bus stopped.

When the younger kids saw him, they had to tell him about their first day at school. The older kids said they still played hoops at four and ran home to change.

After the game, he walked over to see the Hispanic kids. They were all bubbling about their Kindergarten. Although he understood a lot of their comments, he asked their moms to translate. They loved the school and the teachers. They were learning new words in English – so they could talk to him.

As usual, he heard Angie's "Preaker Man" before he saw her. He always hugged all the kids, but he kept the shoulder ride as her special thing. When he finished, he found Dominique and set up practice for tomorrow afternoon.

On his way home he checked on Dave.

"The county picked up the prisoners," Dave said, doing his best to scowl at Joe. "So, Susan and I *might* be able to have a quiet night at home – if you do!"

"I'll try not to let anyone kill me. That's all I can promise," Joe said chucking, as he waved out.

He had to admit, home felt pretty good to him, too. Two nights on the jail floor made a mattress sound divine. He started a pot of coffee and checked his e-mail.

Jack had sent an answer. EXAMINER IS GOING TO THE BANK TOMORROW, ONE OF OURS – WITH INSTRUCTIONS. I'M WORKING ON JURISDICTIONS AND PROSECUTORS. I'M TRYING TO GET MOST OF THEM ON FED LEVEL – TANGLED MESS, AS YOU KNOW. GLAD YOU SAVED THE NURSE AND GLAD YOU'RE SAFE.

After a short nap, he dressed in black, concealed his firearms, picked up some more tapes, locked the door and ran his nightly surveillance. He moved south and set a camera near Max's vacant house. Then he circled around to the bar. It was still closed. He wondered if the redhead lived upstairs somewhere, since she was on all his earlier tapes.

He moved over to the Hispanic section, everything seemed normal. Working his way over to the tape under Max's stairs, he changed it and the one by the hotel. He wanted to see who moved that truck.

He turned north and looked around the front of the storage units. A light was on in the unit Max hid in last night. Apparently, the poor guy was afraid to go back upstairs. Or maybe it was too messed up to live in. He'd have to check on that tomorrow.

Circling around Ben's and Grandma's, he hoped they could have a decent night's sleep tonight – he needed one, too. Everything appeared quiet. He waited a few minutes and just listened – to be sure – before he went inside.

He watched the tapes. It looked like Chad moved the truck. The other tapes didn't have any unusual activity, so he locked up and went to bed.

CHAPTER THIRTY-THREE

THURSDAY – FIFTH WEEK

He woke early, put the ice cream and frozen strawberries in a bag and ran his normal jogging route with his revolver. He enjoyed having a few hours of normal again.

When he reached the storage units, he went up the stairs and knocked loudly on Max's door. When he didn't get an answer, he looked through the window. He was right, the place was a mess. He went around to the front of the facility and knocked on the unit Max had been sweeping. When he heard a voice, he told him who he was. Slowly, Max rolled up the door.

He looks worse today, than he did yesterday, Joe thought. *Sleeping in a storage unit isn't going to help him heal.*

Gently, he coaxed Max back upstairs. Easing him into his bed, Joe put the strawberries and ice cream in the freezer and started cleaning up. *Sweeping up is more like it,* he thought, when he saw how many things had been broken.

He looked in the bedroom to be sure Max was asleep. Then he ran downstairs, retrieved the camera by the hotel and taped the condition of Max's house. He replaced the camera and went back upstairs.

He grabbed a broom and started cleaning out the remnants of the attack. *At least when Max wakes up he'll have his house back,* he thought. He was washing the few dishes that hadn't been broken, when Max walked out. Seeing a man in his house shocked him for a minute, until he realized it was Joe.

Joe gave him a fresh cup of coffee and some toast. He waited to be sure he ate it. Max brightened a little when Joe told

285

him he put strawberries and ice cream in the freezer. Then he gave Max his phone number and told him to call day or night, if he had any more trouble. Max agreed.

It was ten a.m. before Joe went home to shower and clean up for the day. When he started to unlock his door, he heard a noise on the side of the house.

Not again, he thought. He eased his revolver out of the holster, flattened on the ground and crawled along the wall. Looking around the corner, he came face to face with a puppy already down on his front paws ready to play. Holstering his gun, he sat cross-legged on the ground and laughed.

"Where'd you come from, little guy?" he asked, as if the pup could answer. Holding him, Joe could tell he was half starved. His ribs were poking out and he'd obviously been working through Joe's trash looking for food. He took the pup inside and gave him a bowl of milk. Then he saw him circling around his chair.

"Oh no you don't," he said, rushing him back outside. Once the pup finished his business, he stayed right on Joe's heels. Joe played with him for a while outside to see if anyone came looking for him. No one did. Walking back inside, he closed the door on the pup.

He assumed he'd go on his way. Instead, he sat outside the door and whined so pitifully he broke Joe's heart.

"Okay," Joe said, opening the door. "If you're going to stay, we have to have some rules. First you're going to get cleaned up." He drew a tub of water and bathed the pup. Then he showered and changed.

He walked the pup outside again, locked the door and carried him up to the grocery store. Ben and Alice chuckled at him. It was obvious he'd already fallen in love with the little guy. He bought puppy food, chew bones, a collar and a leash.

"What are you going to call him?" Alice asked.

"I don't know," Joe said, "any suggestions?"

"Well, since you found him at the parsonage," she said, "you could call him Parson."

"Parson it is," Joe said. Then he asked, "Do you know anyone with an old playpen?"

"No, why?" Alice asked.

"Because I need a safe place to leave him when I'm gone," Joe said. "Otherwise those sharp puppy teeth will ruin my shoes, socks and anything else he finds."

"How big do you think he'll get?" Ben asked.

"He looks like a German Shepherd mix," Joe said. "I'd guess about sixty pounds."

"Let me make a couple of calls," Alice said. "I may know someone who has one."

"If not," Joe said, "I'll go over to Gene's and buy one."

Alice came back with good news.

"Carmen Montoya has one for you," she said.

"Great," Joe said, "I'll go get it." He put the collar and leash on the pup and left with it bouncing beside him.

He knocked on Carmen's door and waited. When she opened the door, she was carrying the playpen. She giggled at the puppy and sat down on the steps to play with it. Joe offered to pay her for the playpen, but she wouldn't accept any money.

"After everything you've done for us," she said, "I can help you with this."

Joe thanked her and headed home with his puppy, playpen, puppy food and chew bones.

Dave stepped out of the jail just in time to see him coming down the street. He stared in total disbelief at the tough agent laughing and playing with a scrawny little pup.

"What do we have here?" Dave asked.

"A puppy," Joe said childishly. "His name is Parson."

"I see," Dave said, talking the way he would to a child. "Is he your puppy?"

"Yep," Joe said. "He 'dopted me this morning."

Then Joe dropped his antics and told Dave the pup was digging through his trash behind the house when he went home.

"I drew down on the little thing," he said. "I thought he was another thug. I crawled around the house on my belly with my gun drawn and this little guy met me at the corner, down on his front paws ready to play. I fed him some milk and played with him outside to see if anyone was looking for him, but no one was. When I tried to shoo him on his way, he just sat on my step and cried. It broke my heart, so, we adopted each other. "

Dave bent down to look at the puppy.

"I can almost guarantee that someone just dropped him off on the road to fend for himself," he said. "He's lucky he found you. He wouldn't last a week in the wild." Joe agreed.

"Parson," Dave said. "How'd you decide on that name?"

"Alice came up with it," Joe said, "since I found him at the parsonage."

"Here, let me carry that for you," Dave said, as Joe picked up his things. "Is this a playpen?"

"Yep, Carmen Montoya gave it to me," Joe said.

"Why do you need it?" Dave asked.

Joe looked at Dave and said, "You've never raised a puppy. Have you?"

"No," Dave said.

"If you don't put them in a pen when you leave," Joe said, "they'll cut their teeth on your shoes, socks and everything else. Plus they can get into chemicals and other harmful things. So, just like any other baby, they have to have a pen."

Joe opened his door and Parson ran in under his legs.

"See, what I mean," Joe said. "He adopted me."

Dave chuckled and handed him the playpen. "Have fun boys," he said, as he headed back to the jail.

Joe set the playpen up in the corner and put a towel and Parson in it. The pup curled up on the towel and went to sleep, as if he knew he was home. He was.

When Joe went down to the hoops game, he took Parson. All the kids played with him for a few minutes, before Joe tied his leash to a post during their game. Later, he walked Parson over to meet the smaller kids in the field. Parson bounced around and licked all their faces. His wobbly legs gave out on the way home, so Joe carried him. After they both had dinner, he and Joe waited outside for Dominique.

He almost lost Parson to Dominique. The pup loved her. He bounced and played like he'd met a long lost friend.

When they went into the church, Joe took him through the back door and put a towel in the office for him.

Parson slept as long as Dominique played. When she finished, he was up and ready to go.

Joe locked the back door and walked to the front to lock it. Standing outside, he told Dominique that Ralph thought they could probably have the Methodist piano for the Kindergarten.

She was very happy and wanted to know when they could move it to the Kindergarten, so she could work on it.

He told her he'd have to arrange it. He was amazed at how well she understood English. Of course, he was adding a lot of hand signs, too.

He took Parson for a walk and went inside to get ready for his surveillance trip. He put Parson in the playpen, grabbed a stack of tapes and locked the door. He stood outside and listened. Parson seemed content, so he left.

He changed the tape on Max's old house and moved over to the bar. Although it was still closed, he suspected activity upstairs, so he continued to tape the area. He changed the rest of the tapes, noticed a small light in Max's apartment and none in the front storage unit.

Good, he thought, *He stayed in his own place tonight.*

He worked back around the other blocks and went home. He walked Parson and secured the house for the night. He watched the tapes. There wasn't any unusual activity on them.

Parson was content in the playpen as long as Joe was in the same room with him. But he didn't like Joe being in the bedroom. After several attempts to convince the pup to settle down, Joe picked him up and put him on the bed.

Parson curled up at his feet and went to sleep.

Joe chuckled to himself and said, "So much for training him. He's training me."

CHAPTER THIRTY-FOUR

FRIDAY – FIFTH WEEK

Parson made it through the first half of the jog. He piggy backed on Joe's shoulders for the second half.

When they stopped to see Grandma, she played with the pup and handed Joe a foil pack of meat scraps for him. Joe took a few minutes to ask about the Kindergarten.

"The first day was hectic, but the kids are excited about learning English – or, to quote them – they want to be able to talk to Preacher Man. I intend to exploit that incentive," she said, with a twinkle in her eye.

He laughed and told her Dominique thought she could fix the old Methodist piano for them.

"That would be wonderful," she said. "We could add music to our curriculum."

"We need to wait for Charley's approval," Joe said, "and find some movers. As soon as we get it into the Kindergarten room, she can start working on it. Ralph isn't very optimistic about saving it, but we'll see what she can do."

At home, Joe had coffee and cereal. Parson had puppy food and pork chop scraps.

"Something's wrong with this picture," he told Parson.

The pup pulled his head out of his dish and looked at Joe, as if to say –"What?"

Joe laughed and said, "I don't guess you see it the same way I do, do you boy?"

290

He walked Parson and cleaned up for the day. He threw some clothes in the washer, holstered his revolver and walked Parson over to Dave's jail. Parson sniffed out all the cells and curled up on Dave's jacket on the floor. Dave's mouth flew open the same second Joe grabbed Parson.

"See," Joe said, "he'll make you pick up your stuff. Maybe, I should loan him to Susan for a day."

Dave made a threatening comment and Joe laughed.

Joe got the key to the fire station and dug through the garage sale box. He found a large pillow and put it in the corner by Dave's desk. Parson curled up on it.

"Next thing I know, you'll want me to deputize him," Dave grumbled.

"You could do worse," Joe said. He grinned when he realized Dave was petting Parson all the time he was grumbling.

He and Parson walked over to the general store. Ginger spoiled the pup while he purchased a deadbolt, electric drill, bits, screws and steel brackets. Then he and Gene rummaged through the storeroom and found a forty inch piece of two-by-four.

Armed with their equipment, he and Parson walked over to see Max. The stairs were a new experience for Parson. Joe carried the tools upstairs and then showed Parson how to climb up. They knocked on the door. Max answered hesitantly, until he recognized Joe's voice.

When he opened the door, he looked down at Parson and said, "If you brought him for me, I gotta tell you, he's not much of a guard dog."

Joe laughed and said, "No Max, this is my new dog, Parson. I agree that he's not much of a guard dog right now, but I'll bet he will be when he grows up."

He showed Max what he'd bought and explained how he wanted to use them to strengthen his door. Max was surprised at Joe's concern, but he agreed to let him install the stuff.

"You just sit in your chair and pet Parson – and watch a master at work," Joe joked.

It took him a while to get the deadbolt set. Then he mounted the steel brackets on each side of the door and showed Max how to wedge the two-by-four in them. Going outside, Joe showed Max that the two-by-four would make it much harder for anyone else to break in. Max tested the lock and tried the two-by-four a couple of times. He seemed genuinely happy about them. He thanked Joe and was a little reluctant to let Parson leave, but Parson was at the door as soon as Joe called him.

Reversing the situation, Joe showed Parson how to walk down the steps and then ran back up to get his tools. Parson was back on the landing when Joe turned around.

"Okay, smart guy," Joe said, "this time we'll walk down together." Max laughed at them and thanked Joe again.

Joe and Parson went home for lunch. Coffee and a peanut butter sandwich for Joe. The rest of the pork chop scraps for Parson. Joe chuckled. He could see who was going to get the short end of the stick at meal time.

After a quick walk outside, Parson settled into his playpen for a nap while Joe threw the clothes in the dryer and worked on his Sunday sermons. Everything had been so hectic this week, he hadn't devoted much time to his preaching job.

Checking his e-mail, he found an update from Jack. EXAMINER FOUND FORTY FIVE ON CURRENT COZEN PAYROLL. ELIMINATING THE TWO DEAD AND THIRTY-SIX IN COUNTY JAIL, YOU STILL HAVE SEVEN. FOUR ARE NAMES YOU KNOW – THOMAS AND PAULINE TYSON, CHAD ORSON AND ERNESTO. THE OTHER THREE ARE MARCUS SPENSER, KEITH UNGER AND CRAIG RILEY. WE DON'T HAVE ANY INFORMATION ON THEM YET – BUT WANTED TO SHARE WHAT WE FOUND. WE'RE WATCHING FOR ANY NEW NAMES TO REPLACE THOSE IN JAIL.

Joe answered. THANKS FOR THE INFORMATION. I'LL WATCH FOR THOSE NAMES. NEED TO LET YOU KNOW, I HAVE A FOUR-LEGGED AGENT-IN-TRAINING. HIS NAME IS PARSON, BECAUSE I FOUND HIM AT THE PARSONAGE. HE'S ABOUT SIX MONTHS OLD AND SHOULD GROW TO FIFTY OR SIXTY POUNDS IN A FEW MONTHS. HE LOVES MEAT SCRAPS AND MILK BONES.

He laughed. He could see Jack shaking his head about the dog. *Too bad,* Joe thought. *He's part of the team now.*

He'd picked verses for Petey and Lily next week and was working on his sermons when Jack sent his message back. WE'LL TAKE ALL THE RECRUITS WE CAN GET – BUT DON'T PUT HIS DOG FOOD ON YOUR EXPENSE REPORT.

Joe laughed out loud. Jack was always thinking about the budget. He had all the administrative headaches related to these missions.

When he had his sermons ready, he took Parson for a walk before he changed for his surveillance run. Armed and carrying tapes, he put Parson in the pen and locked up.

He walked south to Max's old house, then over to the bar. He was surprised to see it open. Sitting in the weeds, he changed the tapes and watched the crowd through the window. The redhead was tending the bar and apparently running the operation. It seemed to be a pretty quiet night inside. He wondered where Chad and Ernesto were.

Working over to the Hispanic area, everything looked okay. He walked around to the field and looked at the grass.

Need to ask Father Romero to mow again, he thought.

He went over to the truck lot and checked Max's place while he changed tapes. He sat on the side of the hotel and just listened. The night was too still. Something had spooked the insects in the fields. He moved to the shadows around the storage units and listened again. Then he heard a truck. Looking across to the oil rig, he counted four trucks in the area. He looked back at the hatch – it was clear. *Could they be planning to use the tunnel to get into town unnoticed?* he wondered.

He needed to call Dave, but he didn't want to leave. Looking up, he wasn't sure he could convince Max to let him in to use the phone. Taking a chance, he slipped up Max's steps and prayed he still had his hearing aids on as he tapped lightly on the door. *Please don't turn on any lights,* he begged silently, as he waited for Max. Hearing a voice behind the door, he said, "Max, its Joe let me in." A couple of minutes later, he heard Max move the board and unlock the door.

"I need to use your phone," Joe said. "It's important."

Max nodded and Joe dialed Dave.

"Where and how many?" Dave answered.

"None yet, but I need you to roll dark and quiet to the basketball lot and park in the shadows. Bring the two-way radios and some binoculars," Joe said quietly, trying not to let Max hear. He didn't want to traumatize him again.

"Thanks, Max," Joe said, as he hung up. "Now lock up and get some rest." He stood on the landing and waited until he heard the lock catch and the board slide back in place.

Working back downstairs and into the shadows, he startled Dave when he knocked on the passenger door. He described what he'd seen and said, "They may be trying to use the tunnel to get into town quietly." Dave swore.

"Using the tunnel doesn't break any laws," Joe said. "But I don't think they're coming here to socialize. We'll have to catch them breaking the law in town. If we can arrest them without exposing the tunnel, we might still be able to get this group on the smuggling charges, too." Dave agreed.

Joe took the binoculars and one of the radios. He asked Dave to pull back into the shadows between the drug store and the feed store until he heard from him. "Tell Susan to stay out of the jail," he added, as he faded into the shadows.

Back on the side of the storage units, Joe focused the binoculars on the shed. The men had been standing around talking while he briefed Dave. Apparently, they were arguing about something. He could see them waving their arms at each other. Finally, they seemed to reach an agreement and Joe counted five men going into the shed. Watching and listening, he heard voices in the peanut silo. *Angie's ghosts,* he thought.

Then he heard the hydraulics opening the hatch. He'd been updating Dave by radio. He turned his off and waited.

He listened to a voice saying, "This is where the truck will be. All you have to do is unload the women, put them in the silo and go home. The next night, you come down here, load them into another truck and go home again. That's all."

Joe hoped his tape was getting all this. He thought Chad was the speaker. As the hatch was closing, he heard the man say, "Be here Monday night, eight o'clock sharp."

He watched the men exit the shed and drive off. Then he radioed Dave and went around the building to brief him.

"False alarm, Dave," Joe said. "Sorry. Apparently, tonight was just a training run for the new men they brought in for their Monday and Tuesday night smuggling activities. I watched them until they all drove off. So I think we're okay tonight. Thanks for backing me up so fast."

"I'm glad it was a false alarm," Dave said. "But I'd rather be waiting for them, than have them arrive unannounced." Looking around he asked, "Where did you find a phone?"

"Max let me use his," Joe said.

"Max," Dave said, shaking his head. "You've even reached the town hermit." He drove Joe back over to the jail.

"What happened to Max's wife, Ellie?" Joe asked. "I mean, how did she die?"

"She got sick about three years ago," Dave said. "She had a heart attack and died. Max was devoted to her. She was his life. His grief was so deep none of us could reach him. When he lost his house, Cozen offered him that apartment if he'd watch the units. He took it and basically locked himself away from all the rest of us."

"Does he have any children?" Joe asked.

"They had a son," Dave said. "He was killed in Viet Nam. I don't know of any other relatives."

Joe returned Dave's binoculars and suggested they keep the radios on them, since it had been a close call trying to reach him tonight. Dave agreed. Joe thanked him again and went home to Parson.

After a quick walk, Joe and Parson watched the tapes.

The tape on Max's old house showed a lady going inside in the morning and leaving four hours later. Looking closer, Joe thought she looked like Margarita Salazar. She must be the one keeping it clean, but probably not his guardian angel. The other tapes were normal.

Joe sent Jack an e-mail. WE HAD FOUR TRUCKS AND FIVE MEN AT THE OIL SHACK TONIGHT. I SCRAMBLED DAVE, THINKING THEY MIGHT USE THE TUNNEL TO ENTER TOWN AND CAUSE MORE TROUBLE. THEY WENT INTO THE TUNNEL SO ONE MAN – PROBABLY CHAD – COULD SHOW THE OTHER FOUR WHAT TO DO NEXT MON AND TUES NIGHTS. HE HAD THE HATCH OPEN SO I COULD HEAR WHAT HE SAID. HE SPECIFICALLY DESCRIBED LOADING AND UNLOADING THE WOMEN – APPARENTLY THEY'RE READY TO ROLL AGAIN. HE TOLD THEM TO BE AT THE SHACK AT EIGHT SHARP ON MONDAY. I HAD MY CAMERA ROLLING. I HOPE IT CAUGHT THAT INFO. I'LL CHECK IT TOMORROW.

He walked Parson again, locked the house and they went to bed.

CHAPTER THIRTY-FIVE

SATURDAY – FIFTH WEEK

He and Parson jogged around town. Parson was getting stronger, but not quite up to such a long run. Grandma was waiting for them with another pack of scraps. She was working on her Sherie Anderson garden. She'd sent Sherie a picture and Sherie had written back. Joe was right, Sherie was very happy Grace had transplanted her flowers.

"See, I told you she'd love it," he said. "You two had the prettiest gardens in town. Did she mention finding some of them in the truck?"

"Oh, yes," she said. "Sherie said to thank you for helping her daughter dig them up. They survived the trip and she has them thriving at her new home."

"Good," he said, "I'm glad they survived. We weren't sure they would." Laughing at Parson jumping beside him, he said, "I guess I'd better go. I think he wants his five-star breakfast in this foil. Thanks again." He waved as Parson pulled him down the block.

After breakfast and Parson's walk, he cleaned up and rearmed. Before leaving the house, he called Father Romero, checked on his health and asked if he could send his mower back to cut the field.

"I'll send a man in today," Romero said. "Thanks for letting me know. I should've thought about a maintenance schedule for the field. I'll set one up."

Joe and Parson walked to town. First stop was the barber shop. When Roy and Rhonda looked at Joe and his dog, Joe laughed and said, "Just one for a haircut. He says he wants to keep all of his. Do you mind if he sits in the corner while Roy cuts mine?"

Rhonda and Jeanette were already playing with the pup.

Roy chuckled and said, "I guess not." Joe told them a modified story about finding Parson digging in the trash and how Alice named him.

Next, he walked over to see if Ralph and Charley had reached a decision on the piano. Ralph frowned at a dog in his store, but Doris and Danny overruled him. He and Charley had agreed that the Kindergarten could have the piano. He gave Joe the keys to the church so he could move it. Joe left to find a truck and some men.

He walked down to the feed store to ask Charley if he knew of anyone with a truck they could use. Jesse MacKenna and his family pulled into the parking lot in a full-size pickup truck. The kids stopped to meet Parson while Joe talked to the parents. He explained what he was trying to do and asked Jesse if they could use his truck. Jesse was happy to help and tagged Richard and Randall to give them a hand. Sheila took the two younger kids with her. Joe sent Richard into the store to call Chris and snag Jerry for a few minutes. Thirty minutes later, they had the piano out of the church and in the Kindergarten. Joe thanked everyone and returned the keys to Ralph.

Then he headed over to the Sanchez house to tell Dominique about the piano. Once Parson stopped hopping around her, she told Elena about the piano and took the three older kids over to see it.

The kids played with Parson while Joe helped her take off the remaining wood panels. They dusted and cleaned the soundboard, strings and hammers. Then key by key she tuned it. When she sat down and played some scales and chords, it sounded wonderful – and he told her so.

They were reassembling the outside panels when Ralph stuck his head through the back door and asked, "Is that our old piano I'm hearing?"

"Yes it is," Joe said. "I told you she could work miracles with pianos."

"She sure can," Ralph said, as he helped Joe set one of the panels. He went into the storeroom and came back with some wood glue for the broken one. He promised to put it in place after the glue dried.

Dominique played for the children and they danced around the room. Ralph and Joe stood back and enjoyed the moment. Joe knew only one other person who could assemble and disassemble pianos like that – and he missed her terribly. He loved music, especially piano music. Dominique's playing made him happy and sad at the same time.

He wondered what Angelique would say about this little town. Even more, he wondered what he was going to do when he had to leave. Shaking off those melancholy thoughts, he left and went over to check on Max.

When Max opened the door, his face looked better, but Joe guessed he hadn't worked his muscles very much. He was getting stiff and that wasn't good. Joe coaxed Max downstairs to take a little walk with Parson. Then he had an idea. Under the guise of walking Parson, he edged Max over to the drug store – or more specifically, the Kindergarten. He could hear Dominique still playing, so he suggested they go inside and listen – to let Max rest. He eased Max up the stairs and into the room. Max froze. He just stood there and stared at Dominique.

Joe was so worried he was ready to go get Doc, when Max finally took a deep breath and walked over to the piano. He touched it like it was the most sacred thing on earth.

"My Ellie's piano... it's my Ellie's piano," he said again, as if confirming his own recognition. "You fixed it. They broke it the night they killed my Ellie." Joe was stunned.

He pulled up a chair and helped Max sit down. He signaled Dominique to send one of the kids for Ralph. She said something quietly in Spanish. Christina left through the storeroom and came back with him. Joe waved Ralph closer and signaled him to hold on a minute.

"What happened the night Ellie died?" Joe asked softly.

"They came to the house and beat me up," Max said. "When she tried to help me, they hit her. She had a bad heart from all the poison in the water. They hit her so hard she never woke up."

"Who hit her?" Joe asked.

"They wore masks, so I wasn't able to prove it to the Judge," Max said. "But I knew it was Hernando and Felipe."

"Why did they beat you up?" Joe asked.

"Because I wouldn't sign the papers giving them my house," Max said.

"Who was the Judge?" Joe asked. "Do you remember?"

"That Orson guy, Chad's brother," Max said angrily.

"Did you call Doctor Stockwell?" Joe asked.

"Yeah, he came right over, but he couldn't save my Ellie. She was gone," Max said, with tears welling in his eyes.

"Did Doc take care of your injuries?" Joe asked.

"Yeah, he bandaged me up real good, but I didn't care about me. I wanted him to take care of my Ellie," Max sobbed.

"I know, Max," Joe said, hugging him. "It was very hard for you to lose your Ellie. I'm sorry I brought you here. I never would've done it if I'd known it would bring back such bad memories."

"Oh, no," Max said. "Seeing my Ellie's piano fixed is a good memory. Those same men broke into the church and busted her piano, so we couldn't have any more church music. She always played for them. She played like an angel."

Looking at Dominique, he asked Joe, "Does she know *Claire de Lune*? That was my Ellie's favorite song."

"I don't know, Max..." Joe started to say, when the room hushed.

Dominique rippled over that old piano with the most beautiful rendition of *Clair de Lune* any of them had ever heard. Max had tears running down his cheeks when she finished. No man has ever been closer to heaven than he was at that moment.

He got up out of his chair and walked over to Dominique. His gnarled hand gently touched her cheek. He kissed her forehead and said, "You have given me the greatest joy I have known since my Ellie died. Thank you."

With tears in her own eyes, Dominique said, in broken English, "You come back. I play more."

Max nodded and sat back down.

"Max, didn't you work as a janitor at the school when it was open?" Joe asked, as he looked around the room.

"Yes," he said.

"Well, we've just set this room up as a Kindergarten for the little kids," Joe said. "I'm sure the teachers could use some help cleaning up in the afternoons. Why don't you come over and help them? Dominique can play for you while you're here."

"Do you really think the teachers need me?" Max asked.

"I'm sure they do," Joe said. "Why don't you come over about ... he looked at Dominique and she signaled two ..."two o'clock tomorrow and see if you can help."

"I will," Max said. "Now I think I'd like to go home."

Joe signaled Ralph to wait for him. He walked Max home and came back.

Ralph was still in the room with Dominique and the kids. Ralph's eyes showed the same sympathetic pain Joe felt. Walking away from the kids who were playing with Parson, he asked Ralph to write down what he heard Max say and sign and date it. Ralph agreed. Joe said he was going to do the same.

To Dominique, he asked, "Where did you learn to play *Clair de Lune* like that?"

She said something in Spanish to Ralph.

Ralph translated, "It was her uncle's favorite. She memorized it for a recital."

"It was absolutely beautiful," Joe said. "I've only heard one other person play it like that. You truly made an old man very happy. Thank you." He asked Ralph to translate to be sure she understood how deeply he appreciated what she did.

He carried his exhausted puppy over to see Dave.

Dave took one look at Joe's face and knew something had just broken his heart. He looked at the pup to see if it was hurt, but it was okay. So, he just waited. Joe put Parson on his pillow in the corner and pulled up a chair.

"Just listen to what I'm going to tell you and then we'll talk," Joe said.

Dave nodded and Joe started relating the events with Max. When he finished, Dave was bewildered and devastated. He walked to the files and went through three drawers before he pulled out a folder marked Ellie Tipton. Opening it, he looked at the dates and leaned back in his chair.

"I couldn't remember any of the details you just repeated. This is why," he said.

He turned the folder around and pointed to the signature at the bottom of the report. "Susan's mother was very ill and we went to Santa Fe to be with her," he said. "Ellie died while we were gone. *Orson* investigated her death."

"Sometimes I find it hard to be a preacher," Joe said.

"I'm not a preacher," Dave said. "Tell me what you want me to say for you."

Joe sputtered for a minute and then chuckled.

"You're already thinking the same thing I am," he said. "I don't know how or if we can prove what Max just said. But if we can, I want Orson, Felipe and Hernando facing murder charges." Dave agreed.

Joe and Parson made one more stop before dinner. They went to Ben's house to tell Grandma and Ben about the piano Dominique repaired. Then he told them Max recognized it as his wife's piano and how happy he was listening to Dominique play.

He didn't tell them about the murder allegations, but he did tell Grandma about his suggestion that Max come over at two every afternoon, to help the teachers clean up – and hear Dominique play. "I think the music and the kids will help bring Max out of his seclusion," he said.

They were amazed that Joe managed to get Max out and even more surprised that Max agreed to come out each day.

"I'll make sure we have something for him to do," Grandma said. "And I'll work the kids toward him, too."

He picked Parson up to leave when Alice said, "Go wash your hands and put Parson in the corner. It's dinner time." He apologized for not noticing the time and started out the door.

"Joseph Marsh," Alice said, "if you can do this much for our community, we can certainly feed you. Now go wash up and take a seat or I'll give Parson your pork chop."

He whipped around the corner, washed his hands and sat down. Parson whimpered and the others laughed.

Walking home with Parson, he thought about the fun he had with Ben's family. They always made him feel at home. In many ways, he was closer to them than he'd ever been to his own family. He was the *problem child* in his family. His father's sermons came in handy on Sunday, but he knew his dad would never agree with the faith based approach he'd taken here.

301

He certainly wasn't the social climber his rich mother wanted or a financial wizard like Asher.

He did miss Angelique, though. Hearing Dominique play this afternoon made him so homesick for her. He wished he could just pack the two of them off to..... *Where,* he asked himself, *to a place like this? Angelique's concert career is centered on the east coast. Her friends and family are all there. It would be unbelievably selfish of me to expect her to give all that up for small town USA. She'd wither and wilt out here.* He took a hard look at the shabby little town and knew he was right. *Shake this off,* he told himself, *stay focused on the job and then worry about the future.*

He unlocked his door and put his exhausted puppy in the playpen. He changed into his black clothes, concealed his firearms, hooked the radio to his belt, grabbed some tapes, locked the door and did his surveillance run.

The bar was busier tonight with the dance. He changed the tape in the camera and sat in the weeds for a while to watch.

He wondered who the redhead was who took over the bar. He needed to ask Dave about her. He wrote down descriptions and tags on a couple of new trucks. He suspected they belonged to the new guys coming in for tunnel work. The crowd inside was noisy, but not unruly, so he went over to the other cameras and headed home.

He watched the tapes. His camera had caught Chad's instructions and the faces of the other four in the hatch last night. There was nothing new on the other tapes. He logged them in and locked the tunnel tape in his tool box.

After taking Parson out for a quick walk, he locked the door and the two of them went to bed.

CHAPTER THIRTY-SIX

SUNDAY – SIXTH WEEK

He and Parson were up, fed, showered, dressed, walked and armed by seven. He locked the house and took Parson and the two way radio over to the office while he went into the sanctuary to set things up for the Methodist service.

Walking upstairs, he looked at the cramped conditions for the Catholic services. With all the attacks this week, he hadn't remembered to take the walls out. He dusted their makeshift altar and tried to arrange the chairs a little better.

Have to fix this, he told himself.

Back downstairs, he sat in the office with Parson and reviewed his sermons. Dominique arrived at eight with some Catholic music she received from Domingo when he came in to mow yesterday. She didn't have a key to the Kindergarten, so she came early to practice.

While she played, he walked Parson around the church and checked the area again. When the Methodist families arrived, Parson and the kids played for a few minutes. Then he took Parson back to the office, locked the back door and walked into the sanctuary. During his announcements, he told the three families about moving their church piano to the new Kindergarten and Dominique's amazing restoration.

Ralph confirmed Joe's statements and said, "She has it playing better now than it ever did before."

Then Joe told them that Max Tipton had visited the Kindergarten and recognized the piano as his wife's piano that she used to play for their services.

He saw Charley and Mary nodding. "I remember Ellie playing," Mary said, "but I didn't know it was her piano. After it was broken, I guess we forgot about it."

"Well," Joe said, "since Dominique worked her magic and has it repaired, I'm going to order a plaque commemorating Ellie Tipton. We'll attach it to the piano when it arrives."

They all liked that idea.

He also announced that he was going to take out the walls in the church balcony this afternoon after lunch. He invited anyone who wanted to get dusty to join him. After a couple of chuckles, they started their service.

The Methodists were leaving when the Catholic congregation arrived. Joe let the kids play with Parson. Seeing Father Romero's raised eyebrow at Parson, Joe laughed and told him how he found the pup and why they named him Parson.

Angie flew to her "Preaker Man" for a quick shoulder ride, while he told Father Romero about the afternoon project. He asked him to invite any volunteers back to help.

When he started to put Angie down she turned to Father Romero and asked timidly, "Papa Romo?"

When Joe said, "Si," she threw her arms out to Father Romero for a big hug.

Afterward, more than a little embarrassed, Father Romero, put her down and straightened his attire.

Joe smiled and said, "Nothing you're wearing is as precious as that hug, so don't worry about a wrinkle or two."

Father Romero relaxed and agreed. Joe looked around at the crowd and was pleased to see that Father Gordon had arrived with Father Romero – and said so.

"He has a good heart and a lot of potential," he told Father Romero as they walked into the church.

"I agree," Father Romero said. "I guess I'm more cautious after the last two."

"Trust your heart, Father," he said. "It never lies to you."

He went back outside to get Parson. Then he set the church up for the Baptist service.

Before Father Romero left, he told Joe that some of the men said they'd come over around two to help. Then he asked

Joe about all the attacks in town. Joe glossed over most of it, saying they put thirty-six men in jail and sent two to the morgue.

Joe asked if any of the workers at his church had shown signs of drug withdrawal.

"No," Father Romero said, "but I have Father Gordon and my new Field Manager watching for it." As they walked to the car, Joe thanked him for mowing the field again.

He put Parson back in the office and locked that door again. He walked into the sanctuary for the Baptist service. He made a similar announcement about the work this afternoon and announced the opening of the Kindergarten. Then he asked Sarah and Dale to do their recitations. As predicted, Petey and Lily wanted another set for next week. He moved on to his sermon and the rest of the service.

Afterward, he thanked Dominique for playing and thanked her again for making Max so happy yesterday. He locked the church and took Parson for a walk.

Still thinking about Max, he wandered down to the house south of the church. It was such a pretty little house. He could almost see Max and his Ellie enjoying happier times inside. Walking around to the back, he saw what had once been a flower garden and the remnants of bushes.

Moving closer to the filter on the water pipes, he wrote down the name and the specifications on the tank. Then he saw a faded company name that had apparently been stenciled onto the lower rim, Tyson Filter Company, RR 12, Lubbock, TX.

Following the path of the pipes, he saw the loose panel on the outside of the house by the kitchen sink. Too angry to speak, he used his keys to pry it open. Inside he found the same configuration that he had on his house. Parson, apparently impatient to keep walking, started digging at his feet. Turning to admonish the pup, he saw the syringes Parson was digging up.

He ran home to get a camera, rubber gloves and plastic bags. He put Parson in the playpen for a nap, locked up and went back to Max's house. He photographed the filter tank and the interior of the wall by the kitchen. Then he picked up the loose syringes and put them in a labeled bag. He walked to the empty houses north of the church and found the same tanks, back panels to the kitchens and syringes at all three location. He took the evidence back to his house and fed himself and Parson.

He walked Parson and left him in the pen while he grabbed his few tools and went back to the church to work on the balcony. Fourteen men showed up to help him. He was overwhelmed. As they discussed the best way to do the work, he saw the Hispanic men migrating to their employers.

Probably more comfortable with them, he thought.

Ben took Alberto and Archibaldo over to the far room and started ripping off sheet rock. Gene took Alfonso and Manuel to the other side of Ben's wall and started on it. Charley took Pedro and Jorge inside the first room. Ralph, Roy and Roger took the other side of that wall. Jesse and Miguel helped Joe remove the plywood over the balcony half wall.

As they worked, each of the teams was trying to haul their trash downstairs and outside. Joe was looking for an easier way when he heard some familiar voices downstairs.

"Yeah, we can't let a bunch of old men do this by themselves," Chris said.

"Okay, I guess we'd better help before we have to carry all of them over to Doc's," Harry said. Gabbie called the guys a name in Spanish that Joe wasn't supposed to understand.

He kept a straight face and hollered down to them.

"It's about time you deadbeats got over here," he said. "We'd decided you were afraid of a little hard work."

"Afraid? No way!" Chris bantered back. "We were just giving you old-timers enough time to climb the stairs."

"Since you're so worried about us *old-timers* on the stairs," Joe taunted, "you can run the stairs and haul this junk out back." They moaned.

Joe laughed and said, "Its good training for you hot shots." All the time they bantered, they worked – hard.

Eddie and Gabbie were dishing it out in Spanish with their dads and the other Hispanic men.

"Good kids," Joe told the men, "a little cocky – but good kids." Ben translated and the *old-timers* got a laugh.

By four o'clock all the debris was stacked behind church. The plywood that had covered the balcony wall was stacked out front. Since it was good wood, Ben was going to store it for future use.

The kids dusted off their clothes, turned to the men and challenged all of them to a game of hoops. Joe thought it was a great idea, but the others weren't too sure. The kids weren't going to give up. After a few more sassy comments, they'd taunted their seniors into the game of the century – at least for Eutopian Springs – the Old-timers against the Smart Alecs.

Joe locked the church, picked up Parson and locked the house. The kids ran through the street bouncing the basketball and hooting about the game. By the time the men got to the lot, half of the town had come over to watch.

"We should've sold tickets," Joe told Parson.

He found Dominique in the crowd – or more correctly – Parson found Dominique before Joe had a chance to look around. She agreed to hold the pup while he played.

And play they did!

The old-timers had a few tricks to show the young punks. The youngsters had some good moves themselves.

When the game finally ended, the youngsters were worn out and the old-timers were wheezing, but everyone agreed they'd had a great time. The fans were even appreciative.

Doris raided her ice cream box. Alice emptied her popsicle rack. Elena and Carmen carried out pitchers of iced tea and cups. Nadia and Margarita brought homemade cookies. They sat around the lot talking and laughing while the younger kids tried their luck with the big basketball and hoop. Angie sat by herself at the corner of the Kelly's house. She was too afraid to come over. Joe signaled Gabbie and they walked over to her.

"Tell her that as long as I'm with her," Joe said, "I'll fight any ghost she hears. She can still stay away if I'm not here, but ask her to trust me to protect her."

Gabbie translated. They watched Angie debate what she'd said. Then she held one small hand out to Joe. When he lifted her up to his shoulder, she held onto his hair so hard, he knew he was going to be bald by morning. But as terrified as she was, she let him take her over to the lot.

He picked up a popsicle from Alice and split it with Angie. She never left his lap, but that was okay. At least she'd trusted him to keep her safe. Joe was happy – covered with sticky popsicle juice – but happy. When the crowd disbursed, he carried Angie safely off the lot and back to her house. Then he retrieved Parson from Dominique and went home.

What a day, he thought. *Who would've guessed how much fun we'd have getting together to tear out walls. Maybe we tore down more than physical walls today.*

After he showered and fed himself and Parson, he wrote Jack an e-mail about the renovations and the town's response. He sent the data on Max's old home and the other empty houses. He said he'd check the school tomorrow. He asked Jack to check out the Tyson Filter Company, RR 12, Lubbock, TX. He bet it was bogus, but he wanted to add the name to the accounts their examiner was researching. He said he'd give Jack the evidence when he saw him Tuesday.

He assumed Philman stole most of the items he'd seen in the Archer farmhouse from the vacant properties in town. He wondered why no one had stripped Max's house. He changed to his black clothes, armed himself, hooked the radio to his belt, grabbed some tapes and slipped out for his surveillance run.

When he returned, he walked Parson, locked up and sat down to review the tapes – nothing new. He logged them on his laptop and checked his e-mail. He had a message from Jack. HEADS UP! FOURTEEN MEN FROM TEXAS ADDED TO PAYROLL LATE FRIDAY. EXAMINER FOUND DOCUMENTS YESTERDAY – ALSO FOUND TWO VAN RENTALS IN LUBBOCK ON FRIDAY FOR TRAVEL TO PORTALES ON MONDAY. THAT'S ALL WE KNOW NOW. WE'RE GOING TO WATCH THE RENTAL RETURN OFFICE, TO SEE IF THEY DISCLOSE ANY INFORMATION ON THEIR DESTINATION.

Joe answered. THANKS FOR THE INFO, I'LL LET DAVE KNOW. WE'LL WATCH FOR THEM. ARE WE STILL ON FOR TUESDAY NIGHT?

Jack was on-line and answered. SAME PLAN AS LAST WEEK – UNLESS WE DETECT ANOTHER PROBLEM.

Joe answered. OKAY, SEE YOU TUESDAY. PS: BRING ROAST FOR PARSON – HA

Jack sent back: IF I BRING ROAST, IT'S FOR ME. HE CAN HAVE THE BONE. Joe logged off and laughed. He told Parson that Jack was a heartless boss.

CHAPTER THIRTY-SEVEN

MONDAY – SIXTH WEEK

He dressed, armed himself, locked the door and took Parson out for their jog. Parson had already memorized the trail. When he intentionally missed a turn, Parson sat down and waited for Joe to come back. "Pretty soon, I can just send you out to jog for me, can't I, buddy," he said.

As soon as they turned on Grandma's street, Parson literally pulled Joe over to her yard. Laughing, he told Grandma, "Parson knows where you live. Look at him. He pulled me over here and then stopped to wait for you."

She played with Parson and slipped the foil pack to Joe.

"Now you've done it," he groaned playfully. "He'll drag me home and tackle me for those scraps."

She laughed when Parson pulled him down the street.

He fed Parson and himself. He cleaned up and took Parson out for a quick walk. Then they locked up and went over to see Dave. As soon as he opened the door, Parson checked all three cells before he curled up on his pillow.

"I may deputize him after all," Dave said, watching him. "He's pretty thorough." Looking at Joe, he said, "I'm almost afraid to ask what brings you over here this early."

"Yep," Joe said. "You guessed it. My boss has heard that they hired fourteen more men in Texas. They may be traveling from Lubbock to Portales today. We're still on for tomorrow night, unless we have another glitch. But we could have more than the normal number of men in the area. We know they had four new ones the other night. We don't know where these fourteen are going, but I wanted to let you know. Unfortunately, I don't think this is over yet."

"Okay," Dave said. "We'll deal with whatever comes our way. I hear I missed a heck of a ball game yesterday."

"Yes, you did. We had a great time," Joe said. "I wish you could've joined us. We missed you."

"Yeah, well, *someone I know* wanted assault charges written against the thugs that terrorized Max," Dave said.

"Sorry," Joe said, "I can't believe the paperwork you have to prepare."

"It wasn't that bad," Dave said. "When I finished, I went home and watched a football game while you kept everyone else entertained."

"Okay, I won't feel sorry for you then," Joe said, as he headed for the door. "By the way, I keep forgetting to ask you the name of the redheaded lady in the bar."

"That's Roz, Rozalyn Orson," Dave said. "She's Chad Orson's half-sister. She and Clive have been living together over the bar for several years now."

"She's Clive's live-in?" Joe asked puzzled. "He must be pretty liberal about their relationship. I've seen her take several different men upstairs."

"Yeah, well Clive worships the dollar, as you well know," Dave said. "I doubt if he cares what she does with other men as long as she gets paid."

"The bar was open this weekend. It looked like she was running it," Joe said, still thinking about the relationship. "I guess she's taking advantage of his absence."

"She has more brains than Clive ever did," Dave said. "He may not have a bar when he gets back."

"The other question I have is about Max's old house," Joe said. "It's neat and clean and still fully furnished. Is someone living there?"

"No," Dave said. "Max has some sort of agreement with Cozen. He works the storage units for them and they let him keep the house the way it was when Ellie died."

"Doesn't Wellman own the house?" Joe asked.

"Yes and no," Dave said. "Max defaulted on some loan, so technically the house was foreclosed. But they let him keep it and no one cleaned it out like the other places. It's a strange arrangement. Max even pays Margarita Salazar to clean it each week. The same way she did all the time Ellie was sick."

"Who lived in the other vacant houses north of the church?" Joe asked.

"Those were the other teachers," Dave said, thinking back. "The Bartons lived in the house nearest the church, then the Millers and the Swensons."

"When did the school close?" Joe asked.

"The same year Cozen moved out," Dave said.

"Did the teachers leave then, too?" Joe asked.

"Yeah," Dave said. "They lost their jobs so they had to move on. The Swenson's had a sick little boy who died just before they left. I think they wanted to get away from the memories here."

"How did their little boy die?" Joe asked.

"The water…" Dave started to say and stopped. "Damn! Did they do that, too?"

"Very possibly," Joe said, grimacing at the thought. "Max's house and the other three all have loose panels on the back by the kitchen, with fittings just like the ones on my house. And I've found syringes on the ground at all four locations. I'm going to give them to my boss to see if we can get fingerprints."

Dave shook his head and said, "That makes four suspected homicides."

"Technically three suspected homicides," Joe said. "Father Lopez, Reverend Anderson and the Swenson boy. If we can prove what Max said, Ellie was murdered during the attack."

"That's true – if we can prove it," Dave said.

"What about the school?" Joe asked. "Is it a town or county school?"

"It was a county school," Dave said. "When they closed it, they moved all the equipment and other materials up to the schools in Yucca."

"Does the county still own it?" Joe asked.

"No," Dave said. "They sold it to Wellman about four years ago."

"Did it have water problems?" Joe asked.

"It did for a while," Dave said. "Then they bought one of those filters and the problems stopped. Boy, that was a business!

That company was in here installing filters all over town. People were standing in line for them. Everyone was so afraid of the water they took out big notes just to get them. Of course, that happened when the town was booming, so they had no reason to think they wouldn't be able to pay them off."

"Did you get one?" Joe asked.

"No, we couldn't afford it," Dave said. "We bought the Samuels water. But that was one slick salesman. He said we'd all die if we didn't get them."

"How much did they cost?" Joe asked.

"A lot," Dave said. "Something like fifteen thousand dollars." Joe whistled at the amount. Parson thought he was calling him, so he walked over to Joe.

"Okay, boy, I guess it's time to go," he said. "Tell Dave goodbye." Back to Dave he said, "I'll let you know if I get any more information on the fourteen new guys."

He put Parson in his pen and picked up his camera, gloves and plastic bags. He locked the house and walked over to the school. He found the identical filter on the large school that he'd found on the small houses. He followed the pipes and found a similar loose panel and fittings inside the walls. Rummaging around the ground he dug up two extra large syringes. He prayed every one of them had fingerprints on it.

When he'd bagged and labeled the evidence, he walked over to the Methodist Church and did the same thing there. The Church of Christ was next and then its parsonage. All of the buildings had identical filters, regardless of the size of the building or the anticipated number of consumers. He took the camera and bags of evidence back to his house. Locking up again, he and Parson went to the grocery store for lunch.

"I'll bet she gives you the egg salad and me the crust," Joe said chuckling, as he opened the door to the store…. the very quiet store. Parson froze when Joe did.

There was no cashier at the register, no shoppers showing in the surveillance mirrors on the ceiling, no sounds from the coffee shop and no worker at the gas pumps.

He slowly closed the door with his hand over the bell.

Pushing Parson into a cashier's booth, he tied his leash to the cabinet and whispered, "Stay boy and be quiet."

He pulled his pistol and moved toward the storeroom while he mentally clicked off the people who would've been in the store. The kids were at school and Grandma was at the Kindergarten. That would leave Ben and Alice inside and either Archibaldo or Alberto at the gas pumps. He stopped at the rubber swinging doors and listened.

He heard voices. None of them were familiar to him. They were angry and apparently tearing up the storeroom. Laying flat on the floor, he gently pushed one rubber door open enough to see into the room.

He saw Ben on the floor not moving, Alice being held at gunpoint by one man and Alberto on the floor with his hands tied behind his back. He heard two other men tossing boxes around the store room. One man was cursing at Alice and demanding that she show them where *it* was.

"I don't know," Alice said. "We don't have anything to do with drugs here."

"Well, our guy said he put a box in here," one of them said. "He said he told you where it was…so tell us now or I'll finish off that husband of yours."

Joe slipped around to the coffee shop and called Dave.

"Three men are holding Ben, Alice and Alberto in the storeroom," he said. "I'm going to try to bait them out, one by one. Slip up under the loading dock and be ready to move – if I don't make it. Come on foot. No black and white."

Moving back into the store, Joe put his pistol in his waist band, grabbed a pair of sunglasses off the rack and pulled a white *special* pole off one of the aisles. Using it like a cane, he moved to the back of the store.

He banged into some canned goods and shouted, "Where's the creamed corn, damn it! Why can't somebody help me find my food? Where is everyone? Clerk, clerk, come help me. I'm blind, damn it!"

He flailed around, waving a can in the air and banging into others. He heard one of the men in back tell another one to "Go get rid of him."

Walking around the store, still shouting, Joe watched the mirrors as one of the men slipped up the opposite aisle to stalk him. Turning at the same moment the thug intended to pistol whip him, Joe slammed the can into the side of his face.

As the man slumped to the floor, Joe grabbed some rope off the household aisle, tied him up and pulled his body into the coffee shop – out of the line of vision from the rubber doors.

He picked up another can and continued his ranting.

"What does a man have to do to get some service around here? I'm blind, damn it! I need some help to see the food I need to buy. Is anyone here?" Joe shouted, escalating his voice with every demand.

Finally, he heard another man being sent out to shut him up. Using the same ploy, he watched the mirrors until the thug was within reach. He tied him up and piled him in with his buddy. *That should only leave one back there,* he thought. *But that one has Alice. Ranting a third time would seem too suspicious. Let him think the other one got rid of the blind man.*

He dropped the sun glasses and worked back to the rubber doors. *I'll let him come out here to find them.*

Looking for some cover, he moved a cardboard display of a man promoting motor oil beside the doors. He pulled his pistol and waited. He heard the man's temper rising as he hollered for his two buddies. Finally, shoving Alice through the doors first with a gun in her back, he stepped into the store. Joe body slammed Alice to the floor and shot at the same time.

Only when the man on the floor didn't move, did he look back at Alice. She hadn't made a sound since he hit her. She was sitting on the floor, staring wide-eyed at the man. He gently pulled her into his arms. She was obviously in shock.

"Joe?" Dave called from the storeroom.

"Come on in, Dave," Joe said. "It's clear."

Looking at Alice and the man on the floor, Dave walked over to the coffee shop to call Doc. "What the hell," he said, as he stumbled over the other two.

"Some more for you," Joe said, still holding Alice. When the rubber doors moved, Joe shouted, "Who's there?"

"It's me, Joe," Ben said, "and Alberto."

"Okay," Joe said, as he lowered his pistol.

Ben was leaning heavily on Alberto when they came through the door. Joe eased Alice back against the racks and ran over to help. Alberto was trying to hold twice his own weight.

Easing Ben down by Alice, he asked Alberto, "What did they do to Ben?"

"They hit him on the head with their gun," Alberto said. "Then they kicked him a lot while he was on the floor."

Doc came through the front door and looked around.

"Over here, Doc," Joe shouted. "Ben and Alice are hurt." Turning to Alberto, he asked, "Did they hurt you?"

"No," Alberto said shamefully. "They pulled a gun and used me to make Ben and Alice come into the storeroom."

Seeing the anguish on Alberto's face, Joe said, "You were very brave to do that."

Alberto started to argue, but Joe stopped him.

"If you had tried to fight them, they would've shot you," Joe said. "As soon as Ben and Alice heard that shot, these men would've shot them, too. By doing what they said, you gave us time to get here and help. So, in a way, you saved their lives."

Alberto listened to Joe, but he wasn't convinced until he heard Ben say, "He's right, Alberto. All three of us would be dead now, if you hadn't stayed calm and done what they said."

"Don't ever fight with a man who has a gun on you," Joe said. "That kind of person won't hesitate to shoot. You did exactly the right thing."

Doc checked the man on the floor and declared him dead. Then he looked at Alice. She still hadn't said a word.

"Is she going to be all right, Doc?" Joe asked. "I hit her pretty hard to get her out of the way."

"Yeah," Doc said. "She's in shock. Give her a few more minutes and she'll start coming around. You gave her some bruises, but these men terrorized her."

Moving over to Ben, Doc asked Joe to help him get Ben into a chair. Doc checked his skull and said, "You're going to have a heck of a headache for a few days, but it doesn't look like they cracked that hard head of yours." Ben tried to respond, but he sucked air from the pain. Checking his torso, Doc found three cracked ribs and some very sore kidneys. "You'll heal," Doc said. "But you're going to hurt like the devil for a while."

Doc checked Alberto and turned to Joe.

He waved Doc off and said, "I'm fine, but the two in the coffee shop ran into some canned goods while they were shopping." Doc shook his head and laughed.

Sitting back down beside Alice, Joe held her and talked softly. He apologized for hitting her so hard and told her that Ben and Alberto were okay. Finally, she let out a couple of short sobs – and then the dam broke. She sobbed uncontrollably. He was fine with that. At least she was coming out of shock.

When he heard a faint whine, he realized he'd forgotten Parson. The pup had sat perfectly still through all of this. He eased Alice into Ben's arms and went up to get him.

"What is that?" Doc asked.

"That is a dog named Parson, Doc," Joe said. "We adopted each other a couple of days ago. Be nice to him or I'll send you more patients."

"Oh, Lord, not that," Doc said. "I'll be nice, I promise."

As soon as Joe released Parson, the pup ran to Alice. He hopped up and down at her side until she picked him up. Then he started licking her chin and her face until she laughed at him.

"Leave it to a little pup to know how to brighten a day," Joe said, as he and Doc watched. Even Ben was starting to crack a smile at the pup in his lap with Alice.

Dave had disarmed and cuffed the two men in the coffee shop and searched the dead one. Joe saw him talking to Alberto and taking notes. So he wasn't surprised when he walked over to Ben and Alice and kept writing. Then he headed for Joe.

"Okay," Dave said. "Let's hear your story."

"Not much to it," Joe said. "Parson and I opened the door to an empty store. I tied Parson to the cashier booth and peeked through the rubber doors. I saw Alberto tied up, Ben on the floor and a man holding a gun on Alice demanding to know where the drugs were. She didn't know anything about any drugs. They were trashing the storeroom looking for them. That's when I went into the coffee shop and called you."

"The two you left in the coffee shop keep talking about a blind man," Dave said. "Who was he?"

"Me," Joe said.

"I don't believe this," Dave said. "You tricked them by pretending to be blind?"

"Yep," Joe said, grabbing the sunglasses and the *cane* he'd used. Picking up a can off the shelf, he swung the cane and said, "Where is everybody? I'm blind, damn it. Clerk, clerk, I need help finding my food." Everyone was laughing at him.

"I watched them in the mirrors and waited until they were ready to pistol whip me. Then I *canned* them," he said, grinning at Dave. "That took care of two of them. I hid behind the motor oil man and waited for the third one to come looking for his buddies. Since he had a gun in Alice's back, I body slammed her out of his hold and shot."

Alice was shaking her head while he told Dave his story.

"I had no idea who the blind man was," she said. "I was certain they'd killed him."

"I'm sorry I hit you so hard," he said. "But I had to take him by surprise and break his grip on you, before he had a chance to react." She gingerly walked over and gave him a hug.

"It's okay," she said. "I'll be a little sore for a while. But at least I'm alive to whine about it. Thank you for saving all of us. They were already talking about different ways to get rid of us after they found the drugs."

Dave asked him why he came to the store. He looked surprised and said, "Parson and I came over to have lunch."

"Do you normally have lunch at nine-thirty?" Dave asked. Joe glanced at the clock on the wall as he started to answer. It was only ten-fifteen. At his bewildered look, Dave said, "I logged your call at nine-forty."

"I don't know what to say," Joe said.

Dave looked at the others and said, "This is a first."

They laughed while Joe tried to figure it out.

"All I know is I was working around the house and suddenly felt famished," Joe said. "I grabbed Parson and chattered about egg salad sandwiches for lunch. I didn't look at the clock. I never get that hungry before noon."

"I think we have another one of your *feelings*," Ben said haltingly. "I thank God for them. You've saved a lot of people, including the three of us, by following them."

Joe nodded, still stunned at the situation.

Dave and Doc moved the men out of the store.

Joe took Parson out for a long overdue walk.

Then he returned to help Alberto clean up the store room. Since Alberto normally worked the gas pumps, he didn't know where to put the boxes. They moved Ben to a chair in the storeroom to tell them where to put things.

Alice called Archibaldo to come help. Once they told him what happened, Joe asked all four of them what the substitute truck driver said to them last week.

"How did you know we had a substitute?" Ben asked.

"Because I asked Chris if you had any watermelons this week," Joe said. "He said no, because Simms was sick and his substitute didn't know to stop for the fresh stuff."

Satisfied, Ben said he couldn't remember anything other than the man saying he was taking Simms' run.

Turning to Alice, Joe asked, "Did he talk to you at all? Try to remember every word he said."

"He came into the coffee shop for a cup of coffee," she said. "He drank it and left. I didn't like him."

"Why?" Joe asked.

"He made my skin crawl," she said. "He kept giving me...lewd looks."

"Why didn't you tell me?" Ben growled.

"Because he left, so I didn't think any more about it, honey," she said. "But there was something he said..." She rubbed her forehead and tried to remember. "Oh," she said, "he played with the sugar dispenser, while he drank his coffee and said something suggestive about him being my sugar – or bringing me some sugar – something like that. I blew him off. He left after he gave me a creepy look and laughed."

Joe leaned over, kissed Alice on the forehead and said, "Darlin' I hate to ruin your innocence..." Ben growled at him.

"No, I'm not going to steal her, Ben," he said chuckling. "What I mean is, I think the driver was calling the drugs *sugar* and your little lady's so innocent she had no idea what he was talking about." Turning to Alberto, Joe said, "Let's pull any boxes of sugar we find up here." They started digging.

Since Alice used dispensers in the coffee shop, the box labeled individual sugar packets looked suspicious.

"We never order sugar packets," Ben said. Joe nodded and called Dave to pick up the box and have the contents tested.

Dave arrived and carried the box to the patrol car. Joe followed him. With his back to the group on the dock, he opened a packet and tasted a few particles.

"I'll bet this tests out as high grade heroin," he said. "Thanks for giving me some cover. It wouldn't look right for the Baptist Preacher to know how to test drugs." Dave chuckled.

"We have some users around here who are getting desperate for their fixes," Joe said. "Better lock this up tight."

Dave nodded and agreed.

"What I can't figure out is why they thought Ben's was the drop off?" Joe said, thinking about it. "The other stop Simms makes is the Catholic Church. If the substitute dropped it at the wrong place that means we have a distributor out there."

Looking at the packets, Joe noticed a slight difference in the labeling. He opened one of the other ones and tasted it.

"This is just sugar," he said. "Apparently, only certain packets contain the drugs." Dave looked at them and agreed.

"I've got to go back and help Ben right now," Joe said. "Why don't we pull the heroin and send the box of sugar out to the church tomorrow with Simms, since it was a delivery mix up. Then we can watch the box and see where it ends up."

Dave shook his head and said, "We have court tomorrow and you're booked tomorrow night."

"That's right," Joe said. "Thanks, I forgot. Okay, we'll work on this later. Let's just lock it up and I'll come see you after a while to work out a plan." Dave agreed.

"Oh," Joe said. "Did you take pictures of the men you arrested last week?"

"Yeah, why?" Dave asked.

"The substitute truck didn't leave the back lot after we arrested those men," Joe said. "I'm guessing one of them was Simms' substitute driver. If Ben and Alice can identify him, we have him on drug charges."

"I'll bring the pictures over in a bit," Dave said.

"Thanks," Joe said, as he hopped back up on the dock.

The kids came home from school while Joe, Alberto and Archibaldo were still working on the storeroom. After several minutes of assurances, Chris hugged and thanked Joe and Alberto. Then he took over the storeroom so Ben could go rest.

Katherine took over the coffee shop and had a fresh cup of coffee and two egg salad sandwiches waiting for Joe when he came back from putting Ben in bed. Alice stayed with Ben.

Parson had a place at Katherine's feet. He was enjoying the frequent scraps she *accidentally* dropped.

Grandma stayed late at the Kindergarten to get the schedules set with the teachers and arrange some things for Max to do each day. She almost collapsed, when she walked in and heard that the store had been robbed. Searching for Ben and not seeing him, she thought the worst.

Joe caught her as she crumpled. He eased her into a chair and kept repeating, "Ben and Alice are all right."

When he realized his words weren't connecting, he picked her up and carried her over to Ben's. When Ben opened the door, she put her arms around him and broke into tears. Alice walked out of the bedroom and Grandma grabbed her into the hug. Joe left them to reassure each other.

He picked up his well fed pup, an empty box for the evidence at the house and walked back to Dave's office. Since he had two new prisoners in his jail, Joe signaled him outside.

"I put Susan up front with the prisoners while I brought the box of *sugar* through the fire station door," Dave said. "The prisoners don't know we found it. I pulled the heroin packets out and locked them in an old safe in back."

"Good thinking," Joe said.

"How are Ben and Alice doing?" Dave asked.

"We took them home to rest," Joe said. "They're going to be sore for a while, but Doc thinks they'll be okay."

"Thank God," Dave said.

Joe agreed and said, "Since tomorrow is so busy, let's keep the box of sugar until Wednesday. Then I can run it out to the church – as a favor for Ben. I'll brief Father Romero, when he comes to town for court tomorrow." Dave liked that idea.

"Finding that box today explains why Father Romero hasn't seen any people suffering withdrawals," Joe said. "They were still getting their supply. If we can catch the distributor, we have him on federal charges."

"Good," Dave said. "Someone else can do the paperwork." Joe grinned and agreed.

"Does writer's cramp qualify me for a disability retirement?" Dave asked, holding up his version of a deformed hand.

"I hate to disappoint you, but I don't think so," Joe said laughing. "Speaking of court tomorrow, do you know which cases Judge Evermundy plans to hear?"

"Yes," Dave said. "He's going to hear Tobias and Sampson, so I'll need you, Ben and Doc over here at ten. I've already called Father Romero." Then he added, with fake exasperation, "Of course, we have the two new guys you just donated." Joe nodded and grinned at him.

"Seriously," Dave said, "that was a close call. Good work. I love the blind man act. How did you think of it?"

"I don't know," Joe said. "I was just looking for a way to split them up. I knew you and I couldn't take three at once – not with one holding a gun on Alice – so I improvised. I wasn't sure the ruse would work. We're very lucky he didn't get a shot off at Alice." Dave winced and agreed.

Since they'd missed the hoops game, Joe walked Parson for a few minutes and went home to relax. He gave Parson a lot of praise, too. He was amazed the pup had been so good.

Sitting at his table enjoying a fresh cup of coffee, he reviewed his notes on Tobias and Sampson for court tomorrow. If he was right, the box of evidence at his feet would put them away on several more charges. Then he wrote up his notes on today's events at Ben's store.

Ben called at eight, to thank Joe again for saving them. He said Grandma mixed a concoction in a tub of hot water and made both Alice and Ben soak in it. He admitted it had relieved a lot of their soreness. Joe told him how well his two kids took over the store and storeroom for them while they rested.

"Give them extra hugs," he said. "Not many kids are as caring as those two. But tell Alice her coffee shop may run in the red this week, I think Katherine *dropped* most of her profits down to Parson."

"Don't make me laugh," Ben pleaded. "My ribs can't take it right now."

"Oops, sorry," Joe said. "By the way, we have court tomorrow morning at ten. Your two thugs will be there, so you, Alice and Alberto will need to come. I suggest you close the store and leave Archibaldo inside with a shotgun until the rest of you get back."

"I agree," Ben said. "But we can't lock up. Simms will be here in the morning."

"What time does he come?" Joe asked.

"He's usually here by seven," Ben said.

"Okay," Joe said, "call Archibaldo in. He and Alberto and I can unload the truck into the storeroom. They can sort and place the stuff when we get back."

"I'll call them now," Ben said, "and thanks again."

"You're welcome," Joe said. "I'm glad your injuries aren't any worse than they are. I'm sorry I had to hit Alice so hard. She's going to have some big bruises."

"If you hadn't, she might not be with me tonight," Ben said. "I have no doubt you saved her life. She'll survive some bruises, so don't beat yourself up over it."

"Okay," Joe said, "see you at seven."

He pulled out his laptop and started his daily e-mail to Jack. He wrote up the filter evidence he found at the school and the houses north of the church. Then he told Jack about the three men at Ben's and the box of *sugar* packets they'd found. He described his plans for Wednesday and suggested *Reverend Brownstone* might want to join him on this arrest. He chuckled at Jack's cover and signed off.

He cleaned and reloaded his pistol, changed into his black clothes, grabbed his radio, binoculars and extra tapes. He left Parson asleep in his pen, locked the door and ran his surveillance. The bar was closed and the Hispanic area was quiet. Max had one soft light on in his apartment and there were no trucks around the oil shack.

He wondered where the fifteen men were and what they were planning to do. He had no doubt they were going to show up here. Circling the other businesses, he checked the grocery, Ben's house and Grandma's.

He stopped to check on Dave and Susan. Cracking the door softly, he held a hand up when he met Dave's revolver. He asked if everything was okay. Dave nodded.

"Call me when Susan relieves you," Joe said. "I'll come over and stay with her." Dave agreed and thanked him.

He went home, walked Parson, finished his e-mail to Jack and started reviewing his tapes.

Jack sent him an e-mail. FIFTEEN MEN ARRIVED IN PORTALES, HUNG AROUND WAREHOUSE MOST OF THE DAY, THEN CHECKED INTO A MOTEL IN TOWN.

Max's tape and the one at the hotel were clear. No activity at the house south of the church, and nothing on the one at the bar…..until the end.

Late tonight, Roz had opened the side door, looked around and then waved to three cars at the end of the block. Twelve men got out, went inside and up some stairs. All of the men had side arms and most of them had rifles strapped to their backpacks. The other three men, apparently the drivers, walked up a few minutes later.

I wonder where they left their cars. Probably in one of the overgrown fields, he thought, as he watched two of the three walk inside. The third man stood outside with Roz. From the dim lighting around the door, he guessed it was Chad.

Fourteen new hires and Chad, Joe thought, *that's fifteen.*

Looking around the street to be sure it was clear, they started talking. "Are we on for tomorrow night?" she asked.

"Yeah," Chad said. "We're watching for those other men. They aborted last week after we did."

"How do you know they're coming?" she asked.

"José and his uncle are following Tommy," he said. "They saw him go back to the motel where he met the preacher and that other man. We bugged Tommy's truck. We know he's going to pick up the other man tomorrow night."

"Who are they?" she asked.

"I don't know," he said. "But they know that damned preacher and he's been nothing but trouble since he came to town. I just want to make sure they aren't trying to interfere with our shipments."

"What are you going to do?" she asked.

"As soon as the men clean up and get a couple of drinks," Chad said, "I'll wake up Max and get the keys to the hotel. The men can stay there tonight. They'll pick off anyone who goes near our truck tomorrow. They can haul the bodies out and disappear the same way they came in."

"Why so many men, if you're only going after three of them?" she asked.

"We heard part of a conversation in Tommy's truck that talked about ten something," he said. "We don't know if they were talking about ten more people. We're bringing a double load in tomorrow to make up for the shipment we missed last week. We want to be sure it gets through. The guys in Chicago are hot. I don't want to tangle with the syndicate." Roz agreed.

"Let's feed the crew and let them relax before we put this plan in motion," Chad said, as he led Roz inside.

Joe's blood was racing as he listened.

He typed a fast e-mail to Jack: PACK IN AS LITTLE LIGHT AS POSSIBLE. DO NOT MAKE OR RECEIVE ANY CALLS. I'LL PICK YOU UP IN ABOUT AN HOUR. WATCH FOR ME – I'LL BE DARK. DO NOT TALK TO TOMMY UNTIL I GET THERE.

Then he called Dave to come over.

Susan ran to the jail and Dave was there in five minutes.

Joe played the tape for him.

"I need three things," Joe said. "First, I'm going after Max. Follow me in the patrol car and bring him over to the jail so you can protect him. Book him on something – anything, but keep him there. I don't want him beaten up again." Dave agreed.

"Second," he said, "I need you to call someone besides Ben to help you and Susan in the jail tonight."

"I'll call Ralph," Dave said. Joe nodded.

"Third," Joe said, "stay inside unless you're called out. It could be a trap. I'll be gone for two or three hours. I'll call you when I get back. I'm going to call the Judge and try to delay court until next week. These guys could go after him, too, since he removed Orson." Dave agreed.

Joe was packing while he talked. Dave expressed a little surprise at the other firearms, but admitted he should've expected them. He helped Joe put his gear in the van. Joe gave Parson a quick walk in the yard and put him in the front seat. Parson looked around for a minute and sat down. Joe locked the door and told Dave to follow him dark to Max's place.

When he started the van, he hit the choke and rolled silently onto the street. Dave's jaw dropped and Joe laughed. He followed Joe and waited for him to get Max.

"Max," Joe said, when he opened the door, "some of the men who beat you got out of jail. They may be coming back for you." He hated to lie, but he didn't dare tell him the truth.

"I want you to go with the Constable," he said. "He's going to put you in a jail cell to protect you. Okay?"

Max nodded, wide-eyed.

"You aren't in trouble," Joe said. "He needs you over there to protect you."

Max was puzzled, but he trusted Joe. He put on a shirt and turned out the lights.

"Where are the hotel keys?" Joe asked.

Max pointed to a hook behind the door.

"Okay," Joe said. "We'll leave them there in case Simms needs them tomorrow night. Let's leave your door unlocked so he can come get them." Max just nodded and followed Joe.

When he had Max in the patrol car, he asked Dave to roll with lights. "I hope *someone* down the street will see them and know Max is in custody," he said. "Maybe they'll just help themselves to the hotel keys and leave his place alone."

Dave nodded and rolled out.

"Probably asking too much," Joe told Parson.

Parson tilted his head and Joe chuckled. He strapped his leash into the seat belt and drove to Portales.

He parked behind Jack's room and tapped on the bathroom window. "Give me your stuff," he said, when Jack raised it. He put the bags in the back of the van and looked at the small window. "Can you make that?" Joe asked.

"I think so," Jack said.

Together they worked him through the window and onto the ground. Jack walked around to get in the van and found a dog already sitting in the seat. Parson actually growled at him.

"I told you to bring roast," Joe teased.

He walked Parson and put him in the back seat. He pulled away from the motel and parked behind some empty buildings. He gave Jack the tape player and hit the start button.

He borrowed Jack's cell phone, pulled the Judge's personal number out of his wallet and called him. It was late and he was sure the Judge had been asleep. Without exposing the underlying reasons for the new group of heavily armed men in town, he advised the Judge that he and Constable Nelson were concerned that the men might be waiting to ambush him in town tomorrow. When the Judge offered to send extra men, Joe said they thought they could handle things as long as they knew his life wasn't at risk.

"Call me if you need more men and I'll have them there," Evermundy said. "I'll change my docket in the morning. Please call and let me know what happens – and be careful."

"Thank you, sir. You, too," Joe said.

When he got back in the van he waited for Jack to finish the tape. Then he asked what he thought. Jack shook his head, trying to absorb the information.

"What do you want to do?" Jack asked.

"I want to drive to Tommy's house and get him outside for a briefing," Joe said. "Then I want to ask him if he has a couple of friends who could replace you two. We can put one in his house and the other one in your room. Have the first friend load the truck with fishing gear, pick the other one up at your motel and have them talk about the other ten men they're going to meet at the lake. Then have them drive to a lake two or three hours away and fish. I'll take you and Tommy back with me tonight. Both of you will be preachers that I met during theology studies in college."

Joe looked at Jack's face and said, "It's not that bad."

Jack grimaced and nodded.

"Where are the guys in our unit?" Joe asked.

"In another motel waiting for orders," Jack said.

"With nineteen in town tomorrow, how do you plan to bring them in?" Joe asked.

"I'd planned to have them drive in the same way we did the other night," Jack said. "But that may not work anymore."

"I don't think a car load of six men can just slip into the area without being seen," Joe said. "They're on high alert and desperate to get this load through. Let's go pick Tommy up and get back to town. Do you know where he lives?"

Jack did and directed Joe to it.

"Is Tommy married?" Joe asked.

"No, he lives alone," Jack said.

"Okay, I'm going to try to get him outside," Joe said. "His house could be bugged, too."

He pulled into the alley behind Tommy's house and hopped the fence. He tapped on a window he assumed was in the bedroom. Leaving the lights off, Tommy moved the curtains and Joe signaled him outside. He stepped out quietly and Joe took him out to the van so they could talk.

Parson didn't mind Tommy having the other back seat.

Jack noticed the difference immediately. *Two strikes against you with the Boss, Parson,* Joe thought. *Be careful.*

They told Tommy their plan. Tommy said he had some friends who could do the exchange for them. Joe drove him to their houses and Tommy brought them out a few minutes later. They dropped one of them at the motel first, so the other one could see where to pick him up tomorrow afternoon. Then they drove the other friend back to Tommy's house.

A few minutes later, Tommy carried two large bags of *trash* out to the alley. He tossed the bags in the back of the van and they drove off. Throughout the exchange, Joe and Jack didn't speak and they tried to keep their faces in the dark.

"I told my friends that you two were going to give me a ride to California to see my sick uncle," Tommy said. "We needed them to replace you, because Jack's ex-wife had a private-eye following him." Jack sputtered and Joe laughed.

"Good creative thinking, Tommy," Joe said, grinning at Jack. Jack finally chuckled and agreed.

Driving to town, Tommy and Jack talked. Joe was very quiet, but that didn't bother Jack. He knew Joe well enough to know his mind was working overtime on the problem.

At the house, Joe let Tommy and Jack inside, started a pot of coffee, and left them to unload their gear while he walked Parson over to check on Dave. He looked inside and saw Ralph and Susan sitting up front. The two thugs from the grocery robbery were in separate cells. Max was asleep in the third.

Sorry, Max, he thought. *I hated to put you in jail, but it's the safest place for you.* He tapped lightly on the window at the door and just waved at Ralph and Susan. When they gave him a thumbs-up sign, he walked back home.

Inside his tranquil little house, Jack and Tommy were flipping coins to see who was going to sleep in the playpen. Joe settled the debate. He put Parson in it.

He asked them to pour some coffee while he ran after one more tape. Grabbing a spare, he worked his way back to the bar and swapped tapes. He wanted to see if the men left.

When he returned, he put the new tape in the player and they watched all fifteen men leave the bar on foot. Again, Roz and Chad lingered in the doorway, but they just exchanged goodnights.

CHAPTER THIRTY-EIGHT

TUESDAY – SIXTH WEEK

It was one o'clock when they sat down at the table with their coffee. Joe pulled out his map of the town and they discussed possible options. The obvious offset to an ambush from the hotel would be their own snipers – and their guys were some of the best. But geographically there wasn't any location for sniper placement. The hotel was taller than the storage units and the silo, so the agents couldn't conceal themselves there. The open fields around the silo would leave them completely exposed if any light flashed during the operation.

"If we can't get enough cover, we don't use snipers," Joe said. "We'll have to go under and dark." Picking up pencil and paper, he started planning a different strategy.

"Simms makes his grocery stop at Ben's at seven," he said, thinking out loud. "Then he drives out to the Catholic Church and unloads there. If we can get Dave to pull Simms over on his way back to town – and keep him distracted for ten or fifteen minutes – we could pick the lock on the trailer and slip inside." Jack nodded and started making his own notes.

"Dave can close the padlock when he *inspects* the truck for infractions," Joe said. "Then he can follow Simms back into town, let him park his truck in the lot and take him to jail. He'll have to be sure he gets the keys and locks the cab."

"He can slip the keys in the fire extinguisher panel for us," Tommy said.

329

"If Simms isn't involved in the smuggling," Joe said, "he'll walk into a trap at the hotel. If he is involved, he'll be in jail where he belongs." Jack agreed.

"When the panels open in the trailer," Joe said, "we'll knock out the two or three men that hop into the truck to pull the women up. Those men stay in the truck with the women for the next trip. They won't be expected to return through the tunnel. Once the men in the tunnel close the hatch, I can attach a wireless camcorder to the bottom of the trailer so we can monitor the men in the hotel. If the fifteen leave, Jack and I can cover them back to the bar – or their cars. We'll probably need to leave Tommy in the trailer to watch the cargo."

Jack and Tommy nodded.

"Instead of disabling the trucks by the shack," Joe said, "we'll let our guys, capture the men and drive their trucks away, so the men in the hotel will think the operation is a success. Once our guys drive out of visual range, they can put all the men in one truck, cut their lights and circle back across the open Thatcher fields to the oil rig west of Main. They can cuff the men to that rig – with their hands behind their backs."

Jack agreed and wrote the details down for the others.

"Then our guys can drive west on First and park the truck behind the school," Joe said. "From there, they can circle the town on foot and wait for the fifteen men to return to the three cars south of town. If I can find their cars, maybe Tommy can sneak over and disable them."

He grabbed his binoculars and the church keys.

"Come with me," he told Tommy. They slipped over to the church and up to the second floor windows.

"With the fifteen men in the hotel tonight, this would be the perfect time to disable those cars," Joe said. He focused his binoculars south of town and spotted the cars in a field not far from the bar. They went back to the house for Tommy's tools and left to take care of them. With Joe in the lead, it took very little time to skirt the town and cross the field.

Tommy crawled under the cars while Joe covered him. They'd agreed not to do anything obvious. It'd be to their advantage to let the men put their backpacks and rifles in the trunks before they tried to arrest them.

"I cut the starter cables," Tommy whispered.

"Perfect," Joe said, as they headed back to the house.

Apparently Jack and Parson had reached a truce, because they were both nestled in Joe's bed when he and Tommy returned. They grabbed the sofa cushions and made two makeshift beds on the floor. Grumbling something about rank having its privilege, they went to sleep.

Joe's alarm went off at five-thirty. He started a pot of coffee and took Parson on his jog around town.

When he stopped to speak to Jerry and Bart at the feed store, Parson's curiosity gave him the perfect reason to step into the truck they were unloading.

Warning Parson not to *water* any of the seeds, he pretended to let his pup learn the new scents. He bent down to pet Parson and counted two stacks of fifteen empty bags in the front of the trailer. He pulled his curious pup out of the truck and continued his jog.

He made sure he didn't circle the hotel and storage unit. But that was a problem for Parson. He expected Joe to run there.

"Not today, Parson," he said, as he carried him over to the next street. When he rounded the corner to Grandma's house the race was on. She met Parson with a big hug and a foil pack.

That's when it occurred to Joe that he needed to leave Parson with someone today. Maybe Ben could watch him until tomorrow. He rolled his eyes at the joking he'd take if Parson insisted on sleeping in Ben's bed. But it was his best option.

He stopped at the jail, motioned Dave outside and told him about the revised plan. Dave agreed to hide the three of them in his patrol car and distract Simms while they hopped in back. He'd take care of the padlock during his inspection.

"The infraction has to be serious enough to jail him," Joe warned. "We need him out of the way until we can determine if he's part of this other ring."

"I'll take care of it," Dave said.

He told Dave about his call to the Judge.

"I just got a call canceling court," Dave said.

"Good," Joe said. "I'll tell Ben when I go over to help him unload Simms' truck. Can you call Father Romero so he won't make the trip?" Dave agreed. Joe swapped his radio with Dave's fresh one in the charger and headed home.

Jack was sending e-mail instructions to the other agents.

"How do you want them to come into town?" he asked.

"Have them park their car on the west side of the school and travel on foot to the rig. Be sure they're in black," Joe said.

Jack nodded and sent the message.

"I was going to ask them to bring a wireless camcorder," Joe said. "But we'll be in the truck before they arrive."

Jack reached in his gear bag and set one on the table.

Joe looked at Tommy and said, "That's why he's the boss." Tommy grinned when Jack agreed.

"Cell phones don't work over here," Joe said. "We'll have to use two-way radios." Jack pulled two out of his gear bag and set them up on the charger.

"Good," Joe said.

"Anything else?" Jack asked.

"I don't think so," Joe said, looking at Tommy.

"I think we're good to go," Tommy said.

Joe fed Parson and gulped down a cup of coffee, before they went back to Ben's to unload the truck. He told Ben that the court was delayed so they didn't have to rush this morning. Ben called Alice so she could relax, too. He could see Ben was in a lot of pain. He pulled up a chair and made him sit down.

"We'll take care of the truck, you can just be your bossy self and tell us where all these things go," he joked.

"Don't make me laugh," Ben begged. "It kills my ribs."

"Sorry," Joe said. "It's just natural to tease you."

"We'll catch up when I can breathe again," Ben said.

"Could you watch Parson for me until tomorrow morning?" Joe asked. "I have some preachers visiting today. They're not fond of dogs."

Ben's eyes challenged him, but Joe stuck to his story.

"Don't worry about Parson," Ben said. "We'll keep him safe." Joe nodded and thanked him.

Archibaldo and Alberto arrived the same time Simms backed his truck up to the dock – and so did Manuel, Miguel, Alfonso, and Pedro. "Jorge had to help unload Bart's truck or he would've come, too," Alberto said.

Ben was shocked. He thanked the men for helping.

"You helped us with the field and the Kindergarten," Alberto said. "Now it's our turn to help you."

The men formed a relay from the truck to the storeroom. Joe was delighted and said so, but he was also concerned. This would throw Simms' schedule off, because these men would have his truck unloaded in half the normal time.

"Is Alice in the coffee shop?" Joe asked.

"Yeah, she's inside opening up," Ben said.

"Would it be okay if I asked her to fix some coffee and food for Simms and the guys?" Joe asked.

"That's a great idea," Ben said. "Please, go ask her. She can call Ma to help her."

Joe went around to the coffee shop, told Alice about the men and asked her to fix some coffee and food for them.

She agreed willingly. He gave her a gentle hug and asked how she was feeling,

"A little sore, but better," she said. "Quit worrying. I grew up with brothers who tackled me all the time. But I have to admit, that was several years ago."

He nodded and went back to the dock. He took the storeroom end of the relay. Ben told him where things went and he put them on the shelves.

When Ben's load was almost empty, Joe stepped into the truck to see what was left – and to see what accommodations they'd have. There were cargo straps, a couple of moving quilts and a coil of rope. Turning to leave, he saw another box of sugar packets, obviously part of the church order. He put it under one of the Ben's boxes and carried it off the truck. He signaled Ben and put it on the shelf. When he helped Ben walk in to breakfast, he told him to call Dave to pick up the box as soon as the men left. Ben agreed.

Alice served all the men coffee and pancakes.

Simms had two helpings.

Good, Joe thought. *That puts us back on schedule.*

After the others left, Joe thanked Ben and hugged Parson goodbye. He headed for the door with a pack of bottled water. Parson whined, but Ben calmed him. He heard Ben tell Alice, "We're puppy sitting until tomorrow morning. No, I don't know what he's up to and I'm afraid to ask."

Back at the house, Jack and Tommy were dressed in black and had their gear bags packed. Joe rushed to get ready while he told them about the padlock and the items inside. Jack had packed most of Joe's gear for him, so they were ready when Dave pulled up twenty minutes later.

Jack and Tommy piled the three bags and themselves into the back seat. Joe locked up and followed with the water. They crouched down until Dave rolled out of town. Then Joe and Dave picked a remote stretch of road for the traffic stop. Pulling off behind some bushes, they waited. When Simms drove by, the plan went into motion.

Dave threw on the siren and lights behind Simms. Simms pulled over. Tommy had the padlock open in less than a minute. They were stowed with their gear in five. They listened while Dave gave Simms a hard time about his reckless driving and heard the click as Dave relocked the padlock.

A few more minutes of gruff talk had Simms moving into town to park the truck. He argued, but Dave arrested him. They heard the keys drop into the extinguisher box after Dave had Simms in the patrol car.

"Good man," Jack said. "I see why you trust him."

"Most of the people here are good people who have no idea what this group is doing," Joe said.

They checked the floor of the trailer and located the panel the men would open.

"We'll have to check their clothes," Joe said. "If they're wearing jeans and western boots, we can't dangle our combat boots and black pants over the opening. We'll have to belly over the edge to pull them up. If they bring a flashlight, we'll try to partially blind them with it." Jack agreed. They used their gear bags as pillows and stretched out to wait.

At seven-thirty they stowed their bags, put their watches and rings in their pockets and moved against the walls to wait. A little after eight, they heard the hatch open and men cursing when they tried to lift the panel. The first one hopped up carrying a flashlight. They knocked him out and waited for the next one. He followed a minute later. They waited for a third one, but apparently, only two were coming aboard.

Joe helped Tommy quietly carry the men to the far corner. Tommy had them disarmed, cuffed and gagged in seconds. Joe was impressed.

Jack and Joe were at the opening waiting for the women when Tommy tapped them on the shoulder. He handed each of them a pair of boots and whispered, "Black jeans." They slipped the boots on and moved into more comfortable positions. Tommy held the flashlight. After some cussing about the weight of the women, the process started. Thirty women, obviously drugged, were handed into the truck. All three of them were furious over the condition of the women.

"That's all Ron," a voice from the tunnel said. "See you in Portales."

"Okay," Joe mumbled. When the tunnel crew closed the hatch, Joe heard a voice that stopped his heart.

"Angieeee, Angieeee, where are you?" Elena shouted. "Come here, baby."

Oh my God, Joe thought. *Angie's wandering somewhere out there with fifteen snipers in the hotel ready to shoot anyone who comes near this truck.*

Jack recognized the name from Joe's e-mails and signaled Tommy to stop and listen. Joe heard Dominique, Gabbie, and some of the men join the search. A lot of innocent people could be caught in a cross-fire in seconds.

Jack could see Joe's jaw clenching as he fought an internal war between love and duty. He was about to signal Joe to join the search, when they heard Elena shout to the others that they found her.

Sagging with relief, Joe took his first breath in minutes. As he reached down to position the video camera, he heard Gabbie cursing in Spanish and a gruff voice laughing at her.

He turned the camera on and watched Chad drag her over to the tunnel. He had his hand over her mouth and the other around her waist.

"I've been waiting for you for a long time, Gabriela," he said, in Spanish. "Now you're mine. We're going to have a private little party where no one can disturb us."

He clicked something and the hatch started opening again. Apparently, he had a remote to the tunnel. Joe signaled Jack. He was not going to let this happen. Jack nodded.

The hatch opened and Chad dropped Gabbie down the ladder. When she regained her footing, she ran. He raced down after her. Intent on Gabbie, Chad didn't see Joe drop down the ladder behind him before he closed the hatch. Jack and Tommy pulled the panel back over most of the opening and waited. Tommy arranged the women more comfortably. Jack monitored the camera and the tunnel through a crack in the panel.

Following Chad into the silo, Joe knew he couldn't risk a shot down there. The ricochet could be as deadly as his aim. Plus a shot would alert the fifteen in the hotel and the others moving out to the shack. He peeked over the edge of the last step from the storm cellar to the silo and watched Gabbie trying to fend off Chad.

She was using her basketball tactics. She faked left and moved right. She ran center court and faked again. Chad laughed at her earlier. But he wasn't laughing anymore. She was wearing him out and making him angry. Swinging forward, he caught her arm as she turned. His back was to Joe.

"Free throw," Joe shouted, as he lunged for Chad's back. True to form, she responded to her coach's voice and jerked her head back to throw. She busted Chad in the face. When Chad released his grip on her, Joe took over. He vented his rage on Chad's body. He only delivered six punches, but one was guaranteed to change Chad's voice – hopefully for life.

Watching from the side of the silo, Gabbie couldn't believe that man in black was the Preacher Man. But she knew it was – she knew that voice. Somehow he'd found her in time – and boy could he hit!

Joe grabbed some rags off the floor and tied Chad's hands behind his back. He stuffed his mouth with the dirtiest ones he could find. Then he pulled the tunnel remote out of Chad's pocket. When Chad was secure, Gabbie ran to Joe. He held her as she broke into tears.

"It's okay now, baby, you're safe," he said. "Cry it out. You were very brave. You stayed focused and had a strategy. Good work. I'm proud of you." When she calmed down, he debated how to get her out of there. He couldn't yet. He had to know the status of the other actions first.

"I know you have a thousand questions and you want to get out of this place," he said. "But I need you to trust me."

She looked at him and nodded.

"I need you to stay here until I come back to get you," he said. "I know it's a horrible place. But it isn't safe to go back out right now." She hated the place and her face showed it.

"Trust me, Gabbie," he said. "I'll come back for you as soon as it's safe."

"Okay," she said. "Thank you, Preacher Man. Please, come back for me."

"I will, honey," he said, giving her another hug. "I won't leave you down here any longer than I have to, I promise."

He pulled Chad's body over to the other ladder and bounced him down to the storm drain. Halfway out to the shack, he heard the agents coming back.

"Sammy," he called out. "Don't shoot. It's me, Joe."

"If you're really Joe, tell me my favorite food," Sammy called back.

"Hot dogs with mayonnaise," Joe said, with disgust.

"Yep, that's Joe," he heard Sammy tell the others.

"I didn't think you were going to be down here," Sammy said, when he walked up.

"I wasn't supposed to be," Joe said. "But this scumbag decided to grab a town girl for his *personal pleasure*. I had to stop him. He'll be a soprano when he wakes up. But don't put him in a church choir. He's one of the ringleaders. Take him out with the others to the rig."

"Will do," Sammy said.

"How many two-ways do you have?" Joe asked.

"Several," Sammy said. "Do you need one?"

"Yep," Joe said, taking Sammy's. "Was Jack going to call you when the fifteen moved?" Pointing to Chad, he said, "It'll be fourteen now."

"Yeah," he said. "But we need to move these guys first."

"Okay," Joe said. "When he calls, tell him I'm okay. Ask him to tap on the hatch when it's safe and I'll go back up."

"We'll let him know," Sammy said.

"Do you have the others secured?" Joe asked.

"Yep, this was my final sweep," Sammy said.

"Well, it's clear from here on," Joe said, wanting to protect Gabbie's identity. "Add this piece of dirt to the group and head out. See you south of town." Sammy nodded and pulled Chad back through the storm drain with him.

Going back to Gabbie, Joe wondered what to do now. He blew his cover coming after her, but she was more important than any cover. She got up when he climbed the ladder. She obviously assumed he was going to get her out of there.

"Not yet, Gabbie," he said. "We need to wait down here a little longer."

"What is this place?" she asked.

"It was a peanut silo," he said. "When it closed, criminals took it over as a hideout. Some friends of mine are arresting those men and closing this down tonight. That's why we need to wait until they finish their work before we leave."

"Those look like women's clothes over there," she said. "Did they bring other girls down here?"

"They're really mean men," he said. "I'm sure they used this place for a lot of bad things."

She shook her head and shivered.

"I know it's not good to tell a lie," he said, as he gave her a hug. "But I need you to tell a little one to protect me. Do you think you could do that?" She nodded her head yes.

"When you go home," he said, "can you tell people that Chad attacked you and Constable Nelson saved you?"

She gave him a confused look and nodded.

"We don't want people to know about this place yet," he said. "Not until the law has a chance to arrest all the men and process the evidence down here."

She looked around the room again and nodded.

"Before I became a preacher, I was a policeman," Joe said. "I've been helping Constable Nelson and the other lawmen catch these men. If you say I helped you, it would lead to questions about why I was over here."

She thought about it for a minute and said, "And that would lead them back here to see where I was."

Smart girl, he thought proudly.

"That's right," he said. "But Constable Nelson drives all over town on his rounds. They wouldn't think it was strange for him to see your attack and rescue you. When the police finish with their work, I'm sure the story about this place will become public. We just need to protect it until then."

"No problem," she said, finally giving him a shaky grin.

Looking at his watch, he led her back to the ladder in the storm cellar. "When I get a signal from my friends upstairs," he said, "I'll open this hatch. It's under a truck, so don't hit your head climbing out." She looked at the ladder and nodded.

"When you get out, go straight home," he said. "Don't stop for anything. Okay?" She just nodded again.

Jack got the message from Sammy, tapped on the hatch and waited. A couple of minutes later, Gabbie came up the ladder, crawled out from under the truck and ran home. Joe followed her up the ladder and closed the hatch. He watched her until she stepped inside her house. Then he turned back to Jack.

At the question on Jack's face, he said, "He didn't get her. She wore him down for me. He'll have a voice change when he wakes up." Jack chuckled at that implication.

They checked the truck contents, especially the two thugs, before they left Tommy with the truck and followed the fourteen back to the bar.

Since Joe knew the town, he took the lead.

Sitting in the weeds across from the bar, he whispered, "I guess they're hungry and thirsty after a day in the hotel."

Jack looked at his watch and agreed.

Jack had ordered all radios off after his message about the fourteen. He told Sammy to send three blinks from his red flashlight when his group reached the Church of Christ.

When they saw the signal, Joe led them out to the cars.

Jack was still watching the bar when he returned.

"If they're going to leave before the town sees them, they should be moving soon," Joe whispered.

CHAPTER THIRTY-NINE

WEDNESDAY – SIXTH WEEK

About thirty minutes later, the men walked out. Roz held the door for them.

"Sorry, this was a dry run for you boys," she said, "but I'm glad we didn't have any problems with the shipment."

They grumbled and nodded. Looking down the street, she asked, "Are you sure Chad isn't going with you?"

"Naw, he's giving a little Mexican girl a night she'll remember," one of them said, laughing lewdly.

"Probably Gabriela," Roz said, laughing. "He's had the hots for her ever since he saw her playing basketball. Something about her long legs and cute butt really got to him."

Jack and Joe watched her close the door and turn out the light. They waited a few more minutes before they crawled away through the weeds. The thugs were still loading their gear in the cars when they arrived.

Jack had given Sammy the lead in this action, so they waited as backup. They noticed several of the men putting their side arms in the trunks, too – obviously assuming they weren't needed. Sammy waited until all the men were in the cars, before he signaled his team. Two agents moved in on each car.

A couple of the drivers tried to make a run for it, but they couldn't get the cars started – thanks to Tommy. When Sammy's team had them out of the cars and covered, Joe and Jack moved closer for the mop up.

Disarmed, cuffed and gagged, the men looked like fourteen little toadstools sitting on the ground.

They locked the cars and took the keys for the crime lab.

Joe enjoyed watching the men squirm when he told them there were a lot of rattlesnakes in the grass.

"I want Roz and anyone else in that bar who supported this crew," Joe told Jack. Jack agreed. He left four men in the field. The others followed Joe.

Joe knocked on the bar door and waited.

He heard Roz's voice ask, "Who's there?"

"It's Chad," Joe said. "Open the damn door."

"I asked them about you....." she started to say, as she opened the door. When she saw the men outside, she tried to slam the door shut, but that didn't work. Joe was inside and he wasn't moving. He covered her mouth until Jack put some duct tape on it. Joe cuffed her and pushed her upstairs. Using a second set of cuffs, he left her cuffed to the stair railing and fanned out with the others. No one else was inside.

They found several drawers of files on drug deals, truck logs on the transportation of the women, messages to and from Philman on the poisonings, and even some property records with filter contracts. Luckily, one of the men on Sammy's team had brought several sets of gloves, so they could leaf through things without messing up the evidence.

"This was a regular command center," Joe said.

"Hey, Boss," Sammy said. "You two need to see this."

Joe and Jack moved over to see what he found.

"We have a hidden room," he said, as he opened a door in the back of a closet. Inside they found more evidence of sex slavery. "Apparently, some of the *prime stock* was diverted here for *initiation* before being shipped out," Sammy said.

The thought made Joe sick. He turned away.

"Let's lock up and get this garbage out of here," he said, pointing at Roz. She just glowered at him.

Outside, Jack called for the Federal Prison Transport that was waiting in Portales. He told them to come in from the east.

Joe was surprised Jack had one waiting.

"We hauled it in for maintenance yesterday," Jack said.

Joe nodded and called Dave.

When he answered, Joe said, "Step outside so we can talk." When Dave said he was clear, Joe told him they'd ordered a table for twenty and had a dining facility arriving east of town.

"Oh, and Dave," Joe said, "you saved Gabbie from an attack near the hoops lot tonight. I'll fill you in later. Just take the credit and respond accordingly, if asked."

Now it was Jack's turn to be surprised. "Did you add my cover name to the BPD list?" Joe asked. When Jack nodded, he said, "Then I still have my cover. I'll explain later."

Sammy sent one of his men back for the pickup truck behind the school. They had just turned to walk back to the field to collect the prisoners, when a pistol shot rang out.

Spinning and drawing in a single action, they heard a rifle drop and a woman scream. Someone in the apartment over the bar had tried to shoot them. Jack grabbed the keys and took Sammy back upstairs to get the woman.

Joe looked around for the person who'd saved their lives. He couldn't see or hear anything. Judging from the angle, the shooter was in the weeds in front of the feed store.

Good shot, Joe thought.

Out loud he said, "Whoever you are, thank you."

Jack and Sammy relocked the bar and walked the wounded woman out.

Looking at her face, Joe said, "Hello Roberta, I wondered when we'd meet." The shock on her face said he was right. To Jack he said, "This is Roberta Philman, Peter Philman's wife and Homer Wellman's daughter. She's a certified addict. We'll have to put her in a padded cell."

The pickup rolled into the field and they loaded the fourteen men – and two women in it.

Joe hopped in and drove them up to the Transport.

Jack and Sammy went over to get the two from Tommy. They were going to ride with Joe on his second run to transfer the group at the oil rig. The rest of the unit would wait in the truck with Tommy.

Joe made the two connections with the Transport and brought the pickup back to the truck lot. It was almost dawn, when he drove up. The next decision was who was going to drive the semi to Portales. Would the warehouse expect to see Simms or just Simms' truck? Jack's data wasn't complete.

"Given the turnover in the warehouse," Jack said, "I'm guessing it's the truck more than the man. The surveillance reports said Simms just parked the truck and walked home. It didn't mention him speaking to anyone or going inside."

They decided to keep Simms out of the picture. Joe radioed Dave to keep Simms in jail. Dave agreed.

Since they'd need a vehicle to get back to town, they decided Sammy would drive Joe's van behind the truck. Joe took the pickup back behind the school and drove his van over to the east side of the storage units.

"We need to roll, before the town wakes up and sees my van," Joe said, as he tossed the keys to Sammy.

Tommy was in the semi cab. The other agents were already in the trailer with Jack. Joe joined them.

When Sammy started the van, Joe hopped back out and turned off the choke. Sammy gave him a puzzled look. "Later," Joe said. He signaled Tommy and crawled back into the trailer.

Jack was on the radio with the trainees as soon as they rolled out of town. They were in place, waiting for his orders.

While they rode to Portales, the men moved the women behind the cab to give them more room to jump out when the doors opened.

In Portales, Sammy parked Joe's van a block away and hopped in with the others. Tommy pulled into the warehouse at six-thirty. Instead of walking away, he stopped to check the front tire. Then he slipped under the trailer and joined the team.

The warehouse door opened and they heard someone shouting orders to get these women down with the others. Joe shot Jack a look. He wanted that boss.

When the workers unlocked the truck door, Joe and Jack tossed them in to the other agents. They jumped out, identified themselves and took charge. Most of the workers surrendered.

The boss tried to run. Joe was ready for him. He hauled him back cuffed and bloody.

He gave Jack an innocent look and said, "He resisted and ran into some of the equipment back there."

"What a shame," Jack said. "Who is he?"

"Senor Pratt," one of the workers volunteered.

The boss swore at the man and said, "Shut up! You stupid fool!" The worker visibly slumped from the insults.

Joe pulled out the man's wallet and said, "Oh boy! We have Mr. Thomas Tyson with us today." He shoved the boss over with the other prisoners.

The trainees were doing a great job collecting the workers, taking pictures and bagging evidence.

Joe watched Jack inspect their work, make suggestions and give several compliments.

Sammy and his agents were exploring side rooms and stairs. They were securing the building and looking for the other women. Sammy signaled that they came up empty.

Joe turned back to Tyson and asked, "Where are the other women?" Tyson clamped his mouth shut.

"That's okay," Joe said, "*Mi amigo* over here will tell me." He put his arm around the man who had volunteered Tyson's name and walked him away from the others.

Tyson stupidly assumed the agents didn't speak Spanish. He swore and said, "Don't you dare show them the switches to the bays," in Spanish.

"Thank you," Joe told Tyson. He and Sammy started flipping switches. Within minutes they had opened three massive rooms below the floor.

"Jack," Joe shouted. "You need to come see this. Bring some of those cameras."

Each room had one unarmed worker inside who surrendered without incident. They asked the workers for a count of the women in their rooms. They had approximately one hundred and sixty women in pitiful condition.

Looking at Jack, Joe asked, "What hospital can handle this many?"

"None in this area," Jack said. "Albuquerque and Amarillo are probably our best bets."

"Why don't we call the Portales hospital and get their triage teams over here?" Joe suggested. "They can take the most critical ones back with them."

Jack agreed and placed the call. Then he called the other units to move in on the rest of the operation. "Collectively, they should be able to shut down everything from the silo in Texas to the destination outside Chicago," Jack said.

Joe nodded and turned back to the women. They waited while the trainees took pictures and tagged available evidence.

Then the worker Joe used in his ploy with Tyson, walked up and said, in Spanish, "They have our families in Mexico. They promised to bring them over if we helped. But they didn't bring them. We want to help get those women up to the floor, please. Some of us helped a few escape, but most of them were too weak."

Joe called Jack over and asked the man to repeat what he said. Jack looked around the group and saw several men nodding their heads. He ordered Sammy's men to keep them covered, but release them to help. Six men, two to a room, climbed down and started lifting the women up. Joe noticed the care they used and thanked them.

The Portales hospital triage unit arrived as the last women were lifted out. When they saw the warehouse floor and the pits, the two doctors were stunned. But they worked the crowd with a diligence that made Joe proud. Four nurses had come with them. They were rushing equipment and medicine through the crowd on the doctors' orders.

Joe picked up their tempo and began relaying between the nurses. As the other agents completed their duties, they joined him. When the doctors finished the group in the warehouse, Joe told them they had thirty more in the truck. Exhausted, the team stepped into the truck and continued.

The doctor's identified fifteen who needed immediate attention and called the hospital for ambulances. They had another twenty who needed to go to Tucumcari. Again, they called for ambulances. Unfortunately ten had not survived the ordeal. They called the Coroner's office for them. That left approximately one hundred and forty-five that still needed treatment. Joe and Jack were debating the transportation challenge when the younger of the two doctors walked up.

"Excuse me, sir," he said to Jack. "May I volunteer a possible solution?"

"Yes, please," Jack said.

"I'm a member of the Army National Guard medical unit in Portales," he said. "I'm sure my Commander would be more than willing to mobilize our unit to take these women to Albuquerque. We have five doctors and six medics in the unit, so we could give them attention en-route."

"Wonderful," Jack said. "Yes, please call your Commander, but give me his number first. I'll get the approval process started."

Jack snapped open his phone and called his boss to cut through any federal or state red-tape involved.

"Technically, I think this is a state response to the Portales Hospital, since they can't handle the emergency," Jack told his boss. "But call this number and find out what authorization the Guard Unit needs."

The young doctor was outside on his cell phone.

He returned, and said, "My Commander will be here in fifteen minutes. He's mobilized the unit. About half of them will be here within the hour. The rest will take another hour, at the most, to arrive."

True to his word, the Commander drove up a few minutes later. He was a middle aged man with a Colonel's insignia on his jacket. After introductions were made, he and Jack took a few minutes to complete some paperwork.

Then he looked across the warehouse floor and said, "Oh my God. I was hoping Captain Lelano was exaggerating. Obviously, he wasn't."

When the Captain saw the Colonel, he came over to report. The Colonel told Captain Lelano to get on the phone and call the Clovis hospital and the Air Force Base to see how many they could take. As the unit members arrived, they went to work. Litters, IVs and blankets rolled out of the trucks and other members began loading those ready for transport.

Jack's agents fell in anywhere they could. By the time the full Guard Unit had assembled, they were ready to roll. Tucumcari called back with space problems at their hospital, so the Colonel loaded them, too. By ten a.m. the women were in transit to various hospitals and the Federal Prison Transport had picked up Tyson and his thirty-two workers.

"This was a good night's work, guys," Jack told his agents. "I've never seen a unit work better – and I mean that. Joe did a superb job ferreting out this operation. Tommy provided great local assistance. Sammy and the rest of you guys followed the plans down to the smallest detail. Your support made this happen. You're the best! Thank you."

The agents demurred to each other, but they were all pleased with Jack's praise and the fifty-six prisoners they'd rounded up.

"Now," Jack said, "Tommy and I are going back to town with Joe. We still have a lot of reports to write and investigations to handle. Why don't the rest of you go back to your rooms, clean up and get some rest. Once we get our next steps organized, I'll e-mail you."

"Who's going to secure this place for the lab?" Tommy asked when he saw the local police roll up.

"I'll take care of it," Jack said.

"No," Joe said. "The press is with them. Let one of the other agents do it. Otherwise you'll blow your cover with INS and in town with me." He slapped the magnetic signs back on his van for additional cover.

"You're right," Jack said. Turning to Sammy, he said, "Send a man over there to tell them the INS has ordered this area sealed as a crime scene. Then give them my cell number to call." Sammy sent one of his guys over.

Jack's phone rang a minute later. He confirmed the order and gave them a number to call in El Paso. He called that same number and gave his boss the information.

"More details to come," Jack said. "Have the Portales police seal the area and get our lab rolling. Kill all press releases. We don't have everyone yet."

"On second thought," Jack said when he hung up, "we need to protect this site ourselves. Sammy, divide your men into three teams and rotate guard duty here until the lab and backup arrive. The locals may have connections. Call me at Joe's."

Joe provided the number.

"Put your first two inside, away from cameras," Jack said. "The rest of you do some disguising before you relieve them. Assign the first two and let's roll."

They pulled off the lot five minutes later.

"Where are your vehicles?" Jack asked Sammy.

"One in ES, two up here," Sammy said.

"Okay, wait until dark and drive down to get the one in town," Jack said.

"I don't think so," Joe said. "How are Reverends Brownstone and ...Tommy, what is your last name?"

"Rosemeade," Tommy said.

"Okay," Joe said, rephrasing his question. "How are Reverends Brownstone and Meade going to arrive for their visit? In my van?"

"You're right," Jack said. "We'll need that car. If you guys need a third car up here, rent another one – and stop laughing back there."

Sammy nodded and tried to stifle. It didn't work. The back of the van was hooting at the Boss being a *Reverend*.

Joe dropped the chuckling agents off at their motel and drove back to Eutopian Springs. He stopped once on an open stretch of road to pull the signs off his van. Jack spent most of the trip briefing his boss.

In town, he dropped Tommy behind the school so he could drive the other car over to the church.

At the house, he declared first rights to the shower because he had to go see Dave and pick up Parson.

"We have a drug raid at the Catholic Church later this afternoon," he reminded Jack. Jack fell on the sofa and moaned. Tommy unloaded their gear and locked the cars.

Joe was showered, shaved and drinking a fresh cup of coffee when he finished. "That was fast," Tommy said.

Joe handed him a cup and woke Jack up with another one. "I still have my cover, if I get back out there," he said. "I told Gabbie that I'd been a policeman before I became a preacher and that's why the Constable asked me to help him and some other lawmen catch these guys."

Jack agreed it was a good cover story.

"What would you two visiting preachers think about renting the Methodist parsonage right across the yard?" Joe asked. "It'd give us more room and help the church keep the mortgage paid."

"How much?" Jack asked.

"Four-fifty a month plus utilities," Joe said.

"That's a steal," Jack said. "Best budget item I've seen so far. Do it."

"Okay," Joe said. "See you in a bit."

He went to Ben's first to get Parson. He'd missed the little guy and he was worried about him being a problem for Ben's family. Instead, Parson was sound asleep at Alice's feet behind the coffee shop counter.

"I hope he's been that good the whole time," he said, as he hugged Alice and poured a cup of coffee from the pot. Parson hopped up and started yelping as soon as he heard Joe's voice.

"It's okay, little guy, I'm back," he said, picking him up.

"He really was good," Alice said, "until we tried to go to bed. Don't tell Ben I told you, but he felt so sorry for the pup, he put him up on our bed. I never thought I'd see that happen."

They were still laughing when Ben came in to join them.

Looking at Joe, he said, "I don't see any holes in you. Can we say the same for the other guys?"

"What other guys?" Joe asked innocently.

Ben shook his head and said, "Well, it's like I tell the kids, I'll hear about it eventually. Then we'll discuss it."

"Are you going to ground me, *Daddy*?" Joe asked, mimicking Katherine.

"I would if I thought it'd help," he said, laughing at him.

"Well, I have some more stops to make," Joe said, as he finished his coffee. "I have a couple of visiting preachers at my house. I'm going to see if Ralph would like to rent the Methodist parsonage to them."

Ben's raised eyebrow said he didn't believe him for a minute. "Who are these visiting preachers?" he asked.

"Reverend Brownstone and Reverend Meade," Joe said. "We were friends in theology school. They've taken sabbaticals from their churches and just want a place to relax for a while."

"That's nice," Alice said, cutting a look at Ben.

"Yeah," Ben said. "It'll help Ralph keep the church. He doesn't want to lose it."

"I don't blame him," Joe said. "I'll do what I can to help him save it. Thanks for watching Parson. I hope he wasn't too much trouble."

"Naw," Ben said. "He was fine. Alice and Katherine loved spoiling him." Joe winked at Alice and laughed.

On the way to the door, he heard Ben say, "Visiting preachers my ass. I'll bet they haven't been inside a church in years. When is that guy going to tell us the truth?"

"When it's safe for him to do it," Alice said. "We trust him with our lives. That's enough for now."

"Yeah, you're right," Ben said. "I just worry about him." Joe left before Ben came back into the main store.

When he and Parson walked into the drug store, he could hear the kids and the piano in the Kindergarten. He joked with Ralph about the noise.

Then he asked Ralph if he'd consider renting the Methodist parsonage to the visiting preachers. "They're willing to pay four-fifty a month plus utilities," Joe said.

Ralph was ecstatic. The mortgage payment was due soon and he'd been worrying about it. He gave Joe the keys and said, "Let me know if they need anything."

"Did you disconnect the phone?" Joe asked.

"Yes," Ralph said. "I'll call and have it turned on. Is the same number okay?"

"I'm sure that'll be fine," Joe said. "They just need to be able to make calls."

He walked Parson over to the Andersons' and opened the door. The emotional part of him wanted to leave everything exactly the way it was. The logical part, knew Ralph needed the money to keep Wellman from getting the property.

He looked around, plugged in the refrigerator and checked the rooms. They'd have to shop for the basics, the way he did when he moved in. He opened some windows to air the place out and grinned. Since it only had one bed, Tommy would probably have a lot of sofa time over here.

"We'll let them sort it out," he told Parson. "At least, we get our bed back." He locked up and went back to his house.

Both men were cleaned up and looking half human again. He gave them the keys to the Methodist parsonage and suggested they shop for a coffee pot and some food later.

"Right now I need to call Dave over here," Joe said, "so we can update him."

Dave came right over and Jack gave him a thorough, but brief, recap of the night. Dave was amazed at the number of women they found and the cross-country ring they'd trapped.

He wanted to see the tunnel. Jack asked him to wait until the lab released it. If anyone in town saw him over there, they'd have a lot of curious people poking around the evidence. Dave agreed. All three of them thanked him for his role in their mission.

"We couldn't have done any of this if you hadn't helped us get into Simms' truck," Joe said.

"What I want to know is how you come up with these schemes," Dave told Joe. "I don't think I would've ever thought about getting inside a truck and riding it out."

"I don't know," Joe said. "I just try to think of something that'll work."

"I've watched him for years," Jack said. "And I still don't understand, but I'm grateful for his determination."

Dave nodded and asked about the rescue he allegedly performed last night.

"Chad forced Gabbie into the tunnel and I following them," Joe said. "Gabbie knows I was down there and stopped Chad from raping her. She knows about the tunnel and she knows I'm helping you and some other lawmen catch these men – because, before I became a preacher, I was a policeman with the Boston PD. She's cool with the story. She understands if she tells people the real story, they'll start going into the tunnel before we can get all the evidence we need to catch the men."

Dave nodded and sipped some more coffee.

"Oh," he said. "What about that noisy car of yours? It sure was quiet the other night. What did you do?"

"Tommy's our mechanical genius," Joe said. "I'll let him explain that one." Tommy told him what he'd done.

Dave just shook his head. "That's a new one on me," he said. "But it worked."

"Now," Joe said. "Where do we stand on our boxes of sugar? Did Ben give you the second one?"

"Yep," Dave said. "I took it in the back like the other one. I've sorted the odd packets out of it, so it's ready to go when you are."

"We have some addicts who haven't had a fix for two weeks," Joe said. "I think we need to round them up before they get dangerous. Why don't we go out about three? Will that work for you?"

"I still have prisoners," Dave said. "I'll get Ralph to come over with Susan."

"Do we need the Constable?" Jack asked. "We have the authority to arrest them."

"Not as Reverend Brownstone, you don't," Joe said, laughing when Jack growled. Back to Dave, he said, "We'll see you at three. I'll take the two Reverends out with us to meet Father Romero. They can help us watch the sugar boxes."

He walked back to the grocery store and picked up three egg salad and three roast beef sandwiches. He added some chips and cookies and headed home.

After lunch he called Dave. Dave said Susan was sick and asked if they could go ahead and bring the man back with them. Joe checked with Jack and he agreed. Joe asked about Susan. Dave said she just had a headache and needed some rest.

"Okay," Joe said. "I'll come over and relieve you at the desk so you can go to the back and give the boxes to Tommy and Jack." Dave agreed.

Joe locked up. He put Parson in the back with Tommy and let Jack have the front seat. Rolling over to Dave's, they transferred the sugar boxes and drove out to the Catholic Church.

"Whatever, you two remember about religions, be careful," Joe warned. "You're supposed to be Baptist Preachers with limited knowledge of the Catholic Church and its rituals." He heard Tommy groan.

"I'm glad you said that," Tommy said. "I'm Catholic. I would've automatically responded when I entered. This undercover stuff is crazy."

"Something like that," Joe said, laughing.

When they drove up to the Catholic Church, they let Joe handle things. Father Gordon answered the door. Joe made the introductions and then asked to see Father Romero. Father Gordon took them up to Father Romero's chambers.

"Is the Father ill?" Joe asked.

"No, just resting," Father Gordon said. "He spent the morning out in the fields with the workers."

"Really," Joe said. "Is there a problem?"

"No, he just wanted to join them," Father Gordon said. "I think you've convinced him to get closer to the parish."

"That's good," Joe said. "Just don't let him overdo."

"I'm trying not to," Father Gordon said. "But he's a determined man."

"That he is," Joe said, as Father Gordon knocked.

When they heard, "enter," Joe and the others stepped into the room. He and Father Romero exchanged mutually sincere greetings. Then he introduced his two visiting preachers. Father Romero graciously welcomed them. After a few moments, Joe signaled Father Romero for some privacy. Father Romero nodded and asked Father Gordon to take the two preachers on a short tour of the church. When they left, Joe told him about the attack at the Morrison's store.

"The men were looking for drugs that Simms' substitute driver said he delivered there," Joe said. "He said he'd told Alice about them. She had no idea what they were talking about and it almost got three people killed. After the men were arrested, Alice remembered the driver making *sugar* comments. She didn't like him and thought he was just being lewd. Apparently, the sugar was actually the drugs the men wanted. We searched the boxes and found one with sugar packets. It isn't an item the Morrisons use, but it is on the order for your church. The substitute driver left it at the wrong place."

Father Romero was shocked at that information.

"I found a similar box on Simms' truck yesterday morning, while I was helping Ben unload his order," Joe said. "Ben is still pretty sore from the beating. You would've been very proud of the men in your parish. Every one of them showed up to help unload the truck for Ben, except Jorge who had to go to work early. They said he'd helped them with the field and the Kindergarten so they were there to help him. It was wonderful. The community is really coming together, Father."

Father Romero smiled at the pride in Joe's voice.

"Anyway, back to the sugar," Joe said. "We took both boxes to the Constable. Some of the packets are labeled differently. They contained what will probably test as high grade heroin. The other packets are regular sugar. Dave pulled the heroin out of the boxes. I have the two boxes, with only regular sugar, in my van. I'd like to deliver them to your kitchen, and act like it was just a delivery mix up. I want to see who takes possession of them. If I'm right, you have some heroin addicts out here who have missed two weeks of their drug supply. They're going to be desperate. If we don't find them soon, they could get dangerous – like the men at the Morrisons. I hate to always bring trouble out here to you, but I think we need to catch these guys soon."

Father Romero listened closely and agreed.

"I have one question," he said. "Are you the one who caught the men attacking the Morrisons?" Joe nodded.

"I thought so," he said. "Right place, right time, again?"

Joe nodded again.

Father Romero shook his head and said, "If that's the case, I have to believe the same is true of your visit today. What do you want me to do?"

"Walk back to the car with me and lead me to the kitchen to drop the boxes off," Joe said. "Then let's stand around and talk and see who takes them."

"Let's go," Father Romero said.

They met Father Gordon and the two preachers in the hall. They walked outside talking about crops and other things while Joe took the boxes out of the van. Then they wandered over to the kitchen. There were three workers inside. Two of them greeted the Fathers and their guests and went back to work.

The third one saw the boxes and rushed forward to take them. Father Romero expressed concern over her eagerness.

"Were we out of sugar, Juanita?" he asked.

"No, Father," she said, trying to curb her reaction. "I just meant to relieve him of the boxes."

"These are sugar packets," Father Romero said. "I don't remember seeing any on our tables. Where do we use them?"

"We use them for special occasions," she said.

"There are five hundred packets in each box and we get a box every week," Father Romero said. "I don't recall any special occasion that justifies that many. Who are you sharing these packets with, Juanita?"

"It's a sin to lie to your Priest, Juanita," Joe warned, when he saw her eyes flicker. She hung her head and named three members of his household staff.

"Are you using this *sugar*, too?" Joe asked.

She blushed and finally nodded. "Roll up your sleeves," Joe said. She did. He could see the classic needle tracks.

"Who do you contact to get your supply?" Joe asked.

"We used to tell Father Tobias," she said. "But when he was arrested, a lady named Pauline called me and said to let her know. She orders it for us."

"Go get that phone number," Father Romero ordered.

When she returned, he handed it to Joe.

"Who pays for these drugs?" Joe asked.

"The church," she said, shamefully. "It's added to the grocery bills."

"Did Simms know about the drugs?" Joe asked.

"Oh, yes," she said. "He always tells me when he delivers our sugar."

Looking at Father Romero, Joe said, "I suggest we let Juanita call the others and tell them the *sugar* is here."

Father Romero agreed and sent her to do it.

Within minutes three people came rushing into the kitchen. All of them were showing signs of withdrawal. After some more questions, those three named four more who shared their supply. Again calls were made and that four rushed in.

Father Romero was kind, but firm when he said, "You will all be arrested today. After you serve your time, I'll help you get another job and put your lives back together."

They nodded and thanked him.

"But," Father Romero said, "I want all the names today! Right now! If I discover any of you lied to me and left some poor soul suffering from withdrawals, I'll fire you and you will not have my help!" Three more names surfaced.

After questioning those three, he and Joe were fairly comfortable they had all the users.

Father Romero asked Joe to call the Constable.

Joe explained that Dave had prisoners and couldn't leave his jail unattended, since Susan was sick.

"Can we use some of your workers to tie these people up and drive them to town in one of your trucks?" he asked.

Father Romero agreed and sent Father Gordon to get some rope and a truck. An hour later, Jack was driving Joe's van with Tommy and Parson. Joe rode in the back of the truck with the eleven addicts.

Dave came out of his jail and stared at the truck.

"Damn it! I knew I should've gone out there with you. I only have three cells, Joe! Count them, one, two, three – and they're all full! What the hell am I supposed to do with eleven more?" he asked, flapping his arms while Joe laughed at him.

"Call the Feds to come pick them up," Joe said. "These are all drug charges and you can add Simms to it. Then you'll have an empty cell."

Dave mumbled something he wouldn't repeat and went inside to call. Coming back out, he said, "They have a Transport in Portales. It should be here in an hour."

"Am I forgiven?" Joe asked, grinning at him.

"Yeah, I guess," Dave grumbled.

Jack and Tommy went into the Methodist parsonage to see their new home. Joe pulled Parson out of the van for a walk.

"We're going to have to teach those guys how to walk you, aren't we, boy," he said, as Parson raced to a plot of grass.

Joe stepped inside the parsonage and said, "I'm stuck here until the Transport comes in from Portales. Why don't you make a list of the groceries you need and we'll go shop as soon as the prisoners are picked up."

Later, walking Jack and Tommy up to the grocery store, he and Parson showed them Grandma's house and the other homes on the street. He warned Jack and Tommy that Ben didn't believe their cover.

"Be ready for some trick Bible questions," he said. "Ben knows I'm doing things I can't talk about. It aggravates him, because we've become very close and he wants me to trust him. I didn't want to put his family at risk until we broke the sex ring and found the drug connections. Since we've done that now, I need permission to break our cover with him tonight, before he hears about the women on the news."

He could see Jack thinking about it.

"He's the mayor of this town and he's going to have a flood of INS agents in here in the next couple of days," Joe said. "He'd be in a good position to protect us, if he knows what's really happening."

"I think you're right," Jack said. "I trust your instincts on the people here. It's okay to tell him. Set a time at your house and Tommy and I will come over."

When they walked into the store, Joe made the introductions and, as predicted, Alice was warm and receptive, but Ben questioned them. Joe was surprised at Jack's command of Biblical references. *Another preacher in the making,* he thought, as he grinned at Jack. Tommy remained quiet and let Jack handle the discussion.

While the men shopped for their supplies, Joe waved Ben into the coffee shop and asked him if he could come over to his house around eight. Ben agreed, but looked puzzled. Then Joe remembered Ben's injuries and offered to pick him up. Ben waved it off and said he'd walk. When the other two finished shopping, Alice slipped Joe a foil pack for Parson.

"That did it," Joe said. "He'll race me home for this." He hugged Alice and joined the others at the door.

While the guys settled into their parsonage, Joe made some coffee, washed the cups and ate a quick microwave dinner. Parson had puppy food and chicken. After a short walk, he curled up in his pen.

Ben arrived at eight, visibly exhausted and in pain. Joe helped him to a chair. Jack and Tommy came in behind him.

Ben looked at the new guys and frowned at Joe. Joe locked the door and poured four cups of coffee. Jack looked at Joe's questioning face and said, "This is your meeting."

Joe sat down and just as he'd done with Dave, he told Ben, "I need to tell you some things. But before I do, I need to swear you to secrecy."

Ben nodded and said, "Okay."

"I know how close you are to Alice and your mom," Joe said. "But you can't tell them what I'm going to share with you. Understood?"

"Yes," Ben said, getting more concerned.

Joe laid his INS badge on the table in front of Ben.

Ben picked it up and held it for a long minute. "Joseph Morris," he said, almost to himself.

"Before you put me in the same category with those imposter priests at the Catholic Church, let me assure you that I am a qualified preacher," Joe said.

"We knew that the first week you were here," Ben said.

"Thanks, Ben," Joe said. "Now let me really introduce my two *visiting preachers*. Reverend Brownstone is my Superior, Jack Brown and Reverend Meade is my colleague Tommy Rosemeade." Jack and Tommy presented their badges.

"I know you didn't believe they were preachers when you met them, but you have to help us maintain that cover while they're here," Joe said. Ben stared at both badges and the men. He finally relaxed and shook their hands.

"The only other person who knows what we're going to tell you is Dave Nelson," Joe said.

Ben raised his eyebrow at that news.

"You'll understand in a few minutes," Joe said. "Let me give you a brief summary of the situation and then we'll do questions and answers." Ben nodded.

"I was sent here because Eutopian Springs was named as a town involved in smuggling women into the country and forcing them into sex slavery," Joe said.

Ben choked on his coffee.

"No way!" he said when he cleared his throat.

"That was my first reaction, too," Joe said, "but it was happening here, in the closed peanut silo. The Cozen men operated the activities. They entered through the oil rig shed north of the silo. It's fake – there's no pump in there. When they got inside the silo, they hit a hydraulic switch under the trucks that opened a hatch in the pavement. They accessed the trucks through a mobile panel in the belly of the trailers."

"Right here in this town?" Ben asked. "And none of us knew about it?"

"They were slick, Ben," Joe said. "Dave feels guilty that he didn't know. But there was no way he could've found it."

"Then how did you find it?" Ben asked.

"I was looking for it, because of the tip," Joe said. "But it drove me crazy for a while. Then I got a lucky break."

"He gets a lot of those," Jack said.

"Yeah, we've noticed," Ben said, pointing to his head. "He's saved several lives with his *feelings* – including mine and my wife's and one of my workers." Back to Joe he asked, "Every week they were here, they brought women?"

"Yep," Joe said. "Bart brought them in and Simms took them out. We'd planned to move in on them last week. But instead of picking up women, Simms' substitute brought that group of men who tried to break into the jail. We caught the sex smugglers last night."

"Plus fifteen more men waiting to ambush us from the hotel," Jack said.

"You caught them here – last night? How?" Ben asked. "I didn't hear a sound."

"You can thank Joe for that," Jack said. "He devised a plan that protected the town from a potentially deadly gun fight."

When Ben looked back to Joe for answers, Joe waved him off and said, "I can give you the details later. But that's why Dave had to know. If we'd had any gunfire, we couldn't let him get in the middle without knowing who we were and what we were doing. He played a vital support role from the jail. Besides, he needed to know he had another lawman backing him up with all the attempted jail breaks."

"I feel bad that I wasn't helping," Ben said.

"You weren't in much shape to help last night," Joe said. "But you helped in another way, I'll tell you about it later."

Ben stared at him and just nodded.

"Now, back to the women," Joe said. "We arrested the smugglers and the ambushers here. Jack had a Federal Prison Transport ready to haul them off to jail. Then we drove Simms' truck and the women from the silo to their next stop – a warehouse outside Portales. When they opened the doors to unload the women, they ran into us. We had agents all around the place ready to move in on them."

"The transport was waiting for those smugglers, too. "We freed about a hundred and ninety women, ten of them didn't survive. The rest were in horrible condition. It was a massive operation. We had to mobilize a medical unit of the Army National Guard to transport them to several hospitals. If you haven't heard about this on the news yet, you will. The press was pulling up when we left."

Tommy walked over and turned on Joe's TV. It was the top story. They stopped to listen to the report on the condition of the women. Four more had died. Ben could see all three men were hurt by that news.

"What happens to the women now?" Ben asked.

"They're illegals," Joe said, "as soon as they can travel, they'll be deported." Ben winced and nodded.

"The three of us operate in an undercover unit," Joe said. "Our value to the agency and the public is diminished tremendously if our real identity is disclosed. So I need to continue as Reverend Marsh and Jack and Tommy have to maintain their covers. Jack has already called for lab teams and other units to cover the crime scenes. We need to be close to support them, without being exposed. It's going to be touchy."

"I'll help any way I can," Ben said. "Just tell me what you need me to do."

"You probably have less than a day before those teams are going to roll into town," Joe said. "We're trying to keep the tunnel, hotel and shack a secret until they get here. We don't want curious people destroying any of the evidence over there. Or, God forbid, the press snooping around."

"And the bar," Jack added.

"The bar?" Ben asked.

"Yeah," Joe said, "that was their command center for their operations in town."

"There are more?" Ben asked.

"Yeah," Joe said. "I'll tell you more about that later. But let's stay with the smuggling right now."

Ben nodded and Joe said, "We hope to get our people in place before the press arrives. As the Mayor, you're going to be inundated by the press asking questions about this. Be nice and polite – if you can. Defer all their questions to the INS spokesperson who will arrive with the teams. That person is experienced in deflecting any questions that will compromise the investigations." Ben just sat in his chair and stared at Joe.

"Oh, on a local note," Joe said, "one of the men tried to grab Gabbie last night for some *personal pleasure* in the tunnel."

"What!" Ben roared, as he cleared his chair.

"Take it easy, Ben," Jack said. "Joe got him."

Ben sat back down and tried to control his rage.

"I followed them," Joe said. "Gabbie's okay. He's going to wake up a soprano."

Ben could see the temper rising in Joe's eyes, as he discussed the close call.

"Anyway," Joe said, taking a deep breath. "Gabbie obviously knows about the tunnel. But she understands that we need to keep it quiet until the law gets a chance to collect all the evidence. She agreed to tell her folks that a man grabbed her at the basketball lot and Constable Nelson rescued her."

"He would've if he'd seen it," Ben said.

Joe agreed and said, "She was grateful that I was there, but she wanted to know why. I told her that before I became a preacher, I was a policeman and that was why I was helping Dave and the other lawmen catch these criminals." Ben nodded.

"By the way," Joe said, "I was a policeman on the Boston PD until Jack recruited me. And that is my cover story for the town. True, but not complete. I've shot too many people lately for them not to ask questions about me. We've added my cover name to the BPD roster, so it can be proven if someone checks on it." Ben took a deep breath and just shook his head.

"Now," Joe said, taking a sip of coffee, "the smuggling was the assignment that brought me here. The poisonings and attacks on the preachers were not on my initial orders. But they are all inter-related. I won't go into all the details tonight, but Philman and Wellman and Cozen Oil are right in the middle of all this. Oh, by the way, Homer Wellman and Reverend Phillips are one and the same."

"What!" Ben said. "That bas....." He clamped his jaw down to keep from saying what he was thinking.

"Yep, Joe said. "He was right here directing a lot of the activities. He's in jail and so is Philman. Philman ruined the Thatcher and Archer wells to get their land. Wellman and Philman want to own this town." Ben's mouth flew open again.

Joe put his hand up to stop him. "We're not going to let them," Joe said. "But we'll tackle that a little later. A lot of their property will be seized as a result of the smuggling."

"We have other charges against them that we need to sort out with our attorneys," Jack said. "We're probably going to need a lot of help from you on those."

"I'll do whatever I can," Ben said. "Just say the word."

We will," Joe said. "Now, we need to tell you about the results of your beating the other day. The three men who

361

attacked you were looking for drugs. We found them in that box of sugar packets. The substitute driver left them at your place instead of the Catholic Church. Some of the packets contained heroin. The rest were sugar. There was a small difference in the labeling between the two. Of course, the users knew the difference. The second box that I pulled out of the church order in Simms' truck yesterday had drugs in them, too."

Ben did swear this time.

"Anyway," Joe said, "I took my *visiting preachers* out to meet Father Romero this afternoon. While Father Gordon gave them a tour of the church, I told Father Romero what I suspected. We took the boxes of sugar to the kitchen and he took it from there. The users had gone two weeks without their drugs. They were visibly anxious. We hauled eleven people in here on drug charges this afternoon – and they gave us the name of their supplier. Dave had a fit when he saw all of them, until I reminded him that these were Federal charges. A Federal Transport picked them up this afternoon. I wanted to catch the drug users before I told you about any of this. I didn't want to take a chance on you becoming the target of another attack."

Joe poured another round of coffee and let Ben think about everything he'd heard.

Ben took a deep breath, exhaled and said, "Wow!"

"Now," Joe said. "We have three immediate problems. First, Simms is facing drug charges and possible smuggling charges. We impounded his truck at the warehouse. So, as soon as you get public word of this information, you need to arrange a new supplier for your store."

"I can handle that," Ben said.

"Second," Joe said, "I'm pretty sure Bart has been picked up. His truck will definitely be impounded and his supplier's facility will be seized. So, don't be surprised if Charley is looking for a new source, too. Again, wait until you hear this information from a public source." Ben agreed.

"Third," Joe said, "we're going to need a place for the INS teams to set up their offices. We can't use any property Wellman owns, because it's involved in the case. The only vacant property he doesn't own, that I know of, is the Methodist Church. If we protected the altar and stored the pews, do you think Charley and Ralph would agree to rent it to the INS? It would help them pay the mortgage while we sort out the rest of this stuff. It would also be easier for Jack and Tommy to slip over there to brief them. We don't need people asking why Baptist Preachers are going in and out of the INS offices."

"I think Charley and Ralph would love the idea," Ben said, "as long as the church is protected."

"It will be," Jack assured him.

Ben was quiet for a few minutes. Then he said, "I used to play with the Anderson kids when we were little. There was some way their dad used to come over from the church without using the front door. I always wanted to ask him how he did it, but I never did. I think there may be a small passage from the parsonage to the church. If there is, you could use it to go back and forth. If you arrange the offices in the church to cover that path, no one would see you come or go."

Jack and Tommy were delighted. "We'll start checking it out tonight," Tommy said. "Any idea which room it was in?"

"It's been a long time," Ben said. "So, I might be wrong about all this, but I think he walked out of the coat closet."

Jack and Tommy said goodbye to Ben and went home to check on the passage.

Joe poured Ben another cup and sat down to let him ask questions. Ben sipped his coffee and shook his head.

"I know I have a thousand questions," he said, "but I can't think of them yet."

"It's a lot to absorb at one time," Joe said.

When Ben finished his coffee, he got up to leave.

"Oh, no you don't," Joe said. "You're not walking home. I'm driving you back."

"Not in that rattletrap of yours," Ben said. "You'll wake up the whole town."

"We'll see," Joe said, grinning as he grabbed his keys and locked his door.

He helped Ben into the passenger seat, pushed the choke and drove up the block. "What the hell…" Ben said.

"Tommy's a mechanical whiz," Joe said. "He rigged a choke to make the van sound like a rattletrap when I'm in town posing as a poor preacher."

Ben held his head in his hand and said, "This is too much for my brain to handle."

"You wanted to know," Joe teased.

"You're right," Ben said. "I just had no idea how much was going on – but thank you for trusting me. I was afraid you were in over your head with something I could help with – and you were."

"Yeah," Joe said. "I had a plateful. I hadn't expected to find all this when I started. But it just kept unraveling. And there's a lot more to come. But from here on out, I hope we can take it in smaller doses."

"So do I," Ben said, getting out of the car. "I'm too old for this stuff."

"That's your bruises talking," Joe said, as he helped Ben to his door. "Get some rest and we'll talk tomorrow."

Inside, Ben crawled into bed. Alice rolled over and asked, "Did you get your answers?"

"Yep," Ben said.

"Can you tell me?" she asked.

"Nope," he said. "Ouch," he said, when she smacked his arm and rolled over to go back to sleep.

Tommy met him when he pulled up to his house.

"We found the passage," he said. "It was in the coat closet, just like Ben said. That will be perfect for us. Jack wants to know how much rent they want for the church."

"I won't be able to ask until the teams actually arrive and the investigation is public knowledge," Joe said. "But tell Jack whatever it is I'll tell Ralph to double it, because I know how valuable it is to him."

"Don't do that," Tommy whined. "I have to live with him." They laughed and headed into their houses.

Joe walked Parson, did his surveillance run and changed the tapes. The bar tape showed the men returning and the agents entering to arrest Roz. It didn't show Roberta at the window, but it recorded the shot. It was a pistol shot. He wondered who was protecting him. The tunnel tape showed Gabbie's forced entry, her release and Joe's return. The other tapes were normal. He locked up the two evidence tapes and turned out the light.

He and Parson reclaimed their bed.

CHAPTER FORTY

THURSDAY – SIXTH WEEK

Joe awoke from his first good night's sleep in weeks. He didn't realize how much stress he'd been under trying to make this mission work. Now that he had other agents to help, he could relax – at least a little.

He put on a pot of coffee, washed the cups from last night, locked up and took Parson on their jog. He even took some time to play with the pup, who obviously loved the attention. Everything seemed normal as they covered the different streets. He had a new appreciation for *normal* after the last few days. He raced Parson to Grandma's house.

She laughed when he let Parson win. "You're cheating," she said. "He'll never have any self respect if you do that."

"Well, he won't have any if I don't give his little legs a chance," Joe said. "Let him get a little bigger and I'll give him a run for his money and he'll win. German Shepherds are fast."

"All right," she said, "I'll wait and see."

He took some time to ask about the Kindergarten. She was delighted with the kids and Dominique's work on the piano. She admitted that she and Linda Wilson played a little, so they could pick out some tunes for the kids. Of course, they loved it when Dominique played for them. She asked about Max. She heard he was in jail.

"I was worried about some threats I heard from the men who beat him up," Joe said. "I took him over to Dave's to protect him. I'll stop by and ask Dave to let him go to the Kindergarten at two." She liked that idea.

Parson had been sniffing her smock while she talked.

"I guess he's found his treat," she said, laughing at him. She pulled the foil pack out of her pocket and handed it to Joe.

"If you keep feeding him like this, I will win the races," he said, as Parson pulled him home for the food.

"I don't think so," she called after them.

Back home with their breakfasts, Joe checked the date and realized he needed the songs from Gene and Ralph for Dominique's practice this afternoon.

After a shower and shave, he locked up and headed to Gene's store. They chatted about Petey loving Kindergarten – and their daily pocket check for lizards.

"So, are you the *lizard patrol* now?" Joe asked. "Does that apply to Sunday, too?" He looked at Parson and chuckled. "I wonder what Parson would do if he saw a lizard in the church. He'd probably chase it and the whole place would cave in."

After some more joking, he asked Gene for the songs for Sunday. Gene handed him the list. He also asked about the mail. He didn't have any, but he wasn't surprised. Since Jack was over here, there wasn't anyone in El Paso to forward Angelique's letters. He needed to talk to Jack about that. Now that they'd captured the smugglers, he wondered if he could take a short trip back to see her.

He walked over to the drug store. He could hear the kids in the back and Dominique playing the piano. After chatting with Ralph, he collected the music and cut through the storeroom to the Kindergarten. He cracked the door and watched the kids sit spellbound, while she played. She was good with them. She played little songs in Spanish and then had the teachers translate them into English songs.

That's a great teaching technique, he thought.

She saw him at the door and stopped playing. When the kids turned around and saw him, they all ran to their Preacher Man for hugs. Parson ran to Dominique. The teachers tolerated the disruption for a while. Then they took control.

Good for them, he thought, as the kids responded.

He apologized for interrupting and asked Dominique if she could practice this evening. She said she could come over at seven. He retrieved Parson and left.

Stopping to see his *visitors*, Joe asked Jack if they could let Max go home. "The thugs who beat him up are dead and the accessories to the beating are in jail," he said. "Of course, someone went into his apartment for the hotel keys, but I don't think they did anything else in there."

"Let's let the lab look at it first," Jack said.

Joe nodded and explained about Max's job at the Kindergarten. Jack agreed to let Max go over there at two, as long as he came back to the jail afterward.

They talked for a few minutes about the house and the things they were going to need. Jack asked if Joe could take him back to Portales tomorrow to pick up some of the equipment they'd need when the other six joined them. Joe agreed.

"I'll let Dave and Ben know Tommy will still be here if they need him," Joe said.

"Definitely," Tommy said and Jack agreed.

"We have some of Gabbie's attack and the bar activities on our tapes," Joe said.

"Good," Jack said. "Our attorneys will want those."

Joe and Parson ran over to see Dave. Since he still had the grocery store thugs in the jail, they stepped outside.

"The Portales bust is all over the news," Dave said. "It was massive."

"It's going to get bigger when the press hears about this town," Joe said.

"That's right," Dave said. "The agents are going to be coming here, too."

"And the press," Joe said. "I wanted to let you know that we told Ben about us last night. He's going to have the INS and the press on his back in a matter of hours."

Dave winced and agreed.

"Anyway," Joe said, "I trust him the same way I trust you. So, now the two of you can coordinate things without that barrier between you. No one else knows and we have to keep it that way. Even the other agents won't know us. We've told Ben to refer all press and questions to the INS. They'll be in town today or tomorrow and they'll have a person who can handle the press without messing up the investigations."

"Good," Dave said. "We'll defer questions to him, too."

"Another thing," Joe said, "we want to keep Max out of his apartment until the lab gets in there. But he had started going over to the Kindergarten to help with the kids and hear Dominique play Ellie's piano. Can you let him go over there at two and then be sure he gets back here afterward?"

"I'll take care of it," Dave said. "I'll drop him off. Ralph can call me when he's through and I'll pick him up."

"Great," Joe said. "Thanks."

He and Parson walked up to have some lunch with Ben and Alice. This time he looked at his watch to be sure it was lunch time. When Joe opened the door, Parson let out a little *woof*. Joe stopped and looked for a problem. Alice stuck her head around the corner of the coffee shop and giggled.

"*We* learned a new trick while you were gone," she said, holding up a cup of coffee. "Since Katherine's in school, I needed a new announcer for your visits."

She tossed a scrap to Parson and said, "Good boy."

Joe looked at Parson and said, "Now how am I supposed to sneak up on her? I guess I'll just have to leave you at home."

Parson cocked his head at him, as if to say, "No way."

"That dog's smarter than you think," Alice said. "He's waiting for you to tell him he's a good dog."

"Good dog," Joe said and Parson perked up again.

"See, he needed his master's approval," Alice said, handing him his sandwich. "Start working commands with him. He seems to instinctively know what we want him to do, so he should be easy to train."

"I will," Joe said. "I thought he was still too young, but obviously he isn't."

Ben walked in. He was beginning to look like his old self and Joe told him so. While they ate their lunches, Joe told him that he was going to take Reverend Brownstone up to Portales tomorrow, but Reverend Meade would still be in town. Ben nodded and walked out with him when they finished.

Joe said he forgot to mention that the other INS agents would not know the three in town. "So, we have to keep our cover with them, too," he said. Ben agreed.

"Also," Joe said, "you were right about the coat closet passage to the Methodist Church. That will be perfect for Jack and Tommy. Of course, I can't approach Ralph and Charley until the teams actually arrive in town."

Alberto said something to Ben and they turned just in time to see three large INS Mobile Command Post buses drive into town – followed by six press cars.

"Here we go," Ben said, taking a deep breath.

"Yep," Joe said. "Just remember to refer the press to the INS. Good luck. I have to go. I can't be in any pictures."

He ran over to tell Jack.

Jack, in his earlier bearded disguise, had been in radio contact and was going out to direct them to the lot. He asked Joe for the tunnel remote. Joe retrieved it from his house, put Parson in his pen and locked up.

Tommy, in a shorter beard and mustache, blended in with Joe and the crowd that gathered on the street. Since Joe was a local preacher, he didn't need a disguise, as long as he stayed out of pictures.

When the MCP buses turned on Second and back north to park on Luna, the speculation increased. The first two agents on the ground walked deep into the field behind the silo and drove a stake in the ground. Then they ran crime scene tape from that stake to the corner of the hotel, up Main to First, around the outside of the storage units across to the peanut buying station, and back to the original stake.

The crowd was dumbfounded. Everyone was asking the others what was happening. No one knew. *Great,* Joe thought. *None of the townspeople appear to know about the operation.*

Another agent stepped out of the first MCP bus and hit the remote Joe gave Jack. The hatch opened. The crowd was stunned. Three crime scene experts emerged from another MCP bus and climbed down the ladder with their gear.

While the crowd was watching that activity, the original two agents had crossed First Street and staked out a large square around the oil rig and shack. Then they moved behind the crowd

369

and taped off the bar. Now they were out in the field where the cars had been. Joe was impressed.

The press was busy setting up mikes around the front of the hotel, so obviously a press conference was pending.

Joe recognized the agent who stepped up to the mike. He was a no-nonsense public relations man, very adept at handling persistent questions from the press.

He introduced himself and spoke to the citizens of Eutopian Springs, "I know the arrival of these Mobile Command Post buses is a surprise to you. A human trafficking ring used some of the empty facilities in your town for their smuggling activities. The ring has been captured. Our Mobile Command Posts are here to complete their investigative phase and collect evidence." The crowd was visibly shaken by that news.

To the press, he said, "None of the citizens of this town were involved in these activities or aware of their existence. Therefore, we would appreciate it if you would allow the town to continue its normal activities without media harassment. All questions concerning this investigation are to be directed to me."

Although his words were polite, Joe noticed his tone was definitely a warning – which Joe appreciated. The town had no idea how ruthless reporters could be, but the PR agent did.

Then the agent opened the mike to questions. As he answered the press, the town listened in disbelief.

Doc moved beside Joe, looked at the *door* in the asphalt and muttered, "I saw those women in Portales. I can't believe they came through here." Joe didn't answer. He pretended to be listening to the questions.

At the end of the conference, the agent announced to the press, "There are no hotels, motels or restaurants in this community available to visitors. Therefore, I will hold daily press conferences at one o'clock to give you time to commute from Portales for our news releases and return for your evening broadcasts." Again, he issued a clear directive that the press should not linger in the area. *Good,* Joe thought. *Now we'll see if they listen – probably not.*

Then the agent issued his sternest statement, "Anyone, not assigned to the three Command Posts, caught photographing, recording or trespassing in the taped areas will be arrested for impeding a Federal investigation."

That should slow them down, Joe thought. *He watched two photographers, who had been easing over to the tunnel door retrace their steps back to the group.*

To Joe's surprise, the agent went one step further.

"If the press does not comply with my requests and leave town voluntarily," he said, "I have the authority to declare the entire town a crime scene and restrict all press personnel to the open fields north of town."

Let them mull that over, Joe thought, as he watched the reporters. He heard some grumbling about freedom of the press stuff, but the six press cars loaded up and left.

Once they pulled away, the agent softened his voice to the town. "I know our arrival is a shock," he said. "I also know that our Mobile Command Posts and our people will be an inconvenience to you. If possible, please resume your normal activities. We'll try to minimize our interference with your daily routines." The people nodded. They were too stunned to speak.

"We do have two requests," he said. "First, if any of you have office space available for us to rent, please let me know. Second, if you have any facility that can provide sandwiches or light meals for approximately forty people, please let me know. We'll pay for all your supplies and your time. Thank you."

The crowd applauded as he stepped away.

Joe found Ralph in the crowd and pulled him aside.

"You could offer to let them use your church for their office space," he said. Ralph gave him a puzzled look.

"It's a church, not an office," Ralph said.

"Yes, but it has a large open area that they could use for a temporary office," Joe said. "It's close to the work site and they'd pay to use it. That would help you cover the mortgage."

Ralph wasn't grasping what Joe was saying.

"Why don't we get the keys and go look at it?" Joe said.

Ralph nodded skeptically, but he went after the keys and walked over to the church with Joe.

Seeing his reluctance, Joe changed his psychology.

Inside the sanctuary, he said, "Yeah, you're probably right, this wouldn't work. They'd pay good money for this space, but we'd have to move the pews and close the altar...."

"How long will they need it?" Ralph asked.

"I don't know," Joe said. "You'd have to ask them. But it sounds like a pretty big investigation – it might take two or three months. How much would you charge for it?"

"I don't know," Ralph said. "What do you think?"

"I'm not very good at this stuff," Joe said. "But I'd say at least a thousand."

Ralph's jaw dropped. "Really?" he asked.

"Well, that's just a guess," Joe said, stifling a grin. "But it might be worth talking to them about it. What would you do with the pews?"

"They come apart right here at the ends," Ralph said, getting excited about the idea. "We could get some guys over here to help disassemble them. We could stack them in one of the Sunday School rooms upstairs."

"Well, that would work," Joe said, studying the pews closely. He walked over to the altar and said, "We could move the podium and altar table upstairs…and the chairs. We could cover the crosses and just leave them on the wall."

Ralph nodded and agreed with him.

Feigning surprise, Joe said, "We really could clear this in a day or so. Apparently they have their own equipment, because all they asked for was space. If they paid rent and utilities you might get your church books back in the black. Wouldn't that be great? And it'd give you some extra money to cover those mortgage payments you and Charley are always worrying about." Ralph was getting more excited as Joe talked.

"Let me go call Charley to come over," he said.

"Stay here," Joe said, "I'll go to my house and call him."

"Okay," Ralph said, already heading upstairs.

Joe went to his house and called Charley.

Then he called Jack on the two-way and told him to move private. When he did, Joe asked him what the budget would allow for the church space. Jack said they'd budgeted three grand including utilities.

"So would two plus utilities work?" Joe asked.

"Yes!" Jack said.

"Okay," Joe said. "The Elders are still deciding on it, but I'm betting they'll be over to see someone very soon. Let the MCP know you want this space." Jack agreed and hung up.

Joe met Charley walking into the church. He let Ralph present the idea to Charley while he walked upstairs to look at those rooms. There were three medium sized rooms. One could be used to store the pews. The other two could be used for more offices or cots for sleeping areas.

When he went back downstairs, Ralph and Charley were still talking, so he walked into the foyer and looked at the bathrooms. The ladies' was small, but sufficient. The men's had the standard equipment and a shower. *Perfect,* Joe thought.

Wandering back to the two men, he noticed they were smiling. He waited for them to say something.

"Do you really think we could get a thousand dollars a month for the space?" Ralph asked.

"Yes, I do," Joe said. "In fact, I believe I'd ask for two thousand – plus utilities, of course. I didn't realize how much space you had upstairs when we talked earlier. If you can get your pews and alter furniture in one room, they could have two more offices up there."

"We could clear out the preacher's office for another one," Charley said.

"You even have a bathroom with a shower," Joe said. "I'm sure those people will appreciate that after working in the heat all day." Ralph and Charley were staggered at the thought of two thousand dollars. Joe knew this was a dream come true for these two men who'd struggled to keep their church.

"Why don't you go talk to them," Joe said. "Offer it to them at two thousand plus utilities. Bring them over here and show them what you have in mind."

They agreed. As they headed out, Joe told them to call him and let him know how their meeting went.

An hour later, Ralph and Charley were at his door.

"They want it," Ralph said. "And they agreed to two thousand plus utilities."

"I can't believe it," Charley said. "A month ago we thought we were going to lose our church. Then someone makes an anonymous mortgage payment. And now we're getting almost twenty-five hundred a month in rent. It's a miracle!"

Joe poured some coffee and motioned them to the table.

"We're going to have to get started soon, so they can move in," he said. "Let's try to get a crew over there at seven. Dominique was going to come over to practice tonight, but if Ralph takes the music back to the store, we can let her practice in the Kindergarten." Ralph agreed.

"Ben is still bummed up." Joe said, thinking out loud. "I assume he and Alice are trying to get some food ready for this group since they have the only *diner* in town. So, why don't you two call your workers and ask them to come over. I'll ask the hoops kids and Gene. I'm sure others will join us when they hear about the project."

"Let's roll," Ralph said, too excited to sit still any longer. Joe gave him the music for Dominique and called Gene. He said he and his workers would be there.

Then he walked up to talk to Ben. As predicted, he was helping Alice and Grandma prepare food for the crew. Joe told him about the Methodist Church project. Ben said he'd send Alfredo and Archibaldo over after work – and he'd let Miguel know. Chris and Katherine barreled through the door while they were talking. Since their bus stop was across from the MCP buses, the kids had just seen the crime scene.

Once they slowed down with their questions, Joe and Ben answered a few of them. Then Joe asked Chris to call the rest of the basketball crew to go help at the Methodist Church. He wanted Chris and Katherine to stay at the store and help their folks. Chris agreed and headed for the phone.

Joe walked over to the MCP buses and signaled Jack. He told him what they were doing at the church and said it would probably be ready tomorrow.

Then he went over to speak to Dominique as she was walking back to the Kindergarten. He apologized for the change in schedule. She understood.

While they were talking, Jack walked up. After introductions were made, he asked Joe if they could leave for Portales around seven tomorrow morning. Joe agreed.

Dominique politely asked if she could ride to Portales with them. If she could get there early, she could do her errands and catch the bus back. Joe looked at Jack. He agreed.

By seven o'clock, the Methodist Church was under siege. Every able-bodied man and the basketball kids were ready to work. Ralph and Charley directed them, and much like the Baptist Church project, the group fell into a rhythm of friendly taunts and hard work.

Joe and Charley went into the church office and boxed up the records. They wanted to move them over to Ralph's storeroom so they wouldn't get mixed up with the INS paperwork. At eight o'clock, Carmen, Margarita and Sofia walked through the door with a box of cleaning supplies.

A little later, Ben and Chris came in with sandwiches and a large cooler of iced tea. By nine-thirty the church was cleared, cleaned and ready for the MCP. Tired, but pleased with the results, the crews headed home still laughing and joking.

Ralph and Charley were too happy to sit still. As Chris aptly stated, they were "wired." Joe congratulated the two and left them to enjoy the results.

He picked up Parson and walked home with Ben and Chris to see if he could help at the store. Alice, Katherine and Grandma had meat cooking and eggs boiling. He helped Chris pull boxes of supplies out of the storeroom.

Parson helped the ladies sample the food. Joe laughed at his pup. Nestled behind the coffee shop counter, he rotated his head from one woman to the other watching for the next scrap.

"You've got him so spoiled," Joe whined playfully. "He's never going to eat plain puppy food again."

"I have no idea what you're talking about," Katherine said, as she dropped a piece of meat to Parson.

"Oops," she said, giggling at Joe.

Before he left, he walked Ben away from the others and told him that he and Jack were going to Portales in the morning.

Looking at the supplies in the coffee shop, Ben asked, "Since the Mobile Command Posts have arrived, am I cleared to arrange additional shipments of food?"

"Yes," Joe said. "They've publicly asked for it."

"Then, if you don't mind, could you give me a ride up to my *good* supplier in Portales to set up some more deliveries?" he asked. "I'd drive myself, but my kidneys are still giving me some trouble."

"Sure," Joe said. "I didn't think about the drain on your supplies over here. And no, I don't want you to drive yourself – not until you heal."

"Thanks," Ben said.

"We're leaving at seven. I'll swing by here and pick you up," Joe said. "Oh, Dominique asked for a ride, too, so we won't be able to talk freely with her in the car."

"Okay, see you at seven," Ben said, "and thanks again."

"Make your list and double it," Joe said, walking to the door. "These guys work up big appetites. And remember to keep track of the costs, they'll cover it."

Back home, he fed Parson. Parson sniffed at the dog food and left it in the bowl. He laughed and played with the pup for a few minutes before he put him in his pen. Then he called Jack at the parsonage and told him what the town had done.

Jack was impressed – and said so.

"What am I supposed to do about my surveillance cameras?" Joe asked. "I can't collect them without exposing my identity – or getting shot."

"I have the one under Max's steps and the other one by the hotel," Jack said. "I couldn't find the one by the bar. You hid it too well. I told them we had cameras around. They'll return any they find. I think we can discontinue your surveillance. They have several agents posted tonight."

"Okay," Joe said, "see you at seven. Oh, Ben needed a ride so he can get a new supplier and order more food. He's not up to driving yet, so I agreed to take him, too."

"Good," Jack said. "See you then."

CHAPTER FORTY-ONE

FRIDAY – SIXTH WEEK

He showered, dressed, concealed his firearms, fed Parson and himself, and locked up. Parson wandered around the yard while they waited for Jack.

Dominique walked up the same time Jack came out. She was carrying a duffle bag. Joe tossed it in the back of the van. When he tried to put Parson in the back, he whined.

Dominique reached over and put him on her lap. He practically purred as he settled down for the ride.

They picked Ben up at five after seven.

Since Dominique was in the car, he left the choke on for the whole trip. By the time they arrived in Portales, all four occupants were grinding their teeth to keep from cursing the car. Three of the four knew it wasn't a necessary noise.

He dropped Ben at a grocery warehouse and arranged to pick him up at two-thirty. Since Dominique said she needed to go downtown, Joe dropped Jack off with some of his *friends* at the motel. When he asked Dominique the address she needed, she asked him to pull over so she could get it out of her bag.

He pulled off. She reached in her bag, pulled out a sheet of paper and strapped Parson on Ben's empty seat.

Then she moved up front with him.

He was a little surprised at her seating change.

She giggled and said, "Look closer, Joey, don't you know your own fiancée?"

See what happens next in the second novel of the Eutopian Destiny series,
Eutopian Destiny – The Siege
Available at www.EutopianDestiny.com